John 14:2
"In my Father's house are many mansions; if it were not so, I would have told you. I go to prepare a place for you."
Jesus

MOSES' PLAYLIST
"Advent Chant" – Omari T
"Good Life" – Inner City
"Lights Out" – Ronin
"The Tantra" – Gemini Jazz
"A House Is Not a Home" – Luther Vandross
"Here And Now" – Luther Vandross
"Sunbeams" – J Dilla
"Wild Thing" – The Troggs
"We Wish You a Merry Christmas" - Enya
"The Glow" – Casino Times
"I Heard It Through the Grapevine" – Marvin Gaye
"Magic" – Frankie Beverly and Maze
"The Jungle" – Jungle Wonz
"Give It to Me Baby" - Cheri
"Dreamatic" – Audio Trip
"Time" – Leon Vynehall
"Love Is the Key" – Frankie Beverly and Maze
"You Got the Love" – Frankie Knuckles, Candi Staton
"Heard" – DJ Duke

ISAAC'S PLAYLIST
"Breadline" – Megadeth
"Man on the Corner" – Genesis
"Who Cares Wins" -Anthrax
"Another Day in Paradise" – Phil Collins
"The Homeless Song" – Black Sherif
"Left Behind" – Slipknot
"I Need a Dollar" – Aloe Blacc
"Flood" – Jars of Clay
"Young Hearts Run Free" – Candi Staton
"Move Your Body" - Korda

CHAPTER ONE

NBC's lifestyle television show, *Open House,* played on TV in the bedroom of fraternal twins Moses and Isaac Remington, nine-year-old African-American boys lounging in bed of their home in Valley Stream, New York. On this Easter Sunday, the kids gazed at the beautiful townhouse on Manhattan's Upper East Side as an impressive, slender female realtor gave a grand tour of the upscale property on TV. The white-blanket walls displayed different-sized paintings and canvases. The gray, uniquely styled sofa, lounge chairs, and coffee table gave the atmosphere an elegant touch. Moses and Isaac gasped at the kitchen with its high ceilings and three twirling ceiling fans, an island table, and iron chairs with an adjacent breakfast room. Then the realtor introduced the king-sized refrigerator with its deep bins and freezer. The twins loved seeing luxurious homes in magazines, on television, and in real-time.

Moses and Isaac had a bond but were distinguished in their appearance due to their separate DNA. They shared a handful of pastel M&Ms that came in their Easter baskets. The kids were born two minutes apart on August seventeenth. Moses was born with a healthy light complexion, but unfortunately for Isaac, he was born with albinism. His eyes were pink and googly, and he had impaired vision. Isaac wore thick-lensed glasses to help him to see better. He didn't notice anything wrong until people drew his attention to it. Moses always came to his brother's defense.

While the twins enjoyed the real estate television programming, they could hear their mother stirring in the kitchen. The aroma of buttery waffles and sausage filled the air as she called them. Moses and Isaac raced to the table and devoured their food like workers digging ditches. Moses immediately poked his fork into his waffles and shoved it into his mouth. His mother grabbed Moses' hand as he dropped his fork, which clanked to his plate. They bowed their heads and thanked the Lord for their blessings. During prayer, Moses wanted to thank God for everything they had and asked him to primarily protect Isaac from the ills of the world. Then they devoured their waffles with those delicious berries and cream.

Keys rattled at the side door adjacent to the kitchen of their home. It swung open as Calvin Mitchell, a late-forties gentleman strolled into the kitchen with the Sunday paper under his arm. The boys rushed from the table and into their stepfather's arms. He worked nights as an airplane mechanic, earning a good income. Calvin knew that Moses had promised, and he had mapped out Moses' life for success. He and Irene envisioned Moses being the top dog on Wall Street or some executive of a Fortune 500 company. They didn't see a promising future for Isaac since his handicap would burden him. He did not worry about this child too much. It was in God's hands.

Church bells chimed on this sunny morning as the congregation entered the place of worship dressed in their Easter Sunday attire. Moses and Isaac, both dressed in a three-piece suit-clad, marched up the concrete steps. Their arms were around each other like their best friends as their parents followed inside. Minutes later, the congregation crooned with a beautiful organ in the background. The brothers sang from the book of Psalms. Moses nudged his brother because he didn't sing.

"What," Isaac nudged Moses in return.

"Sing," Moses instructed.

"I can't sing! I don't know how," Isaac shrugged his shoulders.

"God understands. Sing anyway," Moses encouraged. Then Isaac raised his voice. The congregation heard this little boy singing his heart out to the heavens. They smirked and smiled at this child with his innocence and his disability, which made strangers pour their hearts out. The congregation concluded in their song and sat down. Then, the reverend approached the altar to read the Bible scripture, John 14:2. "In God's house, there are many mansions." When Moses and Isaac heard that, their faces lit up. The twins wanted to know if God had mansions for good people. Moses glared at the preacher, who proceeded with the sermon. This messenger of the Almighty had been sent down from Heaven to save the congregation of what was yet to come. "God invests in real estate. Wow!", Moses whispered to Isaac. Mesmerized by the scripture, Moses grabbed the Saint James bible, flipping to the scripture of John 14:2. He tapped Issac as they both leaned and read the holy words. Moses placed a religious Bible marker on the page and closed the good book.

That afternoon, several ceiling fans twirled fresh air onto customers eating lunch at a diner. Moses and Isaac ate taco salads while their parents had chicken and waffles. Calvin sat directly in front of Moses, paying closer attention to him. Moses questioned his stepfather about the scripture's meaning of many mansions, to which Calvin told him Heaven was a place of comfort and peace. That is how Calvin interpreted it. Then Moses asked his mother about the Bible verse. Irene believed the same thing: a place of peace and comfort for all humankind. Moses raised an eyebrow because his mother agreed with whatever the father believed. "So, God doesn't have real estate in Heaven?" Moses asked. "Maybe God does." Calvin took a sip of his soda. Isaac ate his salad quietly, taking it all in. "How's your salad, Isaac?" Calvin asked as he stuffed a chicken tender in his mouth. "Good," Isaac chewed his food.

About an hour later, Moses chased Isaac from the diner as they held some leftover food in a bag to take home. The twins chuckled while goofing off in the parking lot. Luckily, there were no cars in motion. Moses almost bumped into the less fortunate man who kept his eyes in front of him. He wore soiled, ragged clothing and shoes and pushed a shopping cart with an old dog by his side. He hadn't bathed or showered since God only knows when. Moses focused on the poor soul walking across the parking lot and looked at the bag in his hand. He then blocked the needy man's path — a bold move for a kid his age — and offered him the leftover food. "Sir, you can have my taco salad," Moses handed the dingy man his food. Isaac observed the interaction between his brother and the homeless man behind his thick-lensed glasses. Then the filthy man took the bag from Moses' hand. "Thank you, young man. God bless you." Moses ran towards Isaac as they watched the homeless man moving on with his four-legged friend. Isaac noticed he still held his doggie bag in his hand and wanted to do the same good deed. He could have given his salad to the man, but it was too late. "What are you boys doing fooling around in the parking lot?" Irene placed her hands on her hips.

On the way home, Christian music played in Calvin's blue Subaru, driving along Sunrise Highway. Moses and Isaac sat quietly in the back, glancing out their windows. Isaac's taco salad sat between them. Moses noticed average homes in the background. They didn't impress him. Then his eyes widened as the properties became more abundant and fancier. Moses did not understand why his father was driving to this neck of the woods. The further Calvin went into the affluent neighborhood, Isaac fidgeted in his seat. He peered over Moses' side window. The luxurious real estate enchanted the twins with its iron gates, trimmed hedges, well-kept lawns, and thick glass and stone houses. Moses and Isaac compared the houses to the ones they saw on television and in magazines.

"When we grow up, we'll sell all the houses in the world," Isaac said.

"Yeah. We will have our real estate firm," Moses added.

The boy's parents were pleased with their kids' ambition. Calvin told his stepsons that they needed to have their real estate license. They could get it at eighteen years of age. Moses and Isaac got excited because they knew that were close.

"You boys have a decade before you can get your license," Irene said, wiping makeup from her face in the mirror with a tissue.

"And you must take the real estate course. It teaches everything you need to know. Then you must take the big exam to get the license."

Calvin drove his car slowly, proceeding to admire the beautiful residential homes.

"Is the test hard?" Isaac's eyes enlarged behind his thick-lensed spectacles. "If you love what you do, then you should have no problem," Calvin started the drive his vehicle faster.

Moses and Isaac drew their attention back to the beautiful properties. One mansion after the other, there was so much to see. A Caucasian gentleman drove his blue Mercedes Benz into the opposite lane. Moses made eye contact with this grumpy man, who rolled his eyes. Calvin took notice of the man's attitude as well. From there, he gave his stepsons a lesson on intolerance and not allowing anyone to tell you that your dreams are too big.

That night, before going to bed, Moses worked on English homework due the next day. He shuffled through his pocket dictionary, looking up words. Moses did not lift his head from his book for a minute. Isaac glued his eyes to the cartoons on television without glancing away for a second. Calvin opened the door, seeing Moses busy with homework, and asked him what subject homework he was doing. He told him he had to complete his English homework. Calvin encouraged Moses to continue working toward his excellent grades to make the honor roll again. Calvin didn't bother to ask Isaac about his homework. Why stress himself out? It was what it was.

"Time for bed." Calvin clapped his hands, getting the kids' attention. Moses packed his English book into his backpack. Isaac turned off the television, hopped into bed, and sighed. He took his glasses off and put them into a case. His eyes googled as his stepfather snickered. Moses knew Calvin always laughed at his brother Isaac. Regardless of how close Moses and his stepfather were, he didn't like it when people made fun of Isaac. Moses glared at his brother, kneeling by his bedside, praying. Moses then bowed down and prayed. While he prayed, Moses gave God as much time as he could; he did not rush his prayers. His family was the most important thing and a prosperous future. He envisioned the many mansions in Heaven, like the Hamptons, Beverly Hills, Palm Beach, Palm Springs, and Whitestone, New York. His biological father, Jacob, occupied one of those mansions waiting to welcome Moses and Isaac when their time was up. Moses believed his Father watched their every move, and if he did something wrong, He didn't want to disappoint his Father and God. So, he and Isaac always did their best to do the right thing. Moses then concluded his prayers with the sign of the cross. As he opened his eyes, he noticed Isaac still praying. Disturbing someone while they were spending time with God was rude. Moses climbed into his slumber, pulling the covers over himself. As he closed his eyes, he then opened one and noticed Isaac bowing down. "Isaac!"

"I'm praying. I got a lot of stuff to tell God!" Isaac murmured and then did the sign of the cross as he leaped upon his bed. He pulled the blanket over his head. "What did you pray for?" Moses whispered. "I prayed we would become very successful in life." Isaac snatched the blanket from over his head and glared at his brother cross-eyed. "We will be," Moses said with confidence. "Do you believe that?"

"Yes," Moses turned his back on Isaac, pulling the blanket over him and shutting his eyes. He remembered what was told to him earlier. "Your dreams are never too big."

CHAPTER TWO

Monday morning, a small mini school bus of clamoring kids honked its horn outside the Remington home. The pupils ranged from first to fourth graders, honor roll students, middle-average students, and special education students. The residence's screen door swung open as Moses approached the school bus. He wore his navy-blue backpack, dressed in jeans, a shirt, sneakers, and a light jacket. Isaac took baby steps, going down the concrete steps with his Spiderman backpack. Irene raised her voice to scare Isaac into getting on that bus. But her yelling didn't intimidate this nine-year-old, who halted at the bottom of the steps. Calvin stormed out of the house in his pajamas and grabbed Isaac, throwing his small body over his shoulder. "I don't want to go to school! I hate it!" Isaac kicked and screamed. His backpack fell to the ground. Calvin grabbed it. Moses escorted Isaac to the front seat of the bus. He begged Isaac to stop crying. The kids snickered as they saw Isaac's skin turning red, with tears cascading from under his thick-lensed glasses. He didn't care what the kids thought; he wanted to go home.

"How are you and I going into business together if you don't go to school?" Moses

encouraged.

"I need this stuff?" Isaac lifted his bifocals, wiping his tears away.

"Yes," Moses shook his head, giving his brother a comforting smile. From that point on, Isaac felt better. No one else could instill confidence besides Moses, not even his mother. Isaac looked over his shoulder, noticing the kids staring and giggling. He took a deep breath and turned around. Moses saw a chubby boy poking fun at Isaac. "That's not funny, porky!"

"Who are you calling porky, peanut head!" The overweight boy insulted, lounging from his seat.

"Leave my brother alone! That goes for all of you!" Moses gave everyone the evil eye. No one dared to challenge Moses. Instead, they focused their eyes in the other direction and minded their business. This bus of rowdy kids became as quiet as church mice. The female bus driver, Martha, did nothing to put these kids in check. They weren't her kids. Moses sneered at her through her rearview mirror. He sneered at this thirty-something woman, who probably hated driving this bus of bratty, boisterous kids to school every day.

Upon their arrival at school, Moses and Isaac stepped off the bus. Then, they hurried towards the uniquely structured school, which would make any parent want to have their child educated there. The twins stuck out their chests and marched as if nothing had ever happened. Moses walked Isaac to his classroom. He informed Isaac about the future and how he needed an education; therefore, they'll be successful in real estate. Isaac smiled, trusting his brother's words, as they gave each other hi-fives. Moses left his brother's side, sashaying down the hallway to his class.

Moses bumped into pretty, African American, Arianna, eight years old, whose notebook fell out of her arms. She had the biggest smile as Moses gave her binder back. They had a crush on each other even though they were in different classes. They hung out on the playground, complaining about too much homework and the future, "So, how was your weekend?" Arianna asked, smiling from ear to ear.

"It was the same ole, same ole," Moses returned the friendly gesture. Then the school bell rang as Moses and Arianna dashed into their noisy classrooms across the hallway from each other.

Inside Moses' class, he took his seat in the second row, second seat. He unpacked his books and placed them on the desk. Then, he gave his friend, Sammy, a high-five. Sammy was a clean-cut young man with an innocent boyish look. Mrs. Neuman, their teacher, rushed into the clamoring classroom. She clapped her hands to get the pupils' attention. "Quiet." The students became silent. The teacher smiled at the children's cooperation. "Thank you."

"Please, I would like you to read the chapter on the history of jazz. Can anyone name a jazz musician?" Mrs. Neuman asked.

Moses raised his hand, and looked around to see if anyone else knew this subject.

"Yes, Moses."

"Miles Davis, Louis Armstrong, Dizzy Gillespie, Lionel Hampton," Moses answered.

"Excellent, Moses," Mrs. Neuman wrote the subject for the day on the blackboard. "Why do we have to learn about jazz? I don't plan on becoming a musician," Moses imagined a twenty-million-dollar mansion where a tall iron gate guarded it. He drove in a Mercedes Benz as the fence opened to the front door of the estate. A maid and butler greeted him at the entrance of his house. Then, a beautiful female, a twenty-something-year-old, greeted him with a kiss. In his fantasy, he did not know this woman. She could be Arianna or some other girl whom he'd meet later in life. She clutched his hand as they waltzed into the foyer, where a massive crystal chandelier hung in the thirty-foot ceiling. A marble table sat under it with a glass vase holding freshly cut roses. A double staircase led to the mansion's west and east wings. Further inside and down a long hallway, photos plastered marble walls of Moses and Isaac's booming real estate firm, Moses' wedding, and other pictures of their family. He created this fantasy in his head. That woman meeting him at the door would be Arianna, who would become his wife. Then the couple entered the marble living room with its cream-colored sofa and lounge chairs. An oval-shaped light fixture hung above the marble coffee table. An aroma of tomato sauce filled the air, where a personal chef cooked a fabulous Italian dish for him and Arianna. They took the private marble elevator up to the second floor, where they entered his master bedroom. Once there, a maid awaited Moses. He threw off his jacket. The maid, grabbing his expensive Armani garment, hung it up. Moses opened the double doors to the stone-crafted balcony, overlooking a keyhole-shaped swimming pool with trimmed hedges and lawns. He looked across at a vast lawn lot of trees. Arianna wrapped her arms around his waist. Then, he turned towards Arianna's face. The couple leaned in for a kiss.

"Moses?" Mrs. Neuman called him.

Moses constantly blinked his eyes, coming out of his fantasy. Then he looked directly at his teacher in a daze. "Answer the question. Who was the jazz artist who composed *A-Train*?" Mrs. Neuman questioned. "Duke Ellington," Moses inhaled. He took sharp breaths, wondering why none of the students knew the answers to these questions. Maybe they knew, but they were too tired to answer. Moses hoped Mrs. Neuman didn't only look at him to answer all the questions. He didn't want anyone riding on his coattail.

Down the hallway, the entire school could hear Isaac's boisterous, echoing class. Isaac sat next to the window in the front. He didn't participate much with the other kids because he couldn't take the name-calling. The class had eight students, so Mr. Reyes, their teacher, could get more one-on-one time. The instructor – a tall, skinny gentleman in a casual shirt, blue jeans, and sneakers– rushed back into the classroom several doors down from the principal's office.

"What's up with you guys? I leave the room for one second, and you go haywire.!" Mr. Reyes stood before the map of the solar system on the wall. "What's the coldest planet?" he asked, pointing with a yardstick. Isaac raised his hand when his classmates couldn't answer the question.

"Isaac," Mr. Reyes paced the floor in front of his class.

"Pluto," Isaac shied away.

"That's correct, Isaac. Pluto!" Mr. Reyes encouraged.

"We're going to learn about every planet and its place in the universe," the teacher continued with his lesson. Isaac's mind drifted off, not into space, but here on Earth. He pictured giving a tour of a penthouse on Park Avenue to a comedian or a billionaire that overlooked Central Park. The image played out in Isaac's head like a movie. Isaac, twenty-eight years of age, sported Armani black dress pants, a sky-blue dress shirt paired with a black tie, a black vest, and pattern-leather shoes. Isaac detailed everything that made up the great room's décor, from the thick ceramic ceiling to the marble floor. The gray-colored sofa, lounge chairs, and unique-styled coffee table were in the center. He and his client waltzed into the red kitchen, with its ebony table and chairs. A massive light fixture was in the ceiling above the table in the breakfast room.

"Isaac, what is the hottest planet?" Mr. Reyes' voice echoed.

"Mercury," Isaac snapped out of his dream.

"That's correct," Mr. Reyes praised. A skinny kid, Angelo, nine years old, sat in the back. He sneered at Isaac every time he answered a question correctly. It vexed him. Angelo drew nude pictures of a woman and concealed them. Then Mr. Reyes spoke about life on other planets. "Do you think aliens live on these planets?" Isaac asked as his eyes crossed through his thick-lensed glasses. "What kind of stupid question is that?" Angelo mumbled.

"It's not a stupid question, Angelo! Scientists have been studying other planets for years, to see if there's life." Mr. Reyes pounded his fist on the blackboard.

Angelo felt like the dumbest kid in the class. He glared at Isaac and punched his fist into his hand. Isaac didn't notice Angelo's intentions because he gave the teacher his undivided attention.

At lunchtime, noisy second-, third-, and fourth-grade students packed the spacious cafeteria with its long, stretched white benches. Isaac sat with his class on the side, looking for his brother's class. He wished he could have lunch with his brother, but he had to remain with his class.

Moses' honor class entered the lunchroom. Isaac scanned the body of students, hoping to see Moses. He felt as if Moses had celebrity status or something. Then he made his presence known. Moses looked around and spotted his brother Isaac calling him. Moses gave Isaac a high-five. Angelo sat at the end of the table behind Isaac and witnessed Isaac's tight relationship with Moses. A few minutes later, students chowed down on burgers, French fries, an apple, and milk. Isaac stuffed some French fries into his mouth without a care. Angelo then sat before Isaac and glared at him. Then, Isaac stopped chewing, wondering why Angelo had a problem with him.

Angelo snatched Isaac's burger from his tray. "Give me back my burger, you ass!"

Isaac tried to get his sandwich back. His outburst only drew the attention of the kids very close by. No one heard the commotion between Isaac and Angelo throughout an extremely clamoring cafeteria. The two boys wrestled over the burger as Isaac climbed over the table. Angelo pushed Isaac to the floor, where his glasses fell off his face. Luckily, the lenses didn't crack. Angelo stood on the other side of the table, guffawing at Isaac. Then Moses put Angelo in the headlock, ambushing him from behind. Moses and Angelo scuffled to the floor as the kids cheered them on. Isaac remained on the floor, witnessing his hero come to his rescue. He then rose as the students flocked to the boys' fight. Isaac tried to maneuver through the crowd but couldn't see anything. So, Isaac stood atop the table to better see Moses kicking Angelo's ass. Suddenly, a teacher pulled the boys apart and dragged them out of the lunchroom.

The brothers bickered with Angelo in the dean's office for the rest of the lunch hour. Mr. Servideo, the dean, rocked back and forth in a lounge chair with his arms folded. He didn't say a word until the boys quit. But they kept on and on. The dean intervened as Moses and Angelo rose, ready to go for round two.

"Quit it!" Mr. Servideo turned tomato red in the face. The principal, Mrs. Darla Pacheco, strutted into the dean's office, where she hauled off Angelo by the collar. The bully kicked and screamed like a little girl. Mrs. Pacheco struggled to get this kid into her office, but he was too much to handle. Then, Mr. Servideo dragged Angelo into her office. Moses and Isaac watched as this adult authoritarian acted. The twins quieted themselves as the principal's door slammed shut. They glared at each other and hoped nothing similar would occur. What was their punishment going to be? Angelo bellowed obscenities towards the principal and dean, and they gave him a piece of their mind. Their angered voices echoed down the hallway.

"What happened, Isaac?" Moses asked in an angry voice.

"He took my hamburger from me!"

"Why did he do that?" Moses clutched his fists in the air.

"Angelo's an asshole!" Isaac cursed.

"His father's probably going to kick his ass good," Moses added. The twins cackled as they pictured Angelo getting a beating from his parents and crying like a baby. The principal's door swung open as Mr. Servideo waltzed out. He wasn't pleased with the twins' behavior, especially since Moses was an honor student. The dean made allowances for Isaac because the kids ridiculed him. He didn't want to call the twins' parents because they were good kids, but still, he had to inform them of what happened.

An hour later, Moses and Isaac sat quietly in Mr. Servideo's office glancing at each other. The dean resided at his desk with his arms folded, not knowing what to think. Not a word was spoken, just looks. Then Irene rushed into the dean's office. Moses noticed his mother's heartbroken expression seeing her favorite son in the dean's office. Irene embraced and kissed him multiple times. While she did this Moses saw Isaac witnessing this display of affection from their mother toward her firstborn. Isaac slumped in the chair in the corner, waiting for his turn to hopefully receive kisses and hugs. Moses then noticed his mother's expression change. She went from a concerned parent for one son to an enraged parent for the other son. Irene abruptly turned to Isaac and blamed him for this whole dilemma. Not with words, but due to the frown upon her face, eyebrows rising, and her turning somewhat red despite her myelinated complexion. Moses had a feeling she held Isaac responsible for this.

CHAPTER THREE

That night, Moses and Isaac quietly did their homework in their dimmed bedroom. Isaac read the chapter on planets from his science textbook. He peered over at Moses reading his textbook on his bed. Then Moses glanced from his English textbook to Isaac, who was doing his science homework. "You're studying planets?"

"Duh," Isaac continued his homework.

"What planet is between the sun and the earth? "Moses yawned.

"Mercury," Isaac shook his head. He turned the TV on with the remote control. He switched through the channels and watched *THE JEFFERSONS*, a seventies sitcom. Isaac guffawing at George Jefferson's jokes. Moses engrossed his attention in the chapter on Dizzy Gillespie from his English textbook. He noticed that his brother kept laughing, but Moses kept on reading.

Finally, he looked at the television and wanted to laugh but held it in. "You know you're in trouble, Isaac," his brother reminded him. Isaac sighed, shrugging his shoulders. But he proceeded to cackle at the TV. Then Moses gave in and laughed along with his brother. It was the episode where George Jefferson slammed the door in Mr. Bentley's face. The twins took a break from their homework and watched the rest of the show. They both knew the storyline of the sitcom. Mr. Jefferson had made it successfully because of his dry-cleaning business. Then, he bought a penthouse overlooking the Manhattan skyline. They had friends and associates from wealthy families who owned profitable companies. Shows like this gave the boys hope and inspired them to achieve their goals. During the commercial break, Isaac danced in front of his brother Moses. He made up his own version of The Jefferson's theme song. "Well, we're moving up to the Hamptons, to a multi-million-dollar cottage between the sand and sky, got the whole pie," Isaac clowned.

"A piece of the pie? Not the whole pie?" Moses cackled.

The boys heard the creaking of their bedroom door amongst the loud television volume.

Irene stood in the doorway with her hands on her hips. Isaac immediately turned the TV off. He hurried to his bed, proceeding with his studies. Their mother gathered their clothing and toys, which had been left scattered around the room. Moses sensed his mother's anger and kept his head in his book. He read the chapter on this famous jazz musician and his peculiar horn. As he skimmed through the paragraphs of the story, Moses could hear the blaring of this man's trumpet in his head. There was tension in the air, which made him very uncomfortable. Moses then glanced at Isaac to see how he dealt with the uneasy presence. Isaac didn't react to it.

"Why can't you guys keep the room tidy?" Irene shoved Isaac's clothes in the hamper. The twins apologized to their mother in a submissive tone. They put their homework aside and helped do their chores. Irene refused their help, wanting her sons to focus on school. So, she would take care of the house. Moses nudged Isaac and whispered in his ear. As Irene threw more clothes in the hamper, she could see the twins talking amongst themselves from the corner of her eyes. "Don't worry; you're in the clear. You did the right thing, Moses, sticking up for your brother," Irene folded Isaac's clean shirts, stuffing them into the drawer. Hopefully, their stepfather would be proud of him as well. Calvin was incredibly proud of Moses because he had leadership. Moses' parents didn't have to check behind him because this kid had authority. Irene knew it was in her son's blood. She believed being first had its privileges. As such, Irene carried the hamper out of the bedroom and closed the door. Isaac then turned the television back on and continued to watch *The Jeffersons*. Moses encouraged Isaac to finish his homework. So, Isaac sat on his bed and continued his assignment for school with the TV still playing. Then a male voice echoed from the first floor. The frats glanced at each other.

"Holy shit! It's Dad!" Isaac turned the TV off with the remote control as his heart pounded in his chest.

"Don't worry! We're in the clear, Isaac!" Moses calmly advised his brother.

"You mean, "You're in the clear!" Isaac shook his head.

"Trust me!" Moses continued with his studies.

Heavy footsteps approached the boys' bedroom. Even though Moses claimed not to be worried, his heart raced. He feared for Isaac. Calvin rushed into the boys' bedroom and sat before his sons in the chair, giving them a light tongue-lashing. "I disapprove of you fighting in school. You're there to get an education," Calvin lectured.

Luckily, the frats didn't get suspended, but his stepfather let Isaac have it. Calvin held Isaac responsible for the fight. Moses came to his brother's defense again as he did in school. Calvin pointed out Moses' problem that he always fought his brother's battles. One day, Moses would have to allow Isaac to defend himself. But he disagreed with his stepfather and stood his ground once more. He sensed Calvin's attempt to break their brotherly bond, even though he loved seeing the twin's interaction. The boys heard that Angelo had been transferred to another school. Angelo came from a dysfunctional family. His mother was an abusive woman who always cursed him out. His father was a no-show, and his nana was no better. She cursed up a storm while she drank day in and day out. The house needed cleaning, and she didn't even cook. That's the reason Angelo stole food. Moses didn't buy the excuses. There was no reason for someone to bully another person because they've got issues. Then Calvin presented three *Unique Homes magazines,* showcasing luxurious properties around the world. The boys flipped through the pages of affluent real estate they loved so much. Calvin then snatched the magazines from the boys and asked if they had finished their homework. It was obvious, the boys had their books opened and were halfway done. Isaac returned to his bed and finished his studies. On Calvin's way out, he tossed the upscale magazines on the side table and winked his eye at them. That was a sign of "Everything's okay." Moses proceeded with his homework, but Isaac rushed through the answers to his assignment. He glanced at the stack of magazines on the side table. He then sprung from the bed and grabbed a magazine from the side table. His eyes widen, mesmerized by a fancy mansion in Palm Springs, California.

"Moses, look!" Isaac showed his brother the colorful page of the fabulous home in the magazine. Moses glanced at the magazine that Isaac held in his hand. Moses 'eyes widen at the breathtaking mansion. The frats turned colorful pages of photos portraying the good life. An estate in Coconut Grove, Florida, had a swimming pool in the rear of the beige-colored villa, built in the nineteen-twenties and recently renovated. This property had an elevator going up three floors and a tennis court on the premises, with five master bedrooms with a patio overlooking views of tropical gardens and palm trees, a spacious living room with a high ceiling, a black and gold spacious kitchen with built-in appliances, a dishwasher, a wine cellar, etc. After reading the description of this home, Moses and Isaac browsed through this upscale magazine like a comic book. "I'd like to sell this property," Moses turned to the next page and noticed properties in different states. He checked the table of contents, where he saw the homes from other regions of the world. One section showcased homes from the United States, the Virgin Islands, Europe, Japan, and South Korea. Moses read the information about the real estate agents and the companies that sold the properties. He placed the periodical aside and proceeded with his studies.

"We've got to get good grades," Moses advised as he finished his homework. Isaac ignored his brother's advice, flipping through the magazine while his eyes crisscrossed behind his lenses.

"Look, Moses. Check out the mansion in the Hamptons," Isaac shoved the magazine page in his brother's face. The enlarged photos of the cottage, the foyer, dining room, master bedroom, and swimming pool made Moses smile from ear to ear. Moses got back to work on his homework. Isaac felt alone as his brother hit the books. Isaac suddenly had second thoughts about Moses' advice toward getting an education and pursuing goals. This made Isaac drop the magazine and finish his school assignments. Isaac wanted to follow in his brother's footsteps and into the real estate market.

CHAPTER FOUR

The mini school bus waited outside Moses and Isaac's home the next school day. The screen door opened as the twins dashed out and hopped on the bus. Irene smiled and sighed, noticing she didn't have to fight with Isaac to go to school. Calvin approached Irene and waved to their boys as the bus sped off. The bus was silent, and none of the kids moved a muscle. Moses and Isaac resided in the front seat. There was dead silence. Isaac whispered in Moses's ear. Moses shrugged his shoulders and didn't pay attention. Instead, he stared at his parents standing in the living room. His mind was blank again and couldn't think of anything that would appease him. Isaac was busy glancing at the kids to figure out what was going on. They didn't say anything or even look at him or Moses. He put a smile on his face because he figured that Moses had everyone in check. Moses had the power to lead and would have everyone begging for mercy.

In gym class later that morning, Isaac practiced shooting the basketball into the hoop. He played by himself and didn't bother to join in with the other students. He'd figured they were probably angry with him because of Angelo. Isaac dribbled the basketball and tried to throw it into the basket. But he missed as the basketball bounced onto the floor. Isaac caught it and attempted another shot. He saw the girls playing jump rope and the boys shooting hoops on the other side of the gymnasium. Isaac continued to dribble the basketball and threw it in the hoop. Once again, he missed the shot. Regardless of Isaac's impaired vision, he tried again but still missed shots. Finally, he got the courage and marched over to his male classmates. Isaac asked them to play. His classmates shrugged their shoulders and concurred. The boys took turns tossing the basketball into the hoop. Some missed as others made the ball through the basket.

In the bigger gymnasium on the first floor, Moses and his friends played a fast-paced basketball game. For a kid Moses' age, he was an outstanding player. Moses' gym teacher, Mr. Dryer, was a muscular and whistle-blowing man in his late forties. He encouraged Moses to go into the NBA if given the opportunity. Moses had his dreams, though, and not someone else's.

Other activities were going on around him. A group of students played volleyball; others wrestled on a mat and others sat on the bleachers, especially the girls. A pretty, stylish-dressed girl named London, and two other girls watched Moses with his footwork on the court. She loved to see him play and beat the other players. Moses dribbled the ball around his opponents and made the perfect shot. Sweat trickled down his face. His shorts were too big with his skinny legs and enormous feet. Moses dribbled and dribbled, making shot after shot. London and the girls cheered from the bleachers. Then the bell rang. The gym period was over, and Mr. Dryer blew his whistle. "Good game, guys. To the lockers!"

London rushed from the bleachers and kissed Moses on the cheek. "Good game," London walked away with her friends. He blushed, got a pat on the back from his coach, and received high-fives from his teammates for being a good sport. One of the prettiest girls in school had an eye for him. It didn't faze him.

That afternoon, Isaac entered the classroom as Mr. Reyes grabbed him by the collar and shoved the drawing of the X-rated photo in his face. Isaac's heart raced in his chest and trembled. He became frightened by his teacher's frustration. "Are you some pervert?"

"What is that?" Isaac's voice trembled.

"You know exactly what this is!" Mr. Reyes hauled Isaac by the shirt out of the classroom.

Minutes later, Isaac cried his eyes out and slumped in a leather chair before the principal's desk. He sobbed like crazy feeling like a tiny mouse. Then he thought about Angelo; he probably drew the perverted sketch. But what was the use of telling Mrs. Pacheco when Angelo's long gone? He had no other choice other than to take the blame for it. Mr. Reyes paced the floor, shaking his head. He couldn't believe Isaac had done such a thing. This was Isaac's second time in trouble. And this time, it was all on him.

"Are you sure this was in his desk?" Mrs. Pacheco rocked in her recliner. Mr. Reyes stopped in his tracks. "Who else could it have been? It was in Isaac's desk," Mr. Reyes paced the floor, shaking his head in disbelief.

Mrs. Pacheco searched through her phone book to notify Isaac's parents. The news would get to his father, and all hell would break loose. Isaac covered his eyes because he didn't want to see his teacher and the principal. *"How could they say that I drew the picture?"* Isaac wished he could be on a beach in Martha's Vineyard with a cottage in the far distance. The seagulls flew above in the ocean's blue sky, squawking as the sea's waves crashed at shore. The interior of the Victorian-styled home had built-in technology. He wished there was no such thing as school. "*Why couldn't I have come into the world, skip the schooling, and go into real estate?"* Isaac thought. But that's not the case.

About an hour later, Mrs. Pacheco handed the X-rated drawing to Irene. She gasped at the picture of a man and woman engaged in penial/vaginal intercourse. Her face turned fiery red like a monster, ready to gobble Isaac up. She charged at him, shaking this small boy.

"Are you kidding me? You little pervert!" Irene hollered. Her voice echoed as it could be heard down the hallway of the school.

"Mrs. Remington. Please calm down!" Mrs. Pacheco stood from her seat.

"Your ass is grass when your father gets through with you! Let's go!" Irene snatched Isaac out of the principal's office.

⁂

Late afternoon, in the twins' bedroom, Irene flipped through pages of Isaac's composition notebook and textbooks to see if there were any more disgusting sketches. Then she shredded the looseleaf paper from his binder and threw it across the room. Isaac couldn't stop crying his eyes out. "What are you doing? Isaac probably has his homework in there!" Moses leaned against the wall. He heard about this drawing and knew it was Angelo who set up Isaac. But he's moved on.

"What the fuck!" Moses murmured to himself. His mother continued to terrorize this little boy who curled up in a fetal position as if he wanted to die. *"I know this hurts Isaac like hell. This is hurting me even more. Shit! If I could get Angelo. I'd fuck him up good for this shit!"* Moses leaned against the wall with his arms folded.

"Where did you learn such filth!" Irene shook Isaac like a rag doll.

Then keys rattled at the front door. It opened with a long creaking sound, and the screen door slammed. "Isaac!" a loud, angry voice called to him.

"You're in trouble now! Your father's going to let you have it," Irene released Isaac from her grip. Heavy footsteps got closer and closer as Calvin barged into the bedroom, shaking Isaac like a doll. "You were just in the principal's office yesterday! And now this! Now, you're going to be suspended!" Calvin grabbed his belt from around his waist. Isaac ran into the corner and begged for mercy. Calvin approached Isaac and raised the belt to hit him. Moses then grabbed the leather strap from his stepfather's hand.

"What the hell are you doing, boy!"

"What the hell are you doing, man!" Moses responded to his stepfather in a disobedient voice.

"Get out of my way, Moses! Before you get it!" Calvin threatened.

"I drew the picture! I drew it!" Moses confessed to his stepfather but lying.

"Don't cover for Isaac!" Irene stomped her foot.

"I drew the picture, and I gave it to Isaac. It's my fault!" Moses and Calvin played a tug of war over the belt. Then Calvin pulled the strap, throwing Moses against the wall. There was a loud thud against it. Calvin then hurled the first lash at Isaac. His skin immediately turned red fast, a deep colored mark. Moses rose to his feet and grabbed the belt from Calvin again. Then there was another tug-of-war between them. Calvin released his grip on the strap as Moses plummeted to the floor. Instead, Calvin grabbed Isaac and pinned him against the wall. Moses intervened again, punching his stepfather in the back. Calvin focused on Isaac. He lifted this helpless little boy, still pinned to the wall, from his feet. He snatched Isaac's glasses off him and threw them to the floor. Moses accidentally stepped on them, cracking the lens. Moses punched and kicked Calvin, fighting for his brother. He didn't care whether he wound up dead.

"You motherfucker! Stop this shit!" Moses then kicked Calvin. Calvin lost his balance as he and Isaac plummeted to the floor. He froze in fear with his hand over his chest. Moses stood over his stepfather like a giant. At this point, Moses wanted to kill him for hurting his brother. He felt his mother creeping up behind him. He abruptly turned, seeing that she was about to intervene. This young man was a brazen soul to get Isaac out of this mess. He rushed to his brother's side and held him. "Look what you made me do! I stepped on Isaac's glasses!" Moses sneered at his stepfather with deep-seated hatred. He grabbed the broken glasses from the floor and handed them to his mother. She stood there feeling like a complete idiot. She did nothing to stop Calvin from going crazy on her son. *"Who was more important? Is it Calvin or your son?"* Moses wondered about his mother's love for this new man in her life and her son. *Whom did she love more?*

"He needs a new pair!" Moses advised in a stern voice. "You're going to be all right," Moses whispered in his brother's ear. Isaac wiped his eyes, and mucus dripped from his nose. He escorted Isaac into the bathroom. Calvin stepped aside. His folks watched Moses take charge as if he were an adult. Moses glared at his parents. He shook his head, disappointed in these adults, especially his mother.

Early that evening, consumers window-shopped inside the busy shopping mall, while others made actual purchases. Moses and Isaac weaved in and out between customers as elevator music reverberated throughout the atmosphere. Moses had his hand on Isaac's shoulder as they entered the Pearle Vision store with their parents behind them. Inside, significant glass cases displayed eyeglasses from prescription to the latest fashion. A few minutes later, Isaac sat on a stool, where an eyeglass specialist checked his vision. The thirty-something optometrist, a slim gentleman, wore spectacles himself and put a new pair of GQ-styled prescription glasses on Isaac. He saw his reflection in the mirror and saw that they were very becoming. Irene kissed Isaac on the cheek, promising him ice cream from Carvel. Moses rolled his eyes at his mother. She knew how to appease Isaac, hoping he'd forget everything. But Moses wouldn't. The glasses made Isaac's eyes smaller, but they still crossed. He felt like he could do anything that Moses could do.

That night, the brothers had the textbooks opened on the bed, doing homework with every light on in their bedroom. Isaac studied his eight- and nine-times tables while Moses read another chapter in his textbook about classical music. Its origins and popularity throughout time. He shook his head and flipped through the pages. It was longer than the chapter on Dizzy Gillespie. *"What strange creative genius is it this time? They say that most creative people are the biggest looney tunes,"* Moses turned page after page to see how much he had to read. He needed to find out when Isaac would return to school. He was going to do everything possible to protect Isaac. *"Don't cover for your brother! Don't cover for your brother, Moses,"* Irene and Calvin's voices played in his head.

An hour later, it was lights out as Moses and Isaac tucked into bed, ready for a night's rest. Isaac slept like a newborn, sucking his thumb. Moses was wide awake, noticing his baby brother with his thumb stuck in his mouth. He never understood why Isaac did this. He's not a baby anymore. Moses exhaled and slept on his side, facing Isaac. Isaac rested across from him in his twin-sized bed. His Spider-man blanket covered halfway around his body. He tossed and turned with his thumb still in his mouth. Goosebumps emerged on his pale skin. A chill swept through the bedroom as a shadowy figure hovered over Isaac's twin-sized bed. His thumb snatched from his mouth; Isaac woke up. Then, someone tossed him over their shoulder. "Moses!" Isaac cried. He reached his hand out towards his brother as Moses awakened to his screams. He sprung from his bed and extended his arms to Isaac. Moses ran behind the unknown person who carried his brother out of their home like a sack of potatoes.

"Mom! Dad!" Isaac cried for his parents. Irene and Calvin calmly left their master bedroom to see the commotion. Moses leaped on this stranger's back, wrapping his arms around this man's neck. Still, Moses couldn't get a glimpse of this intruder because of the murky living room.

"Dad, Mom, do something! Where are they taking Isaac?" Moses bellowed.

His parents didn't move a muscle as this obscure man took the child, which put a strain on them. The intruder abruptly opened the front door, kicked out the screen door, and stormed out of the residence. Isaac bawled like crazy as he reached out for Moses' hand. A dark-colored van parked in front of their home with its engine running, while another weird gentleman slid the door open. A third stranger grabbed Moses off the intruder's back, throwing him onto the cold, cemented ground. Moses screamed in pain, not just physical pain but emotional. The peculiar being hurled Isaac into the van like a corpse and slid the door shut, locking it. His brother looked out of the window, crying for help. Luckily, Moses rose to his feet and limped to the van. The vehicle sped off down the road. Calvin grabbed Moses, dragging him back to the house. "Mom!" Isaac screamed, but it was no use.

In this rickety, junky van, Isaac realized he wasn't alone. He had no glasses, so his vision was blurred. He didn't know what to do or what to think. He then peered out of the small windows of the van and noticed it sped on a highway or a road. Isaac needed to find out where it was going. He looked around, but he couldn't make these people out as he squinted his eyes. With what vision he had, there were people who clustered and shivered in the rusty, bumpy vehicle. He sat down, not hearing a peep from anyone. Isaac wiped his eyes. Then maybe he could see. No luck. He then closed them as the uneven ride drove to a place unknown. Then the van's brakes screeched. Isaac suddenly opened his eyes, and his vision was clear. He looked around the truck, noticing the people huddled together. Then the faceless intruder slid open the van's door, which gave some light.

There were adults and kids who wore torn pajamas and were albinos, just like him. The faceless men grabbed every one of these disposable human beings, escorting them through the entrance of a dark building as the moon beamed in the night sky. The smell of blood, feces, and urine filled the air. Isaac and the group strolled in as the scent became more robust. Isaac held his nose and saw a pile of feces on the floor. He maneuvered away from it to avoid stepping in it. Blood streamed down the walls and even splattered on them. A small puddle of urine was on the floor. Isaac tapped the shoulder of a shivering, seventeen-year-old albino male wearing only his boxers.

"Do you know what this place is?" Isaac asked. The teen glared at him and gestured to Isaac's neck being slashed. Isaac's eyes bulged as his heart raced. Dozens of the faceless robust guards patrolled the premises. They packed loaded firearms, tasers, handcuffs, and pepper spray. Isaac wanted to make a run for it but was too afraid. Screams echoed throughout the entire building as a young albino girl sat in a wheelchair with her hands and feet amputated. She wore drenched bloody bandages with a half-blood-soaked gown.

"Mommy! Mommy!" the eight-year-old girl shrieked. This young girl had her limbs cut off, and Isaac's next. He tapped the seventeen-year-old young man on the shoulder again. "Why are they doing this?" Isaac trembled.

"We're going to have our legs cut off or our heads," the seventeen-year-old albino snickered as if he looked forward to being tortured. Isaac's heart raced in his chest, and he bolted towards the exit. Once again, a robust guard caught the small boy, throwing him over his shoulders.

"No, where are you taking me?" Isaac kicked and screamed. His cries reverberated for all the misfits to hear. The guard hustled through the double doors with this eighty-nine-pound child over his shoulder. He hauled Isaac down a long hallway to surgery.

"Where are you taking me?" Isaac hollered as his voice quivered. Sweat trickled all over his body. An eight-person medical team awaited this pink-skinned child ranting and raving as the security guard placed him on the operating table. The doctors strapped his small body down.

"I want to go home!" Isaac fidgeted on the table.

"You're a curse," the medical doctor said.

"I'm not a curse!" Isaac spat on the doctor.

"You're bad luck. We must rid you and others like yourself from this world!" the doctor held a hacksaw in his hand.

"I'm not bad luck! I'm not a curse!" Isaac cried repeatedly. The surgeon placed the sharp object on Isaac's upper thigh, sawing, starting at the hip. Blood streamed out as flesh popped out of the skin. Isaac screamed, experiencing the most severe pain ever.

Isaac tossed and turned in bed, screaming. Moses sprung from his bed, nudging Isaac. "Isaac, wake up. Wake up."

Isaac opened his eyes and noticed a shadowy figure before him.

"Who are you?" Isaac screamed.

Moses turned the light on and sat on the side table. Isaac didn't bother to put on his glasses because he knew Moses' voice. Isaac embraced his brother, crying, "Are you okay, Isaac?" Moses asked.

"No," Isaac sat up in his bed.

"Tell me about your dream. If you don't mind me asking," Moses said curiously.

"I had a dream that there was a group of people that murdered and tortured albinos," Isaac exhaled on his back in his twin-sized bed.

"No one is going to hurt you." Moses balled his hands into fists, ready to take on anyone.

"Am I a curse?" Isaac asked Moses.

"No," Moses clutched his brother and didn't let him go. He wished he had powers to protect Isaac from the world's evils. Then Isaac put his thumb back in his mouth. Moses held his brother in his arms as Isaac regressed to an infant. He then lay his brother on the bed, turning him on his side. Moses glared at his brother.

Seconds later, Moses crept down the long murky hallway, where a glow seeped through the cracks of his parents' bedroom door. He quickly turned the knob as moans and groans were on high volume — Calvin's hairy buttock was right before Moses' eyes.

"Yuck! Does Calvin wipe his butt when he goes to the bathroom?" Moses closed his eyes to the hideous sight. Irene's legs were over Calvin's shoulders as he thrust aggressively onto her. Moses sneered at them. *"How could any mother not hear their child's scream in the middle of the night? What the hell is wrong with my mother? I don't get it."* He slammed the door shut.

"I bet that got their attention!" Moses commented.

CHAPTER FIVE

The following morning, with light precipitation, frigid temperatures, and cloudiness, made it unusual for April. Moses exited through the screen door of his home alone, wearing his navy-blue raincoat. He didn't feel right going to school without his better half. Irene demanded a kiss from her favorite son. Moses stopped in his tracks, made a bow face, and took his time up the cemented steps. He quickly pecked his mother on the cheek, dashing towards the bus as it waited with its door open. Moses then waved to Isaac who stood in the living room window. Isaac waved back and then stormed away. Moses ran on the clamoring bus, sitting in the front row. Two girls played hand games, some boys threw paper balls and other kids cackled and teased each other. Moses didn't pay any attention to these misbehaved kids. *"Isaac's teacher accused him of drawing X-rated pictures, and then last night, I had to wake him up from his nightmare. Damn!"* Moses thought, leaning his head against the window. Then the school bus sped off.

Moments later, Moses kept his head against the window, his eyes set on the grounds that the bus drove on without a single thought. His eyes watered as a tear trickled down his face. He wiped it away. He felt alone on this bus ride and then set his sights on the traffic lights Martha ran. She sped down the road, making a sharp turn at the intersection. The brakes screeched at a red light, creating a shortstop. A patrol car parked across the street watched out for reckless drivers who zoomed through the area. Moses eyed the white male cop in the driver's seat of the patrol car, wondering if he noticed Martha's reckless driving. The cop glared directly at the school bus driver. Moses set his eyes on Martha through the enlarged rearview mirror. Her eyes shifted from side to side, hoping this cop wouldn't give her a ticket. Moses noticed her face tremble, and within a minute, the traffic light signaled green. She accelerated, making her way out of the cop's sight.

Later that morning, Moses slumped at his desk with his art textbook open. The lesson of the day was about opera singer Andrea Bocelli. Born on September 22, 1958, in Lajatico, Tuscany, Italy, Andrea Bocelli is a beloved classical universal singer who worked with pop star Celine Dion and countless artists. At age twelve, doctors diagnosed Andrea with congenital glaucoma caused by a soccer accident, which resulted in him losing vision completely. Still, he didn't allow his handicap to stop him from what he loved most, which was singing. A music industry executive described Bocelli's voice as the most beautiful in the world.

As Moses kept reading about this magnificent artist, he pictured his future success. A multi-million-dollar estate in the South of France had a private beach. The water was light blue at the shore and further out the ocean got deeper into hue. The crashing waves had a low volume, making the beach quiet. A stretch of stone steps made its way up to the home. An infinity swimming pool had a similar color to the shallow waters of the beach down below. Patio furniture sat along the side of it with the stone mansion in the background. Lavender gardens perfumed the air from every direction. Moses waltzed up the stone steps toward the palace. He opened the glass French double door that led to the blinding white living room. Moses squinted to see the area with a French-styled sofa, matching chairs, and a glass coffee table with stone at the bottom. The curtains were thick white velvet and a crystal chandelier hung from the ceiling. Then two maids dusted the area with feathered fans. Moses gave himself a tour of this jewel in the Mediterranean. He strolled down the hallway with French art on the walls. As Moses approached the kitchen area, a chef cooked a fabulous French dish, whatever it may be. He glanced at the gorgeous staircase, taking his time heading up the steps as if he were creeping into a haunted house. A painting of the Mona Lisa and other artwork hung on the wall. A large black-and-gold vase stood tall on the corridor floor, which resembled a path to Heaven continuing with its blinding white. Still, Moses squinted as he crept further and further to a door. He pushed the door open slowly as another heavenly-lit glow brightened the atmosphere. A king-sized bed was centered in the room, with two nightstands on both sides. Another crystal-like light fixture hung on the ceiling. He noticed a long, white-blanket wall before the bed. Moses caressed his hand across the wall, and then it parted a bit. He opened the wall, which turned out to be a walk-in closet. Again, a white-blinding light revealed three-piece suits, sweaters, denim jeans, tons of sneakers, shoes, and boots. All the clothes were from well-known designers like Giorgio Armani, Thierry Mugler, and Valentino. Moses sprayed on the Angel for Men, feeling super-rich with this musky, wooded with a vanilla base. "What are you doing here!" a stern voice demanded. Moses dropped the cologne bottle to the floor.

"Moses!" the stern voice continued to get his attention.

Then Moses woke up from his textbook and realized his Arts and Culture textbook before his eyes. He had a goofy face and rubbed his eyes from underneath his glasses.

"Moses, are you listening?" Mrs. Neuman asked.

"Excuse me, Ma'am," Moses asked as he blinked his eyes continuously to clear his

vision.

"Did you read the chapter on Andrea Bocelli?" Mrs. Neuman maneuvered between rows of desks of students.

"Yes, I did."

"Tell us what you learned about Andrea Bocelli." the teacher pushed her glasses back on her face.

"Andrea Bocelli was a well-known opera singer, born in Tuscany, Italy. He lost his blindness due to his having a soccer accident. The doctor diagnosed him with glaucoma. But Mr. Bocelli didn't allow his handicap to hinder him. He had the most beautiful voice in the world. A record executive quoted this about the opera singer. The pupils glanced at each other in wonder and snickered. Moses proceeded with a history lesson for his teacher to hear about the well-known singer. The teacher already knew Moses had it all down packed. She only wanted a simple answer.

"Alright, Moses. I didn't need a story!"

"But that's what I read." Moses gave his teacher an attitude.

"Moses, do you want me to call your mother?" Mrs. Neuman pounded her fist on the desk.

"Go ahead. Who am I supposed to be scared?"

"Mr. Remington, what has gotten into you!" His teacher shook her head in disappointment.

"Nothing's gotten into me. What got into you?"

"Go to the dean's office now!" Mrs. Neuman's face trembled, and she pointed towards the door. Moses stormed out of the classroom. He swaggered down the dimmed hallway with Mrs. Neuman behind him.

Minutes later, Moses sat before Mr. Servideo again with his ordeal. The dean and Mrs. Neuman reprimanded Moses for being disruptive. Of course, Mr. Servideo threatened Moses with suspension. The threats didn't faze him. Instead, he shrugged his shoulders and figured he might as well join Isaac. But Moses thought of himself this time. He didn't want to disappoint his parents.

"I'm sorry, Mrs. Neuman," Moses looked his teacher in the eye. Mrs. Neuman's heart softened as she heard those words of sincerity. He had a lot of respect for his teacher. He didn't want to disappoint her either. Mr. Servideo warned Moses to behave and for him to get back to class. He sprinted out of the dean's office. No thoughts crossed Moses' mind. He didn't want to think about the mess he got into over nothing. But it was something.

Mrs. Neuman's heels echoed throughout the hallway as Moses heard his favorite teacher following him back to class. Moses swaggered into the boisterous classroom, where the students became silent. He sat at his desk, not making eye contact with anyone. The students eyed him but wouldn't dare to bother him. Then Mrs. Neuman marched in, closing the classroom door. She grabbed her teacher's edition of the Arts and Culture textbook and picked up where she left off. She asked London questions about Andrea Bocelli. London sat at her desk and confidently answered Mrs. Neuman. Nothing intimated this young lady. London expressed herself in an overly confident posture. The students and anyone else could tell she wasn't convinced. She vexed Moses; sometimes, it seemed as if she tried to compete against Moses. He hoped she didn't sense any weaknesses. He didn't know if he had any shortcomings, but he knew his strengths. London had a four-point average, as Moses did. He shook his head because a girl intimidated him. *"Stop act-*

ing like a chump!" he insulted himself in his mind. Mrs. Neuman wrote the homework assignment on the blackboard. He set his mind on Isaac, wondering about his brother.

Meanwhile, Isaac watched television in his twin-sized bed. He looked at Moses' empty bed in their bedroom. Isaac changed the channels with the remote. There was nothing to watch but repetitious cartoons. He couldn't stand repeats. That's the thing he and Moses hated the most. Isaac ate breakfast alone at the table without his brother to keep him company. He wanted to tell his mother about his nightmare, but her eyes were glued to the television. He wondered if his mother loved him. Irene rarely spoke to Isaac, only to punish him. *I love you* are the words Isaac never heard from his mother.

"I love you" was never spoken. Irene told Moses and showed him affection. She also conversed about his life as a baby, his school, and his plans. Isaac lowered the volume of the television with the remote and placed it on the bed. He opened the door as it creaked. Isaac peered his head into the dimmed hallway. Not a soul in sight. He crept down the corridor as the television played a Reality television. It was just like a soap opera. Irene indulged in a world of glitz, glamor, and toxic romance on a flat-panel screen television while eating popcorn. She didn't feel Isaac's presence behind her. Isaac stuck his chest out, inhaled, and strutted to the couch. He sat next to his mother. Irene didn't even acknowledge his presence. She fixed her eyes on the people inside this box and hoped to live that life someday. Isaac glanced at his mother and then back at the television, which featured a young couple strolling in the park. As Isaac continuously glanced between the TV and his mother, he could tell how involved his mother was. He couldn't stand this reality show crap. Isaac arranged his sentences in his head to tell his mother what was on his mind.

"Mom!" Isaac looked at his mother. Irene was deafened by her son's call. She laughed at the couple's life on TV.

"Mom!" he cried out to her again.

"What, Isaac? Don't you see me doing something here!" She sat the bowl of popcorn on the couch. Behind those stylish glasses, tears streamed down Isaac's cheeks.

"I had a nightmare last night."

"We all have bad dreams. You're not the only one." Irene munched on the snack and focused her attention back on the flat panel screen. "Go back to your room! You're on punishment anyway!" She bellowed. Isaac left his mother's side, his head down in shame. *"Does my mother love me? It's because I have albinism. What can I do to make this albinism go away?"* Isaac marched down the dim hallway; getting to his bedroom felt like an eternity. The corridor reminded him of the one in that dark power plant in his dream the night before.

Isaac's heart raced in his chest. He rushed to his bedroom, closing the bedroom door. Then an enlarged gray rat scurried down the hallway to the twins' parents' bedroom. A glow seeped from the cracks of the door as the television played at a low volume. Inside, Calvin propped his head on a pillow, stretched out in the king-sized bed. He wore his boxers and an undershirt as a blanket covering half his body. A half-eaten bowl of soggy cornflakes, an empty glass of orange juice, one bite of an apple, and his wristwatch were scattered on the nightstand. He dozed off and on as an old sitcom played on television. A squeaking came from the hallway as it got closer and closer. The bedroom door creaked, widening as the squeaks got louder, with tiny feet scrambling beside the bed. Calvin's cardiac muscle raced in his chest. He maneuvered to the middle of the bed. The screeching drowned out the sounds of the box. Sweat trickled down Calvin's face, cringing at the unfamiliar presence that climbed up on the bed. Calvin clutched his pillow, noticing the enormous pest before his eyes. The creature crept closer to him. Then pounced upon his stomach. The rat stared at him as Calvin's widened. His heart throbbed in his chest. "Who are you?" Calvin spoke to it. The red eyes of the rodent resembled hellfire that would scare anyone to death. "I love Irene and the kids. I do. Why are you throwing this in my face? Jacklyn cheated on me. She broke up our relationship. We would get married and get a house, but Jackie lied to me and claimed I abused her. That's a lie! Get the hell out of here! Get out of here!" Calvin threw the pillow at the rat. "Leave me alone!"

While Isaac rested in his twin-sized bed, he heard screams from the master bedroom down the hallway. For a moment, he thought he was dreaming. He widened his eyes and knew it was his stepfather going crazy. He must've been having a bad dream as well. *"Good, I hope Calvin has constant nightmares,"* Isaac sneered. He didn't bother to spring from his bed to see what happened to his stepfather. He had tears of his own. *"Why is God allowing this to happen to me? Did he make a mistake and give me to the wrong mother?"* Isaac wondered about God's error. Isaac sobbed more and then closed his eyes, hoping to wake up in a better place.

Hours passed as the Remington residence felt alive, with voices clamoring from the kitchen on this dreary afternoon. Isaac remained in his bed; the discussions erupted into laughter. Isaac opened his eyes and could eavesdrop from his bed. Moses' teacher planned a field trip to the Museum of Natural History in Manhattan. Isaac always wanted to go there and see the skeletal T-Rex. He attempted to go into the kitchen and greet his brother, but he changed his mind. Isaac didn't know whether to be angry or sad. He heard the happiness coming from outside his bedroom door. *"Does my brother love me? Moses probably doesn't care about me,"* Isaac shut his eyes and went back to sleep.

CHAPTER SIX

Two weeks later, school buses parked in front of the school behind each other, dropping off boisterous kids. They loved to hear themselves scream, gossip, and curse. Parents, teachers, and faculty members made sure that students arrived at their classes on time. Moses and Isaac hurried off the mini school bus. Together they swaggered to the luxurious black and gray charter bus. Moses' classmates boarded the bus as Mrs. Neuman waited by the entrance. Her fourth-grade class hopped on one by one. "Good morning, kids," she greeted.

"You're lucky, Moses!" Isaac's heart raced, patting his brother's back. The brothers got closer to the bus, and Isaac saw its interior.

"That's beautiful!" Isaac gave his brother a high-five. Moses promised he'd bring Isaac something back from Manhattan. Moses boarded the bus and waved to his brother. Isaac waved and bowed as if he had lost his best friend. Moses gawked at the tiny light fixtures in the black ceiling with big, cushioned seats, tinted windows, and two bathrooms. He felt as if he was going out of state. Traveling from Long Island to Manhattan was good enough for him. He looked around, trying to figure out where to sit. There was plenty of room, but he wanted a window seat. Unfortunately, students occupied all the window seats. London sat next to a window in the third row. She grimaced at Moses and pointed at the empty seat next to her. Moses didn't want to be bothered; he wanted to be alone. But he had no other choice. Then the charter bus's quiet engine started up.

Meanwhile, Mrs. Neuman waited for a few more students. The teacher then boarded and alerted the driver to go. Moses plopped his behind into the cushion seat next to this flirty little girl. He kept a straight face without smiling at London as she bragged about her parents bringing home a six-figure salary. London should have given specifics on what they did.

Moses listened but knew she lied right through her teeth. He anticipated the Museum of Natural History and sightseeing in the city. The charter bus navigated onto the Long Island Expressway, driving at a medium speed. After a while, Moses dozed off. London bragged and bragged about her family; she loved to hear herself talk. She didn't even realize that Moses had fallen asleep. He looked like an old man slumped over in the recliner. Only then did London subside her conversation and allow him to catnap.

Around an hour later, the charter bus drove across the Fifty-Ninth Street Bridge. That's when Moses awoke to his classmates' gasps. He leaned over London's shoulder, where he saw enormous skyscrapers. He saw the Empire State Building, the Chrysler Building, and the World Trade Tower, amongst others. Moses' heart pumped heavily in his chest while leaning over London. She sneered at Moses because he didn't hear a word that she said earlier. Moses had a pompous attitude like she did. The charter bus exited smoothly off the bridge and navigated onto Fifty-Ninth Street. The students had their noses glued to the windows of the bus. The big city enthused the students, especially Moses. He had goo-goo eyes over a building in Sutton Place, where NBC's open house advertised these condominiums.

"Oh, Wow, Sutton Place! That's where that condo is for sale for millions of dollars. I hope Mrs. Neuman will tell the driver to drive along Park Avenue. I would love to see those buildings," Moses said to himself. Sunny with temperatures reaching the mid-seventies was the perfect day to walk around the city. Ryan, a slender, chatty boy swaggered over to the empty seat across from Moses. The boys gave each other high-fives and chatted amongst themselves, but the two young men couldn't hear themselves since their class was so loud. Ryan whispered into Moses' ear as if he had a crush on London. Moses shrugged his shoulders and rolled his eyes. Ryan cackled because he knew Moses had played it off. London whispered to the girls who sat directly behind her as well. They knew London had a crush on Moses.

The charter bus parked before the world's leading performing arts center in no time. The bus's automatic doors opened, and one by one, the students exited with their eyes fixed on the majestic white building with its large bright windows. The Revson water fountain was centered in the concert hall. Hollywood motion pictures such as *Ghostbusters* and *Sweet Home Alabama* featured the famous fountain. It pumped sixteen thousand, five-hundred gallons of water a minute, with up to four-hundred, seventy-five gallons, shooting it forty feet high into the air. Three hundred fifty-three nozzles, twenty-four water pumps, and a half-mile of piping were built into the foundation. At night, the Revson fountain gives a magnificent performance of its own with its two-hundred, seventy-two colorful LED lights. Mrs. Neuman's class lined up, and she counted her students with her finger to make sure everyone was present. Moses fixed his eyes on that Revson water fountain. He had seen it on television, in the movies, or on the news. The gorgeous fountain captivated Moses' classmates, as well. Then Mrs. Neuman and her class marched towards the concert hall. They waltzed past the fountain. Moses put his hands in the fountain.

"Don't touch the water, Moses!" Mrs. Neuman raised her voice.

"Sorry, Mrs. Neuman", he apologized in a subservient tone. He turned away from the fountain, continuing to walk towards Lincoln's Center. Then Ryan dipped his hands in the water, splashing it on the girls. They guffawed and screamed, and the teacher turned around. "What did I just say!" Mrs. Neuman repeated.

Then the students gasped as they entered the large lobby with its extremely high ceilings and marble floors. The center displayed different sculptures and photos of the many musicians who played there. Moses scanned the pictures to see if he had read about these artists. Ryan eyed the pictures right along with his friend.

"Who are these people? Ryan asked Moses. Moses didn't know what to say, so he shrugged. These performers were some unknown artists they had never heard of. London rushed to his side and ran off at the mouth. Moses rolled his eyes. He couldn't get this girl away from him. Moses gave her the cold shoulder and stormed away; Ryan followed him. London continued to mouth off as she realized she stood there talking to herself. London hushed up quickly, holding her head down as her class burst into laughter. Moses and Ryan stood over to the side, giving each other a high-five and guffawing.

Moments later, an orchestra tuned their instruments, especially violins and cellos. It created a noise, reversing beautiful sounds into the ears. Moses and his classmates strolled into the David Geffen Hall, where the tuning of the musical instruments became louder. Moses liked the sound of this well-known orchestra while they prepared. The class strutted down the aisle and walked in between rows of fancy velvet cushioned chairs, where they sat down. Moses eyed the stage and its many musicians as he took his seat. The orchestra had eighty musicians who played violins, cellos, trumpets, flutes, harps, horns, and a piano. Moses laid his head back to close his eyes. He enjoyed this so-called noisy classical music. Moses couldn't think of any other place he wanted to be. However, one thing that crossed his mind was how the rich paid thousands of dollars for a seat to see a spectacular show. Then the lights up on the high ceiling dimmed, and the audience erupted into applause. The spotlight beamed on a Caucasian female in her mid-twenties, dressed in a violet dress, singing opera. Her voice had an eerie tone, causing Moses to get chills along his arms. He was curious whether it was the air conditioning or the performance. It was the performance. The music reminded him of one of those horror movies he watched on TV. Either the *Amityville Horror*, *Poltergeist*, or *Nightmare on Elm Street*. Ryan concentrated on the music melodies. "Do you like this?" Moses tapped Ryan on the shoulder.

"What do you think, man?" Moses whispered.

"It sounds haunting," Ryan shrugged his shoulders and sucked his teeth. Moses looked at his other classmates and noticed they didn't seem bothered by the music. He turned back around in his seat, taking sharp breaths. Then the orchestra changed its tune as it became a theme from *Star Wars*. Moses and Ryan glanced at each other, smiling due to a happy song.

After the show, Moses and his class went sightseeing in Times Square. The kids pointed at the colorful billboard advertisements of fashion, food, Broadway plays, movies, and even digital ads. Moses and Ryan wanted to go into the M&Ms store. Mrs. Neuman agreed as Moses, Ryan, and his class rushed into the candy store like a herd of cattle. Moses browsed the wall of chocolate-covered candies in every color. There was plain, peanut, almond, peanut butter, and crispy candy. Isaac loved M&Ms, so Moses loaded some sweets into a plastic bag. Then he grabbed the peanut M&Ms mug for Isaac and a figurine. Moses swaggered to the cash register and threw the items onto the counter. He pulled two twenty-dollar bills from his wallet. He could feel London breathing down his neck. But when he turned abruptly, Moses noticed another female classmate, Amy. A pretty, Asian-American girl who didn't have a crush on him, but she stood too close to him. "Amy, do you mind backing up?" Moses asked politely. Amy took two steps back. Moses then turned around and grabbed his bag.

"This is some shit," Moses mumbled, storming away. Ryan stood at the entrance with some other students and Mrs. Neuman. Moses approached Ryan, giving him a high-five. Ryan didn't purchase anything because he wasn't an M&Ms fan. Instead, he wanted to go to Dylan's candy store, a block away. Ryan wanted some gummy bears and bubble gum. They couldn't wait to go to Dylan's.

"Mrs. Neuman, can we go to Dylan's? It's just a block away." Ryan asked.

In no time, Moses and his class raided Dylan's candy store. Ryan rushed to the gummy bears as if they were going to run out. Moses followed behind his friend and spotted some licorice in different colors, representing different flavors, such as sour apple, cherry, grape, orange, etc. Then he snatched some candy buttons. London bumped into Moses and apologized.

"What the fuck, London," Moses stormed away with his candy in his hand. He dashed over to Ryan's side, criticizing London. Ryan laughed because London had a thing for Moses. Ryan glanced over and saw London smiling at the ordeal. Then the two boys rushed to the cashier and paid for their candy. Moses' face turned red. His classmates cackled and poked fun at the two little lovebirds. Moses paid for his candy and walked out of the store. Ryan then paid for his goodies and went outside with his friend. Moses leaned against the wall of the store, mumbling obscenities.

"Calm down, man," Ryan gobbled his licorice.

"She's driving me fuckin' crazy. Shit!" Moses sucked on his fruit punch jolly rancher.

"You think she's ugly?" Ryan asked, popping gummy bears in his mouth.

"No! She's too clingy!" Moses shifted the hard candy to the other side of his mouth.

Mrs. Neuman rushed into the store, throwing her hands up. "I've been looking for you! Moses and Ryan!"

"We wanted to get some air," Ryan popped some gummy bears into his mouth.

"I don't care what you wanted to do! Back inside now!" Mrs. Neuman pointed towards the store.

Moses and Ryan swaggered back into the candy store with their teacher behind them.

An hour later, the class wanted to stroll through Central Park, but Mrs. Neuman didn't want to avoid taking the chance of Moses and Ryan wandering off. Her students pleaded with their teacher that they'd stay together. Still, their teacher wanted them to experience the famous world park. So, she agreed and closely watched every one of them. Overall, that would be a challenge since she was like a mother with a dozen kids. The fourth-grade class strolled through the park together, making their teacher's job easier by watching out for one another.

"Do you kids want to go to Victorian Gardens?" Mrs. Neuman asked with a slight smile. Nervousness could be seen on her face, hoping the miniature amusement park would keep them occupied. Moses and Ryan wanted to avoid going to Central Park's only amusement park. The two boys wanted to adventure out but hesitated to leave the group. The boys lingered around and watched the rest of the class act like complete asses. Moses and Ryan resided on a nearby bench and laughed at London and the other girls on the merry-go-round. The girls laughed and joked as the carousel went round and round. The loud organ music drowned out Moses and Ryan's conversation.

"This is some bullshit!" Moses kept eating his licorice, chewing with his mouth open. Moses didn't care about his cursing; he wasn't at the dinner table. The boys crammed their mouths with sweets. Moses couldn't help himself and continued to devour his candy. He then thought about his brother and stopped eating the goodies.

Moses and Ryan glared at each other, bored as hell. They wanted so badly to leave that bench.

"Ask Mrs. Neuman if we could walk around," Moses told Ryan.

"You know what the answer will be," Ryan swallowed his candy.

The kids clamoring onto the amusement rides didn't make the scene amusing to Moses and Ryan.

"Try it dude," Moses ate the last licorice. Ryan took a deep breath and approached Mrs. Neuman to see if he and Moses could go sightseeing in the park. Still, their teacher refused, shaking her head. Ryan came back to Moses with bad news. Moses cursed under his breath, determined to go about his business anyway. Mrs. Neuman chatted with the other students as Moses and Ryan eased off the bench. They walked fast-paced away from the group and didn't look back. Their other classmates noticed but didn't say a word.

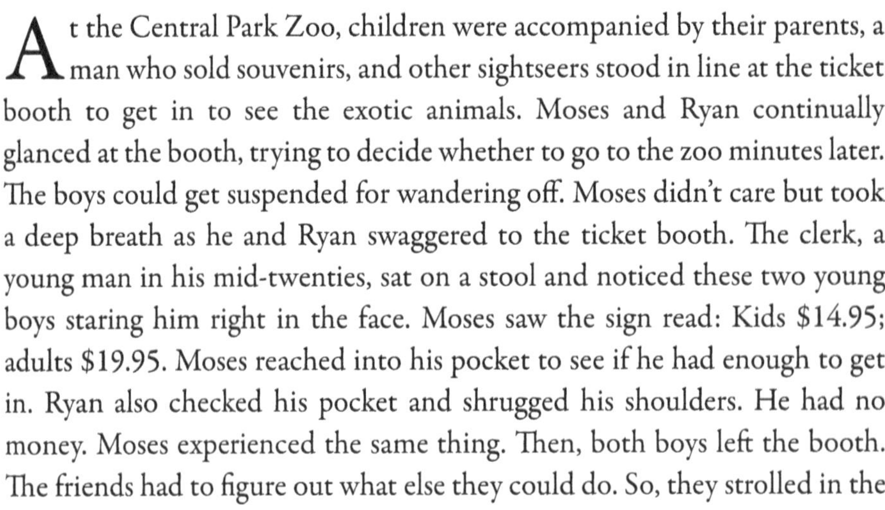

At the Central Park Zoo, children were accompanied by their parents, a man who sold souvenirs, and other sightseers stood in line at the ticket booth to get in to see the exotic animals. Moses and Ryan continually glanced at the booth, trying to decide whether to go to the zoo minutes later. The boys could get suspended for wandering off. Moses didn't care but took a deep breath as he and Ryan swaggered to the ticket booth. The clerk, a young man in his mid-twenties, sat on a stool and noticed these two young boys staring him right in the face. Moses saw the sign read: Kids $14.95; adults $19.95. Moses reached into his pocket to see if he had enough to get in. Ryan also checked his pocket and shrugged his shoulders. He had no money. Moses experienced the same thing. Then, both boys left the booth. The friends had to figure out what else they could do. So, they strolled in the park until they came across something — an endless line of benches going for a least a mile through the park. Trees sat between them with trash cans, and the workers from the park's departments were taking care of the area. Loud house music blared up ahead as Moses and Ryan kept walking. They got closer to the music, and a gathering of spectators watched a guy and a girl dancing.

Moses and Ryan watched their performance. The girl wore a short red dress with glittery red high-heeled shoes, and the guy just wore a three-piece suit. It seemed they were trying to say something or represent something by how they presented themselves. The house music had a big thumping bass sound with synthesized keyboards. Moses liked house music, of course. Ryan bopped his head to the music's rhythm. Moses nudged him as they looked at each other and chuckled. Then the crowd got bigger and bigger. The spectators danced as if they were at a discotheque.

"Hey, what the hell," Ryan got his groove on.

"Are you serious, Ryan," Moses laughed, pointing at how silly Ryan looked.

"This is the only way we can have some fun!" Ryan said.

"I don't think so! Mrs. Neuman could catch us easily," Moses advised. Then Ryan stopped suddenly; it was funny. Moses chuckled at his friend, clowning around. The boys moved along to see what else the park had in store. Moses ran towards the Mad Hatter Tea party of the storybook *Alice in Wonderland* bronze statue. He held on to his brother's candy for dear life because he spent all his money.

"Check this out! "Moses yelled.

Ryan tagged along behind. They stood before the statue and admired it. Moses loved the perfect bronze sculpture. He strolled around the artwork and caressed the Mad Hatter's hat as Ryan ran his hand along with the Rabbit's ears. Moses knocked on it with his fist to feel the statue's strength. "That's tough. I wonder how long it took the artist to do this," Moses ate some candy.

"This is for girls. Come on, let's get out of here," Ryan and Moses swaggered away as they approached the park's entrance. Just then, the friends noticed the *Balto* bronze statue.

"I love Alaskan Huskies," Ryan delighted. The boys walked up to the icon and caressed it with their hands. Then they read the engraved info on *Balto.*

"This dog saved children who were sick in Alaska," Ryan read.

"There are plenty of them where they come from," Moses added.

"When I become rich, I'll have an entire house of Alaskan huskies," Ryan said.

"I would rather have rottweilers. Their good protectors," Moses said and recognized an elegant restaurant in the distance made of glass.

"What's that up ahead?" Moses wandered off without even advising Ryan. Moses slowly strolled to the glass restaurant. He looked up as it read: Tavern on the Green. Moses eyed the guests dining and enjoying themselves. Ryan approached his friend from behind, noticing what captivated him.

"I remember seeing this restaurant in *Ghostbusters*," Moses recalled.

"This must be where the rich and famous dine," Ryan munched on a bag of Doritos.

"It is," Moses responded with a glare in his eye. "I hope to eat here one day," Moses told himself.

"We should be getting back. Mrs. Neuman is probably going crazy right now," Ryan glanced over his shoulders. Then a police car drove up behind them, the siren blaring.

"Holy shit," Ryan held his bag of Doritos tight. A male Latino officer in their early fifties exited from the driver's side and left the engine running. A Caucasian female officer in her mid-thirties dashed out from the passenger's side of the patrol car with her hand on her holster.

"Who are you boys with?" the Latino officer asked, pissed off.

"We're on a field trip," Moses stuck his chest out.

Static emerged from the hip of the female officer as a call came in. She picked up the radio, putting it to her mouth.

"What's up?"

"Did you find the two young boys?" the dispatcher asked with heavy static in the background.

"Yes," The female officer stared at Moses and Ryan.

"You two are fortunate that no one snatched you," the female cop said.

In no time, Mrs. Neuman and the rest of her fourth-grade class tagged behind her, marching toward Moses and Ryan. Then their teacher's voice bellowed throughout the park. Ryan shook in his boots as Mrs. Neuman went crazy. Moses looked at his teacher with an attitude. He was ready for his suspension and didn't care. Surprisingly, Mrs. Neuman seized her anger and didn't bother to say another word. Moses' classmates gasped and looked at one another, whispering. They were shocked at Mrs. Neuman giving Moses such leeway. The teacher thanked the NYPD for their help in tracking the boys down. Moses gawked at the officers; wondering how difficult their jobs must be. Especially, dealing with kids who get lost.

Within the hour, the charter bus drove onto the Long Island Expressway and returned to the school. Moses and Ryan sat next to each other this time and talked about what happened or what could happen when they got back to school. Moses sucked his teeth and had no worries. But Ryan did. His grandmother would knock him across the head with the frying pan.

"Did she do that to you, Ryan?" Moses asked with a glare. Ryan looked away and didn't reply.

"She did. Didn't she!" Moses asked again with a stern tone. Ryan's grandmother was a looney tune; she hollered all the time. Even if someone tried to have a conversation, she raised her voice. Ryan couldn't wait to get older, so he could get away from her. And he didn't even care if she died. Ryan disliked his nana, but it was almost getting to the point where he hated her. Luckily, Moses didn't have that problem with his family.

Later, the charter bus's brakes squealed as it parked in front of the school building. The automatic doors opened as Mrs. Neuman and the students hopped off the bus. The teacher stood at the door with her arms folded. Her face turned cherry red as Moses and Ryan exited the bus.

"I want to talk to both of you," the teacher addressed Moses and Ryan. The kids leaned against the fence.

"You two could've gotten lost or hurt somewhere. What if something had happened, Moses?" Mrs. Neuman's voice quivered. The boys gawked as they saw tears in her eyes. Then Moses and Ryan glanced at each other and saw that this wasn't funny. Guilt filled Moses' stomach like water. He couldn't stand to see his teacher in tears.

"I'm sorry, Mrs. Neuman," Moses inhaled.

"You said that before, Moses," Mrs. Neuman reminded him.

"Are you going to suspend me this time?" Moses asked. His teacher squinted her eyes and cocked her head in disbelief.

"Would you like a two-day vacation, young man?" Mrs. Neuman placed her hands on her hips.

"No," Moses shook his head, looking in the other direction.

"Ryan, what do you have to say for yourself?" Mrs. Neuman questioned.

"I'm sorry," Ryan apologized.

"I'm not going to suspend you. "You two are my favorite, but it seems like you're taking me for granted," Mrs. Neuman said.

Isaac and Calvin waited for him a few feet away. Calvin raised an eyebrow as his stepson's teacher scolded Moses. Calvin and Isaac approached Moses, Ryan, and his teacher. Mrs. Neuman turned and noticed Moses' stepfather and explained what had happened. Moses clutched Isaac and gave him the M&Ms bag as the two adults chatted.

"Thanks, Moses," Isaac devoured the chocolate-covered peanuts into his mouth. Ryan gave Isaac a high-five and shared his candy with him. Isaac then shoved some gummy bears in his mouth, chewing like a cow. Calvin and Mrs. Neuman cleared the air as she said her farewell to them.

Calvin decided to drive Ryan home. They strutted to his vehicle. Moses wanted Calvin to say something about him wandering off. *"Come on. Come on, say something. Isn't he even going to say something to Ryan? Or I forgot, Ryan isn't his responsibility. Maybe, he'll say something to Ryan's grandmother. Shit, that's his ass!"* Moses said to himself. The boys didn't utter a word to one another, but Ryan had terror all over his face. Isaac could even see his brother's friend's fear. His terrifying nana would surely scare anyone. Maybe, that's why Ryan's grandfather or even his mother wasn't around. She was the devil in a rocking chair.

Seconds later, Calvin parked in front of Ryan's house. He shook Moses and Isaac's hands and hopped out of the car. Ryan rang the doorbell of his home, glancing back at Moses and his family as they waited in the car. Then the front door opened with a creek. It was as if Ryan entered hell. Hell bellowed out at this poor kid whose grandmother hit the ceiling. Then Calvin sped away; *"I guess Calvin's afraid of her too,"* Moses said to himself.

Moses was confident that Calvin wouldn't mention anything about the field trip. Calvin kept his eyes on the road and said nothing. *"But I bet you if it were Isaac, Calvin would be on his ass,"* Moses resided in the back with Isaac, continuing to devour the M&Ms.

"Don't overeat candy, Isaac. You must eat your dinner," Calvin peered at Isaac through his rearview mirror.

After dinner, the twins devoured the candies for dessert. They watched episodes of *Open House Videos* on YouTube. Isaac popped some M&Ms in his mouth as Moses chowed down on gummy bears. Calvin and Irene were in their master bedroom doing whatever they did. They didn't even have any concerns about their kids' teeth. Moses stopped as he was about to put the last bunch of gummy bears in his mouth.

"Isaac and I shouldn't be eating so much candy," Moses thought. Isaac kept popping the colorful chocolate-covered candies in his mouth. Moses then grabbed his hand, stopping his brother.

"Isaac don't eat so much candy," Moses said, playing the parent to his brother. Isaac then put the candy back into the bag.

"You're right," Isaac smiled.

The boys watched the episode of *Open House* as an interior designer gave a penthouse tour on the Upper West Side of Manhattan. Ivory marble decorated the entire apartment from the corridor leading to the highly lit living room with a black and white couch, loveseat, and lounge chairs; black and white photos were on the wall, and black lion face décor. A black opal light fixture holding over several bulbs in the ceiling made the room bright. Moses and Isaac eyed each other and nodded at the luxurious condo.

"We saw this one two weeks ago. How was Manhattan?" Isaac wanted to know about his brother's field trip.

"It was beautiful. We drove along Park Avenue, where you can see all the luxury apartment buildings," Moses lied.

"And what else?" Isaac eagerly asked.

"Then we went to FAO Schwarz at Rockefeller Center," Moses lying his tail off some more.

"Did you see any movie stars?" Isaac asked enthusiastically.

"Nah," Moses nodded.

"How was Lincoln Center?" Isaac asked with his fourth question.

"It was okay. It wasn't that great, just a bunch of stuck-up musicians," Moses answered.

"What other places did you see?" Isaac asked as his eyes enlarged from his glasses.

"My class and I ate lunch at the Tavern on the Green restaurant in Central Park," Moses continued to tell his brother more stories. Isaac frowned and could tell Moses was fibbing.

"No, that's a restaurant for the rich!" Isaac corrected Moses. Moses snickered because his brother figured that he made that part up.

"Wow, I wish I could go. We could ask Dad to take us to the city," Isaac said.

"I'll ask him," Moses said.

The boys looked back at the computer screen again as a realtor gave a tour of a home in Coral Gables, Florida. The computerized glass house cost fifteen million. Even though Moses and Isaac had watched this episode before, they were still captivated by the property's beauty.

Isaac grabbed a hand full of sweets and put it in his mouth. Moses followed suit, disregarding his advice. The twins shared the bag of M&Ms and put a handful of the chocolate goodies in their mouths.

CHAPTER SEVEN

On the last day of school, kids looked forward to upcoming vacations, the Fourth of July weekend, amusement parks, swimming, camping, etc. The sun peeked from the clouds as if God were checking on Moses and Isaac. The twins lay in their beds, the bedroom darkened with bits of beams of sunlight peering through the shades, but then, it became dismal. Moses squinted his eyes when bits of sunlight bothered his vision. He rubbed his eyes to clear his vision and sat up in slumber. Moses scanned the murky bedroom, seeing his brother sleeping like a baby. Moses hoped he and Isaac didn't have to go to school; it was the last day. There would be nothing to do but have a stupid farewell party, wishing their classmates a happy summer vacation. The clock read: 7:58 a.m. Then the school bus's horn beeped; then the front door opened. Moses heard his mother's voice. "No, it's the last day! See you in September." Irene hollered to Martha as the minibus sped away.

An hour later, *The Today Show* played on the television as Irene and Calvin's angry voices were heard from the living room. Cursing and sudden outbursts caused Moses to spring into action from his slumber. When Moses' birth father was alive, he didn't recall any verbal fights. Maybe, he's imagining things, or it's no big deal. Hopefully, his mother and stepfather will patch things up. Moses wanted to chat with his parents about his upcoming summer vacation but gazed at the ceiling in his bed. His eyes shifted in his head, and he heard Calvin yell, "*Bitch*!" Moses' eyes widened as his heart raced in his chest. *"I know he didn't call my mother a bitch. I hope it's just my imagination."* This young kid hoped this man didn't come into their lives to raise hell. Heavy footsteps approached the boys' bedroom. Moses shut his eyes and pretended to be asleep. Calvin entered and looked at both twin-sized beds where Moses and Isaac rested.

"Today is the last day of school, and you don't have to go!" Calvin said aloud. Moses sprung from his bed as he and his stepfather wrestled to the floor. Moses wrapped his arm around Calvin's neck, deliberately choking him. At first, Calvin didn't realize this kid's ill intentions. But Moses' grip on his stepfather's neck got tighter and tighter. Calvin turned red in the face, trying to get this kid's arm from around his neck. For someone so little, Moses had a lot of strength. And then, Isaac joined in the fun. All three scuffled on the carpeted floor. Moses backed out of the fun as he glared at Calvin wrestling with Isaac. Calvin didn't notice his stepson's glares as he turned hell-red. Then Moses rushed back and wrapped his arm around Calvin's neck again to protect Isaac. Calvin held Moses' hands behind his back. "What are you doing boy!"

"Get the fuck off me, you asshole!" Moses wrestled himself out of his stepfather's grip.

"Are you trying to kill me, kid?" Calvin cringed at this small child taking steps toward him. Calvin's eyes bulged and trembled.

"I heard what you called my mother," Moses balled his hands into fists. He saw the terror on his stepfather's face and didn't want to hear any excuses. This kid's fists tightened even more. Isaac stood there, cocked his head, and gawked at his brother. He then realized his brother's fury. He patted Moses on the shoulder to calm him down from whatever got him hot.

"I love you guys. Your mother's the best thing that ever happened to me," Tears streamed down Calvin's face. Isaac embraced his stepfather. Then Irene rushed to her boys' bedroom door in wonder. Calvin then embraced their mother, kissing her on the forehead.

"You're my family," Calvin became teary-eyed.

Irene and Isaac fell for Calvin's bull, but Moses stood his ground. He didn't believe a word he uttered. He could spot a person who shed crocodile tears. Or he could be telling the truth. Moses had to give this man who provided for him and their family the benefit of the doubt. So, he wrapped his arms around Calvin and let it go.

On top of that, the boys had a birthday coming up, and Calvin had big plans for them. Moses had to find something to do for himself and his brother.

"It's the last day of school, Dad. What's up for today?" Isaac leaned his head on his father's shoulder.

"I don't know. What do you want to do?" Calvin gave them a choice.

"I know...the carnival," Isaac's face lit up.

"Where?" Moses sneered at Isaac.

"There's one over in Bethpage," Calvin recalled seeing on his way home from work. He suggested they hurry and get dressed. Then, they could grab a bite to eat.

Later that morning, waitresses served customers breakfast at a slightly crowded diner. Pop music played from the ceiling stereo as a waiter sang along with his favorite song, entertaining their guests. Moses swaggered in first as Isaac followed and then Calvin. A hostess greeted them, grabbed three menus, and escorted them to a booth. Irene stayed home. She didn't want to miss her soap operas. From what Moses knew, Calvin got Irene down. She probably cried her eyes out after having this man call her names. He hoped this man wasn't putting his hands on his mother. Moses and Isaac sat beside each other across from their stepfather at a booth. The frats didn't bother to look over the menu; they wanted waffles with syrup and whipped cream. The twins were easy to please when it came to food. Calvin tried to figure out what he wanted from the menu.

"You know you two are going to have to wait a while before you go on any rides," Calvin peered from his menu. The kids agreed that they would get nauseated. He hated the uncomfortable feeling he couldn't explain. Isaac listened to Moses and Calvin talk about amusement parks. Moses told how he went to Walt Disney World with his grandparents who were his birth father's parents when he was seven. But Isaac didn't go because his mother feared he would get sunburnt from the Florida sun. So, Isaac was kept home in the summer in a darkened bedroom with little to do. He heard that Isaac cried and cried all weekend long. "No, I didn't!" Isaac interjected. He was about to get up in his brother's face.

"That's what mom said," Moses shrugged his shoulders.

"That's not true! "Isaac sat back down. He sucked his teeth, looking in the other direction. Moses could see the red on his face. Isaac was embarrassed because he hadn't experienced the happiest place on earth.

"I watched real estate videos and repeats of Open House on YouTube! What's wrong with that?" Isaac said abruptly. Moses knew his brother didn't watch any real estate on TV or look through any magazines because he wanted to go to Disney World. He heard that Isaac sobbed all weekend. The frats glared at each other as Calvin eyed both his twin stepsons. "Don't worry Isaac you'll get to go there one day," his stepfather said with a smile. He dropped his smile immediately and ignored Isaac as if he wasn't there. Then a waiter hustled to their booth, placing three glasses on the table, and pouring water from a pitcher.

"Thank you," Calvin smiled slightly. Then Moses spoke about Space Mountain, the Pirates of the Caribbean, and Madder Hatter's Tea Ride. Isaac stared at them, noticing how Moses wasn't angry with Calvin. Earlier, his brother wanted to kill this man for some reason he really didn't know. And now they're *Buddy, Buddy*. For now, it was time to dig in as the waitress sashayed to their booth with plates of waffles. She placed the food in front of Moses, Isaac, and Calvin on the table. Then the three of them dug their forks into their food, and grunted like pigs, devouring their breakfast. Isaac then stopped chewing the waffle, squinting his eyes. He sipped his water. *"Aren't we supposed to say grace?"* Isaac then continued to eat his waffles, slowly. *"I guess not."* Isaac took notice of his stepfather's lousy table manners but simply chose to ignore them. He enjoyed his waffles, which had his mind occupied. Moses swallowed his food, telling Calvin more about Florida. Calvin washed his food down with his glass of water. "Florida is a wonderful place; palm trees all over. And, of course, it's hot. There's the smell of orange blossom in the air." Moses fidgeted in his seat, giving Calvin more Floridian details. "How much does it cost to go to Disney World?" Calvin grasped his glass of orange juice.

"How should I know? I'm just a kid," Moses sucked his teeth. He shrugged and continued eating.

"I guess it's expensive." Calvin shoved a bacon strip in his mouth.

"So, Walt Disney World is in Orlando. Am I right?" Isaac asked bashfully. He hoped he didn't embarrass himself.

"Yes, it is," Moses nodded to him.

"Have you been to Palm Beach or Jupiter?" Isaac asked with stars in his eyes.

"No. I would've told you that before. I'm sure it's beautiful," Moses said.

Isaac shied away, eating his waffles. Moses noticed Calvin continuing to eat and knew he wouldn't take Isaac to Disney World even if he could. "Hey, Isaac, when we get older, we'll travel all over Florida and every state and country in the world. Vacation-wise and business," Moses embraced his brother.

"You two sure will," Calvin guffawed, putting on a phony smile. He patted Isaac on the shoulder. Moses kept his eye on this grown man who was full of crap. Calvin asked this pint-sized gentleman who seemed to have more experience than himself as an adult question about Florida and traveling. Moses wanted to avoid answering because he didn't want to hurt Isaac's feelings. He just wanted to eat and looked forward to the amusement park.

Hours later, after the breakfast burnt off, Moses and Isaac drove on the bumper cars together. Moses drove as Isaac sat in the passenger's seat. Moses steered the bumper car well, especially since Isaac had impaired vision. Calvin watched. His stepsons from the sidelines. Moses noticed Isaac was having a good time and didn't mind that he couldn't drive a bumper car. Isaac was impressed with how well Moses drove this bumper car. *He'll probably drive an expensive supercar someday.*

Within a few minutes, the boys and Calvin stood in line for the roller coaster. This was Isaac's first time on a roller coaster. Of course, Moses was on a roller coaster before. Space mountain. Isaac saw the other kids about the same age as he and Moses were. As the line moved forward, a cut-out sign stood for kids, "Are you this height to ride on this ride." Moses measured himself; he passed. Then Isaac stood against the sign and measured up. Moses gave Isaac a high-five. The coaster seated three people, so Moses entered first and sat on the side. Isaac sat beside him in the middle, and Calvin sat on the other end. Isaac's heart raced in his chest. He knew the ride was going to be fierce. His eyes googled behind his glasses, fidgeting in his seat.

"Are you nervous, Isaac?" Moses saw the fear in his brother's face.

"No," Isaac laughed it off.

"Yes, you are. I can see that you look scared. Give me your glasses before you lose them," Moses advised. Isaac grabbed them off his face. Moses held his brother's glasses in hand as it became sweaty. Calvin didn't bother to tell Isaac about taking off his eyewear. Then they pulled the safety shoulder restraint over themselves. After it was locked, the coaster operator checked every rider to ensure the restraints were secured. A bell rang as the train coaster moved slowly from the station. The coaster made a curvy turn and ascended a steep hill. Isaac inhaled and nervously glanced over his shoulder. Moses assured his brother everything was going to be okay. Isaac had to trust his brother's words while the coaster proceeded up the hill. Moses shoved Isaac's glasses in his pants pockets, hoping not to lose them. The coaster reached its peak, turned, and descended a steep drop. Isaac screamed for dear life. He felt as if he were going to fall out of the coaster. Moses shouted and laughed. He saw the fear in this kid. The coaster then went upside down, up another steep hill, and came down again.

"Stop the ride!" Isaac sobbed. Calvin found this child's terrifying experience amusing.

"Close your eyes! Close your eyes, Isaac!" Moses screamed. Isaac shut his eyes, only to feel the hot breeze on his face and hear the other passengers' screams. Then the coaster made another drop down a steep hill. Isaac held onto the silver handles as the coaster made a sudden stop. It entered the station slowly.

"Let me off!" Isaac wept.

"The ride is over now," Moses patted his brother on the shoulder. The other riders on the coaster looked at him with sympathy. Moses used words of endearment to calm his brother. Calvin guffawed and guffawed at the child. The riders on the coasters sneered at this immature adult.

"It's not funny," Moses turned red in the face.

The roller coaster stopped as the riders got off. Moses clutched Isaac who sobbed like crazy. Calvin cackled.

"What the hell is so funny, dude," a thirty-something man asked, accompanied by his girlfriend.

"Why don't you mind your business!" Calvin insulted the stranger.

"Fuck you, man. He's a kid," the girlfriend bitched.

"You're poking fun at a child! Are you serious!" a second female stranger hugged Isaac. Moses bickered with his stepfather as if they were the same age. Spectators shook their heads in disappointment at the adult acting like a child.

"Let's go home!" Moses hollered at Calvin. Calvin didn't utter a word to this child genius who would even embarrass him if he didn't get out of there. Moses wiped Isaac's tears away and put his glasses back on him. He wrapped his arm around Isaac and stormed out. Calvin followed right behind them.

Minutes later, in the car, on their way home, no one talked. The radio wasn't even on. Calvin focused his eyes on the road without glancing in the rearview mirror. But Moses did glare at his stepfather through the rearview from the backseat. Isaac slept all the way home. That roller coaster had knocked him out. Isaac's feelings were hurt due to Calvin's behavior, and Moses felt his brother's pain. Moses started to hate Calvin, wishing their real father was still alive. He knew that Isaac wanted the same thing. If his father were here, Calvin wouldn't be in their lives. Not only did Moses resent Calvin, but he also began to resent his mother for dealing with this loser. Right about now, Moses knew his mother's eyes were glued to that television, watching *Reality TV.* Moses watched his brother as if he were a night watchman. *"What the hell is going on here? What kind of man is this? He comes into our lives, curses my mother, and pushes my brother around. What will he do to me? My mother's so into him. It's like she doesn't care what happens to Isaac or even herself. I didn't know what to do. What can I do?"* Moses thought. Even though he was young he had to protect Isaac.

CHAPTER EIGHT

Independence Day started with a bang as neighbors set off firecrackers in the morning hours. Sounds of the holiday forced Moses from his sleep as this bright-eyed young man sprung from his bed. He glanced at Isaac, who was still asleep. Isaac was probably experiencing another dream, but it couldn't be a nightmare since he rested peacefully. Moses hoped his brother would continue to have pleasant visions in his head. Mansion after mansion, Isaac and Moses would sell properties to the rich and famous. The brothers, both adults, would live in separate cottages on their private beach in Martha's Vineyard. They shared a brunch under the sunny sky, with squawking seagulls soaring above.

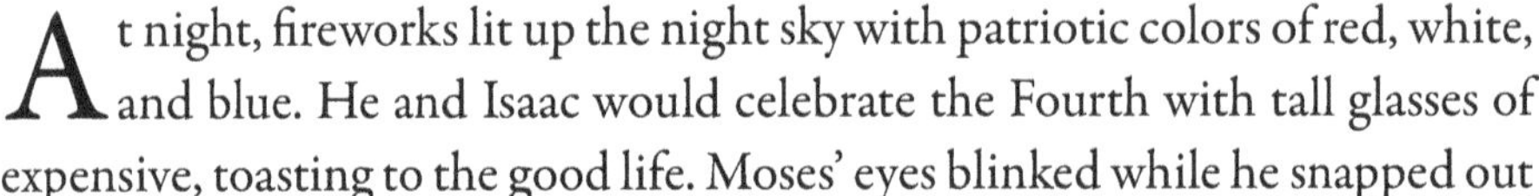

At night, fireworks lit up the night sky with patriotic colors of red, white, and blue. He and Isaac would celebrate the Fourth with tall glasses of expensive, toasting to the good life. Moses' eyes blinked while he snapped out of his one-minute fantasy and rushed to Isaac's bed, nudging him.

"Wake up, Isaac!" Moses shook his brother. Isaac opened his eyes slowly, and he could see only a blur. "What?" Isaac tossed and turned in his twin-sized bed.

"It's the Fourth of July!" Moses could hear more firecrackers popping from outside his window. He dashed to it and saw the next-door neighbors starting the holiday fun. Isaac wasn't crazy about the Fourth of July; Christmas was his holiday. No one got gifts on Independence Day. He sat in his bed and heard the outside cracking and popping sounds. Isaac grabbed his glasses from his nightstand and put them on, storming the bedroom. Moses felt as if his brother's presence wasn't behind him. He gave chase and heard the bathroom door slam.

"Aren't you excited?" Moses chuckled on the other side of the bathroom in the hallway. Isaac's pee echoed from the bathroom, and it was a long one. Moses was curious to know if his brother heard him or not. He ambled from the bathroom door and entered the bedroom. Moses resided on the edge of his bed and turned on the television. It wasn't Sunday, so *Open House* wasn't on. Moses thought of YouTube and typed in the title in the search column. Dozens and dozens of episodes on television appeared. He clicked on the first video with the remote control and watched it alone. He stretched out on his bed with his arm over his head and indulged in the house. Isaac strutted in, not saying a word. He laid on his back in bed and watched the screen.

"Good morning," Moses glanced at Isaac's bed.

"What's your problem?" Isaac asked with an attitude.

"You woke up on the wrong side of the bed," Moses insulted.

"I don't think so," Isaac replied.

"I just saw you when you got up. You usually get up between our beds," Moses pointed to the center of the floor.

"Why are you watching my every move?" Isaac pointed at Moses.

"Did you have another bad dream?" Moses sat up, glaring his brother right in the eye. Isaac looked away from Moses, and no words escaped. Moses shook his head in disappointment because he knew it. He wished he could eliminate bad dreams from Isaac's mind. Moses encouraged Isaac to talk, but he refused. The visions frightened him too much.

Later that morning, Calvin's blue Subaru drove along the Long Island Expressway toward the city. Moses and Isaac rode in the backseat while devouring M&Ms and drinking water to wash the sugar down. They sang along with a House song that played on the radio. Irene snoozed in the front passenger's seat, probably dreaming of an affluent world of her own. Calvin kept his eyes on the road as cool air from the air conditioner made the vehicle comfortable, which helped no one to experience the sweltering weather. Moses then gazed out of his window as he quickly subsided his singing.

"Look!" Moses pointed at an ocean blue Lamborghini driven by an older gentleman, mid-sixties, speeding along the expressway, wearing sporting sunglasses. Isaac tried to peer over to the window at Moses but couldn't because he had on his seatbelt. He then unbuckled his safety belt to get a better look at the sporty vehicle. The safety belt alert rang.

"Put your seat belt back on, Isaac," Calvin eyed his stepson's bold move through the rearview mirror.

"Why?" Isaac leaned forward to the front of the car.

"I'll get a ticket, Isaac!" Calvin reduced his speed, eyeing this kid.

"No, you won't," Isaac replied, being a smart ass.

"Shit, kid. Put your seatbelt on now!" Calvin slowed the vehicle down even more.

"No!" Isaac stomped his foot on the floor.

"Fuck! Put your seatbelt on, Isaac!" Moses hollered at his brother, who had Isaac shaking in his boots. Isaac sat back and buckled his safety belt. The brothers eyed each other. Moses had the power here. He glared Isaac down, which made Isaac cringe in his seat and shy away. For the rest of the ride to the big city, the music played and played, song after song.

Surprisingly, Irene still slept through this minor ordeal with Isaac and Calvin, which forced Moses to handle the situation. Moses leaned forward as he sat behind his mother. Irene's eyes were still closed as if she was dead. *"How could she not hear that?"* Moses didn't know what to think of this woman who really didn't give a rat's ass. Especially Isaac. He leaned back in his seat and shook his head. He then looked over to Isaac, who had his head down. Moses hoped Isaac wasn't shedding any tears like a girl. Moses didn't want his brother to be a wimpy baby whenever he advised or told him to do something. He placed his hand on Isaac's shoulder and apologized. Isaac always accepted his brother's apologies because he knew they were sincere. Moses poured another handful of red, white, and blue M&Ms into Isaac's hand. This candy that the twins shared kept peace between them.

As the Subaru drove down Queens Boulevard, Calvin had to park his car in Long Island City. Then, they could take the train into Manhattan.

The twins were ecstatic about the subway ride because they'd never experienced it. Irene woke up, looking around.

"Are you going to take my kids on the nasty subway?" Irene yawned.

"Yes. It'll be a real New York experience," Calvin grinned from ear to ear. Irene sucked her teeth because she hated the subway. Moses would shut up and go back to sleep. The rumble of the number seven train up on the elevated train tracks drowned out the bickering between Calvin and Irene. Also, the traffic got more massive due to so many cars driving across Queensborough Bridge. Moses couldn't wait to hop on that New York ride to the city. He loved it. Calvin searched and searched for a parking space. He consistently made turn after turn onto each block, trying to find a safe place for his car.

"Parking is hard to find around here." Calvin twirled the steering wheel of his vehicle.

Irene shook her head. She didn't want to get on those stinking trains with every germ in the world. Irene remembered it was a holiday and wanted her sons to enjoy themselves. So, she kept her mouth shut. Finally, the blue Subaru pulled into a good parking space with ease. Then Calvin shut its engine down as Moses and Isaac stepped out of it on opposite sides of the vehicle. Moses noticed that neither his mother nor Calvin had come out of the car. Then, loud talking and cursing erupted. Moses swaggered towards the front, where Irene was blowing her top. "That's why I moved to Long Island!" she bellowed. Initially, Irene moved from a bad neighborhood and hated it with passion. It was like a third-world country, and it wasn't safe to go outside.

"Irene, you're acting like we're going there," Calvin bellowed in return.

"I don't like the city," Irene bitched.

Calvin walked away from the argument Irene had conjured up. He slammed the door, locking it. She wasn't budging.

"What the fuck is she doing!" Calvin marched towards the passenger's side and thrust the door open.

"I'll wait here," Irene refused to go.

"Are you out of your mind!" Calvin couldn't believe his wife's behavior.

"No." Irene folded her arms.

"Why didn't you just stay home?" Calvin yelled.

"I would have if I had known we were taking the train!" Irene remained still in the passenger's seat.

"So, you're going to stay in this car in the empty parking lot," Calvin questioned.

"Mom, stop and come on," Moses rushed between them.

Shockingly, Irene removed her rear end from the passenger's seat without thinking. Calvin slammed the door and locked it. Then the family marched towards the subway station. Moses and Isaac dashed up the concrete steps, where they noticed two number seven trains going in opposite directions. Moses' heart raced in his chest as he and Isaac ran along a ramp that led to the station's entrance. Moses saw the different trains that stopped at the station. Not only the number seven train but also the W and N trains. When he noticed the other numbers, he was a bit confused.

"Dad, what train are we going to take?" Moses felt like a dummy for the first time.

"We're taking the seven train," Calvin smiled. Then Moses and Calvin looked at Irene with her frown upon her face.

"Dang, how could Mom be so miserable? Have some fun," Moses mumbled. The family entered the station as the stink hit their noses hard.

"Pew! What's that stink," Isaac held his nose.

"Don't worry. It'll get better," Moses put his arm around Isaac, ensuring him their time in Manhattan was memorable. Calvin approached the MetroCard vending machines and paid for three cards. He gave one to Isaac and another to Moses, but the boys didn't know how to use them. Moses watched a man swipe his MetroCard through the turnstile. Then Moses caught on quickly, swiping his MetroCard through it. He pushed through the turnstile. Isaac, of course, watched his brother and followed suit as he made their way to the subway platform. Calvin and Irene eyed each other in disbelief. Irene snatched the extra MetroCard from Calvin's hand and got through the turnstile. Calvin wanted to let Irene have it so badly, but he tried to enjoy the holiday. Moses witnessed the friction between his mother and her husband, noticing they had issues. The brothers dashed up the steps as the train pulled into the station. It rumbled like an earthquake. Moses stopped and looked back to see if his parents were right behind. Calvin and Irene ran up the steps as fast as they could. Moses looked up the steps towards Isaac, who waited at the top. Moses continued up the steps to his brother's side. The bell rang, and the automatic doors opened. Suddenly, a bunch of passengers rushed out.

Moses and Isaac boarded the number seven train with their parents behind them. The bell rang as the doors closed. The train chugged out of the station, heading into the city. The frats glued their eyes to the window, where the Manhattan skyline displayed before them. Skyscrapers were up close and personal. Moses and Isaac stared at the majestic buildings. It was the perfect time to daydream by staring at such a sight. The kids didn't even bother to see where their parents were. But Calvin and Irene stood watching the kids loved the view from the window.

"Beautiful, isn't it?" Calvin smiled.

"It sure is," Isaac answered with a loud tone.

"Shh, quiet," Calvin whispered.

"Sorry," Isaac cringed in embarrassment, whispering.

An older man noticed the boys and enjoyed their sightseeing on the train. Calvin focused on Irene, who found a seat, her face displeased. He tried to figure out what her problem was. Moses' parents bickered during the train ride. He looked away from the window and witnessed this embarrassing moment. This verbal fight caught the attention of other passengers. He hoped this day wouldn't be ruined due to the likes of his mother and Calvin.

"What is her problem?" Moses asked in his mind.

Moses focused his attention on the skyscrapers as the train made its way underground. Now, there was no more to see. So, the boys turned around in their seats and noticed the people on it. Moses eyed the older gentleman, who graciously smiled and nodded to them. Moses nodded back in response. Isaac's eyes wandered as he noticed a gentleman residing in the corner with soiled clothing. He carried lots of bags and a cup to beg for money; therefore, he could get a bite to eat. Isaac nudged Moses, focusing on the destitute gentleman. He imagined the things the homeless man experienced every day of his life. *Where does he sleep at night? How did he get food to eat? How does he stay warm in the winter and cool on hot summer days like today? Where's his family? Or did he have any family?* This poor soul didn't even notice the nine-year-old young man staring at him throughout the train ride. "Fifth Avenue, Battery Park," the train conductor announced as the train pulled into the station and stopped.

"Moses, let's go!" Calvin gestured to his sons. The twins snapped out of their trance. Isaac took a last look at the man and wished the best from his heart. The double doors automatically opened, and the passengers got off. Moses ran to catch up to his family and reached their side.

Within minutes, Moses and his family sashayed down Fifth Avenue. Battery Park is famous for its musical and theatrical performances. Speaking of music, a jazz band played while spectators lounged on the enormous green grass. Moses could hear a trumpet blaring, a bass thumping, and drums banging through the air. The twins marched ahead of their parents while they tried to keep up with them. Moses and Isaac acted like they knew how to get around the city. Moses, of course, didn't see the city, even though he had been there before. Someday he'll know this borough like the back of his hand.

"Moses, Isaac," Calvin called to his sons as he and Irene ran up to them.

Calvin clutched his sons, letting them know to stay close. The Remington-Mitchell family proceeded to stroll around until they found somewhere to eat before the Macy's Fireworks show. The patriotic fireworks show launched from the East River. Since this was Moses' second trip to Manhattan, he had some suggestions. The M&Ms store in Times Square, FAO Schwarz at Rockefeller Plaza, and a summery stroll through Central Park. Calvin was impressed by Moses' knowledge of the city and that he remembered everything. When people have a good experience, they'll live with them forever. Moses and his family waltzed down Fifth Avenue, pointing, and gasping at every tall building, fashion store, and expensive car that drove along the street and the entire atmosphere. As the frats enjoyed the sights, Moses eyed his mother, Irene. He noticed something wasn't right. *"Is my mother sick? She's not interacting with Isaac and me!"* Moses scratched his head. Isaac then tapped him on the shoulder, drawing his attention to two clowns on the streets performing before a small crowd. One of the clowns honked a horn and told corny jokes. Isaac chuckled at their colorful, goofy outfits and make-up. Moses raised an eyebrow, frowning because these street performers weren't funny. But Isaac guffawed and guffawed. And so did Calvin. Then Irene grinned her teeth, pulling Isaac to the side.

"How would you like for someone to laugh at you!" Irene shook Isaac. Isaac's jaw dropped while his cross-eyes watered from behind his lenses.

"Their clowns, Mom. What do you expect!" Moses stood in front of Isaac, looking in his mother's face. Irene released her son from her grip as Isaac burst into tears. Moses put his arms around his brother as Isaac let it all out. Irene stood in a daze as if she had no idea of her actions. Moses glared at his mother along with spectators on the street, who took notice. Calvin stood dumbfounded for a moment. Then threw his hands up. He didn't know if they should go home or try to enjoy the day. "Irene, what's with you?" Calvin took a deep breath.

"Are you all right, Isaac?" Calvin asked in a gentle tone.

"Are you really concerned now?" Moses advised his stepfather, who forgot about the incident on the roller coaster ride. Calvin shrugged his shoulders.

"Don't think I forgot," Moses said. Calvin didn't allow it to bother him. He rubbed Isaac on the head and kissed him.

"Let's go, get some ice cream," Calvin said, patching things up. Then the family continued sightseeing along Fifth Avenue. The fraternal twins stormed ahead of Calvin and Irene, acting as if they were alone. Moses didn't know who his mother was, so he kept ignoring her and her new husband.

"Sorry about that, Isaac. It's not like Mom," Moses patted Isaac on the shoulder.

"Why is she treating me so mean?" Isaac whined. The twins stormed at a fast pace as Calvin gave chase.

"Wait, guys!" Calvin touched Moses's shoulder.

"Go on, get out of here!" Moses shouted, pulled away from his stepfather. He was upset about Calvin's antics. And even his mother's. People passing were wondering about this young child arguing with this grown man who felt embarrassed. Calvin couldn't even look anyone in the eye. His eyes shifted side to side, feeling stupid.

"Do you want to go home? "Calvin asked since someone's unhappiness ruined their fun.

"No! Where's the ice cream?" Moses hollered.

Minutes later, Moses and Isaac enjoyed their vanilla and chocolate ice cream with the sprinkles and mini-M&Ms. The twins gravitated to a bench along the stone wall of Central Park. Calvin sat across from them on another bench. Irene sat two seats down, her arms folded. *"What would happen if Calvin and my mom decided to give us up? Mainly Isaac,"* Moses thought as this terrifying question popped into his head. He stopped eating his ice cream; then, he sobbed like he had never. Isaac then wrapped his arms around Moses.

"What's wrong, Moses," Isaac wrapped his arms around Moses. Calvin stopped eating his ice cream and noticed his favorite son in tears.

"Are you alright, Moses?" Calvin consoled Moses.

"I'm sorry, son. I'm sorry our day of fun isn't going well. Hey, look at the bright side. We got the fireworks show tonight," Isaac patted his brother on the shoulder, smiling. He then offered to trade ice cream with his brother to make him feel better. They did just that, but it didn't make his worries go away. Moses didn't even make eye contact with his stepfather.

"When do we eat some real food?" Moses scooped the ice cream into his mouth.

"Let's get some grub," Calvin wrapped his arms around both boys. They strolled past Irene, who remained on the bench with a negative disposition. "We're going to get something to eat, Irene," Calvin told her. She rose from the bench and followed her family. At some point, she would stop acting so stubborn.

About an hour later, pop music blared from the ceiling speakers of a themed restaurant. Its wall décor consisted of nostalgic memorabilia. Moses and his family sat at a booth with soft drinks by their sides, looking over menus. Irene and Calvin sat beside each other while their sons sat across. Surprisingly, Irene eyed the food on the list and used her finger to skim. Moses raised an eyebrow, shocked at his mother coming out of her shell. *Maybe, she needs food. People go crazy when they're hungry.* "The chicken salad looks good," Irene continued to look at the menu. Her family was shocked to see this angry woman's persona mellow. Her eyes rose from her menu with softness on her face. She apologized, kissing Isaac. She leaned over the table and gave her sons loads of affection. Isaac accepted his mother's apology, but for Moses, he didn't know what to think. "I'm sorry, Moses," Irene grasped his hand. Moses pulled his hand away and focused back on the menu. Her firstborn's coldness surprised Irene. Calvin gestured that Moses would get over it. Then a waitress strutted to the booth, taking the family's order. Irene wanted the chicken salad with lots of olives, if possible. *"Why don't you be quiet? Who cares what you want to eat!"* Moses thought to himself. This young man peered from his menu.

"What would you like, Isaac?" Calvin asked.

"Oh, oh. Do you have taco salads?" Isaac asked the waitress in an innocent tone.

"Again," Moses nudged Isaac, looking away from his menu.

"I like tacos and salads," Isaac raised his voice, embarrassing Moses.

"I like taco salads," Moses mocked Isaac and then shut up. He focused on his menu, ready to place his order.

"Moses?" Calvin called his name.

"Again. I'll have a taco salad, too," Isaac embarrassed his brother in return. They both snickered as Calvin ordered a steak with French fries. The waitresses collected the menus and walked away.

"So, do you guys like the city," Calvin looked at the wall décor. The kids nodded. Isaac liked Manhattan, but Moses didn't say a word because he was upset at his mother. He had already experienced the city, but Moses wanted Isaac to experience the sights and sounds of the grandest city in the world. They had to go to the M&Ms candy store. Calvin agreed to take the kids there, so they could devour all the chocolate they wanted. But now, they must eat healthy food first.

About an hour later, Moses and Isaac swaggered along the busy, crowded streets of Times Square as their parents ambled behind. These young men seemed to know how to take care of themselves. But Calvin didn't let these kids out of his sight. He continuously trotted behind them, trying to keep up.

"Kids, wait up," Calvin grabbed Isaac and Moses.

"The M&M store is across the street!" Moses swaggered away from his stepfather.

"Alright! Be careful, Moses!" Calvin stood there, feeling like an unfit parent with his hand still on Isaac's shoulder. He saw Moses standing at the corner, waiting for the traffic light to change. Then, he could cross this three-lane street with massive motorists. Moses had a mind of his own and seemed to be very independent. Calvin believed this daring kid could survive independently in the real world. Moses wouldn't need any parents.

"I bet he would love for Isaac to get lost. That would be his way to get rid of him. And I'm not going to forget that rollercoaster incident," Moses thought as he crossed the street. He then saw Isaac dash to his side as they entered the candy store.

In minutes, the frats shared their love for chocolate-covered candies in the M&Ms store. "My class and I came here. Remember when I brought you all those candies?" Moses reminded Isaac.

"Yes," Isaac's face lit up like a bulb. Due to Independence Day, the twins filled the M&M's plastic bags with red, white, and blue candies. They didn't even think about the other colors. Calvin and Irene filled their bags with different shades of chocolate.

"Don't you want the other colors," Calvin held up his bag of colorful treats.

"No," Isaac continued to fill his bag with blue, then another with white, and the final bag with red. Moses mixed patriotic colors into one bag. Isaac finished filling his bags of candy and browsed around the store. The world's famous candy had a brand than just sweets. Moses and Isaac shoved their candy bags into their parents' hands and hopped on the escalator to the second floor. The second level had another chocolate candy wall with more flavors of toffee, jalapeno, coffee, etc. Isaac stood before the peanut M&M wall, where he grabbed another plastic bag. He filled it with red, white, and blue. Moses filled another plastic bag with peanut M&Ms, multi-colored this time.

"Isaac let's try the jalapeno," Moses filled a branded plastic bag with the spicy goodies.

"Just a little bit," Isaac saw the colored walls and displays of the M&M characters everywhere. Colorful t-shirts hung on the wall, drawing Isaac's attention. He left Moses' side and browsed the clothing department.

"Isaac, where are you?" Moses looked over both his shoulders.

"I'm here," Isaac raised his hand, waving to his brother. Moses dashed to his brother's side with their parents, finally catching up.

"Boys, you've got to stop doing this," Calvin wanted to grab them, but he didn't want to draw attention to himself. The boys acted as if they didn't hear their stepfather.

"Can we get some T-shirts?" Isaac asked excitedly. Calvin inhaled and gave in to his stepsons. Irene smiled as she whispered in Calvin's ear. Moses gave his mother the most dead-hard stare ever. *"What the hell is she telling him? She's probably telling Calvin not to buy anything for us,"* Moses thought, but his stepfather strolled over with some cash in his hand.

"Pick out whatever you want." Then the boys scrambled all over the floor like deranged kids from hell, grabbing almost every piece of merchandise such as mugs, coin holders, belts, and two navy blue patriotic M&Ms shirts with red, white, and blue candies on them.

That evening, dusk soon approached as the sun set in the summer sky. Along the boardwalk, spectators waited for the first bursting firework to light up the night. Moses and Isaac maneuvered through the crowd as they resided on a bench. Both were surprised it wasn't occupied. Most people had their portable lounge chairs or preferred to stand. The boys ate their M&Ms as if it was popcorn at the movies. A thin, red, white, and blue patriotic-clad Caucasian gentleman; with salt and pepper hair; in his mid-seventies; ambled with his cane and service dog, an old golden Labrador. The old man resided on the end of the bench, glancing at these two unattended boys. The brothers noticed this gentleman, as well. They both looked at each other and smiled. "Are you two here alone?" the elder eyed the twins head to toe.

"No. My parents are around here somewhere," Moses chewed a mouth full of gooey chocolate. Isaac smiled at the gentleman and took notice of the Yellow Labrador.

"I like your dog," Isaac stroked the dog's coat.

"Charlie likes you too," the elderly gentleman chuckled.

"Were you in the war?" Moses popped more candy in his mouth.

"Yeah, Vietnam. You can tell by the medals I'm wearing, right?" the elder asked.

"Yes," Moses smacked on his goodies.

"Was it scary?" Isaac smacked his mouth of the chocolate and the colorful shells while his eyes crossed behind his thick-lensed glasses.

"Moses! Isaac!" Calvin weaved in and out amongst the crowded boardwalks.

"Over here, Dad!" Moses waved, holding his candy in his hand. Calvin and Irene ran with the large M&Ms bag.

"What am I going to do with you two?" Calvin raced out of breath. He noticed the veteran sitting with his sons.

"This is..." Moses stopped in the middle of his sentence. "What is your name, Sir?" Moses addressed the veteran with the utmost respect.

"Isaiah," he answered.

"This is Isaiah," Moses introduced the veteran to his father.

"Nice to meet you, sir," Calvin politely shook the veteran's hand.

"I'm Moses."

"And I'm Isaac," the boys introduced themselves.

"Wow. That's nice. Moses and Isaac."

"Isaiah is nice," Isaac added.

Calvin wanted to confront his sons about running off; but changed his mind. Irene hugged Moses and Isaac without saying a word.

"Do you boys know what the three of us have in common?" the veteran asked.

"We have biblical names," Isaac responded.

"Smart kid," the veteran shook Isaac's hand.

Their parents listened as Moses and Isaac interacted with this war hero who indulged in conversation with them. Isaiah told a little about his war stories but refrained from getting explicit. Moses enjoyed listening to stories from this war veteran, not some creep off the street. He hoped that when he and Isaac got older, they would make the right choices, associate with the right people, and do everything right. This time, Moses thought about Isaac's future instead of his own.

"I'm sorry you lost your friend, Isaiah," Moses swallowed his last bit of candy. Isaiah took a deep breath, looking across at the East River. He halted in the middle of his war stories. The sixties veteran became watery-eyed as he closed them to fight back the tears. Then he opened them, and the boys saw his red, watery eyes filled with sadness.

"You know what! The day is beautiful on this cloudy July fourth, and you're alive," Isaiah looked at the bright side.

"Hold your hand out, Isaiah," Isaac said. The veteran held his hand as Isaac poured the red, white, and blue M&Ms into his hand.

"My favorite candy in the right colors," Isaiah chuckled, popping the candies into his mouth.

"Mom?" Isaac offered to pour some M&Ms into her hand.

"Thanks, son," Irene crunched on the candy.

"Here, Moses," Isaac poured candy into his brother's hand. The boys, their parents, and this veteran shared the American chocolate treats until the sky darkened that evening. Then a boom of the first fireworks burst into the air in red. Then white, blue, and other colors mesmerized the spectators below watching Macy's spectacular fireworks show.

"Happy fourth, everybody," Isaac greeted.

The twins put their arms around each other and watched the show.

CHAPTER NINE

A blue and white banner reading "Happy Birthday" hung high on the fence behind Moses and Isaac as they blew out ten candles on their cake. Everyone from Moses and Isaac's friends from school and the neighborhood, Irene's family, Jacob's kin (the twins' biological father), and Calvin's relatives were in attendance. A long picnic table stored lots of candies, snacks, food, and drinks for their guests. The twins had the first piece of their favorite ice cream cake; vanilla, chocolate crunchies, and chocolate ice cream on the bottom. The party was off to a good start. Everyone socialized while enjoying the food and music.

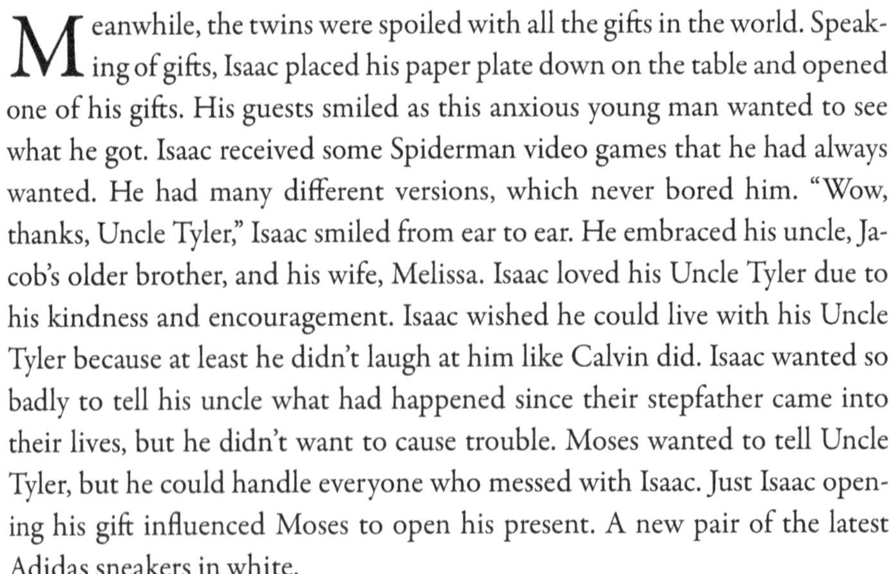

Meanwhile, the twins were spoiled with all the gifts in the world. Speaking of gifts, Isaac placed his paper plate down on the table and opened one of his gifts. His guests smiled as this anxious young man wanted to see what he got. Isaac received some Spiderman video games that he had always wanted. He had many different versions, which never bored him. "Wow, thanks, Uncle Tyler," Isaac smiled from ear to ear. He embraced his uncle, Jacob's older brother, and his wife, Melissa. Isaac loved his Uncle Tyler due to his kindness and encouragement. Isaac wished he could live with his Uncle Tyler because at least he didn't laugh at him like Calvin did. Isaac wanted so badly to tell his uncle what had happened since their stepfather came into their lives, but he didn't want to cause trouble. Moses wanted to tell Uncle Tyler, but he could handle everyone who messed with Isaac. Just Isaac opening his gift influenced Moses to open his present. A new pair of the latest Adidas sneakers in white.

"Thanks, Uncle Tyler," Moses jumped from his seat.

"You're welcome, son," Tyler embraced Moses and Isaac.

Irene stood in the background, happy her sons got what they wanted. On the other hand, Calvin stood around with family and friends with fake smiles, sucking their teeth.

"They're spoiled as shit," Calvin mumbled under his breath. His friend Joe heard what he uttered. As far as Calvin's family went, they treated Moses and Isaac so-so, but sometimes they were mean. Sometimes, Calvin's relatives treated Moses better than Isaac. Isaac dreaded family gatherings with Calvin's kin. They were devils - especially Calvin's mother, Monique, a pudgy woman in her early-sixties with cantaloupe-sized breasts. She smelt like stale perfume and cursed like crazy. When she arrived at the party, she went off on Calvin about not keeping Moses and Isaac in check. She advised Calvin to keep a closer eye on the boys because she could sense they would get out of hand. Irene overheard Calvin's mother gossip about her and her sons. Monique wasn't too keen on her son marrying a woman with two children from a previous marriage. She didn't care if their father was alive or not.

Meanwhile, Moses and Isaac kept opening their gifts. Calvin's nephew, Ronnell, eleven years of age, dark-skinned, thin kid, buck teeth, wearing a basketball jersey and jeans, sneered at them. His older brother, Winston, was not that skinny, medium-brown-skinned, nicely arranged teeth, and wore some old jeans, a worn T-shirt, and old kicks. He snatched the Adidas sneakers from Moses' hands.

"What the fuck!" Moses jumped from his seat.

"You need to check that boy!" Monique lit up a cigarette.

"What the hell are you doing? Give those back!" Tyler stood up from his chair.

"He's just playing!" Monique blew smoke into the air.

"Give the sneakers back, Winston. Stop acting like an ass!" Calvin insulted him.

"You know I'm playing with you, Moses," Winston gave the kicks back.

Moses shoved his new kicks in the box.

Then Ronnell grabbed Isaac's Spiderman video game from his hand and ran around the backyard with it. Isaac gave chase, trying to get his gift back.

"Uncle Tyler! Uncle Tyler!" Isaac's voice quivered.

Tyler snatched this kid by the arm with an irate expression.

"Let go of my brother," Ronell demanded as this seventeen-year-old would go toe toe-to-toe with this adult man. Then Calvin's brother, Troy, intervened. Being an X-con, Troy would defend his sons, Winston, and Ronnell, to the death even if he had to return to the slammer. Calvin diffused the situation too late. Tyler and Troy hurled fists at each other. Calvin, Ronnell, and Winston punched Tyler as he did his best to defend himself. Isaac and Moses stood in shock as Calvin's relatives ambushed his favorite uncle. Isaac dashed into the house and dialed 911. Moses jumped in and fought these hoodlums off his Uncle Tyler. As Moses did this, Ronell threw a punch at Moses. He hit the ground but thankfully landed on the grass. Moses rose to his feet and punched this unwanted relative in the face. Then two boys went toe to toe. Moses put up a good fight which Ronell weakened.

Isaac, in tears, waited outside on the sidewalk for the authorities. In seconds, a patrol car sped up to the residence, stopping short with screeching brakes. A Caucasian male officer hopped out from the driver's side as a female Asian officer in her mid-thirties rushed to Isaac. "They're beating up, my uncle," Isaac said, wiping his tears from behind his glasses. The officers could hear the commotion. They dashed towards the rear of the house, calling for backup on their radios with their hands on their holsters.

Moments later, the cops diffused the confrontation, questioning guests at the party. Monique kept giving Isaac the evil eye as an officer noticed it. Monique then turned around, leaving. "Why did you call the police? Are you serious?" Calvin threw his hands in the air. "He had every right," the Asian officer got in Calvin's face with her hand on her firearm.

Irene embraced her sons, who seemed timid. The officers asked Irene questions, but she was too afraid to answer. Irene had no idea Calvin had a crazy family. If she had known this beforehand, she wouldn't have married him. The police did a background check on Troy; they found out he just got released a few months earlier. And so, three officers gave him a real tongue-lashing. They did everything the officers said and fled the premises. Before leaving, he whispered in Calvin's ear and gave him a high-five, swaggering away.

As Irene consoled her sons, Calvin stood alone as his family left the scene. Moses figured it out. Irene was frightened of Calvin and his weird family. *"When you marry someone, you're not just marrying the person, but you're marrying the family. I hope Calvin's mother doesn't do anything to my mother. Or anyone in his family. Who the hell did she marry? I'm going to be careful who I marry when I get older. I don't want to be in a marriage where I must walk on eggshells,"* Moses embraced his mother and Isaac.

Nine-thirty at night, Moses and Isaac shared their birthday M&Ms as they heard the bitching from the master bedroom. "I hate Calvin. I'll never call him dad again," Isaac chewed the chocolate candy. "Why couldn't she marry a nicer man? Boy, I wish Dad were here. We wouldn't be going through this." Isaac rambled on and on. Moses took in every word his brother spewed out but couldn't help the situation. "Calvin just had to invite his relatives to our birthday party. We had plenty of kids from the neighborhood and school to help us celebrate. We didn't need his family there," Moses pounded his fists on the bed.

"What the fuck!" Isaac shouted, but Calvin and Irene didn't hear Isaac curse because of their friction in the master bedroom. Then, when Calvin's bitching intensified, Moses marched out of the bedroom. Moses barged into the master bedroom. "My brother had the right to call the cops. Your family is a menace."

"My brother just got out of jail," Calvin waved his arms like a maniac.

"And our birthday party that he messed up!" Moses stared him dead in the face.

"I'll make it up to you, Moses," Calvin felt guilty. He was about to embrace Moses as he pushed him away.

"Take me to my father's grave!" Moses demanded. Irene's eyes enlarged by what came out of Moses' mouth, his posture firm. Her son didn't fear anything or anyone other than God. Calvin then nodded his head and agreed.

A week later, Moses and Isaac took baby steps through a graveyard, holding flowers in both hands. On this dismal summer morning, it was still hot and humid with only peeks of sun. Moses felt something in the air, being in the cemetery and visiting the one person who protected you from harm. Moses and Isaac could only count on each other for protection. The brothers arrived at the tombstone. It read: Jacob Remington. It also had his date of birth and date of death. The brothers placed their arms around each other, giving comfort. Calvin and Irene stood in the background. Calvin respected the children's wishes, giving them their time at the gravesite. The twins looked at each other in wonder. "Do you want to say something to Dad, Isaac?" Moses asked.

"Can he hear us?" Isaac wondered.

"Yes. But he won't answer back," Moses said.

"Why not?" Isaac added.

"Dad's in heaven," Moses shrugged his shoulders.

Then the boys became quiet and focused their eyes on the sky.

"Dad, I know you have a new home in Heaven with God. We wish you could come home to visit us for a while, but it is what it is. All I can say is I love and miss you," Moses then looked to his brother. Isaac looked nervous. He didn't know what to say.

"What do I say?" Isaac whispered and shrugged.

"Just do like I did," Moses encouraged.

Isaac was quiet for a second, then he poured his heart out.

"Dad, I hope that..." Isaac got lost for words. He didn't want to copy Moses' words. He took a deep breath.

"All I can say is.... I want to be with you," Isaac's voice quivered, and he burst into tears. Moses embraced his brother as he and Isaac both cried. Calvin noticed the twins sobbing before the tombstone. He wanted to comfort the children but kept his distance. Irene stepped in and embraced her children as tears streamed from her eyes. Calvin witnessed his new wife's tears for her husband, who's now long gone. He didn't know what to do or feel. But Calvin felt disheartened.

CHAPTER TEN

Seventeen-year-old Moses, sported a t-shirt, jeans, and sneakers while he dribbled a basketball on a nearby neighborhood basketball on a warm September afternoon. He was now even more of an item with the ladies in the community, school, and aboard. Beneath those good looks, Moses was an intelligent bookworm with a promising future. He, Isaac, and Ryan were in their senior year. All were ready to head out to make a life for themselves. For now, Moses had to plan for college while they looked forward to the prom and graduation. Speaking of the prom, he didn't know who to take. Moses had plenty of time to think about that. He showed his fancy footwork on the court with his best friend Ryan, playing a one-on-one game. Ryan, now a handsome devil at six-foot-one, had talented skills on the court.

"Come on! Come on! What! What!" Moses dribbled the ball toward the hoop and scored. "Damn. You got blessed, Moses," Ryan fell on his rear end.

"That's right," Moses reached his hand out, helping his friend up off the ground. They gave one another a high-five for a good game. Twelve pretty girls sitting on two benches applauded Moses and Ryan as they played another round of one-on-one. Isaac, dressed in jeans and a t-shirt, was now seventeen. He sat alongside the group of ladies. Regardless of his condition, he got somewhat share of the ladies. Isaac had his eye on one girl, in particular, Valentina. She was a dark-skinned girl, who turned a man's head when she strolled down the street. She wore stylish jeans, and cute blouses, and her hair was in a cute bun. Isaac befriended Valentina, but he knew she had eyes for his brother. The women picked Moses first, although a couple of girls had an eye for Isaac. Some young ladies were turned off by Isaac being albino. So, they gave him the cold shoulder. Isaac knew Valentina was going to be his brother's prom date. He could picture the couple slowly dancing to Luther Vandross. Moses was dressed in a black tuxedo and Valentina wore a beautiful red gown with red and white carnations on her wrist. He'd hold Valentina close to him, pelvis to pelvis. And, of course, that night, they'll make love in a fancy hotel. He shook the notion of lovemaking, hoping it would be just a night's *fuck.*

Isaac, Moses, and Ryan played again as the girls watched like cheerleaders sitting on the sidelines at the NBA game. Isaac felt like a sucker seated on the side. He wished that he and Moses could have that one-on-one game instead of Moses and his best friend. "I'm his best friend, not Ryan. He's a stranger," Isaac glared at them playing b-ball on the court. The girls clapped and laughed at how Moses and Ryan insulted each other during the game. It was all fun. Isaac couldn't stand the sight of them and swaggered away. The girls rooted Moses on as he made a shot with the basketball in the hoop. Valentina rose from the bench and hugged Moses along with the other admirers. No one even noticed that Isaac was gone.

At home, Isaac lay in his full-sized bed with a black comforter in his dimmed bedroom in the basement. He closed the blinds with only a peek of light in his small space. His bedroom had bare walls, a laptop on his desk that he didn't use, a medium-sized bookshelf against the walls with some books, a lounge chair, and his school bag on the floor. His small flat-panel television played an old eighties cartoon at low volume. He consistently opened his eyes, waiting for Moses to come downstairs. Isaac stashed a butcher knife under his pillow. He never had such vile thoughts about his brother. Moses always had his back, but things changed. Moses had gained popularity as Isaac walked in his shadow. Now, he hardly existed. The front door creaked as footsteps entered. Then, the door shut. Isaac wanted to sneak up on his sibling and gut him like a deer. But instead, Isaac lay in wait for his prey to enter the trap. Then, the side door's hinges squeaked, and the screen door slammed. Isaac heard Moses' panting. He knew he was alone.

"Moses!" Isaac raised his head from his pillow. He gripped the butcher knife.

"Isaac!" Moses' voice bellowed from the head of the basement steps.

"Down here!" Isaac laid back on the pillow. He held an even tighter grip on the knife. Moses' footsteps pounded down the steps, opening his brother's bedroom door with a squeaky, eerie, and ominous sound. Moses plopped his rear end into the lounge chair across from Isaac's bed.

"Who told you to sit there?" Isaac gripped the butcher knife tighter and tighter.

"What the fuck is with you? You called me down here!" Moses, out of breath, shook his head.

"Get the fuck out of my chair!" Isaac stood to his feet, concealing the large blade behind his back.

"Fuck it! What kind of shit is this!" Moses stood from the lounge chair, turning his back to storm out of his brother's bedroom. And then, the silvery blade plunged into his back. He fell to the floor face-first. Moses turned over with his brother on top of him, wrestling over the butcher knife. Moses saw the evil in Isaac's eyes. Isaac wasn't himself; it was as if he were possessed. Isaac thrust the enormous blade into Moses' chest, with blood spewing everywhere. Repeatedly, the knife thrust into Moses's abdominal area. Blood continued to spread all over the place. Moses took his last breath as Isaac then took sharp breaths, standing over his brother's corpse.

Isaac's eyes widened, looking at his bloody hands as he bellowed in horror. Isaac abruptly raised his head from his pillow, sobbing. He rushed from his slumber and swung his bedroom door open. Throughout the house, not a soul was in sight, complete silence. His parents had gone out to dinner, so the twins had to fend for themselves for the evening. Isaac ascended the staircase to the second floor. As he got to the top, moaning and groaning came from down the hallway. Isaac crept towards the sound of sexiness, which had an eerie tone. He looked over his shoulder steadily. Isaac approached Moses' cracked door, where he saw Moses and Valentina in the nude, thrusting hard and fast. Valentina loved every moment of it. Isaac shook his head and leaned up against the wall. He wouldn't stand there and listen to them get it on. Nor was he going to barge in on his brother and Valentina. *"What about me? Why aren't the girls going for me? They may associate with me or have me as a friend, but not as a lover,"* Isaac gently banged his head against the wall.

"This is some fucked up shit," Isaac left his brother's bedroom door. He swaggered down the stairs, thinking about the dream he had. He wanted to

tell Moses about it but was busy getting it on. *"This bitch and everyone's taking my brother,"* Isaac spoke in his mind. He regressed to that small kid back in the fourth grade, where he felt alone. None of the kids would play or associate with him. Instead, they made fun of him, and Moses always defended him. But Moses wasn't there. *"How will we have our own business if my brother isn't communicating with me or including me in his world?"* Isaac entered his bedroom in the basement and plopped on his bed. He stared at the ceiling and thought about his dream of murdering his beloved brother. Isaac slept off the hurt, closing his eyes, and thinking about nothing.

That morning at Hempstead High School, the late bell rang. Moses and Isaac dashed up the concrete steps. As Moses approached the steps, students greeted him with high-fives and handshakes while the girls embraced him. Isaac stood in the background, watching his brother— *"the star"*—get all the attention. He pictured the word "Loser" written all over his forehead. Everything was *Moses, Moses, Moses*. No one ever rooted for Isaac, only a few students embraced him. Then Ryan met up with Moses. They entered the building as if they were brothers. Isaac's face turned red, very red. Afterward, he calmed down because he didn't want the students or faculty to. think he was ill. He reversed his anger into tears, crying like a baby. His eyes got watery, and a few tears streamed down his cheeks. Isaac wiped them away quickly. He stormed into the classroom, hopping in his seat, and made no eye contact with anyone. He kept his head down, not bothering to look up. A whiff of a flowery fragrance caused Isaac to lift his head. Upon doing so, he noticed beautiful Clarissa Roberts, a sixteen-year-old who frequently smiled at him. Right then, she did just that. Isaac reciprocated the smile as his eyes crossed behind those glasses he wore. This gorgeous gem's friendly gestures confused Isaac.

There were no words exchanged, for now, only hello and bye. Isaac didn't want to make a fool of himself in front of the school. But he knew one thing; if it were Moses, she'd be all over him. So, he chose to stay to himself and allowed Clarissa to make the first move. In front of the classroom, a girl named Rhonda sat chatting with some other girls about the popular guys in the school. From the middle, where Isaac sat, he heard Moses' name called amongst the girls' gossip. *Did they even know that Moses had a brother right under their noses?* Isaac listened to what they were saying. It was nothing but how beautiful Moses was and how he was so fuckin' smart. The girls talked about Moses' penis size and how they would love to get it on with him. The English teacher, Mr. Donovan, hustled with his paperwork under his arms, slamming it down on his desk, ready for the day's lesson.

Thirty minutes into the English session, Isaac read a passage from the book *Of Mice and Men*. As Isaac read the chapter, Clarissa couldn't keep her eyes off him. She saw past his condition and was attracted to his intelligence. Isaac answered every question. He had a three-point-five grade point average and was an available guy. Isaac glanced at this girl, who continually cracked a smile. All Isaac knew was that he was going to take his time. He didn't want to get his feelings hurt.

In the library, students studied silently at wooden tables and chairs. A librarian resided at her desk to keep an eye out for any disruptive pupils. Moses and Valentina resided at a table; their textbooks opened before them. Moses sat close to Valentina as if he had the opportunity to engage in a passionate kiss. The librarian raised an eyebrow at Moses' motives. She gestured for him to back his chair away from Valentina a bit. Moses inched his chair away from Valentina, but when the librarian looked elsewhere, he pushed his chair closer to her. He laid a kiss upon her. Surprisingly, the librarian didn't notice the kiss, or maybe she let it go. As the two love birds got friendly, Isaac stood in the distance from the aisle of books. He stared at his brother, enjoying his life that came out of the blue. *"This was supposed to happen for both of us — girls, parties, and success. Not just him,"* Isaac hid behind a bookshelf. He slid his back against the side of the bookcase, moping in his own misery.

CHAPTER ELEVEN

That night, Moses and Ryan watched real estate videos on YouTube. Both gasped at every property they saw. The friends scrolled through the properties on a computer. Then Irene opened Moses' door with a squeak and leaned in the doorway. "What are you guys up to?" Moses' mother folded her arms. "We are checking out some real estate properties," Moses glanced away from the computer screen, acknowledging his mother's presence.

"Check this mansion out!" Ryan pointed at a home. Irene marched over, glancing over her son's shoulder at the eighteen-million-dollar Santa Barbara, California home. It had an infinity swimming pool with a waterfall, an enormous living room, a spacious kitchen, and seven bedrooms with panoramic views of the estate. Irene fell in love with the home and hoped to live in a house like that someday. The friends discussed how they would get their start in the real estate market. They kept talking about their dreams, while Irene had high hopes for Moses and herself. As the three spoke about the future, Isaac hid in the hallway, where he listened to their every word. *"What the hell are they talking about? Why is Ryan so important? I'm Moses' brother, not Ryan. I know I keep repeating myself!"* Isaac stormed away, turning red in the face.

He burst into his bedroom and paced the floor, punching his fist in the palm of his hand. *"Did he forget me? Moses doesn't even acknowledge me in school. Half of the school doesn't even know that he has a fraternal twin brother,"* Isaac mumbled. He wanted so badly to ransack his bedroom but didn't. *"Maybe Moses is going through something. He could talk to me about it. How did Ryan get in the picture?"* Isaac realized he was having a conversation with himself and stopped. Instead, Isaac thought about what happened to him and his brother's bond. *"It's because I'm albino. That's it. Moses is ashamed to tell anyone that I'm his brother. Why did God curse me? He cursed me with hardly any friends, no girlfriend, no family. They don't care about me. And my brother who was there for me through thick and thin, has now gone astray,"* Isaac fell to his knees, sobbing. It was as if he were at God's feet. *"Why?"* Isaac shouted at the top of his lungs. He continued to cry, curling into a fetal position. Isaac cried and cried. He then opened his eyes, noticing that no one had come to check on him. Isaac crawled into his full-sized bed and pulled the covers over his body. He didn't care that it was too hot. Sweating, like crying, would do Isaac some justice.

The following day at school, Isaac sat in his seat in English. He glared at the front door and waited for Clarissa to enter. He could already smell her flowery fragrance contacting his nose. She hustled to her desk with her book bag over her shoulder, wearing tight light blue jeans, a pink blouse, white sneakers, and holding her notebook. Additionally, she would be carrying *Of Mice and Men* in her arms. Her French braided hair gave her a sophisticated look. Clarissa smiled at Isaac, which made his eyes cross when he got excited. She laughed at his cookie monster eyes. "Good morning, Isaac."

"Good morning, Clarissa," Isaac smiled from ear to ear. She snickered at this googly-eyed young man.

"What's so funny?" Isaac gave a goofy smile.

"Nothing," Clarissa tried to control her amusement.

"Is it my goofy look?" Isaac leaned close to Clarissa.

"No," She cleared her throat with a straight face. She didn't back away when Isaac leaned close to her wearing this heavenly scent. He sniffed the perfumery air, wanting to kiss her, but Isaac sat back in his chair. He didn't want to feel like an ass. He proceeded to eye her and smile. "What fragrance are you wearing?" Isaac inhaled more of the fragrance through his nostrils.

"Flowerbomb," Clarissa smiled.

"Is the bottle shaped like a hand grenade?" Isaac wondered.

"Yes, it is," Clarissa laughed.

"My mother has that fragrance. It's pretty," Isaac smiled even more.

The students clamored to anticipate Mr. Donovan's arrival. But then, a substitute strolled in, Mr. Rakoff. In his mid-eighties, he was very slender and wore clothes that were too big. He also had dumbo ears. He stood in front of the rowdy class.

"I don't care what you do. You can talk and whatever." Mr. Rakoff sat at the teacher's desk in front of the class.

"Do whatever?" Isaac asked loudly.

"No! Not whatever! Just chill out for the day," The substitute replied, gluing his eyes in a book.

The students laughed and socialized with one another. Isaac focused his attention back on Clarissa. Out of nowhere, Isaac grabbed her hand and caressed it with his thumb. "You know I'm attracted to you," he smiled slightly.

"It's obvious," Clarissa smiled.

"You know that Moses is my brother?" Isaac asked.

"I know," she nodded.

"When can I see you?" Isaac then held Clarissa's hand tight.

"What kind of question is that, Isaac.? You're seeing me right now," she said.

"Beyond school," he said.

"Whatever, babe," Clarissa gently smacked his hand.

"You just called me babe," Isaac's face lit up like a Christmas tree.

Clarissa caressed Isaac's hand, gazing into his googled eyes. Isaac had a pretty girl who seemed to be into him and overlooked that he had impaired vision. Hopefully, they can take things further.

That afternoon, Clarissa lounged in Isaac's bed. She watched an old movie on television in his darkened bedroom. No one was home, so the two lovebirds had their place to themselves. Clarissa waited for Isaac as he brought cans of soda and chips from the kitchen and headed downstairs. He entered his bedroom as Clarissa lay nude in his bed, waiting for him to take charge. Isaac stood in the doorway, glaring at her with his eyes which enlarged behind his spectacles. The soda cans crashed to the floor, and two bags of chips followed. He rushed to lay a passionate kiss on Clarissa. Isaac unfastened his pants and inserted himself in Clarissa. She wrapped her legs around his waist as he thrust hard and fast. Their bodies glistened with sweat as they took sharp breaths and moaned.

"Isaac," Clarissa whispered his name during their lovemaking. "Isaac!" Clarissa cried his name. Isaac snapped out of his fantasy, noticing the two busted soda cans bubbling on the floor.

"Fuck!" he picked up the dented cans with more soda bubbling and squirting everywhere. Clarissa, fully clothed, sprung from the bed to aid him.

"Be careful, babe," she spoke in a loving tone. Isaac gazed into her eyes and kissed her on the lips. They engaged in a passionate lip-lock, but then, Irene barged in. She witnessed her son's first kiss. Then, she cleared her throat.

"Mom," he smiled. Clarissa then smiled with her pretty brown eyes that warmed anyone's heart.

"Hello. I'm Isaac's mom," Irene shook Clarissa's hand.

"How are you? I'm Clarissa," she introduced herself.

"Boy, you're a beauty," Irene complimented.

"Thank you, Mrs. Remington," Clarissa added. Isaac grabbed the bags of chips from the floor.

"Look at the soda all over the floor. Be careful! Don't slip!" Irene entered his bedroom.

"Your Mom seems nice," Clarissa said.

"She's alright," Isaac shrugged his shoulders.

"Isaac, move. Let me get this mess up!" His mother gently hit him with the mop.

"I got it," Isaac and his mother played tug of war over the mop.

"It's my mess. Let me clean it up," Isaac snatched the mop from his mother's hand. Clarissa stood there, shocked. His mother stormed out of his bedroom, glancing back at her son with a frown. Isaac mopped up the soda from the floor. From the corner of his eye, he saw that his new love wasn't pleased with him scuffling with his mother. Clarissa grabbed her books and purse.

"Where are you going, Clarissa?" Isaac threw the mop down and blocked her from leaving. He kissed her on the lips. Clarissa didn't smile or melt due to his affection. "Why did you do that?"

"Do what? Oh, that. It's no big deal," Isaac grabbed Clarissa around the waist.

"It's no big deal! It's a big deal to me," Clarissa pushed Isaac's hands off her hips.

Isaac then kissed her passionately, and Clarissa, just like a girl, gave in and melted away. He hoped Clarissa didn't think he mistreated his mother because he would most likely do it to her. Isaac also hoped that she would forget the whole thing.

Minutes later, Irene sweated over a hot stove. She stirred a large pot of spaghetti and a smaller one with tomato sauce. Isaac stood right behind her as she made her way to the refrigerator. Isaac followed his mother, apologizing. Clarissa stood in the doorway, watching the scene play out before her eyes. Clarissa gestured to Isaac that she had to leave. He gave his mother a peck on the cheek.

"I love you, Mom," Isaac scrambled from her side.

Irene gave her son the cold shoulder, not uttering a response. She continued stirring the pot of raw spaghetti. Isaac halted in his tracks for a second. *"She does hate me. Shit!"*

He and Clarissa exited the house as Moses and Ryan swaggered toward the front door. Ryan greeted Isaac with a high-five. Then Moses and Isaac just nodded at each other. Clarissa's eyes widen, noticing Moses. This handsome guy is very popular with the ladies.

"What's up, Clarissa," Ryan greeted her with a hug. Isaac turned cherry red and looked away, hoping no one would notice.

"Hi, Ryan," Clarissa smiled.

"Do you two know each other?" Isaac asked, surprisingly.

"Yes, we had some classes together last year," Ryan answered.

Moses smiled at Clarissa from ear to ear. He extended his hand to her.

"How are you, Clarissa? I'm Moses. Isaac's my brother. We're fraternal twins," Moses answered with a phony smile.

"I didn't know that," Clarissa said. Isaac noticed Moses' attitude, and this made his blood boil. Isaac shoved Clarissa away from his brother's sight.

"Let's go, Clarissa," Isaac hauled her down the street like a caveman in the Stone Age.

"What is your problem, Isaac?" she broke away from Isaac's grip.

"I don't have a problem!" Isaac followed right behind her.

"Look! We hardly know each other, and already you're possessive!" She ambled even faster. Isaac wanted her so bad, but he wasn't going to beg. He stormed away from the scene as well, not glancing in return. She crossed the street and didn't even look back at Isaac. As Isaac marched down the block, he balled his hands into fists. His heart pounded in his chest. He approached his house and thrust open the front door. Loud, pounding footsteps entered the house as if it were coming down.

"What the fuck is with you, Moses!" Isaac bellowed throughout the house. He dashed up the steps.

In Moses' bedroom on the second floor, the chaos echoed out of the cracked opened window. Ryan got between Moses and Isaac, trying to keep them apart. Then Irene rushed in and noticed her sons going at it.

"What's going on, Isaac?" Irene asked him.

"Get the fuck out of my room, Isaac!" Moses looked for something to defend himself with. "Mom, he came in here like a crazed fuck!"

"Go downstairs, Isaac!" Irene pointed towards the door for him to exit.

Isaac retreated, storming out of Moses' bedroom. Irene turned to Moses.

"What's going on with you two? Whatever it is, resolve it, please," Their mother left as Moses closed his bedroom door.

"Clarissa," Moses and Ryan both *hit the nail on the head.*

In Isaac's bedroom in the basement, he lay in bed, glaring at the ceiling. His mother stormed with the laundry basket. She then swept his floor with the broom. They didn't utter a word to each other. It could be better this way because Isaac wanted so badly to curse her out. He couldn't understand why his mother didn't get to the bottom of Moses and Isaac's broken bond. She didn't care. All she thought about was Moses' future and probably getting all his money if he ever became successful. Isaac believed that Moses would be successful in whatever field he chose. Still, Irene didn't make eye contact with him. Isaac kept glaring and glaring at her. *"Fuck! It's as if I'm not even here! Holy shit!"* He kept his eyes focused on his mother. Then Irene swept the dustpan and emptied it into the trash can. She rushed out of her son's bedroom. *"Wow! I'm invisible!"* He folded his hands behind his head. He shook his head. Isaac recalled when he told her about his nightmare, and instead of hugging him, she gave him a nasty attitude. Just like now, his mother is doing the same. He wondered how she must've reacted when he was born. Of course, Moses is favored, and Isaac is just invisible. Irene swept the dirt in the dustpan and emptied it in the trash. "Take out your trash," his mother grabbed the laundry basket, exiting his bedroom.

CHAPTER TWELVE

The following day, Moses was dressed in his black jeans; and a red and black shirt, paired with black sneakers. He prepared for another school day. He threw his backpack over his shoulder and made his way downstairs. At the same time, Isaac marched to the front door. The brothers both halted in their tracks and glared at one another.

"Go!" Moses demanded.

"After you!" Isaac opened the front door.

"You first!" Moses then said.

"You're the big shit around here!" Isaac exclaimed.

"I'm the big shit! I'm the big shit, Isaac!" Moses stormed out of the door as Isaac exited behind him, slamming the house's front door.

"It's all about you," Isaac followed Moses a few feet away.

"Isaac, give me a fuckin' break, alright!" Moses stomped down the street with Isaac close behind.

"Moses! Moses! Fuck!" Isaac was antagonized.

Moses stomped even faster, ignoring his brother's insecurities. Isaac wanted to patch things up, but his brother was wrapped up in his little world. Then Isaac got angry and thought about taking his brother's life. *"It wouldn't be so bad not having Moses around. Then I would get admiration from people,"* Isaac thought.

He erased those crazy concepts and headed to school.

Later that morning in gym class, Moses played basketball with Ryan. Each insulted the other during their play. The other students played volleyball and lifted weights, while additional resided on the sideline — notably, the girls. From outside the gymnasium, Isaac stood in the window of the gym's door, glaring at Moses. He noticed the females cheering for him. His twin's popularity crushed Isaac's soul as he swaggered from the gym's door. He made his way back to class. As he took his time up the steps, he noticed a girl and a guy kissing in the back staircase. Valentina was lip-locked with a guy named Wallace, the football team's captain. Isaac didn't know if he should tell his brother about Valentina messing around since they were on bad terms. So, Isaac decided to keep his mouth shut and allowed Moses to find out for himself.

At noon, the students studied in the library with the librarian's watchful eye. Moses sat at the long table with Clarissa this time. Isaac peered from the aisle of books, watching. *"I had a feeling Clarissa had a thing for my brother. She's smiling from ear to ear and chatty. When Clarissa and I met, she was more reserved,"* Isaac shifted his vision away from Clarissa and Moses. He took a deep breath and felt the heaviness in his chest again. And fuckin' Ryan got under Isaac's skin as well. Moses hugged Clarissa tightly. It wouldn't be such a bad idea to plunge a butcher knife through Ryan's heart as well. But, Moses and Ryan had all the promises in the world.

Isaac strutted into the guidance counselor's office later, and Mr. Gersh, a Caucasian gentleman in his mid-fifties with a receding hairline, shuffled through some paperwork. He aided students in the right direction for their classes, colleges, and career goals. Mr. Gersh greeted Isaac with a handshake as his glasses slid from his nose. Isaac sat at his counselor's desk without saying a word. Isaac seemed disturbed, and Mr. Gersh could sense it. "Are there any problems at home?" Mr. Gersh pushed his spectacles to his eyes. Isaac shook his head. "I know you're not having any problems academically. You have an A-average. What's up, Isaac?" Mr. Gersh's glasses slid away from his eyes again, so he pushed them back.

"My brother's loved by everyone. Why didn't I come out normal," Isaac hopped from the chair, paced the floor, and sobbed. Mr. Gersh gave Isaac a tissue to wipe his tears. Isaac held back his tears as much as he could. His guidance counselor had a popular brother with all the girls, but Mr. Gersh attended college, earning his bachelor's degree. He advised Isaac not to worry and that the right woman would come along. From that little conversation, Isaac felt better and hopeful. But he still felt bitter towards Moses.

In English class, the students were rowdy while others sat quietly at their desks. Isaac - already pissed off - stayed in his seat. He spoke to no one. Then Clarissa marched in, laughing and giggly like a schoolgirl. Isaac glared at her and wanted to curse her out. Every negative notion came to mind. *"Did she just fuck my brother in the back staircase?"* Isaac squinted his eyes.

Clarissa sat down and turned to Isaac smiling. Her smile dropped because she could see the distress on his face.

"Isaac, what's wrong?" Clarissa touched his hand. Isaac snatched it away, continuing to glare at her.

"Isaac, what's the problem?" she squeezed Isaac's hand gently.

"You know exactly what," Isaac's face read: MURDER. Clarissa could see his expression. It made her hands tremble and her heart race.

"We met up in the library, that's all," Clarissa's voice quivered.

"Exactly! You would love for Moses to fuck you. Right?" Isaac embarrassed Clarissa with a fiendish smile. Even though the class was noisy, some students heard Isaac throwing insults at Clarissa. She noticed her fellow classmates staring and overhearing the friction between them.

"Would you please keep your voice down, Isaac?" Clarissa's eyes watered.

"Why? Because you don't want people to know you're a fuckin' slut!" Isaac was insulted again.

"It's not like that, Isaac!" Clarissa raised her voice.

When the bell rang, Mr. Donovan hustled in. He put on his glasses ready to begin the day's lesson. Clarissa turned around at her desk, weeping. Isaac proceeded to smile like a devil. He then leaned in towards Clarissa's ear.

"Would you love to have a threesome? You can be down on all fours while Moses fucks you in the ass, and you could give me....," Clarissa turned abruptly in her seat and pounded her fist on Isaac's desk.

"Go to hell, Isaac!" Clarissa stormed out of the classroom in tears.

"What happened, Isaac?" Mr. Donovan took his glasses off.

"I guess I said something wrong," Isaac shrugged his shoulders.

At home, Moses and Ryan watched television as the radio played in his bedroom. Isaac barged in, glaring at Moses, and balling his hands into fists. Ryan sprang into action to avoid another confrontation between the twins. The brothers came face to face. Then, Isaac held his hand out to patch things up. Moses automatically accepted and gave his brother a high-five.

"Valentina's a hoe," Moses turned red from embarrassment as he looked in the other direction.

"How did you find out?" Isaac lifted an eyebrow.

"She was the topic of conversation in the guy's locker room," Moses shrugged his shoulders.

"Alright! Are you guys cool now!" Ryan guffawed. Moses and Isaac embraced, giving each other a high-five.

"This is beautiful, man!" Ryan exclaimed.

A couple of weeks later, Irene pinned a red carnation on Moses' Vera Wang black tuxedo as he stood in front of a full-length mirror that evening. The three-piece suit was made of polyester and velvet with a white shirt and black tie. On his feet were his patten leather shoes. He couldn't stop smiling at his reflection and, of course, smiled at him in return. Irene took a few steps away from her son to get a good look at how handsome Moses looked. "You look like you're going to get married."

Moses lifted an eyebrow at his mother speaking about weddings instead of his prom. "Let's not jump the gun here, Mom. I'm going solo to my prom." Moses straightened his jacket, taking a couple of steps back from the mirror. He glanced at his mother and waited for an answer beside the wedding bells.

"You're going to dance with all the girls tonight! You look so good!" Irene embraced her son. Then a car horn blared from outside. Moses rushed to the window, noticing a black Audi. "I'll be right down," Moses hollered. "Shit! I can't wait to get my own car."

"Watch your mouth, babe," Irene pecked Moses on the cheek.

"Sorry," he smiled and dashed out of his bedroom.

As Moses raced downstairs, Calvin rose from his lounge chair with the television blaring. Upon seeing Moses going to his prom without a date, his stepfather grinned from ear to ear. Of course, it's not because Moses was single but because he could have his pick of the litter. Surprisingly, Moses didn't think about getting it on with anyone. He just wanted to have a good time. Calvin embraced Moses, giving him fatherly advice on being safe and handing him some condoms. Moses lifted an eyebrow again for the stepfather showing that much concern for his well-being. Isaac strutted into the kitchen as they chatted a bit about his night. He sat at the small table, grabbing an apple from the fruit bowl, and biting. Isaac saw how good his brother looked in his tux. He shied away from his brother in the distance of the living room. Then, he glared at Moses even more. He couldn't stop the glares and wanted so badly to tell Moses that he looked good and to have a good time. But Moses didn't even recognize his brother in the kitchen. *"I'm right in the kitchen here. And my own brother doesn't acknowledge my presence!"* Isaac thought as his heart raced and felt the heaviness in his chest. Tears streamed down his cheeks. He placed the bitten fruit in the bowl and ran to the basement. Then a door slammed from the lower level, shaking the entire house. Moses and Calvin snapped out of their chit-chat.

"Don't slam any doors around here, Isaac!" Calvin hollered.

Moses didn't say a word, shrugging his shoulders. Then the car horn blared again.

"Moses! What are you doing? Let's go!" Ryan beeped the car horn repeatedly.

"I got to go! Thanks, Calvin!" Moses rushed out of the house. He slammed the front door just as hard, which also shook the house. Calvin cringed at the loud sound that could bring the home to the ground. All he could do was shake his head.

Through the basement window, Isaac stared at the Black Audi with its running engine, which wasn't that loud. It was the kind of engine a person could hear, but it was not that disturbing. Isaac saw Ryan occupying the driver's seat while dressed in his tuxedo, and then Moses hopped in the passenger's seat. They spoke loudly about their exciting night. Isaac thought about how many girls were going to be there. He envisioned every beautiful girl from his brother's graduating class in prom dresses in every color and style while guys escorted them sporting their tuxedos into the ballroom. House music blared from the speakers with a disco ball spun in the center of the ceiling. It reflected lights on the dance floor as couples danced. Moses and Ryan would make their presence known. But then a fiendish smile surfaced on Isaac's face.

By Moses and Ryan going to the prom together, the students in their class would think they were a couple. Isaac knew that thinking ill of someone was wrong. So, he flipped his evil thoughts into something positive for his brother, like Moses fucking all night. Then the black Audi sped off as Isaac stared out of the window even though his brother and best friend were off to have the time of their lives. His mind was blank. He stared and stared and then thought of himself. The sun was ready to set, and still muggy outside, he wanted to take a walk. But he had no idea where to go. Then Clarissa crossed his mind. Maybe this would be a good time to apologize for disrespecting her. *Would she even forgive him? Maybe? Maybe not?*

He figured that he'd take that walk.

Minutes later, Isaac strolled down the streets of Floral Park, another beautiful community not too far from his home. Since some students resided in this quiet community, he hoped to see someone from school. Isaac heard from students that Clarissa lived in a blue Victorian house with an American flag that hung high above the porch. The flag always blew in the wind. Isaac didn't know exactly where she lived, but he hoped to find out from someone in the neighborhood who did. A male pupil said that Clarissa always sat on her porch swing, eating, or working on her laptop. Isaac made it his business to find this woman, so he could spill his guts out of apologies to her. Several cars drove on the road with engines echoing in the distance, including an eighteen-wheeler truck. This monster truck made so much noise that Isaac lost his thought. He didn't even know what he was doing or going for a second. Then the long trailer truck sped down the road as its engine echoed in the distance. Miraculously, a blue Victorian home appeared before his eyes, located on the corner that befitted the perfect suburban home. Trees, bushes, and a well-manicured lawn surrounded the property. It was quiet and not a soul in sight as the wind ruffled through the leaves in the trees.

"Holy shit! This is it! And there she is!" Isaac eyed this beautiful young girl precisely the way he pictured her. He also could hear the wind chimes loud and clear. It was like the chimes were calling him. *"I hope Clarissa will forgive me. She probably won't. We'll see,"* Isaac approached the blue Victorian home. An American flag hung above the porch, blowing in the wind. There were a couple of plants, and those wind chimes called him just like everyone said. Clarissa rocked on the porch swing while clicking the keys on her laptop. Isaac slowed down his pace because he didn't want to intimidate her. The light summer breeze swept through the air as Isaac slowed down even more. Finally, he stood still. He glared at Clarissa, hoping she'd look up. Clarissa noticed this pale young man staring at her in the distance. Isaac wondered what she would do, so they participated in a glaring match. Isaac wanted to see who was going to speak first. But it was Isaac's responsibility.

"Clarissa!" Isaac took several steps towards Clarissa's home.

Clarissa stormed into her home and slammed the door. Isaac stomped his foot on the ground. He felt so stupid and embarrassed. He wondered if Clarissa's neighbors were peeking from behind their curtains. Isaac didn't even bother to look around to see if he had an audience, but it felt like it.

"Shit!" Isaac marched down the block and constantly glanced at Clarissa's home.

"Damn! What a fucked-up evening!" Isaac mumbled as he made his way home.

A few hours later, Isaac propped his head on his pillow, resting his arm behind his head in bed. The air conditioner blew cool air through his dimmed bedroom. The television wasn't on, and there was absolute silence. He didn't hear trampling footsteps from the upper floors of the house. So, his parents had gone out to dinner. Isaac checked the time on his cellphone that read: 10:14 p.m. For sure, Calvin and Irene went out to eat or went to cruise around some fabulous neighborhoods on Long Island. His stomach growled because he had only eaten a bite of that apple earlier. His mother usually fixed him dinner, but tonight, he was on his own. But he was too tired to march upstairs to the kitchen floor to find something to fill his belly. So, he continued to prop his head on his pillow and stare at the ceiling. His mind was blank for a second. Then, he thought about making it up to Clarissa. He was going to beg for forgiveness. Hopefully, she'll forgive him for his dirty, disrespectful language. Moses then crossed Isaac's mind. He wondered what his brother was doing, how many girls he danced with, kissed, or if he would get lucky at the end of the night with one girl or maybe several? Isaac erased the thought and focused on himself. "*What about me? There's nothing I can do now. I didn't have the guts to ask any girls in the senior class to the prom because they would've rejected my offer, and Clarissa is only a junior. Now, if there was a prom for high school students regardless of status, then Clarissa would be my date.* The rumbling in Isaac's stomach told him it needed food. He took a deep breath, rose from his slumber, and dragged his feet out of his bedroom.

Within seconds, Isaac marched to the kitchen table, where the apple he took a bite of turned brown from the inside. Even though his stomach continued to rumble, Isaac wouldn't take another bite of the fruit. He sneered at the delicious red apple, tossing it in the trash. He swung open the refrigerator door, scanning the food from top to bottom while trying to see what he could find. Corned beef, honey chicken, American and Swiss cheese from the deli, a head of lettuce, mayo, and bread. Then he looked at the leftover roasted chicken, rice, and broccoli. Everything looked so good to Isaac. He shrugged his shoulders and did whatever.

About an hour later, a half-eaten chicken sandwich and scraps of roasted chicken, rice, and vegetables were left on a plate with two water bottles. Isaac sat up in his bed, trying to let his food digest. He wanted to stretch out in his bed so badly, but he didn't like sleeping on a full stomach. So, he closed his eyes and figured he could sleep sitting up. Some people do that, so why couldn't he? Then he did.

Several hours later, tires screeched from outside of the Remington home. Isaac widened his eyes, noticing a peek of sun peering into his bedroom. He checked the time on his cellphone. It read: 6:39 a.m. Voices echoed from outside. Isaac rushed to the window and saw the black Audi's engine running. Ryan hopped from the driver's seat with no tuxedo jacket on, no tie, and three buttons unfastened. He looked as if he had been in a fight. Then Isaac noticed Moses slumped over in the passenger's seat. He lifted an eyebrow and mouthed *"Holy shit"* to himself. The trampling footsteps of his parents could be heard above his room. The front door crept open, and Isaac saw his parents rushing to the car. Irene screamed and cried in agony. Moses looked dead. Or maybe, he fought with a guy over a girl he wanted to dance with. As Isaac kept his eye fixed on his brother, Ryan opened the passenger's side door. Moses slumped in the seat even more. Then Isaac figured it out; Moses was drunk.

Ryan and Calvin unfastened Moses' seat belt as both men wrapped Moses's arms over each of their shoulders, hauling him into the house. Irene opened the front door as they got Moses inside. Isaac looked up at the ceiling, still hearing his mother's cries for her firstborn. Calvin and Irene argued with Ryan about what happened to Moses.

Isaac crept out of his bedroom and took baby steps to the first floor. The voices became louder, as if they came from a radio with the volume turned up. He halted at the foot of the steps, hearing more details of his brother's prom. Isaac thought his brother would've danced with every girl that night or would've had sex with every one of them. Instead, he had gotten drunk. Isaac lifted an eyebrow, surprised Moses would stoop so low to do that. Why?

Isaac sniffed the air lightly of the stint of alcohol. Isaac knew that, had he come home drunk, he wouldn't have heard the end.

Then Moses regurgitated into the toilet from the bathroom. Isaac eased up the second floor to the bathroom. His parents and Ryan hovered over Moses spilling his guts into the toilet. Isaac stood in the background, watching the whole thing unfold before his eyes. He wanted to do something, but what could he do but watch? He hoped his brother was going to be okay. Ryan stormed out of the bathroom and glared at Isaac as if he was going to blame him for Moses' drunkenness. Ryan stormed away and exited the house. Moses sobbed, apologizing to his mother for his bad behavior. Of course, Irene and Calvin had no problem with what Moses did. She embraced him, telling him that everything was going to be okay. And all Calvin could do was shrug his shoulders. Throughout all this drama, Irene and Calvin still didn't acknowledge Isaac's presence. "What the hell! This is my brother!" Why didn't you ask me to help Moses from the car!" Isaac's heart pumped heavily in his chest. His complexion turned fiery red. His face and arms were noticeable due to his wearing a tank top. Isaac stormed away, not feeling sorry for Moses.

CHAPTER THIRTEEN

Graduation day arrived as graduates left their high school memories behind. Moses, Isaac, Ryan, and their classmates all looked forward to a bright future. The sun peeked in and out of the clouds on this summer morning in June, sometimes making it dismal. Over one hundred students were decked out in their caps and gowns, ready to receive the honors they won.

Moses and Ryan were accepted to Long Island University, whereas Isaac got into Hunter College. Intimidated by his brother's achievements, Isaac felt the college he was accepted to didn't have as much status. As the three young men sat together, Isaac observed Moses and Ryan chatting. His brother rarely said a word to him. "*This celebration is about me and my brother. Our plans, not Ryan's,*" Isaac wanted to punch the shit out of Ryan and tell him to find a new best friend. Though, what could Isaac do but deal with it? The principal stood at the podium, announcing students by name as each student came to receive their diplomas. Friends and family applauded and cheered students who walked on stage. "Moses Remington! Isaac Remington! Ryan Smith," The principal called the names of these three young men. The applause from the crowd, family, and friends went crazy as if they had won the Nobel Prize. Isaac appreciated the cheers, but he knew they were mainly for Moses. He played along and pretended to be as popular and loved as his brother.

At the end of the ceremony, graduates took photos. They signed yearbooks; and gave hugs and kisses and warm wishes on their future endeavors. Irene, Calvin, Uncle Tyler, and Melissa embraced the twins. Irene hugged her first child, and then she welcomed Isaac. Isaac's heart dropped like an apple from a tree. As his mother held him in her arms, Isaac felt the hug wasn't genuine. It felt like she was trying to suffocate him. *"Wow; is she trying to kill me on my special day?"* Isaac wiggled out of his mother's arms. She glared at Isaac for a second and then smiled. Then, she focused her attention on Moses. Isaac didn't know what to think of his mother. Afterward, his Uncle Tyler and Aunt Melissa embraced him. Isaac felt that their love was real. As Isaac chatted with his aunt and uncle about lunch, he noticed Ryan taking photos with his family. Ryan had a huge family, which included both of his parents, grandparents, and all his extended relatives. Isaac hoped he would spend time with his family instead of hanging around Moses. Then, speaking of the devil, Ryan rushed over to Moses. The two graduates embraced one another for a mission accomplished. Uncle Tyler shook Ryan's hand and invited him to join them for lunch. Isaac's face turned fiery red at the offer. Uncle Tyler asked the young men where they wanted to eat. Moses had a thing for Red Lobster, while Ryan wanted Italian. As the two best friends bickered over food, he tried to tell them to *"Shut the fuck up!"* These two were arguing over something so petty as *food.*

An hour later, elevator music played through the ceiling of a themed restaurant while waiters and waitresses took orders and served meals to guests. Everyone celebrated the same occasion, graduation. Moses and Isaac sat at a booth before their Uncle Tyler and Aunt Melissa sat at a separate booth, where they ate shrimp scampi with Ryan. They had seltzer water in tall glasses with a slice of lemon. Calvin and Irene decided to allow the twins to spend time with their aunt and uncle since they hadn't seen them in a while. Calvin and Irene would have their own surprises waiting at home for the brothers.

Moses and Ryan did most of the talking about the future as Isaac kept quiet. He wanted so badly to punch Ryan right in the face. *"Shit! Ryan has a fuckin' family! Why doesn't he spend time with them? Why is he stuck up under Moses? Or is it something else?"* Isaac lifted an eyebrow while his brother and Ryan blabbed about the real estate market. *"I hope he doesn't try to come on to my brother,"* Isaac continued glaring at the two, giving each other high-fives on their plans. *"Oh, well! What the fuck should I care about! I don't count anyway!"* Isaac shoved a shrimp in his mouth and focused his eyes on his plate.

As the conversation proceeded, Tyler recalled the fight at their birthday party when they were kids. That incident left a bad taste in the twins mouths. And they hadn't seen nor heard from Calvin's relatives again. The twins lived peacefully with no more crazy outbursts from people they barely knew. The brothers mainly had eruptions over girls.

Tyler and Melissa were shocked to hear about their favorite nephews fighting over girls. But Tyler knew the reason for the dispute over the young ladies, Isaac's condition. His uncle smiled at Isaac and told him that, one day, the right woman would come into his life. As Isaac heard those words from someone he loved dearly, he had doubts. *"Who will make love to someone who looks like a ghost with awkward eyes? I know Moses is going to marry a fine woman, and he will be successful. I can picture it,"* Isaac thought, staring into space.

Uncle Tyler told his nephews that their birthdays were coming, and he had information about a real estate course in October. Moses' eyes widened upon hearing about the seminar. Isaac wasn't thrilled as he shied away from his dreams and future. He couldn't help but notice how Moses, his Uncle Tyler, and Ryan engaged in their futuristic conversation. Moses dominated the talk, only thinking of himself. Uncle Tyler then handed the brothers two envelopes. Moses pulled out a graduation card with a twenty-five-hundred-dollar American Express gift card. "This is so cool, Uncle Tyler," he shook his uncle's hand. Isaac noticed Moses' gift card. He rushed to open his envelope, pulling out the same card. It was another twenty-five-hundred-dollar American Express gift card.

"Thanks, Uncle Tyler," Isaac shook his uncle's hand.

That late afternoon, Moses, Ryan, and Isaac watched real estate properties on YouTube in his bedroom. Moses lounged in his swivel chair, turning the volume up on his computer. The three young men got along for the moment, watching successful realtor Marcus Ivan giving a tour of a mansion in the Hamptons. The thirty-one million-dollar, eighty-six-room home was built in the early nineteen-thirties and was completed six years later. Mr. Ivan had the opportunity to purchase and renovate the property in the late nineteen-eighties and sold it to oil tycoon Andre Ritz. Then Mr. Ivan repurchased the home after Mr. Ritz died of a stroke. So, all the back and forth of this fabulous property made these three young men even more ambitious, especially Moses. Suddenly, Irene opened Moses' bedroom door abruptly.

"Moses, there's a surprise waiting for you," his mother jingled a set of keys, grinning from ear to ear. He gasped as he rose from his desk. "Are you serious!" He rushed towards his mother. Isaac and Ryan gasped at the shiny silvery keys Irene held in her hands. Moses grabbed the keys from his mother's hand, kissing her on the cheek. Ryan dashed out behind his best friend. But Isaac remained behind and took a deep breath. "Come on, Isaac," Irene could tell that her son felt depressed. Isaac knew why she handed Moses a set of keys. His mother walked ahead of Isaac, cheering for Moses. Ryan's voice echoed from outside, also rooting for Moses. Isaac came downstairs, dragging his feet to the living room window. He heard an engine rev and a rumble. *"Holy shit! Are you fuckin' kidding me!"*

Moses resided in the driver's seat of a brand new black matte Dodge Challenger. He rolled down the window of his new ride on the passenger's side. "Come on, Ryan!" Ryan dashed into the passenger's side of the muscle car. Isaac's heart dropped not due to his brother getting a new set of wheels but offering Ryan a ride. *His best friend and not his brother.* Calvin and Irene cheered as Moses sped off in his new Challenger. Irene saw the hurt on Isaac's face from the living room window. He knew why he didn't get a car. His parents waltzed into the house. Calvin also noticed Isaac's glum expression. Calvin then slammed the front door angrily. The door slamming shook the house and Isaac as well. Isaac titled his head, wondering what that was about. He could tell Calvin was upset about something that had to do with him. "Why are you slamming the door like that?" Isaac wondered.

"I was about to ask you the same thing. Why are you standing in the window pouting like a bitch!" Calvin insulted.

"What! Where's my graduation gift?" Isaac's sorrows turned to anger.

Irene's jaw dropped, and they ambled towards Isaac. She placed her arms around him. "I'm sorry, Isaac. "We didn't have enough money to get your gift," She pecked him on the cheek.

"Is Moses your only son? I don't exist around here!" Isaac threw his arms in the air.

"I'll make it up to you, Isaac. I promise," Irene hugged him.

"I wasn't the one who came home drunk! Oh, you forgot about that shit!" Isaac stepped away from his mother.

"Are you mad because I didn't get you a car, Isaac!" Calvin got in Isaac's face. Irene stood between them, trying to keep them apart.

"Calvin, cut it out! I promise to keep your graduation gift in mind, Isaac," Irene hugged Isaac again.

"You didn't have me in mind when you guys were at the car dealership!" Isaac wiggled his way out of his mother's arms. He ran downstairs.

"Don't push your mother! Are you crazy!" Calvin hollered. Isaac gave his stepfather the finger from the bottom of the basement steps.

"He didn't push me!" Irene raised her voice.

"That's why I didn't get you a car! You're blind, and you would kill everyone on the road!" Calvin continued hollering.

"Don't go there, Calvin!" Irene continued to shout.

Out of nowhere, Isaac charged up the steps, knocking Calvin to the floor. Luckily, Moses and Ryan rushed inside, seeing Isaac and Calvin wrestling on the floor. The best friends ran in to break up the scuffle.

"What the fuck!" Moses pulled Isaac off Calvin.

"Stop, Calvin!" Irene shouted at her husband.

"Get the fuck off me!" Isaac pushed Moses.

The twins got up in each face, ready to go at it. Both young men turned fiery red, balling their fists.

"You want to hit me, Moses! Take your best shot!" Isaac challenged his twin.

"Is there a reason I should? Maybe, so!" Moses hurled a punch at Isaac as they plummeted to the floor. The brothers hurled punches at each other. Calvin, Ryan, and Irene tried to separate them. The twins had a firm grip on each other. "You've been acting like a real asshole!" Moses yelled at the top of his lungs.

"Come on! What are you going to do?" Isaac raised his arms in the air, ready to go for round two.

"Fuck you, Isaac," Moses yelled.

"Fuck you too, Moses," Isaac dashed into the basement, slamming the door hard. Moses opened the door back, attempting to scramble downstairs to the basement, but Ryan then grabbed his best friend. He tried to calm this chaotic situation again.

"Moses, chill, man. Cool off!" Ryan patted Moses on the back.

"Let me talk to him," Moses tried to go downstairs, but Ryan continued to block him.

"Come on! Just chill!" Ryan pleaded again.

"I just drove around the block. I was coming to get you! You cocksucker!" Moses hollered at Isaac.

"Cocksucker! That's a discussion for you and your best friend!" Isaac inched to the middle of the staircase.

"Don't fuckin' go there!" Moses tried to get at Isaac again. But Ryan and Calvin both grabbed Moses away from the basement stairs.

"Moses don't bother with him. Let me talk to you about something," Calvin advised.

"Go talk to your father and chill, Moses," Ryan pushed Moses further away from the basement door. Shutting it as Isaac stood at the bottom of the staircase.

Moments later, Irene and Calvin spoke extensively with Moses in their master bedroom. Moses sat in the leather recliner, listening to his stepfather's every word. His parents sat on the edge of the bed. Ryan pulled a chair, also listening as if he were a family member.

"He's jealous, plain and simple. You've got a promising future; all the ladies love you. Your brother is only going to hinder you. I know you don't want to believe me, but you'll see it, and it'll be too late. Now, I don't want you to fail and have your plans screwed up because of an envious sibling," Calvin threw his hands up in the air, pacing the floor. Moses glared at Calvin and then his mother, shaking his head. He wanted to give his brother the benefit of the doubt.

Meanwhile, Isaac nestled in his bed as he heard murmuring from the upper floor. He crept out of his bedroom. He then inched up the staircase as every word became louder and clearer.

"You need to fly solo, Moses," Calvin murmured.

"Why don't you and Ryan go into business together? Take the exam that I heard is coming up in October and see if you two can do something," Irene suggested.

Isaac alternated blood red with anger as his heart raced. The most significant loss would be his brother. *"What the fuck! My brother has built a bond with Ryan and broke it with me,"* Isaac thought to himself. He punched his fist in the palm of his hand and stormed away.

Minutes later, Isaac dragged his feet along the sidewalk without knowing where it would lead him. Motorists sped along the road with their reverberating engines. And no, Isaac couldn't really think straight again. The hot breeze didn't give too much relief in this weather. Isaac felt as if he was struggling in the knee-deep sands of the Sahara Desert with no food or water. The fiery ball in the blue sky gave him a slight headache. He didn't care if he got sunburnt and died. It would be his way of committing suicide. He glanced at his skin to see if it had turned red, but nothing yet.

As he kept walking, he wished this road would lead to a better place. Maybe, Heaven was where he could be with God and his Father. The rest of his kin who had passed on would be there too. There wouldn't be any more trouble. There was nothing but problems here on Earth, which was a sin. *"I'm albino. I feel as if I should be in a horror movie or something. I can't see that well. I won't be able to drive. My eyes are crossed. I fought with my twin. I don't have a girlfriend. I could've had one, but I screwed it up. Clarissa is the one for me. She probably wants to beat the living shit out of me!"* Isaac strolled along a road where a few cars passed him. And then another eighteen-wheeler truck zoomed past him. After that, he figured out his destination.

Shortly, Clarissa rocked back and forth on the porch swing of her blue Victorian home, surfing the internet on her laptop. She sipped her iced tea and continued to surf the web. Then she noticed someone walking in her direction. The person looked exhausted and was in need. Clarissa put her computer on the swing. She stood up and recognized that it was Isaac. Isaac made eye contact with her as he stopped in his tracks. He glared at her while she stood on her porch.

"I came over to apologize, Clarissa," Isaac wiped the sweat from his forehead, standing at a distance. He looked at this beautiful girl standing on her terrace as if she were a fairy tale princess. Clarissa smirked.

"Why are you saying it at a distance?" Clarissa folded her arms.

"Clarissa, baby, please. I'm sorry for what I said. I was in the wrong," Isaac pleaded. He took small steps towards her home.

"Are you begging me right now?" Clarissa asked.

"Are you loving it?" he replied with a question. Isaac held his arms open. He continued to convince Clarissa to come to him. She wasn't too sure about Isaac's apology, so she took baby steps down from her front porch. Clarissa approached Isaac with ease. Isaac wrapped his arms around Clarissa.

"I'm sorry. I'm an asshole," Isaac whispered in her ear.

"Come on and get in the house," Clarissa laughed as Isaac continued to whisper sweet nothings in her ear. The lovers wrapped their arms around each other, hurrying into the house.

Minutes later, the Roberts' home was air-conditioned from the top floor to the basement. Isaac ate a bowl of spaghetti in Clarissa's kitchen. He grunted at every serving and gulped the grape juice from a tall glass. He acted as if he hadn't eaten in days. Clarissa sneered at his table manners. She wanted to ask Isaac about the prom and graduation, but she allowed him to enjoy his food. Isaac slowed down his eating and noticed Clarissa staring at him. He cleared his throat and told her about his relationship with Moses. His stepfather broke their bond and all kinds of drama. Isaac was positive that Clarissa knew why the low self-confidence. He asked her if she could see herself with someone like him. And she said yes.

Isaac smiled slightly, but he didn't want to get his hopes too high because he hadn't yet met her family. They would discourage Clarissa from seeing him. Her mother worked as a union representative for supermarket employees, and her father lived in Riverhead in Suffolk County. He worked for the Long Island Railroad. Clarissa only saw her father occasionally, especially around birthdays and holidays. Isaac wondered about this Victorian home that Clarissa and her mother occupied. A home like this would be a full house with kids clamoring in the house and yard.

After Isaac finished eating his last serving of food, Clarissa led the way, giving him a tour of the upper floors of her home. The corridor's walls were painted baby blue with photos of Clarissa. They ranged from her childhood years to the present with her family. She had aunts, uncles, and cousins who used to reside at home in her earlier years, but they had all since moved out. Isaac could tell by the empty bedrooms as they walked past them. "Doesn't it get a little creepy with no one in these bedrooms?" Isaac asked with caution.

"At first, it was a bit eerie. But I'm used to it," Clarissa shrugged her shoulders. Isaac felt as if he were a potential buyer of his first home. And, of course, Clarissa was the real estate agent. Isaac left her side and stepped into one of the bedrooms. He looked around and didn't feel any uneasy about the bedroom. Isaac felt comfortable with the unlived-in room. A queen-sized bed in the center of the room with a blue comforter, a dresser, and a desk made of dark cherry wood. The glossy wooden floor shone. It had perfectly painted ocean blue colored walls and a rocking chair with a teddy bear.

"This is nice," Isaac exited, closing the door easily.

There were other bedrooms Clarissa probably wanted to show him, but Isaac hoped that she would give him some. He had to play it cool and finish up the tour. As they continued down the hallway, Clarissa opened the door to her bedroom. "This is my room."

Isaac saw the red candy cane-colored walls with a cherry wood desk and armoire. The floor was glossy with a small red rug. Also, a cherry wood mirrored dresser held a vase of red carnations and perfume. Her full-sized bed had a red bedspread with a nightstand. Isaac got turned on by Clarissa's bedroom, but he had to control himself. Then he took his chances, grabbing Clarissa and kissing her passionately.

"Clarissa!" a voice cried out. The young couple halted their kiss. Mrs. Roberts strutted into the room and noticed her daughter accompanied by an obscure young man.

"Hi. Mom, this is Isaac. Isaac, this is my mother," Clarissa laughed it off. Mrs. Roberts extended her hand as she frowned at this pale-skinned, pink-eyed male.

"How are you, Isaac?" Mrs. Roberts nodded.

"I'm good. And yourself?" Isaac added shyly.

"Can I see you downstairs in the kitchen, Clarissa?" Mrs. Roberts sashayed away. Isaac knew what Clarissa's mom was going to say.

"I'll be right back, Isaac. Don't go anywhere," Clarissa strutted out of the room, but Isaac kissed her lips quickly.

Minutes later, Mrs. Roberts unloaded groceries from shopping bags in the kitchen, putting the food away. Clarissa rushed in, helping her mother with the food. Mrs. Roberts held a can of tomatoes in her hand. Clarissa grabbed it and put it in the cabinet. Her mother glared at her daughter for a second and had to think before she spoke.

"Clarissa," Her mother sighed.

Clarissa put the meat in the freezer. She ignored her mother calling her name. Clarissa put the milk in the refrigerator.

"Clarissa!" Mrs. Roberts in a stern tone.

"Yes, Mom," she turned from the icebox.

"Are you getting serious about him?" Mrs. Roberts sneered.

"Maybe?" Clarissa shrugged her shoulders.

"Aren't you embarrassed? What would the family think?" Mrs. Roberts continued to unload more of the groceries.

"Please, I can't worry about what others think," Clarissa threw the ice cream in the freezer. Mrs. Roberts sucked her teeth and saw the unwashed tomato saucy dishes in the sink. She didn't say a word, instead pouring dishwashing liquid onto a sponge and washing the plates.

"Why, Mom? Is it because Isaac is albino?" Clarissa leaned against the refrigerator.

"No," Mrs. Roberts shook her head and washed the dishes.

"Yes, it is. You want me to be with someone with more promise. Right?" Clarissa hung onto the handle of the icebox.

"Yes, I do. He isn't going to help your future," Mrs. Roberts said.

Suddenly, Clarissa felt someone's presence listening to their conversation. She heard the front door open and then close. Clarissa rushed out of the kitchen and through the living room.

"Isaac!" Clarissa cried out. She ran to the window, seeing Isaac storming down the road. Isaac knew he was the topic of conversation. People made fun of him and disapproved of his existence. Clarissa dashed out of the screen door and gave chase. "Isaac, wait!"

"What?" Isaac stopped in his tracks.

"Where are you going?" Clarissa embraced him.

"To hell!" Isaac bellowed.

"My mom wanted to get to know you," Clarissa gently kissed Isaac.

"Really? Are you serious about me, Clarissa? What would your family think?" Isaac mocked Clarissa's mother. Isaac swaggered away.

"Fuck, family!" she stomped her foot on the concrete ground and folded her arms. Anyone could see some redness in Clarissa's brown-skinned tone. Isaac halted suddenly like a car that almost missed a red light. He turned around slowly and glared at Clarissa. They stared at each other and knew what the other was thinking. Like forbidden lovers in a romance novel or movie from opposite ends of the spectrum, Clarissa and Isaac engaged in a passionate kiss.

At dinner, Isaac told them about his family situation, from that kiss to a sit-down conversation with Clarissa's mom over steak, broccoli, and potatoes. Isaac mentioned how he and his brother, Moses, were close as kids, but now they had become the worst of enemies. Moses had gotten so caught up in himself that his twin didn't exist. Isaac yapped and yapped about the bad blood between them. On top of that, Isaac didn't bother to talk about his prom or graduation. Those two special events in his life that didn't involve him. So, there was nothing to talk about. Mrs. Robert's heart melted, listening to this young man's struggles with his condition and inability to keep up with his brother's popularity. She admired him for his bravery and for trying to be the best person he could be. And since Moses and Isaac were still young, their broken bond would mend in no time. Isaac had his doubts about that.

Afterward, Clarissa's mother agreed that Isaac could stay with them in return for work around the house. He could also get outside employment and go to school. As soon as Isaac and Clarissa heard that, they were happy. But not so fast because Mrs. Roberts didn't want any hanky-panky all hours of the night. She understood that Clarissa and Isaac were adults, and they will get intimate. "Just don't disrespect her house; everything will be cool."

CHAPTER FOURTEEN

Happy birthday, America! It was the Fourth of July in this Floral Park neighborhood, where there wasn't a sound. Only the birds sang or communicated with one another through the air. The humidity and heat brought the best of unpleasant and appreciated weather most people either loved or hated. A grassy scent filled the air as Isaac mowed the lawn in Roberts' backyard. He pushed the lawnmower across the grass around seven that morning. He did everything in his power to keep himself from getting dehydrated. He wore a hat over his head and held a water bottle in his hand. As Isaac proceeded to run the machine up and down on the lawn, he continuously looked up at Clarissa's bedroom on the third floor. He hoped that she'd wake up. Isaac's bedroom was adjacent to Clarissa's, but nothing happened between them. He wanted to sneak into Clarissa's bedroom, but there's a thing called "self-control." And so, he was learning to allow things to happen at the right time. Throughout the roaring lawnmower, he heard a sweet voice calling him. He looked up at Clarissa's window and saw her beautiful face. Isaac smiled from ear to ear as she wore her summery silk pajamas. He hoped that he could get her out of them soon. Then Isaac stopped with his wet fantasies and focused on her beauty.

"How are you, babe?" Isaac wiped the water bottle droplets along his forehead.

"I'm fine. You woke me up with that machine and grassy scent," Clarissa shouted from the third-floor bedroom window.

"I'm sorry," Isaac quickly turned the lawnmower off. He took three gulps of water from the bottle.

"Happy fourth," Clarissa greeted with a sweet tone.

"Happy fourth! So, what's up for today?" Isaac asked, out of breath.

"My Mom's inviting our relatives over," Clarissa responded, smiling. Isaac looked away nervously. He wasn't too comfortable about meeting new people. He always experienced stares, whispers, and odd questions that came with the territory. Despite this, Isaac couldn't tell her how he wasn't too crazy about meeting her family because he didn't want to overstep his boundaries. So, he had to deal with whatever came along with his stay. Surprisingly, he didn't even think about home. *Was his mother even worried about him? And Moses probably didn't care.* Clarissa spoke about her family and how great they were. They had wonderful careers and enjoyed their lives. Even though Isaac was crazy about her, Clarissa never knew when to shut up. So, Isaac paid some attention to her yapping.

"Did you hear what I said, Isaac," she shouted from her bedroom window.

"I heard you, Clarissa," Isaac responded in a daze. He took another gulp of his water. He only recalled Clarissa's uncle being a bank manager and making eighty thousand dollars a year. *"Fuckin' good for him!"* Isaac sarcastically said in his head.

"I'll make breakfast, babe," Clarissa added.

"Cool," Isaac waved with a smile. He pulled the cord of the lawnmower, turned it on, and continued his duties.

Later, Isaac wrapped a towel around his waist, covering his essential parts as he strolled into his bedroom from the bathroom. He sat on the edge of the full-sized bed and turned on his cell phone. Isaac, of course, had to wait for it to load. He then relaxed in his slumber and gazed at the ceiling. As he waited for his cell phone to load, he experienced a slight headache. The pain started on the side and alternated to the middle of his head. "I shouldn't have stayed in that sun too long. And I didn't eat either," He figured it out. He checked his cell phone and noticed how long it was taking. He sucked his teeth. "I'm not going to wait forever for this phone to load. I'll check my messages later."

Moments later, Isaac poked his eggs onto his fork, shoving it in his mouth. Then he stuffed the entire strip of bacon into his mouth. Clarissa glared at Isaac and wondered what was going on with him. "Babe, slow down before you choke," Clarissa grabbed his hand. Isaac inhaled and ate his breakfast slowly.

"So, what time are your folks going to get here?" Isaac asked in an unpleasant tone.

"There'll be here soon." Clarissa sipped her orange juice.

"Soon?" Isaac's heart pounded in his chest whenever he felt a threat.

"You look disturbed, Isaac. Don't worry; they're cool," Clarissa held his hand tight.

"That's what they all say. Shit, I've got to go through the fuckin' interrogation from her relatives. From one hell to the next," Isaac checked the caller ID on his cell phone. He had no messages on his phone. His mother must have been really upset after he disrespected her. He didn't mean to lay his hands on her. And there weren't any messages from Moses either. Moses would probably never forgive him for disrespecting their mother or for the fight they had. Moses would have called if he was concerned with Isaac's whereabouts. And this proved that his brother only thought of himself; *what a self-centered fuck*! Or maybe, Isaac should apologize. The holidays were supposed to be special for the twins, but Moses has another brother, Ryan. *"Moses and Ryan are probably going to get stoned drunk and get all the pussy on this fiery, sparkling occasion. I could see Moses doing some hot girl!"* Isaac thought.

"Why am I thinking about my brother getting some when I got someone here right next to me," Isaac glared at Clarissa as a devilish smile surfaced. Clarissa squinted, trying to figure out why he had a fiendish grin. He then kissed her on the lips, and nothing went further.

That night, a strike of a match lit the main fuse of some fireworks as they burst into the dark sky. Red, white, and blue fireworks boomed over the Roberts' home. Clarissa's cousin, Billy, lit up more fireworks for the family's entertainment. There was plenty of leftover food from the barbecue. Clarissa's mother insisted her relatives take some home. The kids cheered at the colorful, fiery display along with Clarissa's kin, who watched on the porch enjoying the private show. She and Isaac held hands as they sat on a loveseat, watching their so-called Macy's spectacular fireworks. Isaac recalled that he and Moses watched the Macy's fireworks in the city as kids. Isaac squeezed Clarissa's hand tight as he felt a sensation in his pants. They smiled at each other and clutched. *"She got to give me some,"* Isaac thought in his mind.

In the dimmed hallway of the Roberts' house on the third floor, where Clarissa and Isaac's bedrooms were adjacent, the two lovers breathed heavily, kissing while continuing to take things further. Isaac unbuttoned her blouse. Then he took off her bra and sucked on the nipples of her breast. They were so into each other. They kissed and caressed their way into the bedroom and didn't bother to close the door. Hopefully, no one would hear them. Isaac placed Clarissa on his bed, pulling her jeans off and using his teeth to remove her panties. Then Isaac pulled off his pants and boxers and inserted himself in Clarissa's warm, wet vagina. She moaned and moaned as Isaac thrust in and out.

Clarissa's thighs wrapped tighter around Isaac's waist. *"Clarissa loves me. She better love me with all the fuckin' that I'm doing. I'm probably taking her virginity, but she's also taking mine,"* Isaac began to thrust harder and faster. Clarissa moaned and groaned even louder. He didn't give a fuck if Clarissa's mother heard her daughter in the heat of passion. Isaac cleared his mind and looked Clarissa in the eyes, enjoying each stroke. In the corner of his eye, he sensed someone was watching him and Clarissa in this private moment. He wasn't sure who it was, but he would give them a show. Isaac pounded and pounded Clarissa, faster and harder. In the hallway, Mrs. Roberts cringed as she noticed Isaac's pale-skinned body on top of her daughter's gorgeous brown body. Of course, she heard Clarissa moaning and groaning as it intensified. Clarissa reached her climax. Mrs. Roberts gasped as she dashed downstairs.

Moments later, Clarissa and Isaac eased out of the house as if nothing happened. Something happened, though, and Clarissa noticed her family sitting on the side of the porch. Her grandmother frowned at her knowing her granddaughter was doing things she wasn't supposed to be doing. Clarissa sensed her relatives knew where she and Isaac went off to beforehand. Still, they knew she wasn't hurt. If so, her relatives would've dashed right into that house and let her attacker have it. Mrs. Roberts glared at Isaac and her daughter, shaking her head. Isaac knew that Mrs. Roberts witnessed him giving Clarissa some love. He smiled devilishly at Mrs. Roberts. She turned away because she could tell Isaac knew she had witnessed him pounding her daughter.

The next morning, a heatwave with lots of humidity brought no relief. The birds sang while the sun beamed over the Roberts' home. In Isaac's bedroom, the air conditioner blew cold air through the entire area. Isaac lay in his bed as he tossed and turned. He shivered from the extremely cold air and needed a blanket. Then he felt someone next to him in bed. Isaac turned as his eyes bulged out of his head. Clarissa slept right by his side with her sweet face. Isaac didn't wake her; he could read her face. *"She loves me. I hope I am her first; I'm hers."* He lifted the sheet from Clarissa's body to see if she was nude. Wrong, Clarissa wore her nightshirt. Isaac wondered if she had panties on, but he didn't check. Isaac stood in the middle of the bedroom, not knowing where to look for a blanket. Then, it hit him "The smart thing was to turn off the air conditioner," Isaac wanted to kick himself in the ass for not thinking straight. He turned off the cooling system. A feminine voice coughed. Isaac turned around, noticing Clarissa tossing and turning in his bed.

"Can't sleep?" Clarissa stretched and yawned at once.

"It's cold," Isaac shivered.

"There's a blanket in the closet," she sat upright in bed.

Isaac grabbed a blue blanket from the top closet shelf, wrapping it around himself. He then sat on the edge of the bed. Clarissa snuggled him in her arms, kissing him on the cheek.

"I want to see what's going on with my family," Isaac sighed.

"Okay. Do you want me to come with you?" Clarissa asked.

He didn't want Clarissa to see what was going on in his household, especially between him and Moses. Isaac exhaled. Then, he looked into her eyes. He hoped Clarissa cared about him. He shook his head, kissing Clarissa with a *"yes."*

That afternoon, the heat continued with its murderous humidity over the Remington home. Meanwhile, the block felt like a ghost town. There weren't any neighbors around. Nobody wanted to experience thirst, sweat, or even heatstroke. Then a small red Honda with screeching brakes parked in front of the home. Clarissa occupied the driver's seat while Isaac sat in the passenger's seat. Sitting on the passenger's side of a vehicle embarrassed the hell out of him. As they both exited the car, not a soul was in sight. He wanted Clarissa to take him right back to her house because, after all this time, he didn't deal with his family. And on top of that, Isaac wanted to avoid dealing with the heat. He wasn't wearing his hat. He could drop dead right in front of his home. His family might then come around. He took his time up the concrete steps towards the front, opening the screen. Luckily, he had his keys, so he inserted the key into the keyhole. Then Isaac opened the door with ease as he looked around. Clarissa followed him into his house.

"Mom!" Isaac headed into the tidy living room.

"Mom!" Isaac cried. Still, there was yet to be a response.

"Check the rest of the house, Isaac," Clarissa said in a worrisome tone. Isaac scrambled upstairs while she waited in the living room. Clarissa browsed the immediate area of the Remington home. There were pictures of Moses and Isaac as tots alongside a birthday photo of the twins blowing out five candles on their cake. Clarissa smiled. She knew that they were close. There were even more photos of the frats on Halloween, vacations, Christmas, and plenty of baby pics. Clarissa's heart melted when she came across the twins' pictures at six months old in baby boy frames. Especially Isaac's picture. She cradled it as if she were holding Isaac as a baby.

Meanwhile, Isaac rummaged through Moses's drawers, searching for cash. No one was home, so why not take advantage of whatever was available. Isaac threw his brother's clothes all over the floor, stepping on them without caring. Then, he thrust open the closet door and threw more of Moses' garments around. He looked up at the closet's top shelf and grabbed whatever. Nothing but old board games he and Moses played as kids. "Those days are over. It's every man for himself," Isaac murmured.

While Clarissa proceeded to tour the living room of Isaac's home, there was the rattling of keys at the front door. Still cradling the picture, Clarissa froze in fear. She didn't know whether to hide or run or even call out to Isaac. The front door swung open as Moses and Ryan swaggered inside. They noticed Clarissa holding the baby boy framed in her arms. Moses's eyes widened, but he didn't utter a word. He heard the rummaging from the second floor. He dashed upstairs. Then loud arguing and cursing echoed throughout the home. Ryan ran up the stairs again to break up another sibling rivalry. Clarissa's heart pounded in her chest as the brothers' chaos intensified. She placed the picture on the table and scrambled upstairs. The twins wrestled on the floor, repeatedly hurling punches at each other. Ryan tried to avoid getting hit.

Then Calvin and Irene sprinted up to the second floor as the twins battled it out. Calvin intervened, gaining control of the situation. Then he shoved Isaac to the floor and became more attentive to Moses. Ryan held Moses back as well. Isaac knew that, by Calvin pushing him, he felt deep-seated hatred. And his mother wasn't even by his side. She was attentive to Moses. Isaac's face turned fiery red as he stood firm on his feet and charged at his stepfather. Isaac and Calvin then scuffled to the floor. Isaac threw as many punches as he could to his stepfather. In return, Calvin hurled those punches at his stepson. Again, Ryan, Irene, and Moses had to diffuse another altercation.

Minutes later, the brothers exchanged words back and forth. Clarissa pulled Isaac as hard as she could away from his home. He had too much strength. The rage that flowed through Isaac's body made him feel like stone. Finally, Isaac's body became lightweight, and he went to Clarissa's car. Moses cursed at his brother from the living room window. Due to the yelling and screaming echoing throughout the air, the neighbors peered out from their windows. Calvin stood there, glaring at Isaac. Not saying a word, he attempted to utter something. Then Irene stormed out of the house, calling her son's name. As Isaac turned, his mother slapped him across the face. "Don't come back! I don't want to ever see you again!" Irene marched back into the house without glancing at Isaac. Just by that slap, Isaac's eyes watered up as the tears streamed down his face. Moses sneered at Isaac from the living room. Isaac hopped into the passenger's seat, looking at his twin in the window. Isaac could tell his twin's face seemed satisfied by their mother laying the slap upon his face. Moses stormed away from the glass window as Clarissa entered the driver's seat and sped away.

That evening at the Roberts' home, Isaac propped his head on his bed pillow and gazed at the ceiling. His mother hated him. Since Irene met Calvin, things have changed. Isaac truly believed that his mother didn't love him. Irene loved Moses without a doubt. And Ryan was the new addition to the family. Clarissa knocked at the door, opening it slowly. "Dinner's ready, babe," she said in a loving tone.

"I'm not hungry," Isaac turned his back on Clarissa while he stretched out in bed. Clarissa's smile turned upside down. She sat on the side of the bed and kissed him on the neck. Isaac wasn't in the mood for lovemaking, food, or anything. All he wanted to do was die.

"Come on, babe," Clarissa slithered her tongue on the back of Isaac's neck and into his ear. He shoved Clarissa away and had a tight grip on her wrist.

"Stop! Clarissa, I'm not in the mood!" he said sternly. Isaac pushed her hand away.

"I'm sorry," she marched out of the bedroom, slamming the door.

Isaac rolled from his side on his back, staring at the ceiling again. He reflected on his stay at Clarissa's house. Isaac promised to keep the house up in exchange for room and board. Speaking of keeping the house up, he had to trim the hedges, paint the fence, and do other housework. He couldn't stay in Clarissa's home and not do anything. Isaac had to decide on what to do. *"I've got to leave. Where am I going to go? I don't want to impose on my Uncle Tyler. I don't want my problems to become his problems. I'm going to have to figure it out,"* Isaac closed his eyes. A tear struggled from under his eyelid, then streaming down his face. He wiped his tears away.

As the night went on, Isaac tossed and turned in his bed as he overheard Clarissa and her mother from the kitchen. His eyes kept opening and closing, trying to stay awake to see if they were talking about him. He couldn't keep his exhausted eyes open for anything. Isaac's sorrows wouldn't allow him to sleep. Hours later, the clock read: 2:17 a.m. Isaac opened his eyes, inhaling. He quickly got dressed and was quiet as a mouse. He peered out the cracked bedroom door, ensuring he didn't wake anyone up. He slithered his body through the broken bedroom door, leaving it open, and didn't care. Isaac crept downstairs and opened the front door. He easily closed it back. He hurried away from the Roberts' residence, not looking back. It wasn't his home. He had no idea where he was heading. Once again, he swaggered along that long road to wherever it took him.

CHAPTER FIFTEEN

The enormous blue sky had a few clouds as the birds soared across it. They chirped away in search of food for their young. Then a pigeon released its droppings down below. The bird's feces splattered on Isaac's face while sleeping on a bench. He jumped up, wiping the slimy, ugly-colored, stinky turd from his face. He didn't want to rub it on his clothes, but some got on his shirt. Isaac looked at his disgusting hands, noticing a water fountain across from him. So, he darted towards it, washing the nasty waste from his hands and face. It was then he saw joggers in the enormous park. A woman walking her dog, a man reading his newspaper, and kids clamoring in the playground. Isaac didn't know what time it was. He looked at his wrist, but he had no watch. After he washed off the bird feces, he flung the drips of water from his hands and waved it through the air. The sun would dry him off in a matter of no time. For now, Isaac had to get a new shirt.

Later, Isaac snatched a black t-shirt from the rack in a clothing retail store. But then, he realized it was too hot for that color. A blue color would suit him. Isaac grabbed three sporty blue shirts and threw the garments on the counter. The cashier turned around and spoke to another co-worker, but then she noticed Isaac glaring at her. It seemed as if he were looking somewhere else. Isaac was in a trance. He then snapped it out and smiled at the clerk.

"Hi. I'm sorry. I'm in my own little world," he placed his American Express gift card on the counter. He was using it for the first time and wondered what other plans he had for the day. He didn't want to go home and engage in another scuffle with Moses, and just looking at his stepfather was sickening enough. Isaac didn't know what to think of his mother. He didn't want to go there, so he erased the bitterness from his mind. He didn't even want to burden his aunt or uncle with his issues since they always went away on cruises or something like that this time of year. Realistically, Isaac dreamt of falling in love with the right woman and having a bank full of money. And having a normal complexion. He had never thought of it before. But this time, for the first time, he imagined himself able to walk in the sunlight, lay in the white sand on a beach in the Virgin Islands with the woman he loved and who loved him. Fairytales weren't just for little girls. Boys had them too.

"Hello, sir," Isaac snapped out of his daze again. He felt embarrassed.

"I'm sorry," Isaac hoped no one was looking. Then he turned around and noticed there wasn't a line behind him. He swiped his American Express card through the card machine, keying in his information as it approved his purchase. The cashier packed his bag. Isaac scurried out of the establishment with his head down.

Minutes later, Isaac put on the brand-new blue Adidas shirt in a men's bathroom stall. He exhaled, feeling good about wearing something new on his body. He swaggered out of the booth and balled up the soiled shirt. Then, he tossed it into the trash can. He washed his hands in the sink, lathering them with liquid soap and cleansing the germs away. Isaac dried his hands with the towel, glaring at himself in the large mirror. He felt brand-new.

Alone, Isaac ate a bowl of chicken pasta at a booth in a diner an hour later. Eating alone was a first for him; he wasn't used to it. He noticed customers in the restaurant staring at him as if he didn't belong there. *"They must think I'm homeless or something. It is because I'm a freak of nature,"* he said in his mind. He cautiously peeked over at a family with three teenagers. They pointed and snickered at him. The boy's mother yelled at the top of her lungs, advising them to mind their business before someone kicked their ass. Isaac smiled. *Correcting your children when they're wrong is a mother's responsibility.* His cell phone buzzed. Isaac checked the caller ID and it read: Clarissa. Isaac poked some pasta with his fork and shoved it into his mouth. Isaac didn't bother to answer the call. *"I guess I don't have a family anymore."* He didn't check his call log because he knew there were not any calls from his family.

"Maybe, they'll get to me later when they miss having me around," Isaac reflected in his mind again. He finished his lunch as the waitress slid the bill on the table.

Minutes later, Isaac strutted outside, wondering what the next best thing was. Then, in the distance, was the Long Island Railroad. A trip to Manhattan put a smile on his face. He could experience all that *"New York, New York"* goodness. In no time, Isaac stood on the platform, waiting for the train to Penn Station. Then the long silver locomotive slowly pulled in without making a sound. Isaac squinted his eyes. He recalled the New York Subway making a lot of noise upon its arrival and departure. The LIRR was Isaac's first ride. He looked down at the gap between the train and the platform, taking a few steps back as the train doors opened before him. Then, of course, he stepped onto the train from the platform. Isaac noticed the rows of cushioned seats like that of an aircraft. Isaac raced for the empty window seat. He placed his plastic bag on the seat next to him. Isaac knew he'd have to remove it because someone might want to occupy it. So, he focused on the world outside the train's window. There was nothing more than a railroad yard with trains coming in and out of the station. He sat back and couldn't wait to get to Manhattan. The train pulled out of the station with ease. The wheels' high-pitched squealing moved with a low chug. The ride had no bumps, so Isaac could rest his head against the glass window. His eyes became heavier and heavier. He did his best to stay awake because he didn't want to miss anything. He couldn't help himself when his eyes got the best of him.

Surprisingly, as tired as he got, Isaac kept opening his eyes at every train stop.

"Jamaica Station," the automated conductor announced. The train pulled in slowly and made a complete stop. Isaac opened his eyes and stretched, looking around. He then laid his head against the window, dozing off again. Then Isaac eyed the automatic doors opening. A reasonably small number of people got on. Amongst the passengers was a fair-skinned, African American male, his hair nicely cut and good-looking. He wore a three-piece suit while carrying a small backpack over his shoulder. *"Holy shit! He looks just like Moses,"* Isaac murmured. He looked around to make sure no one saw him talking to himself. The young gentleman sat a few rows ahead of him. Isaac eyed this look-alike since the train doors opened. Then his cell vibrated. He looked at the caller ID: Clarissa. Once more, Isaac didn't respond to his girlfriend's call. He decided to nap until the last stop.

About an hour later, the LIRR train pulled into Penn Station. Isaac's eyes widened for this moment he anticipated. He realized the young Moses look-alike was getting off at the same stop. Moreover, he wondered what type of job he had. Maybe, he was an executive or in some well-paid position. "Penn Station is the last stop on this train. Please take all your valuables with you and have a nice day. Thank you for riding the Long Island Railroad," announced the automated announcer.

The train halted. Isaac rose from his seat and exited. He almost forgot about the gap between the train and the station platform as he looked down. If he didn't look, he would've been a goner. Isaac headed through the nicely well-kept station and gasped. *"The station looks like a museum. Many rich people must come through here every day — stockbrokers, entrepreneurs, authors, musicians, etc.* As Isaac strolled further and further through the station, classical music echoed in the distance. A symphony orchestra of five musicians, two violists, and three cellists. An African-American woman played the cello, smiling at the crowd. The music she played was beautiful, just like her. The cellist a dark-skinned female in her early twenties, smiled at Isaac. She proceeded with her musical talents, impressing the hell out of him.

A donation box sat before the artists as they performed. He pulled a twenty-dollar bill from his wallet and put it in the money box. She eyed Isaac with a big smile and mouthed, *"Thank you"* to Isaac. The aroma of coffee and pastries filled the air as Isaac noticed a donut shop that sold beverages, books, and newspapers. Isaac wasn't hungry, but everything smelled good. He went on his way and hopped on the escalator, which led to the ground level above the station.

As he glanced over his shoulder, he realized it was becoming overcrowded. They probably had the same agenda as Isaac's: to experience the Big Apple. As Isaac reached street level, he stepped off the escalator with ease. But then, a young woman rudely pushed him out of her way. Isaac sucked his teeth and didn't bother to exchange words with the lady. He realized people were in a rush to their destination. The streets were packed with cars, trucks, and taxis blaring their horns through the air. That's all Isaac – or anyone else – could hear. Madison Square Garden stood right behind him, with its concerts and sporting events scrolling across the screen. Isaac weaved himself in and out of the New York crowd. *"Why are they in such a rush?"* Isaac asked himself and avoided any confrontation with these people. A man cursed at an invisible person he believed to be a couple of feet away from Isaac.

Isaac's heart raced as he strutted through the crowded streets. *"Why am I so nervous about New York? I'm a New Yorker. I'm from Long Island, that's why. We don't have packed streets. Well, I'll get used to it,"* Isaac placed confidence in his mind. The Empire State Building was just a short distance away. Isaac couldn't help but see it. He remembered coming to the city on the Fourth of July when he and Moses were kids. One thing Isaac noticed was that no one stared at him. He wondered if people would see him as a human being, not as a freak of nature. What was Isaac going to do? Walk around the city all day? He took his first steps while thinking about his life. Isaac could at least call his Uncle Tyler and Aunt Melissa to say hello. But then, he erased the idea from his head and continued walking. The New York City Public Library stood majestically with those two lions of stone. Even though Isaac had his cell phone, he didn't bother taking a picture. The street numbers kept getting lower as Isaac swaggered further and further downtown. He grabbed his cell, typing Google locations in for Park Avenue.

Suddenly, he stopped in his tracks and jumped out of the way of the crowded people. Park Avenue was in the direction where the street numbers went up and on the west side. He could do some sightseeing along the way. Within a few minutes, Isaac approached Times Square. Its digital displays advertise fashion, music, celebrities, television, movies, books, and other products. He smiled at the colorful displays. Then, the M&Ms store with its massive logo was right in his face. Isaac wanted to go and purchase some candy, but it was too hot. The sweets would undoubtedly melt in his hands. It was just that hot. But still, Isaac already felt tired. A hot dog stand was behind him, so he bought a Sprite from the vendor. He gulped the soft drink, tossed the aluminum can in the trash, and continued his sights of the city.

Finally, the beautiful, tall buildings constructed of glass, stone, and other earthly materials made this block very ritzy. Some of the high-rises were different in shapes, sizes, and colors. Isaac strolled along one of the most charming streets in the world. He couldn't see inside, but because of the exterior of the superstructures, it said a lot. Also, Isaac noticed that men at each building's entrance greeting residents.

Then, a black Rolls Royce Wraith pulled to the curb. Isaac stopped in his tracks. He wanted to see if it was a celebrity or an imperative person with high social status. The tower doorman raced to the luxury vehicle, opened the door, and tipped his hat to a well-dressed Caucasian male; in his mid-thirties, who must've been someone of the elite. He looked like a stockbroker on Wall Street or in real estate. Isaac couldn't move from where he stood. He was a bit starstruck, even though this gentleman wasn't seen on television or anything. Isaac then dragged his feet slowly and glanced back at this gentleman. *"I know he's busy with business deals, taking important phone calls, and having lunch. This businessman had no time to talk to little old me — a nobody. I'm only seventeen years old,"* Isaac swaggered down the avenue.

Across the street, construction workers hammered and drilled diligently on a new tower. Isaac stopped in his pathway, where construction workers used glass and stone to construct the building. Those materials must be a trend in architecture. *"I wonder how much they charge residences for an apartment per month?"* Isaac wondered. Then a young, tanned female, probably Italian or Latina in her early twenties, sashayed while walking her Pomeranian pooch. Isaac gave a friendly smile as the model-like girl gave a quick smile. She then went on her way. *"She must be a Victoria's Secret model or something like that. She probably lives in one of these penthouses. Her boyfriend must be the luckiest dude to have a woman like her,"* he kept his eyes fixed on this alluring woman while she jay-walked across the street. His eyes shifted from one corner to the other, hoping she didn't get hit by a truck or anything. Isaac was ready to spring into action just in case. Luckily, she made her way to the other side safely. Then Isaac's cell phone vibrated. The caller ID read: Clarissa. He took the call.

"What?" Isaac asked sarcastically.

"Isaac! What do you mean, what? Where are you, baby! I'm worried sick about you!"

"Really?" Isaac responded.

"I love you, Isaac," Clarissa's tender voice answered.

Isaac's heart dropped as he heard those endearing words coming from Clarissa. *Did she mean it, or was it because she didn't have a handyman around the house? He loved Clarissa too, but he wasn't going to tell her. She was probably pulling his leg.* Then Clarissa sobbed on the other end of the phone. She pleaded with Isaac to return home.

"Forget about me. I'm pretty sure plenty of guys are dying to be with you!" he disconnected his call. He proceeded along the Manhattan Street.

Sunbathers soaked up the sun while laying on their towels on Central Park's great lawn. Dogs played with their owners, and families had picnics. Isaac strolled across the green grass, looking at everyone enjoying their day out. He could've had a good day, but things didn't look too good. Moments later, Isaac sat on one of the benches that stretched endlessly throughout the park. Almost behind the bench was a large tree that gave plenty of shade. He needed it since he was tired. He ignored the joggers, the dog walkers, the parents, and the clamoring children. "Young Hearts Run Free," a seventies disco song, echoed in the distance. Isaac noticed the dancers just several feet away, dancing. He saw the people lounging on the nearby benches as he pulled his cell from his pocket. He took his focus off the parkgoers, gazing at his phone. Isaac didn't know if he should call Clarissa to apologize, but he couldn't face her now. She had probably told her mother what was going on. Mrs. Roberts wouldn't forgive him because she didn't care for Isaac. Anyway, he thought about giving his Uncle Tyler a call. Maybe he would be worried about him. Isaac pushed the keys on his cell and put the cell to his ear. On the other end, there was a connection tone.

"Hello, Isaac. How are you?"

"I'm good," Isaac's voice trembled.

"What's up?" Uncle Tyler answered.

Isaac's uncle didn't know that he was missing in action, but at the same time, Isaac wouldn't tell him anything. He acted as if everything was fine.

"Nothing much. I'm just chilling,'" Isaac said.

"Alright. How about you and I do lunch?" his uncle insisted.

"That's cool," Isaac tittered.

"I'll give you a call later, alright?" Uncle Tyler said.

"Yeah, cool," Isaac said.

His Uncle Tyler disconnected his call.

"Holy shit," Isaac mouthed. He glanced over both of his shoulders as he sniffed the air. There was a hot dog stand not too far from where he sat. He wanted to get something to eat, but he didn't want to lose his spot. Isaac was comfortable with a large tree behind his bench, where he relaxed. He took his chances. He dashed to the hot dog stand, but two customers were ahead of him. Isaac was anxious to get his food and sat on the bench under the oak tree. No one seemed to want that spot. Still, Isaac continued to glance at it while waiting in line.

"Good afternoon, sir? How may I help you?" The food vendor greeted Isaac with his foreign accent, smiling. "Two hot dogs with mustard and onions, a soda, and a pretzel," Isaac pulled a twenty-dollar bill from his wallet. The food vendor prepared Isaac's order. Isaac scoffed when a female jogger sat in his spot. The runner was out of breath, so she tried to relax for the moment and tie her sneakers.

"Fuckin' shit," Isaac cursed under his breath. He and the food vendor exchanged money; then, Isaac got his food. He stared directly at the female jogger, who got up from the bench and jogged away.

"Yes," Isaac quickly sat back and ate his hot dog. He loved this bench. It was as if this were his new residence. Homeless people claimed park benches, street corners, corridors, and other unusual places for shelter. Isaac slowed down his eating and thought about housing. *"What the fuck am I going to do? I don't have enough money on me. And I don't want to go back home to where it doesn't feel like a home,"* Isaac's heart pounded heavily in his chest. He shoved the rest of the hot dog in his mouth. He sipped his soda.

"Why hasn't Moses contacted me? Let me know you're concerned," Isaac pushed in his brother's number and then a dial tone.

"Fuck it," Isaac disconnected his call immediately. His eyes became watery, holding in his emotions. *"They say it's not good to hold in your feelings. Just let it spew. You'll feel a lot better,"* Isaac remembered people saying. Even if he did cry, he probably wouldn't feel any better. Suddenly, a large arm wrapped around Isaac's neck. He smelt potent marijuana. Isaac didn't get a good look at this stranger who had him in the headlock from behind. "Don't mother fuckin' turn around? Don't look at me. Where's your wallet and cell phone?" The menacing voice whispered in Isaac's ear. Isaac did everything this perpetrator asked him. He kept his eyes forward and noticed that people didn't even bother to see what was happening to him. Isaac handed over his wallet and cellphone. Then he was released from the chokehold. Isaac took a sharp breath and slowly turned around. His eyes widened, but he couldn't figure it out.

"Where the fuck is he?" Isaac wondered about the person who mugged him. He wanted to pinch himself and wake up from this nightmare. The robbery was real, but now he had no money or cell phone to call home. Isaac stood to his feet and reached into his pockets. There was neither a wallet nor a cell phone. He panicked and wanted help, but no one saw anything. If Isaac had been average-looking, maybe people would have noticed. Isaac sobbed and sat back on the bench with his head down. He was really in a bad situation now.

CHAPTER SIXTEEN

August seventeenth arrived, the day Moses and Isaac would celebrate their eighteenth birthday. Moses lay in his bed, his face up with the ceiling fan twirling slowly. It wasn't that hot, and the room temperature was comfortable. It's been a month now. Neither Moses nor anyone in his family has yet to see or hear from Isaac. Moses hoped to God nothing had happened to him. Clarissa had no idea about his whereabouts and had been the last person to speak to him.

"He'll probably show up. Let me stop worrying and focus on me," Moses sat on the edge of the bed. Moses and Isaac had always had family and friends gathered around them with many gifts on their birthdays since they were little. But on this occasion, Moses flew solo for a second time. Moses immediately got up from his bed, went into the bathroom, and showered.

Later, Moses searched through his closet for the best clothes to wear. He wore expensive blue jeans, a royal blue shirt, and sneakers. Afterward, he brushed his hair in the mirror and sprayed some cologne. Then, he put his earring in his ear. Moses opened his bedroom door with ease, closing it back. He crept down the hallway and peered into his parents' bedroom. A ray of sunshine shone on the empty king-sized bed, beaming through the shades of the window.

"Calvin's probably at work. I know Mom must be in the kitchen fixing me a special birthday breakfast," Moses said to himself, going downstairs. He saw his mother sitting in the lounge chair, facing the window. Nothing but silence. No television or radio on. Moses cautiously approached his mother because he didn't want to frighten her. As he stepped before his mother, he could tell by her facial expression. Irene fixed her disturbing eyes on the living room window. She neither moved a muscle nor acknowledged Moses stand-

ing right before her eyes. "Mom," Moses called. Irene still didn't budge. Instead, she sobbed.

"I shouldn't have hit Isaac. What did I do? I shouldn't have hit him!" Irene sob even more.

Moses kneeled before the woman who gave her all to her sons. He wrapped his arms around and told her he loved her, adding that it wasn't her fault.

"So, whose fault is it then? It's surely not yours," Irene fought back her tears.

"It is my fault that Isaac's gone," a tear streamed down Moses' cheek.

Moses convinced his mother that Isaac would return home. Moses' shirt had a wet spot in it from his mother's tears. He wanted to unwrap his arms from around his mother, but he couldn't. She was in emotional need. Then Irene lifted her head from her son's chest and grimaced.

"I'm sorry, Moses. Happy birthday," Irene sniffled. She kissed him on the cheek.

"Thanks," Moses smiled.

"It's Isaac's birthday too. He loved sharing his birthday with you. You're his brother," She wiped her tears with her hands.

Even though he and Ryan would hang out, Moses didn't have the guts to leave his mother's side. He had no idea where they were going to go. Maybe they could invite some girls to his birthday celebration in their backyard. Moses and Isaac always had their birthdays in the backyard, but Moses wanted to try something new this year. When a horn beeped from outside, Moses peered over his mother's shoulder and saw Ryan. He and Ryan would cruise in their vehicles and go somewhere. Irene looked at him with saddened eyes.

"Where are you going, Moses?' Irene's voice quivered.

"I don't know. "Somewhere, I won't be long," Moses smiled.

"Please don't stay out late. You never know. Isaac might come home," Irene added. Moses kissed his mother again before heading out the door with his car keys in hand. As he was about to close the door, Irene stayed in the recliner as if waiting for Isaac to come home from war. Moses stepped on the front porch for a second as Ryan greeted him with a high-five.

"So, what's up, Moses? Where are we going?"

"I know we planned to hang out, but my mother's upset," Moses said.

Ryan understood. He agreed to spend time with his best friend, even if they didn't hit the town.

That same morning in an urban alleyway behind a Manhattan diner, Isaac hid behind one of two dumpsters. During the night, he came across this place. He had hoped to get some sleep where no harm would come to him. Surprisingly, when restaurant employees came out to either dump the trash or smoke, they never noticed him. Rats and cockroaches scurried alongside him and even crawled on him. He was so tired that he didn't see the rodents. And fortunately, the rats didn't bite him. Isaac still had the same clothes on. He stunk, and his hair had become matted since it hadn't been combed. As the sun beamed upon his face, he heard the squeaking door of the diner. He squinted, watching a cook toss a trash bag into the dumpster. Luckily, the restaurant employee didn't notice Isaac hiding in the corner. Isaac needed shade because it was way too hot for him. Where would he go? He was still tired and starving. He knew there was some good food that customers didn't eat. People were very good when it came to wasting food. He eased his way up from behind the dumpster. But then, he ducked behind it. The diner's rear door opened again. Two chefs communicated in Spanish, tossing out more trash. The chefs reentered the restaurant, slamming the back door shut.

Isaac crept back from around the dumpster and lifted the heavy lid. He held his nose as the foul odor hit like a fist. Cautiously, he untied the plastic garbage bags. "God, please let there be something delicious here," Isaac prayed. There were half-eaten salads, chicken, fresh bread, a steak bone, etc. Isaac grabbed the pastry, half-eaten veggies, some cooked rice, and a cake. Isaac found a brown bag into which he shoved all the unwanted food. He then leaped out of the dumpster. The manager stood there with his hands on his hips.

"What are you doing, young man?" The diner manager asked in an unpleasant tone.

"I was hungry," Isaac said in a humble tone. The restaurant's manager couldn't help but feel sorry for this miserable person on the street.

"How old are you?"

"I'm seventeen, eighteen. Today's my birthday," Isaac continued in his modest tone.

"Happy birthday. What's your name?"

"Isaac," he told the manager with a slight smile.

"Where's your family.... Isaac?"

"They're on Long Island," Isaac replied. He hoped that this manager didn't call the authorities on him.

"Isaac, next time, when you're hungry, knock on the door so I can give you fresher food," the restaurant manager said.

"Okay. Thanks," Isaac scrambled away with the food in the brown paper bag.

That evening, R&B music blared from the speakers in the backyard of the Remington home. Moses, and his family and friends, ate and drank while celebrating his special day. Moses indulged in a rib steak Calvin had cooked on the barbecue grill. His Uncle Tyler and Aunt Melissa attended their nephew's birthday since they had already spent time with him and Isaac on graduation. Tyler wondered where Isaac was. He had another gift card with even more money on it for college. Tyler tried asking Moses, but Ryan interrupted. On his iPad, he showed Moses the latest show: *Beautiful Homes and Garden Estates.* As the saying goes: "There's a time for business and pleasure." Moses' birthday was a pleasure rather than a time to talk business. But Ryan didn't care. He continued to shove the iPad in his friend's face. Moses couldn't help but see the mansion in Malibu, California, going for sixty-three million. The two best friends disengaged themselves from their realtor talk and continued eating the food. His Uncle Tyler attempted to ask about Isaac again, but Irene grabbed Moses' hand. She wanted to dance. Moses shied away from his mother because he wanted to answer his uncle. But then, he gave up and accepted the dance with her.

"Happy birthday, son," Irene kissed him on the cheek.

"Thanks," Moses replied.

Uncle Tyler knew something was wrong, causing him and his wife to make eye contact with each other.

Isaac devoured a chicken leg at a red table alone in Times Square, which was well kept. The claustrophobic glass skyscrapers were vivid, colorful, and twinkling virtual advertisements. The bleacher-like red-ruby steps, the TKTS booth, and Father Duffy Square were there. Isaac inhaled the summery air into his lungs. Right before his eyes, the area had large gatherings of tourists and native New Yorkers. Suddenly, a monstrous sound of house music blasted from a speaker while dancers got their groove on. Isaac observed the entertainment just a few feet away. He didn't think about anyone trying to hurt him because there were so many people in Father Duffy Square. He didn't know much about this Canadian soldier and a Catholic priest, Francis P. Duffy, who had served as chaplain for the sixty-ninth infantry regiment, a unit for New York's National Guard from the city's immigrant and Irish population.

Since Father Duffy was a man of the cloth, Isaac wondered if Father Duffy aided the locals without any shelter, food, or a place to rest their heads at night. Isaac had to have faith that no harm would come to him. But then, he had a flashback of the same scenario, where dancers danced to house music. That's when he was mugged. He swallowed the piece of chicken and glanced over his shoulders. His heart pounded in his chest. Isaac lifted his hand and noticed it trembling. Isaac took a three-hundred-sixty-angle view of the surrounding area as he stood to his feet. Uniformed NYPD Officers, a K-9 unit and surveillance cameras were in proximity of this famous tourist attraction. The traffic surrounding the area was filled with trucks, taxis, and other cars going about their way. Then he set his sights on the Father Duffy statue. He crossed himself and sat back in his chair. He could only imagine what was happening at home with his brother's birthday celebration.

At the Remington home, eighteen candles glistened on a three-layered ice cream cake that read: Happy birthday, Moses. It was supposed to read Moses and Isaac. Moses felt horrible that his brother wasn't there. Isaac was out there in the world somewhere. As Moses' guests sang "Happy Birthday," Moses' eyes watered up with tears trickling down his face. There was no way that Isaac would miss his birthday, their birthday. His mother tried to hide her tears throughout the entire party, but she couldn't help it. Irene ran into the house to have her tearful moment. Moses had his own tearful moment right before those candles. He missed Isaac and wished he'd come home wherever he was. Moses closed his eyes. His wish was evident.

Back in Times Square, Isaac snapped out of what his brother must be doing or have. Instead, Isaac focused on what he had. Isaac had nothing. Isaac wished that someone would bless him with a slice of cake and offer him birthday greetings.

"Happy birthday, Isaac," a woman greeted him with a kiss while holding the leash of her golden retriever. Then a gentleman, in his mid-forties, jogged past Isaac and waved.

"Happy birthday, Isaac, and many more."

Echoing, harmonious voices played out like a surround sound stereo. "Happy birthday to you! Happy birthday to you!" Meanwhile, house dancers danced their way to Isaac's table. As the singing continued, more strangers descended from the red ruby staircase with a rectangular ice cream cake with eighteen glistening candles. "Happy birthday to you! Happy birthday to you! Happy birthday, dear Isaac; Happy birthday to you!" the imaginary crowd sang. Isaac closed his eyes. He hoped to see his brother someday. Isaac opened his eyes, noticing that no one was around. Instead, it was just him and that piece of cake. *"Happy birthday to me. Happy Birthday to me. Happy birthday, dear Isaac; happy birthday to me!"* Isaac sang in his mind. Then he bit out of a piece of cake that he had gotten from the diner.

Someone then tapped him on the shoulder. He chewed the dessert in his mouth and noticed a young woman with a very angelic smile. She presented herself with concern and only asked him his name. Then, she asked if he had a place to sleep for the night. Isaac trusted this woman without even thinking about any harm she could inflict on him. The navy blue T-shirt read in bold white letters: VOLUNTEERS FOR THE HOMELESS. Isaac smiled as soon as he saw the woman's shirt. He noticed there were other homeless volunteers making attempts to the homeless some shelter. Without hesitation, Isaac nodded as this woman escorted him to a green van.

That night, Isaac propped his head on a small pillow on a bed in the corner. He appreciated having a place to sleep; but wanted someone to confide in. The homeless volunteer who aided Isaac was nowhere to be found. He noticed a woman, maybe in her twenties or early thirties, wearing an old gray jogging suit. She lay on her side, facing him. She wasn't really that pretty from Isaac's point of view. But, then again, Isaac shouldn't be judging anyone. Her hair needed to be combed. It wasn't matted, just kinky and dry. She seemed to grimace at Isaac, but she shut her eyes and went to sleep.

Isaac sucked his teeth and looked at the entire large room of beds, all filled with New York's homeless population. Only a small portion of this room would get to rest for the night. Isaac laid back down on his pillow. He glared at the very high ceiling as all sorts of things crossed his mind. *"Moses probably got drunk again or got some pussy for his birthday. Maybe, he's taking a vacation somewhere, or God only knows,"* Isaac speculated, envisioning his brother possibly adventuring the world. He ceased his ideas, thinking about himself. *What was he going to do about his circumstances? He had to think about his future. Where would he lay his head down in the future? Where would he get food or clothes or bathe?* Isaac could only think about this night when he could sleep comfortably without looking over his shoulders. His eyes became heavier and heavier, hoping his days ahead would be promising.

CHAPTER SEVENTEEN

In mid-October, Moses swaggered onto the Campus of LIU with his backpack strap on his shoulder. He wore blue jeans and a casual shirt with a denim jacket. The ladies on campus seemed to be into him. But he could never tell when someone was honest. Moses stayed focused on his goals because he had to maintain his GPA. Because Moses majored in business administration, he had economics, business management, and accounting courses. He still had the information about the real estate course his Uncle Tyler gave him and Isaac.

As Moses proceeded to his next class, he had to acknowledge that his brother wasn't there with him or coming home. And so, Moses expunged his brother from his mind. He had to think of himself. Isaac probably wasn't even thinking about him. Moses swaggered into the business building to his economics class. Within seconds, he rushed to his seat next to pretty, melanited, nineteen-year-old Shawnette Crawford. She was an African-American young lady who gave him a pen to write. "Why are you rushing? You're never late, Moses," She had her eyes glued to the blackboard as their economics instructor, Professor Merrick, jotted down notes for the day's lesson.

"It's a habit," Moses couldn't keep his eyes off her. She turned to Moses and smiled. He noticed that her flawless skin had neither a blemish nor a pimple. Shawnette loved Moses' good looks and charm. He was an intelligent gentleman and a sharp dresser.

"You're beautiful," Moses smiled, pleased with the fascinating woman before his eyes.

"Thank you," Shawnette whispered as she proceeded with her classwork. Moses glared at her for a second and jotted down a note on a blank paper.

"Do you really like this class?", the note read that Moses wrote. Shawnette read it and jotted a response on the blank paper. She slid the message before his eyes. It read:

"Yes! Why do you ask?"

Moses wrote again on the paper. He slid it to her. It read: *This class is a complete waste of time.*

Shawnette frowned at Moses's response and jotted down her response. She slid him the piece of paper. It read: *This is important, so get with the program.*

Miles away at Hunter College, along Park Avenue on the Upper East-side of Manhattan, was where students entered and exited the buildings hoping to accomplish greatness. Isaac noticed the pupils strolling onto campus and making their way to class. He glared at the historic-looking building, probably built in the nineteenth century. His clothing appeared increasingly ragged and filthy while having a stench of body odor.

Freshman year was supposed to be Isaac's most significant accomplishment in his life. He dropped his head down, not making any eye contact with anyone. Because of his insecurities, Isaac had thrown away his college and his entire future. He hoped none of the pupils noticed him or snickered. Isaac wondered about his college years. He eyed the young Indian or Arabian young man in his early twenties. He had potential as an engineer or something in medicine. Then a young Caucasian female, also in her early twenties, looked the lawyer type. A young Arabian man, perhaps in his late twenties, was bound for his master's degree in his major. "These kids with big dreams. I had a dream once, and now I threw it away; anyone would say," Isaac envisioned himself on this campus engaging in intellectual talks with students about their future goals. And of course, having a normal complexion like his brother and not being treated like an alien. The relationship with his parents would be good and he would get the admiration of many beautiful young women.

He scurried along Park Avenue, approaching those luxury buildings again where the rich and famous lived. He didn't think much of the surroundings this time. His brother crossed his mind, and Isaac wondered what Moses could be doing now. Moses was probably studying in the library, dorm, or maybe at home. Or he was perhaps up in some pussy. Every girl on campus was dying for Moses to fuck them. Isaac wanted to go to a pay phone and call his Uncle Tyler collect, but he didn't want to stick him with the bill. *"Let me go on and live my life. I'll die out here, and no one will care because I'm an invisible man,"* Isaac thought while walking down an endless street to nowhere.

Isaac hadn't eaten and didn't want to beg, but he had no choice but to return to the diner. Minutes later, Isaac swaggered into the alleyway of the Manhattan diner, where garbage piled up with rats scrambling about. Hungry, diligent New Yorkers grabbed a meal after work that early evening at around six-thirty. Isaac peered around the brick wall to ensure no one was around. He remembered that the manager told him to knock on the door to see if he could get fresh food, or he could have lied. Isaac eyed the dumpster anyway and wondered about the food in it. Isaac dashed towards the trash and opened the lid slowly. The workers had thrown away more rolls. *"What the fuck is up with throwing away bread? People like me are starving. I've got this dumpster for my refrigerator."*

"Hey Isaac," a strange voice called him. Isaac stepped out and saw the manager again.

"Hello," Isaac greeted with a slight smile.

"Hungry again? I told you I could get you some fresh food."

Isaac nodded his head, cringing. He could tell that the manager was lying his ass off.

"Isaac, do you need work?" the manager snickered.

The manager told another bald-faced lie. Then, he refused the offer. Isaac couldn't trust anyone because he was homeless on these dangerous streets. People make promises but never come through with them.

"Where are you sleeping?" the manager asked, having more questions.

"On a park bench," Isaac answered.

"That's dangerous," the manager raised an eyebrow.

"I'll be okay," Isaac held his head down like a peasant.

He took leftover rolls, half-eaten meats, and whatever else before he scurried away.

“There’s a shelter over on Prince Street. They may have a few beds left. You never know,” The diner manager’s voice echoed. Isaac turned and nodded, continuing his way.

Moses and Shawnette devoured their pasta dishes at a themed restaurant in Westbury, Long Island. Pop music is played from the speaker in the ceiling. The young college couple engaged in conversation about their plans. Shawnette wasn’t sure what she wanted to do, but it had to be something she loved and lucrative simultaneously. She already knew what Moses wanted to do. He had to decide whether to take that real estate exam. Moses didn’t even pay for the course yet. Shawnette advised him to hurry up and make up his mind. He was still ambivalent about what to do. Moses brushed all those issues aside and wanted Shawnette to do more talking. He hated doing all the talking. Shawnette hinted at heading down the aisle. Moses’ eyes widened since he wasn’t into marriage yet. He also had to think about not getting too intimate with her either. After all, it could wind up resulting in pregnancy. Moses wanted to do things right. First, get a career and make money; then, get married and have a family. In any case, he felt he was a good candidate for his future. Only time will tell. While Moses spoke of being careful, he and Shawnette still got it on in the backseat of his parked Dodge Challenger later that evening in Lover’s Lane. The steamy back windshield concealed the entire passionate moment. Hopefully, no one would witness the two sweaty lovers' nude bodies.

Meanwhile, in a park in Manhattan, Isaac ate the rolls as he sat on a bench. He tried to eat what little meat was on the steak bone. Then he noticed a couple of beautiful women around him. Isaac being in such a misfortunate situation, pictured a fabulous restaurant with a gorgeous woman seated across from him at a candle-lit dinner. Three violinists played “Spring La Primavera” by Vivaldi. Isaac and this woman conversed as if they had known each other all their lives. Then this female was Clarissa; Isaac knew this young woman. She wore a black evening gown with a side split, and black pumps and wore her hair in a bun with glistening floral hairpins. *Boy, did Isaac miss this girl? She had probably long forgotten about him and moved on to another guy. What if she missed him? He sure did miss her.*

During their conversation over dinner, Isaac slipped an engagement ring on Clarissa's finger. She wrapped her arms around me and said, *"I do."* Then Isaac snapped out of it and saw no more women. He shoved the last piece of bread into his mouth. He would never find happiness in his situation. Isaac felt tired from walking around the town during the day. He needed a good night's rest. He recalled what the diner manager had said about sleeping on the bench. It was a dangerous thing because a lot of crazy things could happen to someone. He also said there might be a couple more beds at a shelter on Prince Street. So, Isaac made his way to Prince Street – wherever that was. Isaac asked a young man in his mid-twenties for directions. He had to take the number six train to Union Square and then get on the Q train to Prince Street. *"That sounds easy, but I forgot I'm not from the boroughs. I'm from Long Island. Holy shit. I don't have any money to pay my fair. I'll have to hop the train,"* Isaac weaved into the crowd of people going down into the subway. He followed the people, attempting to get on this train. Isaac noticed a line of people purchasing their MetroCard at the MTA booth. Other subway riders were at the MTA vending machines buying Metro Cards or scanning their OMNI from their cell phones while a few passengers opened the gate and made their way through without paying their fare.

Isaac followed a woman. She looked behind her and screamed as soon as she saw Isaac. In contrast, Isaac smiled because the woman had quickly moved out of his way. She sat on the bench and cringed, hoping Isaac wouldn't do anything to her. Passengers on the platform noticed the minor incident and glared at Isaac as if he had stepped out of a horror movie. *"What the fuck is everyone staring at! Okay, this is nothing new. I've been through this my whole life. Stares and stares and stares,"* Isaac's heart raced in his chest. He couldn't take it anymore. Isaac wanted to fuck someone up on that platform. Too tired to think about it, Isaac ignored the ignorant people who pretended to have peachy lives. The rumble of the number six train pulled into the station, halting with its squealing brakes. The automated doors opened as the passengers got off. Then, the people on the platform got on. "Sixty-eighth Street, Hunter College. The next stop is Fifty-Ninth Street and Lexington

Avenue. Please stand clear of the closing doors. *"Bing-Bing,"* the automated conductor announced. The double doors closed as the locomotive pulled out of the station. Isaac stood and held on to the pole as the train picked up speed. He didn't make eye contact with anyone but sensed people watching him. Isaac kept his eyes glued to the floor without anything on his mind. Then he lifted his head up, at which point he recognized a pretty girl sitting in the corner reading a book. Isaac didn't bother to read the title, but she reminded him of Clarissa. He told himself not to stare because she might be intimidated by him. So, Isaac focused his eyes on his feet and thought about this young woman's name. He further wondered if she had a boyfriend or was married. Or if she was single? But it was not for Isaac to mingle.

He peeked up a bit as her eyes stayed glued to the pages of this novel, engrossed in another world. He still didn't bother to read the title. His eyes were glued to her like the story she held dear in her hand. Isaac wondered about this woman's destination and all that good stuff. He then got the courage to glance at this pretty lady again. She was shocked by Isaac's pale-skinned and worn glasses. Yes, his glasses were getting old. He often worried about his vision since these spectacles were no longer helpful. Then the train pulled into Fifty-Ninth Street station. She had her eyes fixed on the double doors as the train stopped. The automatic doors widened as she strutted on her way. Isaac felt ugly inside and out. He had dropped his head as if he had lost his best friend, which he did. The world was cruel, heartless, and thoughtless with no compassion, but people who find love and happiness are beautiful.

Moments later, the train pulled into Fourteenth Street Union Square. The automated double doors swung open as the passengers got off; of course, Isaac was one of them. He made his way to the Q train platform, where passengers packed like a can of sardines. Then the rumbling train arrived at the platform, stopping as the doors departed. The passengers got off as Isaac and another group of passengers hopped on. Prince Street was only a couple of stops, so Isaac didn't have a long train ride. During his short train ride, Isaac sat in the corner and kept his eyes on himself. He couldn't help it again when he saw another beautiful girl reading her iPad. Either Indian or Arabian, her glasses were clad and black-suited. Another beauty sat across from him; she looked and noticed Isaac. Isaac immediately put his head on because he assumed he would get the cold shoulder. He then peered up again and recognized her smiling at him. Isaac then quickly smiled at her.

"Prince Street," the automated conductor announced.

Isaac rose to his feet and gave a more giant smile to the Arabian woman. He glanced at the attractive woman once more and grimaced. The double door opened as Isaac exited.

Along Prince Street, the buildings were taller than others. The traffic was lighter than on the Upper Westside or Midtown. Isaac had to find this shelter as quickly as he could, to get some shut-eye. An old-looking building once used as a factory was where an older, mid-sixties Latina female stood with the door open. She welcomed the city's impoverished population. She gazed down, noticing Isaac approaching with his old worn clothing.

"Are you looking for shelter, young man?" the homeless shelter director asked.

"Yes," Isaac answered without hesitation.

"Hurry, we've only got a few beds left," the director encouraged. Isaac dashed up the stairs and nodded to the director.

"Thank you," Isaac said as he hurried inside.

Beds were everywhere, occupied by homeless women, children, and single persons. Isaac scanned dozens and dozens of beds with his eyes, trying to find a place for himself. He spotted a bed in the corner where no one would bother him. Isaac stomped his way to the twin-sized cot. He took his sneakers off, placing them under the bed. Then he lay down and stared at the ceiling. How could anyone get any rest with the cursing and loud chattering? Isaac snuggled in his slumber, shutting his eyes. He felt as if he had gone in time when he had his bed next to Moses' bed as a kid. Snug in his child-sized bed with two fluffed pillows, sheets, blankets, and a Spider-man comforter, how he wished to go back and experience the warmth and safety from his childhood. A baby's cry echoed throughout the shelter. Isaac looked up to see if the child was okay. A woman wrapped with a veil over her head and face catered to the nettled infant. She reached into her bag and fed the child a bottle. Isaac placed his head back on his pillow as he frowned. His pillow felt like a rock. He had to endure the amenities that the shelter provided. "How are you?" an unfamiliar voice spoke to Isaac. He lifted his head from the cot and squinted his eyes. A strange-looking gentleman about his age, wearing dingy clothes, was over-friendly. "I'm Jason. How are you? What a crazy night this is. Right? Tomorrow will be a better day. Hey, what's your name? Wait, don't tell me? Let me Guess. John? Steve? Patrick? Mike? "Jason yapped. Isaac couldn't get a word in edgewise due to his constant talking. There was a profound alcohol smell on his breath.

"I'm Isaac," Isaac said, trying to hold his breath.

"Isaac, what a cool name. That's biblical, you know," Jason took a sip of his liquor bottle stashed under his pillow.

"Do you know the story of Isaac?" Jason belched.

"Sort of," Isaac turned his nose up and turned his back on Jason. It didn't bother Jason that Isaac gave him his back. He kept on talking and talking and talking. Isaac tried his best to go to sleep, but Jason's mouth was like a motor. Isaac couldn't help but hear word for word what this guy Jason recited. "In the beginning was the Word, and the Word was with God, and the Word was God, John Chapter One, Verse One." Drunk Jason kept reciting more verses from the good book and in order. *"How could someone know the Bible so well and become wasted?"* Isaac stopped with the question in his mind and went on to sleep. He still heard Jason reciting the Bible. Isaac didn't know the good book very well, but this guy sure did. Isaac believed every word Jason quoted.

Hours and hours went by as the homeless shelter became vacant. The clock on the wall read 7:34 a.m. Then a loud-mouthed director of the housing cried out to Isaac. She clapped her hands to awaken him from his sleep. Isaac raised his body from the mattress slowly and yawned. Rubbing his eyes, he saw Jason's empty bed. Isaac put his glasses on and reached down under his cot and didn't feel his sneakers there. He got down to the floor and realized they were gone. Isaac's heart pounded severely in the chest. He knew Jason had taken his kicks.

"Let's go, young man! Let's go," the homeless shelter director hollered, clapping her hands loudly, echoing throughout the atmosphere.

"My sneakers are gone! My sneakers are gone!" Isaac panicked. He searched under every cot fearfully. "I'm sorry, young man. You should have kept your sneakers on! A lot of people get their things stolen! I'm sorry, but you've got to go!"

Isaac rose to his feet, only wearing his socks. He strolled around and lowered his head. He desperately tried to see if he could find his footwear. His eyes became watery. He had no other choice but to enter the world with nothing on his feet.

That same morning, Moses woke up and stretched for the heavens as he yawned. Moses sat on the edge of the bed with no shirt and only wearing his boxers. He and Shawnette had a good night. Moses' sexual experiences have been good, but not like this. Maybe, that night of passion was more than sex. He cared for Shawnette and wanted to go steady. Most guys would've just looked at this type of night as a *wham-bam- thank you, Ma'am.* Moses' feelings got mushy on Shawnette. She was the kind of girl you took home to Mama. He could tell that she wanted more between them. Shawnette slept in bed with covers concealing all crucial parts, looking radiant in the break of dawn. On this new day, things were looking up for Moses. He had to pay the tuition for the real estate course. He looked forward to taking more business classes on campus, internships, and being in a steady relationship. Later, Moses strode on the school grounds with Shawnette by his side. He held his backpack strap on his shoulder while wearing his brand-name construction boots. With every step Moses took, anyone could tell he knew what he wanted. He knew which path to take toward his future.

CHAPTER EIGHTEEN

On Christmas Eve, Enya's "We Wish You a Merry Christmas" bellowed from Bose radio as it sat on a living room side table in the Remington-Mitchell home. A seven-and-a-half-foot flocked Christmas tree with bright lights glistening with red and gold ornaments stood in the corner. Holiday décor adorned the entire living room and into the dining room.

Irene loved to decorate when it came to the holidays, especially Christmas. Despite losing her son Isaac in the cold, brutal world, she kept her holiday spirit. Irene sat in the lounge chair, facing the bay window with Isaac's graduation photo in her lap and her cell phone in her hand. She needed to seek help from the authorities regarding her son's whereabouts. Moses sat in the middle of the couch with his head down and hands clasped together, praying. His Uncle Tyler and Aunt Melisaa embraced him. All sorts of crazy things ran through Moses' head on where Isaac could be or what Isaac could be doing. Calvin paced the floor, acting as if he cared.

Moses then regressed to that little kid again, where he knew how his stepfather operated. "He didn't care about Isaac; he always wanted Isaac out of this family. Calvin was the stranger who infiltrated their happy home. *"Why was Mom so weak? I know she missed our father, but we could have managed,"* Moses stared at his mother. She rose from her seat as flashing red and blue lights reflected on the glass window. He hurried to the front door, beating his stepfather to it. Moses swung it open as four officers made their way into their home. They took off their hats as a matter of respect. It seemed as if Moses and his family would receive some bad news. Irene looked at the officers teary-eyed, hoping for something positive.

Within minutes of engaging with officers about his brother, Irene proceeded to bawl every time a cop had doubts about his disappearance. This Irish-American officer was dubious whenever Irene mentioned that something terrible happened to her son. "Isaac probably got in the car with someone stranger who promised him a place to stay, or maybe he went to the club, seduced by a green-eyed beauty. No, Isaac loves Clarissa too much to fall into the arms of another female," Moses quoted. Officers could tell in Isaac's pictures that he was albino. Therefore, he could be easy to locate. Another thing, Isaac had turned eighteen years of age, so why didn't the family report Isaac missing months earlier? At this point, the officers didn't know what to do or where to look. Tyler blamed Calvin for breaking his nephew's bond. Calvin had moved into a home that his brother Jacob purchased and was a freeloader. Tyler lunged at Calvin as the officers broke up the scuffle. Irene couldn't take it anymore, dashing upstairs in tears. Moses knew he had to be there for his mother, but right now, he had to pull his uncle off his stepfather before they both landed in jail. He then rushed to the second floor and approached his mother's bedroom door. He knocked and knocked.

"Go away," Irene sobbed.

"Mom, it's me," Moses informed her. From inside, Irene got quiet. Still, she didn't bother to open the door. Downstairs, Tyler, and Calvin exchanged words over the ruling of the house and Moses and Isaac's well-being. Moses ignored the two gentlemen from the lower level, tapping on the bedroom door with his fist.

"Mom, open up," Moses suggested.

"Go away, Moses. I don't want to talk," Irene cried.

"I'm not leaving until you come out," Moses slid his back against the wall until he landed on his rear end on the floor.

"This is all my fault," Irene blamed herself out loud from inside her bedroom.

"It's not your fault," Moses convinced her.

"Who's is it, then?"

"It's mine," Moses stood to his feet and stood directly in front of the bedroom door. The master bedroom door opened slowly as the hinges squealed. Moses glared at his mother with watery eyes and sobbed. Irene embraced the only son she had left. Then both mother and son cried, feeling the same guilt.

An officer slowly went upstairs and witnessed the mother and son moment. Moses had to act quickly to bring his brother home safely.

Along the streets of Manhattan, three musicians played "Have Yourself a Merry Little Christmas" on violins. Heartfelt New Yorkers dropped some change into the donation bin. On this overcrowded sidewalk, holiday shoppers rushed in and out of stores purchasing gifts for their loved ones regardless of the frigid temperatures. The nineteen-degree air had an icy feel, which caused people to catch a cold, or, worse, the flu. Isaac shivered on the corner with his hand out needing spare change. His glasses became foggy.

"Please, Ma'am. Can you help me? I've got nowhere to go," Isaac pleaded to a pretty, twenty-something young woman rushing to her destination. She noticed Isaac's frosted glasses, only wearing socks and no coat. He snatched his glasses off, wiping his lens with his finger. He placed them back over his eyes. She smiled and gave him a dollar.

"Thank you, Ma'am," Isaac nodded and smiled. He shivered and shivered, but he felt good that he left a good impression on the woman who gave him a dollar. He wondered if he could do anything else to impress someone. Some homeless become street performers to survive on these rough streets. But Isaac couldn't do anything but hope to God that something would come through. Then a businessman/entrepreneur saw Isaac and that he had no shoes or a winter coat. He knew Isaac probably had a cold and was hungry. He approached Isaac with a mostly angelic smile and handed him twenty dollars.

"Hello, young man. How are you?" the businessman asked.

"Fine. Oh, thanks," Isaac cringed. He didn't know how to take this guy or what he might want in return. The three-piece suit-clad gentleman looked down at Isaac's feet and saw that his socks were filthy. "What happened to your shoes?"

"Someone stole them," Isaac's teeth chattered.

"What size shoe do you wear?" the businessman continued to eye Isaac from head to toe.

"An eight and a half," Isaac replied with a grimace.

"What size are you in a coat?" the good Samaritan asked again.

Isaac frowned and couldn't believe the question the stranger asked him.

"A medium," Isaac continued to shiver.

"Don't move," the businessman hurried away. Isaac sneered at this stranger who demanded that he remain on the corner. He sucked his teeth at this rudeness as his feet felt like ice. Isaac was not able to feel his feet or hands. Within seconds, the businessman rushed towards Isaac. "Here you go. Put the coat and boots on," the good Samaritan insisted.

Without any hesitation, Isaac opened the box and saw the brand-new pair of winter boots, along with a pair of socks. His eyes were ready to jump out of their sockets. He immediately snatched off the old filthy socks and slipped on the fresh ones and then his boots. Then, he finally slipped on the winter coat. Isaac felt his body heating up. Isaac and the good Samaritan embraced, shaking hands. Despite the freezing weather, pedestrians captured the act of kindness on cellphone video. Dozens and dozens of people caught the video of Isaac. Isaac didn't want to be seen, for it was humiliating to have viewers see his ugly face on social media. Isaac knew he had to hide from these cameras of everyday people. It was as if he were a movie star and had to flee from the paparazzi. Isaac shoved the shoebox in the plastic bag and hustled away. He didn't even say thank you; the strangers taking videos scared him. The businessman smiled as the people videotaping asked him a couple of questions.

"Do you do this for people you see in need?" asked a female cellphone owner.

"Not really. You know, it's the holidays, and you've got millions of people in need. It was a gift to him," the businessman shrugged his shoulders.

"He didn't even say thank you," a male cellphone owner continued videotaping him.

"It's all right. Homeless people are on the streets alone with nowhere to turn, so that's fine. I did a good thing. Happy holidays everyone," the businessman waltzed down the street.

Isaac rushed down into the subway. He noticed the platform was half full of straphangers. Isaac kept his eyes on the ground and hoped no one followed him. He was going to get something to eat with the twenty bucks. He didn't know where to sleep tonight because someone would steal his coat and boots.

"I've got to keep warm. I've got to keep warm. I must find a safe place to sleep, so I don't have to worry about a fake preacher taking my property," Isaac murmured. He took a seat on the wooden bench for three people. An older man sat in the middle seat, but as soon as Isaac sat down, he got up immediately. No one wanted to be next to him. Evidently, Isaac scared some people off by being homeless, but it was due to his condition.

"My look scares the hell out of people. I don't mean any harm. I'm on these dangerous streets alone. I've got no one to protect me," Isaac whimpered to the people on the platform. They looked at him sneering, rolling their eyes, and turning away. The train pulled into the station with its screeching brakes. The automated double doors opened as they got on. Everyone went about their business. "You're not alone, young man. You've got God to protect you," said another so-called Jesus freak who might attempt to steal his clothes. A sixty-year-old gentleman approached him with matted hair, a beard, a mustache, wearing filthy clothes, and down on his luck. Isaac saw this guy was in the same boat.

"Hey, there, young fella. I'm an okay guy. I've experienced a lot of crazy shit out here. You must always keep your eyes open. I'm Bob," He offered to shake Isaac's hand.

"Isaac," Isaac answered cautiously, a bit standoffish.

"You're on the streets like me?" Bob noticed Isaac didn't trust anyone.

"You don't have to answer that. My journey started on these streets twenty-eight years ago. I lost my house on Long Island and a lucrative restaurant. It wasn't so. Restaurant business is tough," Bob exhaled, shaking his head in disgust.

"I'm from Valley Stream," Isaac added with a slight smile.

"I'm from Smithtown," Bob extended his hand to Isaac. Isaac then gave in because he was meeting another Long Islander. *He wondered where Bob slept. How did he keep warm at night? "Why didn't Bob get another job? Or get an apartment? I really should be asking that question. Maybe, he couldn't take it anymore and gave up on the world, just like me. Should I ask him where he rests his head? He might get offended or think something crazy?"*

"Where do you spend your nights?" Bob took the words right out of Isaac's mouth.

"Over in a home shelter on Prince Street."

"I don't trust shelters. You can get killed in those places," Bob sighed.

"Where do you stay?" Isaac asked hesitantly.

Bob detailed his mole-like living conditions. Isaac couldn't believe what Bob had told him. When Isaac and Moses were kids, they watched a documentary about the homeless living underneath the New York subway system. Isaac faced the harsh reality that he would be one of them. It was the best protection from the cruel outside world. Caution: You still must keep your eyes open regarding other poor souls like yourself. Isaac knew all about trusting. He wasn't sure if he should live amongst other misfortunate beings or remain on that platform. Isaac envisioned the tunnels as extremely dark. A person could freak out. You didn't know if a deranged person would slit your throat while you slept. Also, by Bob talking about the dark haven below, Isaac never forgot the nightmare he had as a child. Recalling that weird dream gave Isaac the notion that another homeless person might attack him. "It's up to you, Isaac. You either stay on this platform at your own risk or be safe below," Bob gave him a choice. Isaac cringed in his seat and had to think fast. He needed to be safe before night arrived. God was the only one who could guide Isaac to make the right choice.

"I've got something for you to eat," Bob opened the crumbled paper bag and pulled out a cup of chicken soup, handing it to Isaac with a plastic spoon. Isaac's eyes popped out of his head because he usually rummaged through dumpsters in back allies of restaurants. And of course, so did Bob because he said he was in the restaurant business.

"Thanks," Isaac dipped the spoon in the soup, sipping it. Bob also sipped his soup. The two gentlemen didn't even notice the passengers on the platform. Since people saw them as invisible, they saw people as invisible too. As Bob shoved the noodles into his mouth, he noticed a group of boisterous teens entering the platform end, swaggering towards them. The rowdy bunch looked in their direction. Bob's hands trembled as he turned to Isaac, who pigged out on his hot beverage. "Isaac, do you want to live or die? Your choice!" Bob's face quivered. He rushed from his seat, dropping his soup on the platform.

"Are you coming, Isaac!" Bob ran for dear life.

Isaac noticed the teens running towards him, so he also dropped his soup. His heart pumped in his chest and trembled. He ran as fast as he could, trying to catch up to Bob. Bob reached the end of the platform and ran down the small set of yellow steps. Isaac halted at the end of the platform, where the small steps ended. He didn't know what to do. Isaac looked over his shoulder as the teens got closer. The set of yellow set leads to the train tracks. *"Holy shit! I could be killed by a train! Or be killed by these crazed teens!"* Isaac then raced down the small steps to the tracks. "Bob, where are you? Where are you!" Isaac's voice echoed throughout the tunnel.

"I can't see a thing! Bob, where are you!" Isaac's voice echoed. He kept running on the train tracks. He hoped to be on Bob's trail. He had to focus on getting somewhere safe to stay. Isaac stopped, continuing to pant, and put his hand in front of his face. "I can't see a fuckin' thing! I can't see a fuckin' thing!" Isaac's voice bellowed through the tunnels. Then a beam of light flashed in his face as he saw Bob directly in his face. "Keep running, keep running, keep running!" Bob advised. "Holy shit! You scared me!" Isaac's face trembled. He fixed his glasses correctly on his face. The two gentlemen looked over their shoulders and saw that the teens had a lot of guts to come down on the tracks. "Keep running, keep running! Keep your pace! Remember, you see that third rail there?" Bob echoed. He shined the flashlight on the third rail.

"Yeah!" Isaac tried to keep his glasses on his face while running out of breath.

"Don't touch it because you'll get electrocuted," Bob panted. Then Isaac looked back, noticing the train pulling into the station on the other side. It stopped picking up passengers.

"I think we better move a bit faster!" Isaac held his spectacles tight to his face.

Bob glanced over his shoulder and saw the train sitting in the station.

"Much faster, that is," Bob hollered. The two men ran as fast as they could. The train pulled out of the station, chugging along the tracks. When Bob made it to his cut-off on the side of the tracks, Isaac was right behind him.

"Be careful of the third railing!" Bob warned again.

A condemned area with a "DO NOT ENTER" tape was streamed over the deteriorating wall. Bob removed a piece of concrete and squeezed his body through it. Isaac wasn't sure about entering this dangerous area, but he followed suit. He wedged his body through the medium-sized hole and reached the other side. Then Bob placed the piece of concrete back in place. Bob led Isaac into this murky deserted section of the station. The smell of this abandoned part of the station had the usual subway odor, but as the two men made their way further, it smelt like urine and feces. Isaac couldn't see a thing and hoped he didn't step into anything disgusting. They descended an iron staircase with a bright bulb screwed into the wall socket. Isaac kept his glasses pressed close to his eyes with blurriness and clearness. His vision confused him, but Isaac still made his way down a second staircase as another light bulb shined from the wall socket. At that point, it got even murkier. Bob and Isaac proceeded down the third flight of steps, where a homeless woman slept in the corner. Isaac's jaw dropped at the deplorable conditions she faced. A half-eaten sandwich, rotten apple, and day-old soup piled in the corner. Isaac held his nose due to the potent fecal odor. He kept his head up because he didn't want to see any waste. On the fourth staircase, a mother and her infant were wrapped in a dingy pink blanket, huddled in the corner with a dimmed light bulb above their heads. Old, soured formula baby bottles, wasted diapers, and soiled baby wipes were piled up in a corner adjacent to them. A couple of steps away, the woman had a few cans of baby formula, boxed crackers, half-empty milk in a container, and a cup of noodles stacked close to them. *"Holy shit! Why is she down here with a baby?"* Isaac didn't want to ask Bob because it was none of his business. The people down there would ask Isaac his story. They headed down a fifth staircase, lit by another dimmed light bulb.

"Okay, watch your step, Isaac," Bob warned as he walked three short steps. He occupied a small space the size of a jail cell. The MTA construction used to section it off for office space. Bob grabbed a bottle of soda from the corner, where he stashed his food. Bob slept in an old sleeping bag, with an empty bag right across from him. "Isaac, make yourself at home."

Isaac stepped into the candle-lit area. Photos of Bob's family were plastered on his side. He didn't want to ask him anything about his life on Long

Island. Bob poured some soda into a cup, gave it to Isaac, and then poured some for himself.

"Here's to making new friends. Joy to the world and Merry Christmas," Bob toasted. Isaac couldn't help but accept this new life.

"Merry Christmas," Isaac bumped their foam cups together and drank the soda.

CHAPTER NINETEEN

Real estate guru Mike Eves stormed into a packed New York hotel ballroom, with excited, applauding students ready to hear his success story and the home market. The realtor expert pinned the microphone to his light blue dress shirt, greeting the massive crowd of primarily Caucasian students just like himself. Mr. Eves started investing in real estate in the late eighties and made his millions two years later. He put his funds into luxury homes for the rich and famous living in New York and Miami. As Mr. Eves relayed his success story, he spoke about his financial freedom. He could do whatever he wanted, spend quality time with loved ones, and travel. But there was a catch; a person had to put in ten hours daily to achieve this type of freedom. Moses was interested in luxury real estate and was curious about getting investors into his company. If possible. He felt embarrassed asking this tycoon about investors or any questions at all. Moses further noticed there wasn't another person that looked like him. He didn't even bother to debate the reason why. He wouldn't fit in being the only African American, plus these people were from an older generation. Then Mr. Eves spoke about flipping houses, either on-market properties or off-market properties. Moses had to strategize and make a way out of no way. Mr. Eves also discussed rental properties, where someone is the landlord, especially with section eight homes.

From that point on, Moses attended every seminar and studied from the expensive real estate textbook. Between college studies and this real estate course, Moses felt the pressure. He paced the floor of his bedroom in the middle of the night. Fortunately, he had a small apartment off campus, so he had the freedom to do whatever he wanted - like having Shawnette stay with him. Spending time with her was an oasis when he had to escape the books.

During this time, Moses had doubts about his goals that seemed impossible. Shawnette encouraged him to stick with it, and you never know in life. With Moses taking this course, Shawnette, too, thought about getting her real estate license. That made him smile because he wanted his woman to be in the same field. "Maybe, this would be the right time to introduce Shawnette to my mother," Moses clutched her hand, pulling her body close and giving her a passionate kiss. He had already met Shawnette's kin, which consisted of her father and five male siblings. They seemed fond of Moses and his persona, his going to school, and his aspirations.

Shawnette's mother died of cancer when she was eleven years old. This young lady was raised in a house of men. Her brothers watched guys like a hawk regarding their little sister. Shawnette carefully chose guys wisely and was taught not to wear her heart on her sleeve. But from the moment she and Moses met in economics class, they were destined to be an item.

About a week later, Moses inserted his key into the keyhole of the front door of his childhood home. Shawnette stepped in first with her beautiful smile that lit up any home. The cozy living room made anyone comfortable who entered. R&B music played from the Bose radio where peace settled in the atmosphere.

"Mom," Moses' voice echoed throughout the house. Irene peered out from the kitchen while drying a dish. She noticed the young lady who accompanied her son.

"Hello," Still drying the plate, Irene smiled cautiously. Moses turned the volume down on the radio.

"Mom, this is Shawnette. Shawnette, this is my mother," Moses introduced proudly. He was proud of the woman who had brought him into the world and the one who would spend the rest of his life with him.

The two women shook hands and got acquainted. Irene returned to the kitchen as Shawnette and Moses followed through the swinging door. His mother offered Shawnette a glass of soda with a napkin. "Oh, thank you, Mrs. Remington," Shawnette sat at the kitchen table. Moses kissed his mother on the cheek, bitching about his studies and the real estate course he was taking. Irene encouraged Moses to win and not let anyone discourage him from anything. Shawnette, listening to his mother's endearing words, nodded in agreement.

Minutes later, Shawnette browsed around Moses' bedroom, where she noticed his desktop computer, shelves of books from high school, and personal reads. There was a full-sized bed with a blue comforter and a small blue rug. His mirrored dresser on the other side with his colognes, two framed photos of him and Isaac on their fourth birthday, and a graduation photo, which neither of them smiled. Noticing the disgruntled picture of the twins, Shawnette raised an eyebrow.

"Who is he?" Shawnette held the five-by-seven framed photograph in her hand.

"That's my brother, Isaac," Moses smirked and didn't say anything else about Isaac. He hoped she wouldn't hound him with questions about his brother. Moses certainly knew she noticed Isaac's abnormal condition. She gently placed the photo back on the dresser and didn't ask anything. She turned to Moses, smiling. The lovebirds engaged in a passionate kiss on his bed. He slapped her on the rear end several times, playing around like lovers do. Then Moses felt a presence in the doorway of his bedroom. Calvin stood at the door, noticing his son with this new young lady. Moses and Shawnette subsided their goofing around, showing respect as they stood to their feet.

"What's up, Dad?" Moses and Calvin embraced.

"How's school?" Calvin eyed his stepson's love interest and how pretty she was. And then he scanned her girly figure shaped like an hourglass.

"Dad, this is Shawnette. Shawnette, this is my stepfather," Moses introduced them. Shawnette and Calvin shook hands. Calvin held a tight grip on her hand. Shawnette lifted an eyebrow, not knowing what to think. Was this on purpose, or was it nothing? She snatched her hand from his grip, turning away. Moses and Calvin engaged in some small talk. Shawnette proceeded to browse Moses' bedroom.

"Nice meeting you, Shawnette," Calvin said, exiting and keeping his eyes fixed on her like a predator stalking its prey. Moses snuck up behind his girlfriend and kissed her.

"What's wrong, babe?" Moses could see the frown on her face.

"Nothing," Shawnette played it off.

Moses and Shawnette kissed again as Moses' bedroom door cracked open with a pair of eyes on the other side. Shawnette sensed someone was watching her and Moses but brushed it off.

Later that evening, the screeching wheels of Moses' Dodge Challenger took off in a flash as Irene and Calvin waved to their son and his girlfriend. Irene had the biggest smile, whereas Calvin only smiled a little. He gaped at this new hot thing that he'd love to know better.

"Shawnette's so beautiful," Irene said, entering the home, and inhaling. Calvin didn't utter a word, scowling. He took his time going up the concrete steps of their residence and slammed the front door. Then a loud smack and thud as Irene screamed from inside.

"Calvin, why! Please don't hurt me!" Irene pleaded.

"Shut up! That spoiled ass son of yours!" Calvin hollered.

Back at Moses' apartment, a desk lamp brightened the desk while Moses studied from his real estate textbook. Shawnette slept in his bed, facing the wall. As he read more and more about properties, he looked them up online and checked out the addresses. He wasn't optimistic about what the instructor had taught in the course. He was dubious about his future. But all Moses had to do was pass the exam, get his license, and find out. "I hope this isn't a con game," Moses murmured while looking up more of the online properties.

Eight weeks later, Moses got his New York state real estate license. He shared the news with his mother at his childhood home. A pot roast cooked in the slow cooker and rice and beans with broccoli on the stove. He wanted to share the information with his stepfather, but Calvin had to work overtime. Minutes later, Moses and his mother ate dinner at the kitchen table. He devoured his rice and beans and everything else on his plate. Irene smiled at her firstborn, placing her hand over her face. Moses gawked at his mother, chewing his food. He then squinted his eyes, noticing her discolored cheek. He grabbed Irene's wrist away from her face.

"What happened to your face, Mom?" Moses sneered.

"I bought some facial cream, and it broke me out. I've got to get to a dermatologist," Irene laughed it off and placed her hand over the bruise. Moses continued to eat his meal but slowed down. Seeing that red and purple mark on his mother's cheek made him lose his appetite. Moses wanted to be frank about the situation but kept his mouth shut. He recalled when he heard Calvin call his mother out of her name. As soon as this man entered the room, Moses strangled him when he was a kid. *"Do I have to put this man in the headlock for trying to hurt my mother again?"* Moses threw his fork down on the plate and lost his appetite. He leaned back in his chair, frowning, and balled the napkin in his fist. Irene noticed her son's complexion turning fiery red. She knew her son had a feeling that something wasn't right. This was his mother, but what could Moses do but hope that nothing happened to her?

Later, Moses drove in his Challenger with a blank expression. He worried about his mother's situation. *"Why the hell doesn't she tell me anything? She's covering for him as usual. Most women do this when they're supposedly in love,"* Moses thought and focused on getting his college degree and figuring out what he was going to do about his real estate endeavors. So, he drove and drove, not knowing where he was headed. He wound up on the borderline of Queens and Long Island, which was the beautiful upscale community of Douglaston. The neighborhood resembled Beverly Hills but there were no palm trees and hot weather all year around. The lavish properties he saw made his eyes widen like a kid in a candy store. He smiled at an enormous three-stored light blue colored mansion with trimmed hedges, manicured lawns, beautiful windows, and a giant fence surrounding the property. Moses loved seeing these homes because it was therapy for him. His mother's dilemma was in the back of his mind. Then Moses' Dodge Challenger brakes screeched as he stopped at an alluring white/grayish mansion about two stories high. And of course, the home had a surrounding iron fence. Every window of this house was lit as the residents inside enjoyed their American reality. All Moses had was the American dream. *"Wow, this is amazing. All this beauty is right before my eyes, and I've got to make it my business to sell these beautiful homes. Let me see what other homes I can find,"* Moses swerved the steering wheel of his Challenger through more of the neighborhood. Again, he slowly drove past an English Manor with enormous cut lawns and beautiful trees adjacent to the property. On the lawn was a sign that read: Barbara Levi realtor investor. He took a picture of the sign with his cell phone. He drove away, holding his cell phone in his hand. Moses put back his cell in its holder on his dashboard before he got pulled over by authorities. As Moses drove through the upper-class community, he typed in Mrs. Barbara Levi's information on Google. A beautiful photo of Mrs. Levi popped up on his screen with a written history of her success. Moses had to find somewhere to park, so he could find out more information on this amazing woman.

Within minutes, Moses parked his fast car in the parking space of a fast-food restaurant. There was the aroma of burgers and fries. He debated on getting something to eat, but his mother had already cooked for him. Moses proceeded to read the article on Barbara Levi and how she's been an investor in real estate for over thirty years along with her husband, Gary who passed away a few years earlier. On her own, Barbara mastered networking with other big investors to achieve her dreams, continuing her husband's legacy. She has a son, Gary Levi Jr. who also works in the field. *"Very impressive. I need to work with someone who has connections and who could help me. Should I call Mrs. Levi or not? She might not even talk to me,"* Moses was about to dial the phone number. He started to dial Mrs. Levi's cell number but halted in the middle of the last four digits. He was curious if she would do business with an eighteen-year-old kid. Then Moses took a deep breath and punched in the final two numbers of her number. There was a ring, then one more ring as a feminine voice introduced herself and greeted him on the other end of the call. Moses's heart raced in his chest, clearing his throat, and introducing himself. He rambled over his cell phone about this English manor property that he hoped to sell.

A week later, Moses swaggered through a glass door of New York Realty Investments, a company that developed, bought, and sold properties in the New York Tri-state area. He figured he would give this a shot and he had to pretend that he knew what he was doing. Moses approached the receptionist's desk, greeting her with a smile. He gave Mrs. Barbara Levi's name and that she was expecting him. The receptionist picked up the phone, alerting her boss of Moses's arrival. And within seconds, a short, blond-tress woman dressed in a pink dress, resembling, Barbie marched in. She looked around seeing that Moses was the only one in the waiting room. For a second, she hesitated to even approach him because he was so young.

"Moses Remington? Hi, I'm Barbara Levi. How are you today?" the beautiful woman short in stature gave Moses a firm handshake. Moses stood up with his six-foot, one-inch stature. Barbara took a step back to get a good look at Moses.

"I'm good. And You?" Moses shook her hand.

"Wow, you're a tall young man. Do you play basketball?" Barbara smiled.

"No, that's not my thing," Moses smiled, grinding his teeth. He hated stereotyping.

"Step into my office," she escorted Moses towards her large office.

In a matter of no time, Barbara shook her head at the fact of Moses working for her at his young age. He had no experience in real estate even though he had his license. If something went wrong, Barbara could lose her license. And Moses hadn't even finished college yet. Barbara held his real estate license in her hand while residing behind her dark cherry wood desk. She glared at Moses sitting erect in a leather chair before her.

"You're a handsome young man," she complimented. Moses stuck his chest out, feeling optimistic. "But, no!" Barbara gave him back his real estate license abruptly.

"Mrs. Levi, I've got to start somewhere! Right?" Moses rose from his seat, pacing in front of her desk.

"Yes, that's true. But you're a huge risk!" Barbara glared at him. Moses stopped in his pacing and knew the exact reason. But he attempted to bargain with this affluent woman of means. He even gave Barbara his social security number, so that she could do a background check on him. "I've never been to jail!"

"You're still in school Moses? How would you maintain your hours between classes and working in this field? Working for me, that is," Barbara stood from her seat.

"I will! I'll make that English Manor livable," Moses held a tight fist to let her know that he would get the job done. *"God please make this possible,"* Moses prayed in his heart.

Barbara knew this kid didn't have experience in selling properties, so she wanted Gary to do a joint tour of this Open House to test Moses' determination. She had to test him. She's never given opportunities to people with little or no experience. She always worked with people who were qualified in the business. As soon as Moses exited Barbara's office, she dialed her son's number on her cellphone.

"What's up, Mom?" Barbara's son greeted his mother.

"Hello, Gary. I need your assistance in an Open House," Barbara sat on the edge of her desk.

On a cloudy afternoon, an open house sign sat on the lawn of the English Manor a week later in Douglaston. Moses wore black trousers, a white dress shirt, a tie, and shoes. He shook the hands of the Kelly's, a young married couple in their mid-twenties with their six-month-old baby girl. He escorted the new family to the front of the home, rambling about their adorable baby. Moses inserted the key in the lock and pushed the heavy wooden door open. They stepped into the living room with its high ceilings and fireplace. Moses escorted them into the dining room with an enormous chandelier and the spacious kitchen. Mr. Kelly and his wife browsed around the island that resided in the middle. Mrs. Kelly held her baby girl on her hip while caressing the marble counter with her finger. The couple was impressed with what they saw. Moses stood at a distance, allowing the couple to figure it out. He wondered about what Mr. Kelly did for a living? All he knew this man was going to give his baby girl the best life ever. And Moses would hopefully make his first sale. Mr. and Mrs. Kelly kept browsing around.

"There's more," Moses smiled.

Minutes later, a brightly lit large bedroom, with yellow blanketed walls, and baby animal wall decor gave that nursery ambiance. Moses widened the white door, allowing the mother to enter, where her daughter would possibly spend her days and nights sleeping and playing. Mrs. Kelly's eyes popped out of her head, falling in love with the room that her daughter would occupy. Mr. Kelly, impressed by the home so far, strolled into the baby's room which would be his daughter's. He strutted to his wife's side checking out the spacious bedroom. Then he saw the private bathroom. He clicked on the light and saw the toilet, tub, and sink with child décor on the tile. Then the mother browsed around as well. Moses folded his arms giving the family time to get a feel for the home.

Seconds later, then Mrs. Kelly had her eyes fixed on the ceiling because of the light fixture. Her baby girl began to whine. "Ok, Melinda. It's time to eat," Mrs. Kelly rocked her baby.

"Do you like the house so far, honey," Mr. Kelly kissed his baby girl.

"Yes," Mrs. Kelly nodded as the baby became more irritable. She exited the master bedroom.

Moses' cardiac muscle raced in his rib cage and his hands became sweaty. He switched his black folder from one hand to the other with the company's name. NEW YORK REALTY INVESTMENTS in gold lettering and a symbol of a luxurious home.

Mr. Kelly shook Moses's hand feeling confident about the purchase of his first home. He wanted to ask Moses his age, but he let it go because he didn't want to offend him. If anything went wrong all he had to do was call his boss. Then there was a knock on the door, Gary Levi, Barbara's son swaggered to Moses shaking his hand. Gary introduced himself, out of breath because he got caught in traffic. *"What is he doing here? Oh, I forgot. I can't be trusted. That's the way the cookie crumbles,"* the negative thoughts crossed Moses' mind. Moses shook Gary's hand. Gary then shook Mr. Kelly's hand. Moses wanted to continue with the tour of the English Manor to Mr. Kelly while his wife attended to their baby. Moses hoped his new boss' son didn't intervene in the deal. This was a deal that Moses wanted to have a say in. But Gary had to make sure the deal went smoothly. He took a few steps back, nodding to Moses to proceed with the tour of the home. Moses and Mr. Kelly strolled further into the master suite where they entered a stone patio.

Two days later, Irene washed the dishes in the kitchen sink. Again, the aroma of roast chicken, potatoes, and mixed veggies cooked in the oven this early evening. R&B music played on the radio. Moses strolled in with a mesmerized expression on his face. "Hey, Mom," he greeted his mother. He showed the check to his mother. Irene gasped that her son sold his first house. She kissed her son. "I'm so proud! My son's a real estate tycoon." Moses noticed his mother's cheek was back to its normal tone, and Calvin wasn't home again. He wondered if his stepfather had another woman. Irene fixed her son a plate as Moses sat at the kitchen ready for dinner.

The following week, Moses inserted the key into the lock of a fancy-looking apartment door in the hallway in Forest Hills, Queens. Moses stepped into the enlarged wooden space of the living room, adjacent to a dining room and kitchen. The sunlight brightened the atmosphere with its large windows. Moses swaggered to the middle of the living room giving a tour to a bachelor, in his mid-thirties, who relocated from the West Coast. Moses marched to the double doors in the living room that opened to a brick balcony. The eligible bachelor followed Moses on the patio with two chairs. He sat down and immediately decided.

"I'll take it," the bachelor stared off into space.

Moses raised an eyebrow because this bachelor didn't see the rest of the apartment. He shrugged his shoulders, pulled out the paperwork, and got down to business.

Two weeks later, Moses gave another Open House tour to a couple with three rowdy kids who were busy playing while their parents focused on their new home. The two-story brick home sat on grass and trees surrounded the property. The established family marched into the living room as the kids dashed to the second floor. Moses had to chase after these kids that weren't even his. "Hey! You kids want a tour!" he shouted.

"Yes!", the kids shouted as they stomped to the different bedrooms on the second floor.

The parents had to give themselves a tour of the first floor. From this property on, Moses continued to sell homes to buyers. And Gary Levi trusted him with the Open Houses.

In Barbara Levi's fancy office, a week later, she resided at her desk writing Moses a check for selling that brick home. Moses fidgeted in his chair, biting his nail. She peered at him and tilted her head.

"What's wrong Moses?" she asked. Barbara continued to cut the check.

"Nothing," Moses shrugged his shoulders. *"I want to ask Barbara about starting my own firm. That could wait until later. Hopefully after graduation. It's best that I get my feet wet some more."* His boss then ripped the paper check from her checkbook and handed him his salary.

"Here you go, Moses! Good work!" Barbara smiled.

Moses smiled from ear to ear due to the amount of his pay. *"Wow! All this pays for a home. I've got to keep up the good work. But I'm getting tired because of this and school. Do I drop out of school and continue in real estate? I've got my license. I might as well. Let me just stick it out,"* Moses thought in his mind. He yawned.

"Are you getting enough sleep, Moses? "Barbara wondered.

"I've been-," he yawned again. Then Barbara's phone rang, which interrupted Moses.

"Hello, Barbara Levi. How may I help you?" Barbara answered her call, putting it on speaker.

"Mrs. Levi. Is Moses in your office?" the receptionist asked with a muffled tone.

"Yes, he is," Mrs. Levi answered.

Moses slouched in the leather chair right before Mrs. Levi's desk. His eyes became heavy as his boss and receptionist chatted. And then his eyes widened as the receptionist informed Barbara that Moses had a visitor.

"I've got a visitor? Who? Is it from a TV personality? They probably heard about me selling these properties," Moses lifted an eyebrow, smiling from ear to ear.

Barbara then cut off the speaker from her phone. "You have a visit from an old friend,"

"Who?" Moses stood from his chair, gripping the check in his hand.

"Your guess is as good as mine. Don't spend all that in one place," Barbara escorted Moses out of her office.

Seconds later, Moses swaggered through the office of his fellow colleagues, approaching his desk. He noticed a tall, bald young man lounging in a chair. Moses got closer and closer, recognizing this familiar face. "Oh, it's you. What are you doing here?" Moses' eyes shifted from side to side, feeling awkward. He kept his head down, not making eye contact.

"What's up, Moses!" Ryan stood from his chair, embracing his friend.

"What do you want?" he asked Ryan, not even saying his name.

"What do I want? I came to check you out. Your mother told me you made a name for yourself in real estate. We're supposed to start our own firm. Right?" Ryan expressed it loudly. Moses didn't want to cause a scene, so he gestured to Ryan to sit down. Ryan proceeded to blab away. Moses sat in his recliner, rocking back and forth. He tried to figure out how to get Ryan out of his office.

"How have you been Ryan?" Moses rocked in his recliner and swerved side to side.

"I'm just chilling," Ryan chuckled.

"Where have you been? I haven't seen you in a while," Moses stopped swerving in his chair.

"I got into some trouble," Ryan sighed. He eyed Moses' name sign on his desk.

"What kind of trouble?" Moses tilted his head.

"I was in jail for speeding," Ryan shrugged with his head down. He then peered up at Moses. Moses slid his recliner back as a sign of distrust.

"Speeding?" Moses asked.

"Yeah," Ryan nodded his head.

"So, you didn't enroll in college?" Moses questioned his former friend.

"How can I enroll in school if I was in the pen?" Ryan replied with an attitude.

You've got to go! You're a risk! I've worked too hard!" Moses stuttered, waving his arms in the air.

"What! I thought we were going into business together!" Ryan stood from his chair.

"Good luck to you, Ryan," Moses stood up from his recliner, shaking his former best friend's hand.

"What the hell's gotten into you!" Ryan raised his tone.

"Look it was nice knowing you, but the past is the past! And I cannot allow my past into my future," Moses escorted towards the exit.

"I'm not your brother," Ryan said.

"You're right. You are not my brother!" Moses opens the door, gesturing for Ryan to leave.

"Holy shit! You're full of yourself now! Payback is a bitch!" Ryan stormed out of the office. Moses closed the door as Barbara and his colleagues witnessed him and his former best friend's outburst. Moses noticed all eyes were on him, he smiled and played it off.

"I apologize for the commotion everyone," ensured the firm and his boss.

"Are you sure everything's ok?" Barbara placed her hands on her hips.

"It's cool," Moses said.

"Because I was ready to dial 9-1-1!" Barbara added.

"No, no, there's no need to get the boys in blue. That guy won't show his face around here anymore," Moses, Barbara, and the realtors at the firm went back to business as usual.

Three years later, Irene helped Moses with his black Graduation cap and gown in front of a full-length mirror in his bedroom on a Saturday in

June. Moses had earned his bachelor's degree with top honors. Calvin took photos of Irene and Moses with pride and joy. She couldn't help but shed a tear and consistently embraced her son. Marching down the aisle with your classmates was the greatest accomplishment. Then something popped into Moses' head. There would've been two graduations. One for him and the other at Hunter College for Isaac.

"Irene, stand next to your son," Calvin insisted. He was ready to take a picture of Moses and his mother on this special occasion. Moses received his real estate license, earned his degree, and was ready to conquer the world.

Speaking of conquering, that's what Moses did. A month after graduation, he set up a meeting with Barbara and two investors for his real estate company "Remington Realty." He had cards printed and a binder of his business plans for wholesale and short-sale properties, which included homes and apartments. He looked up the information online, which included homes for sale from the owners. Moses was a diligent genius, working long hours, and gathering information on real estate with the help of Shawnette. He got access to several apartments in Forest Hills and two upscale homes. One in Whitestone and the other in Brookville, Long Island.

In a matter of no time, Moses interviewed potential realtors in his Forest Hills office. Some of the candidates had experience in real estate while others were newbies who just got their realtor licenses. He interviewed lots of women, who were pretty. Looks weren't everything, but he had to go with knowledge and smarts. Zahira, a beautiful middle-aged woman, kind of starting over in life just received her license. She wanted to step into a more lucrative career, coming from the medical field. This former nurse spoke about her experiences in the hospital. Moses' eyes widened as she talked about the horrors of sick patients and some who met their demise. He hired Zahira because she came from a horrible and stressful job. And maybe, this would help to put her mind at ease. Then a twenty-something pretty woman smiled from ear to ear at Moses. She was excited to have such a handsome boss. She flirted with him as she touched his hand. Moses quickly pulled his hand away. And immediately made up his mind that this young woman might be trouble. Moses then interviewed Kevin, a gentleman in his late forties with a son and a live-in girlfriend. He had some experience flipping houses and already had his real estate license. So, he was good to go. Seconds later, a sassy young lady, Jocelyn, sat before Moses' desk, wearing tight blue dress pants, and a white ruffled blouse with white shoes. Moses looked over her resume and saw that she worked in a law firm for several years. Jocelyn might have been covered up, not showing any important parts. Her clothes left an imprint on her body which made any man's head turn. Her breasts were right in Moses' face. He kept his eyes focused on her face as she kept talking about her experiences. Surprisingly, Jocelyn held the interview very professionally. Moses shook her hand, welcoming her to the team. For three weeks, Moses interviewed people who were enthused to join his team.

Remington Realty was established a month later as a company party took place. Moses, Barbara, investors, realtors, and other team players were dressed professionally, mingling over appetizers and drinks. Shawnette looked as beautiful as ever while she chatted with Jocelyn. And Jocelyn, of course, was breathtaking wearing a pink fuzzy sweater and black dress pants that complimented her curves. Moses approached Shawnette kissing her on the cheek, complimenting, and acknowledging Jocelyn's presence. He gave her a firm handshake that was strictly professional. Jocelyn took a couple of steps away from Moses and Shawnette allowing the loving couple to chat. She sipped her drink, looking around and greeting colleagues. Jocelyn sensed that someone was watching her. Her eyes shifted from side to side. She set her eyes straight in front of her as Calvin glared at her. Calvin was right by Irene's side, gossiping with Barbara about Moses' life growing up. Calvin glared at Jocelyn so hard it was as if he could see through her. Or imagine her in the nude. From across the crowded room, Calvin eyed her from head to toe. Jocelyn smiled slightly in return, feeling a bit uneasy. Then Moses rubbed her arm as he could tell she seemed nervous.

"Are you all right, Jocelyn?" Moses asked.

"Yes, I'm fine," she responded playing it off.

An hour later, Moses, Barbara, Shawnette, Calvin, Kevin, investors, and other realtors, gathered for a company photo.

"One, two, three!" the photographer said.

"Cheese," everyone said, smiling. Then the photographer snapped the shot.

CHAPTER TWENTY

On this summery afternoon, Central Park had its joggers, bike riders, and dog walkers. Parents pushed strollers while everyday New Yorkers went about their daily routines. People sat on long benches, where the trees kept perfect shade for comfort. Bob and Isaac strolled into the park, looking for anything they could find for survival. Bob walked fast paced as Isaac lagged. He had slowed down his pace. He recalled the time someone demanded his valuables at gunpoint. Isaac wanted to make a bow face and march in the opposite direction, but he didn't. Bob kept scrambling for whatever it was that he wanted to find, whether it be on the ground or in the garbage can. Isaac stood, not moving a muscle. Then Bob noticed how Isaac remained at a distance. Bob frowned and wondered, "What was wrong with Isaac? Did something scare him? Bob rushed towards his friend and placed his hand on his shoulder.

"Are you alright, buddy?" Bob glared at him directly in the eyes.

Isaac shook his head, playing it off. Isaac had to let his terrifying experience roll off his back like water rolling off a duck's feathers. He then followed Bob, as they both searched for plastic bottles and cans. He stayed as close to Bob and continuously looked over his shoulders. Isaac found a two-liter plastic soda bottle; then he found a second and a third. He noticed a man tossing a soda can in the trash bin on the other side where more benches were. Isaac glanced over both shoulders again, rushing to the trash can to grab the aluminum can. Surprisingly, the trash bin had no more wasted bottles and cans. Isaac rummaged through the bin angrily and kicked it.

"What the fuck! People throw bottles and cans away every fuckin' minute!"

"My friend, you must remember we've got some stiff competition. Here, you can have some of my bottle returns," Bob offered his new friend at least eight dollars in recycled cans.

"I can't take that," Isaac refused.

"It's fine. Don't worry; I don't know how much time I'll have left on this earth anyway," Bob shoved the bottle receipts in Isaac's hand. He proceeded to rummage through another trash can for more recyclables. *"Why is he giving me his bottles? He can't be this generous,"* Isaac noticed Bob was on the other side, a few feet away from him. Isaac hustled to his friend's side so that he wouldn't be another target to get mugged. Isaac and Bob maneuvered through a crowded Manhattan sidewalk where people went about their day. Bob taught Isaac about survival in New York as a homeless person. He took every word because Bob had been in this situation for years. Being new to the streets of New York, Isaac stuck by Bob's side like glue. As these two unfortunate souls marched on this well-known pavement, Isaac felt eyes following him. He noticed a chunky, pretty, classy woman in her mid-thirties, sneering at him. Isaac recognized this snobbish woman through his spectacles. *"She must be over two hundred pounds,"* Isaac insulted this rude woman in his mind. "Jesus, what's that smell?" Isaac noticed three teenage girls holding their noses at him and Bob. Isaac had some serious challenges ahead of him by living as a homeless person with his condition. The only thing Isaac could do was pray. That's all he could do for his sanity.

Then Isaac and Bob rushed into an upscale supermarket. The produce department was stocked neatly with fresh fruits and vegetables. The store had dimmed lighting, beautiful wooden ceilings and elevator music played from speakers. The deli section smelled of rotisserie chicken. It had cheese and Boar Head products stocked neatly in the deli case. Donuts, cookies, Italian bread, and other pastries filled the air as Isaac and Bob passed the bakery. Also, a neighboring winery sold the world's most expensive wines and cheeses.

Isaac's face lit up. He loved this place. It was as if he had died and gone to food heaven, where God served his best and healthiest foods grown from the earth. Isaac hoped to purchase something good to eat that would make his day. His mouth watered at everything he saw. The shoppers seemed upscale and snotty, though, and looked down their noses at Bob and Isaac as they waltzed through the aisles. Isaac noticed more of the dirty looks that he got from these customers. He had no other choice than to ignore it. The friends marched towards the back of the store and outside into an alleyway. Four recyclable machines stood where a couple of homeless people inserted their plastic bottles and soda cans. The friends approached the fourth bottle's machine that accepted plastic. One by one, Bob slowly entered his plastic bottles. In return, a receipt was ejected from the device. Isaac's mind wandered, looking in the alleyway, where a delivery truck unloaded groceries onto the loading dock. Isaac then focused his attention on his friend and noticed that he pulled out his final bottle receipt from the vending machine.

Minutes later, Isaac and Bob stood in line at the register. The cashier had an attitude that wouldn't quit. She smiled at specific customers, like a well-dressed Caucasian gentleman in his mid-twenties wearing a three-piece suit. He looked like a stockbroker on Wall Street or an entrepreneur. *"If I were a real estate investor with a three-piece suit, she would kiss my ass. I know that successful people have got the world in the palm of their hands. I pretty much sense how she's going to treat me. I bet she going to roll her eyes and suck her teeth. This stuck-up clerk will probably have the manager throw Bob and me out of this jot. Maybe, I could be wrong,"* Isaac foreshadowed the incident. Next, it was Bob's turn. He handed the small stack of bottle receipts to the cashier. The clerk snatched the bottle receipts from him.

"Don't disrespect me, young lady!" Bob raised his voice. The cashier handed Bob his cash, and Isaac was next in line. She was stunned when she saw Isaac being albino and homeless. Isaac felt that attitude coming from the clerk and knew she would do just that. *"If I could get away with murder, I would jump over this counter and choke the fuckin' shit out of her!"* Isaac's vile thoughts ran through his head. The cashier snatched the bottle receipts from his hand, just like Bob. She rang up the amount and threw the money at Isaac.

"Don't disrespect me!" Isaac bellowed.

"I'm not disrespecting you, sir. Have a nice day," the cashier said sarcastically. Then the store manager rushed to the scene.

"Your cashier is nasty. She really is," Bob complained.

"Give me my money in my hand! And treat me with some respect!" Isaac's eyes watered as tears streamed down his face from behind his glasses. A short woman stood behind Isaac and witnessed the scene. She shook her head in disappointment at the clerk.

"Give him his money, please, young lady," The woman in line addressed the cashier. The store manager stomped to the register.

"What's the trouble, Donna?" the manager rushed to the scene.

"Nothing," Donna replied with an attitude. She placed Isaac's money in his hand. She gave a phony smile.

"Bitch!" Isaac stormed away with Bob right behind him out of the store.

"Donna, you're suspended! Close after these last customers!", the manager shouted.

Later underneath the New York City subway system, Isaac lay face down on his sleeping bag across from Bob, sobbing like a baby. Bob didn't say a word. He allowed Isaac to get it out. He would ask Isaac questions about his journey later. The woman cradling her infant baby in her arms heard cries coming from one flight from where she resided. "Are you alright?" the homeless mother shyly asked. Isaac choked back his tears, wiped his eyes, and sniffled. He heard the feminine voice with its pretty-sounding tone. He didn't look at who it was precisely because Isaac felt embarrassed. A grown man crying over fucked-up life. Some guys would've toughened up. Standing right before Isaac was the mother and her infant baby girl. The child was wide awake and quiet.

"What's wrong?", the mother gently touched Isaac shoulder.

"How are you, Jessica?" Bob asked.

"Fine, thank you," Jessica responded with a bright smile.

"I heard someone crying," Jessica added.

"I'm sorry," Isaac sniffled.

"Jessica, this is Isaac. Isaac, Jessica," Bob introduced.

"Are you alright?" Jessica asked as she cradled her baby in her arms.

"I'm fine. This is all new to me," Isaac said.

Jessica gave Isaac some encouragement and told her sob story. And boy, did Jessica have a tale to tell. While she spoke, Isaac saw her beauty underneath the filth upon her skin. Jessica had enchanting, ebony eyes, and he couldn't tell what kind of figure she had under that large clothing on her small frame. Jessica most likely had a Victoria's Secret model shape, which was extra thin. He grinned at her as she told her life before living like a mole under the New York subway system. Isaac couldn't believe his ears about how she had escaped an abusive relationship. Jessica and her husband, Gerard, had been married for about three years and lived in a three-bedroom apartment. Her husband had an excellent job in human resources for the city. Suddenly, she and Gerard were very loving and intimate, but then it became less and less. He must've had his eyes on someone else. Jessica would stay up waiting for him at night, and when he arrived home, she demanded an explanation. Gerard said the usual; *he had to work late.*

Jessica knew her husband was lying right through his teeth because city employees leave work around five or six o'clock. When she did the laundry, she noticed lipstick on his collar, and perfume on his shirt. One day, his cell phone rang, and Gerard was in the bathroom. Jessica answered the call, and sure enough, a feminine voice asked for her husband. She yelled and told the woman that he was married. Moreover, he was expecting a child. Then, she hung up.

Jessica stomped into the shower, drew back the curtains, and hollered until Kingdom Come. Her husband denied knowing the woman and asked why Jessica answered his cell. As Isaac listened to this young woman's story, he asked himself, "Why didn't she leave him?" He wanted to ask her that, but it was none of his business. The usual response is, *"I loved him. Or I wanted to make our marriage work."* After a while, things between Jessica and Gerard got better. But the calls from other women kept coming in. Jessica answered and noticed sexy text messages. Gerard weighed over two hundred pounds and was six-two. He was a stock guy with mood swings who slapped her for checking his cell phone. On another occasion, Gerard pushed Jessica down a flight of steps, which resulted in a sprained ankle. And, of course, there were apologies with flowers, candy, and lovemaking. As he ate his dinner, Jessica told Gerard she was three weeks pregnant. He tossed the dish across the kitchen, crashing to the floor. From that point on, things got worse. And, of course, being called every name in the book. Again, Isaac thought, *"Why didn't you leave sooner? And why did you give him all those chances to continue to hurt you?"*

"Why don't you sleep in my space? I can sleep one flight down," Isaac offered and interrupted her simultaneously.

"That's fine. My baby and I are fine down here," Jessica rocked her baby in her arms.

"I asked her a million times, and she refused. Let me sleep in your spot," Bob offered, giving up his area to the mother and child.

"That's perfectly fine," Jessica held her infant. Bob moved out of his space and hustled up the steps where Jessica and the baby slept.

"How do you like it, Jessica?" Bob hollered from the staircase landing. Jessica stood there and heard Bob's question.

"My space is fine!" Jessica stomped her foot on the floor.

"Jessica, please. Take my space," Isaac offered with his sincere eyes. He moved his sleeping bag out of the way. He gave Jessica and her baby all the room they needed. She laid her child down in Bob's sleeping bag.

"Thank you," Jessica said with a smile.

"You're welcome, sweetheart," Bob said.

Isaac nodded, letting her know she was welcome to it. Isaac then had an epiphany. "Jessica, do you have milk for the baby?" Isaac cried out to her from the bottom of the steps.

"A little bit!" she replied.

Early the next morning, on the jam-packed streets of Times Square, vehicles beeped their horns as motorists cut each other off and ran traffic lights. Street performers dressed in costumes of popular cartoon characters, and superheroes took pictures with tourists. Isaac smirked at them, making fools of themselves. At least they were trying to make a dollar. He wondered if he could get in on the act. Isaac didn't say anything to Bob because he might discourage him from doing so. "Maybe, I'll look into that later," Isaac thought.

The sidewalks were no different from the streets; people weaved between one another like guests at a crowded party. Bob and Isaac had no other choice than to do the same. As they marched through the mass of New Yorkers, the two gentlemen scanned their eyes for a small convenience store. A Duane Reade drugstore stood right before them. The two men strutted through the automatic open door and knew what they needed. A security guard watched the monitors of the business. Because Isaac had previously had a bad experience at the supermarket, he didn't allow another merchant to discourage him. Isaac marched over to the dairy case, grabbing a half-gallon of milk, a Minnie Mouse baby bottle with a pink top, a pink baby rattle, and ice cream, shoving it in a plastic bag. He then shoved a chicken sandwich, salad, and soda into the bag as well. Isaac then stormed right through the exit. Bob grabbed a few jars of baby food, a pink baby bottle, and baby wipes shoving them into bags on the other side of the drugstore. He grabbed a package of diapers from the shelf. He wished he had enough money to pay for everything. But, next time, he and Isaac would work on that one. Bob stormed right out as the security guard tried to stop him.

"Get the fuck off me!" Bob shouted. He wrestled his way out of the guard's grip.

"You're stealing!" the guard had a grip on Bob.

Bob then kicked the guard in between the legs. The security guard fell to his knees, holding his pelvis. He curled in a fetal position in agony on the ground.

"No, shit Sherlock!" Bob dashed down the street.

Moments later, Isaac and Bob weaved in and out of the crowd on a packed Manhattan sidewalk. Bob gulped down an orange soda while holding the items from the store. Isaac munched on his sour cream and onion chips, smiling. He stole some baby stuff for Jessica's little girl. Isaac breezed past a young couple pushing a baby stroller. He glanced back at the new family. He turned back looking forward and pictured himself and Clarissa maneuvering a baby stroller on this city sidewalk. The happy-storybook fantasy proceeded in Isaac's head. He cradled his healthy complexioned baby boy in his arms while strolling in Central Park. He even imagined himself with a healthy complexion as well. And even without wearing glasses. His vision was twenty, twenty. Isaac and Clarissa engaged in a kiss on top of it all. "Isaac! Isaac!" Bob hollered to his friend from the packed sidewalk. Isaac stopped, looking around, and noticed Bob.

"Oh, I'm sorry," Isaac tried to snap out of his daydream. He trotted towards his friend.

"I lost you for a second, buddy," Bob shoved his soda can into his bag. Then the two gentlemen hurried into the Times Square train station.

Underneath the busy streets, a couple of hours later, Jessica rocked her baby girl in her arms. She fed her baby from the pink bottle Bob supposedly purchased. She kissed her daughter and was thankful to these two men who spared her worries. Isaac and Bob shared the chicken sandwich and whatever else they had. "Jessica, do you want some of this sandwich? Here!" Isaac offered her a piece of the sandwich and gave her a bag of sour cream and onion potato chips.

"No, that's alright," Jessica didn't want to seem greedy.

"It's fine. Take it, Jessica, please," Isaac shoved the food in her face. She took the bag from Isaac's hand upon noticing her baby girl was fast asleep.

"She's knocked out," Jessica whispered. She took a bite of the sandwich and continued to rock her baby.

"What's her name?" Isaac asked with a mouth full of food.

"Shereza," Jessica swallowed her food and replied softly.

"That's pretty," Isaac complimented. He became quiet, trying to figure out what to say next. He wanted to know more about her troubled life as if he knew how to help her. He couldn't even help himself. *"What the hell does he know?"*

"So, what's your story, Isaac?" Jessica asked gently with a smile, rocking Shereza while waiting for an answer. He had no choice but to tell her his situation after Jessica spilled the beans about her life. "You'll probably kick me in the ass for this one," Isaac said. He spoke about how his mother remarried another man after he and his brother's father had passed away. Isaac felt like the black sheep in the family. His brother Moses had gotten all the attention. Later, their bond broke due to their stepfather's crafty ways. Isaac wrapped it up in a nutshell with how he couldn't stand the way his family, so-called friends, and strangers treated him because of his condition. Tears streamed down Isaac's cheeks as he abruptly turned away.

"Don't cry, Isaac," Jessica handed him a tissue. *"Again, crying in front of a woman. What a punk. Get it together, Isaac,"* he thought, being hard on himself. He eyed this lovely woman who had experienced horrors herself. Isaac took a deep breath and cautiously asked Jessica. "Why didn't she do something about her situation much sooner? She took sharp breaths and explained the love, hopes, and dreams she wanted for her family. The conversation went on between the two for the entire night.

CHAPTER TWENTY-ONE

About a decade later, an open house sign reading Remington Realty sat on the front lawn of an upscale home in Garden City, Long Island, priced at $1.8M. Within a few minutes, Moses, now twenty-nine years old, gave a tour to newlyweds Mr. and Mrs. Ira Salzberg, a middle-aged Caucasian couple, in their mid-forties. They were starting their lives over after struggling to find the right person. Moses and the happy couple marched to the sunken living room and descended a few steps to the large wooden floor. He stood in the center of the room with his stocky build, GQ-styled royal blue dress shirt, black and blue tie, black vest with matching trousers, and black and gray shoes. Moses gave details of the light fixture hanging above their heads. The chandelier looked identical to the ball in Times Square on New Year's Eve. Then he swung open the dining room's double doors, revealing a built-in breakfront with enough space for a ballroom. Minutes later, the married couple gasped at the spacious kitchen Moses waltzed through. It had a large island, a built-in refrigerator, a separate freezer, deep sinks, a deep fryer, and many cabinets. Mrs. Salzberg caressed her fingers across the marble island as her husband checked the roomy cabinets. "I love this, babe."

"I could stir up a meal here!" his wife added with a snicker. Mrs. Salzberg turned red in the face. Moses' heart raced in his chest because these newlyweds seemed eager to purchase. He pointed to the large breakfast room, where a bay window overlooked the backyard with a massive lawn. The new wife dashed to the breakfast room table while her eyes widened at the panromantic views of the yard. She was like a little girl who fell in love with her first dollhouse, but this was the real deal. Mr. Salzberg sat at the table, gazing at his wife, mesmerized by the property. They talked amongst themselves as if Moses wasn't there. He understood the Salzbergs were married, in love, and wanted to decide quickly. But they didn't see the rest of the home. Moses scratched his head, waiting for them to snap out of their little world. They held hands and proceeded to glare out of that glass picture window. Then Moses cleared his throat. "Hello, Mr. and Mrs. Salzberg?" The newly married couple turned to Moses and apologized for their rudeness. Of course, Moses smiled, which indicated he accepted the couple's apology. He wanted to show the couple something else as they descended a small flight of steps. Moses swung the door open. Mrs. Salzberg screamed as if she had won the lottery and hugged her husband. Mr. Salzberg gasped as they entered the pool house with a large sparkling marble swimming pool.

"This is fabulous!" she bellowed, guffawing.

"Wow, this house is amazing," Mr. Salzberg strolled around the pool.

"Outside, you've got your outdoor kitchen and large patio," Moses pressed the button as the door opened to the brick patio. He strolled outside while the Salzbergs' followed behind him. Mrs. Salzberg opened the refrigerator, checking its compartments. She caressed her hand along the marble counter and noticed the eight-burner stove. Her husband opened the oven door and saw the small microwave that it had. And once again, he checked out the spacious cabinets. "These are as big as the ones in the main kitchen."

"He's into lots of space for food. "Junk food, that is," Mrs. Salzberg smiled.

On the second floor, the double door of a master bedroom opened with a sunken sitting area with another bay window overlooking the backyard. The newlyweds gasped at the suite fit for royalty. Moses sauntered behind and allowed them to check out every nook and cranny. "Honey, we could put our bed here," Mrs. Salzberg suggested.

"Right," her husband agreed.

"Then, over here in the seating area, you could place your flat panel on the wall," This new bride continued with her decorating ideas.

"Where's the closet?" Mrs. Salzberg asked. Moses pointed to the other side of the master bedroom. She swung the massive closet door open. The lights automatically came on from a beautiful fixture in the ceiling.

"Oh, my God! Babe, look at this!" Mrs. Salzberg gasped. Her husband rushed into the closet.

"A walk-in closet?" Mr. Salzberg asked in disbelief.

Moses stood in the doorway, smiling.

"I could put all my shoes over here. And my suits in here," Mrs. Salzberg proceeded with more of her creative ideas. They noticed Moses staring at them, waiting for an answer.

"So?" Moses asked.

"We'll take it," Mr. and Mrs. Salzberg responded in unison.

At dusk, Central Park's Tavern on the Green restaurant where servers hustled fancy dishes to customers as they enjoyed a luxurious evening. Moses and Shawnette ate filet mignon while sitting at a fancy booth. Tall wine glasses sat on the side of each of their fabulous dishes. Elevator music blared from the establishment's speakers as waiters hustled food orders to customers. Moses proposed a toast to the sale of another property, a successful firm, and his blessed life. He and Shawnette clanked their wine glasses and sipped.

Then, Moses thought of Isaac. He wondered if Isaac was dead or alive. Has Isaac achieved any success? Is he married, or does he have kids? Moses felt guilty about having his career without his brother. Blame, remorse, regret, and other feelings surfaced within Moses' mind like spirits rising from the dead. He had a dead side to him, which was his brother not being present. Every holiday and occasion, he felt like his soul died. When someone becomes successful, they share it with family and friends. Moses did that, but the only person missing was his brother. He thought about hiring a private investigator to locate Isaac, but it would probably bankrupt him. The only thing he could do was put it in God's hands. Moses focused his mind off Isaac and on his beautiful fiancé Shawnette. Shawnette wore a light blue mini-skirt business suit that was cute and sexy. The soon-to-be husband and wife eyed each other. He placed his hand on Shawnette's knee and slowly caressed it. Then pleasure surfaced on her face as she tried to keep her composure.

That night in Moses' master bedroom of his lavish home, he and Shawnette thrust up a storm in his California king-sized bed. Their bodies were uncovered from head to toe, with balls of sweat emerging on their skin. Shawnette's heavy breathing was pleasurable to Moses' ear. He loved her sexy moaning and groaning; it turned him on. As they reached a climax, Shawnette's moan continued its sexiness and then subsided. After a moment of passion, he sat on the edge of his luxury slumber and looked at the fancy cherry wood armoire that cost a fortune. He directed his eyes on the wall, a walk-in closet, and looked up at the light fixture above his bed. Moses stood to his feet and put on his boxers, jeans, and a t-shirt with sneakers. He glimpsed Shawnette as she slept. Moses crept into his walk-in as the light automatically lit up the atmosphere. He opened his drawer, where his sweaters and T-shirts were neatly tucked away. He reached his hand underneath the garments and grabbed a ring box. When he opened it, the rock glistened before his eyes. He pictured himself slipping this fancy jewel onto her finger. Moses descended the spiral staircase to the main floor, where the foyer's light fixture dimmed all night. He switched on the lights in his entire from his automated house system. The four-bedroom, four-and-a-half-bath brick manor home lit up like a Christmas tree. His estate resided on three-and-a-half acres with English gardens, manicured lawns, floral plants, and apple trees. The patio, made of bluestone and brick, is perfect for entertaining family and friends. Security cameras were surveilling the property twenty-four-seven, day, and night. He strolled into the family room and looked at the photos of him and Isaac as kids. Moses stopped and stared at the picture of them at Christmas. Then, he glared at a Halloween photo of them eating their candy. A caribou painting hung on the wall. Moses opened the artwork as if it were a door with a safe behind it. Moses punched in the combination. It clicked, and he swung open the sturdy door. He had cash, bonds, and personal information like credit cards, social security, etc. Moses placed the ring box inside and then locked the safe after closing it. He swung the picture back against the wall.

Minutes later, CNN played on the television in his brightly lit sitting area. He almost changed the channel, sitting in his recliner and listened to a report of a missing young white male from Santa Ana, California. Residents searched high and low to find this young man, twenty-one years of age. "But he's over eighteen," Moses murmured. When Isaac went missing, even though he was eighteen, the authorities didn't bother to look for him. Moses rose from the recliner and paced from room to room. He opened the glass door of the backyard and strolled alongside the in-ground swimming pool with its reflecting lights. He consistently roamed around and around, glaring at the gleaming blue water. Moses fixed his eyes on the lights; he couldn't figure out why. Suicide was not on his mind; Moses had much to live for and worked hard for his company. Suddenly, Moses halted in his tracks and gawked at a particular light at the bottom of the water. The heavenly clear reflector gave Moses a calling from God. Maybe, taking his own life would be the thing to do so he could be with Isaac. If Isaac's dead. *If so, then they could own the Many Mansions in heaven.* Tears outpoured on Moses' face. He immediately sat in a patio chair and sobbed like never before. He balled his hands into fists and hit them on his head.

"God, my brother. Where's my brother? Where's Isaac?" Moses sobbed. Then Shawnette stood in the distance, witnessing her boyfriend and boss crying like a child. She cautiously headed towards him and embraced him. He didn't tell her the story about his brother and how he'd been gone for over a decade. He had to find his brother. Private investigators are probably as greedy as lawyers. Moses didn't want to jeopardize his business due to searching for Isaac. He looked up at Shawnette's beautiful eyes with his watery eyes and smiled. He wrapped his arms around Shawnette as if she were his wife. The hug was long and tight. Anyone could tell that Moses was hurt.

CHAPTER TWENTY-TWO

Meanwhile, throughout this murky underground refuge, Isaac, now twenty-nine years old, slept across from Bob. Two lit candles gleamed between the two friends, giving a heavenly glow to their surroundings. Bob constantly coughed as Isaac heard the mucus bubbling in his chest. He couldn't do things like he could before since he was much older now. He gained weight and was more sluggish. Isaac opened his eyes, noticing his friend with the vision he had without wearing his glasses. Bob consistently coughed. Isaac immediately placed his glasses on his face. He patted Bob on the back to relieve his cough. Bob cleared his throat and began to snore. Isaac crawled back to his sleeping bag and slipped into it. He rested his arm behind his head, thinking about how he and Jessica now had to provide. He hoped Bob wasn't seriously ill and hopefully, it was just a common cold. He'd be better in no time.

As Isaac lay awake, he noticed a gleam from the upper area, where Jessica and her daughter, Shereza slept. A candle gleamed between them as well. Jessica still looked the same as she did when Isaac first arrived down here. Bob then turned on his back, snoring as the mucus continued to bubble in his nostrils. Isaac sneered and couldn't stand that thick, bubbling sound. Shockingly, Bob didn't even spit. Dreadlocked and matted hair grew on Isaac's head as he sat in his sleeping bag. He ran his hand through his coarse locks. His mustache had grown, and his goatee had spurted long on his chin. Isaac attempted to keep his facial hair neatly trimmed as much as possible; sometimes, he could get his hands on a razor or go without shaving. His clothing was no different than before; old and stained. Isaac did his best to keep his spirits up through his circumstances.

Ten years have passed as Isaac forgot that he had a twin. His childhood memories had been expunged from his mind as he lived underground. When holidays and birthdays came about, Isaac didn't think about it. Bob reminisced on his holiday memories. He spoke of how he and his wife drove from Long Island to Manhattan to see the tree lighting in Rockefeller Center, go shopping on Fifth Avenue, and eat at the Russian tearoom. He felt like a millionaire when he brought jewelry for his wife. In the summer, he'd rent a summer home for them in the Hamptons or go to Hawaii. As Bob talked about his past life, Jessica sighed and pictured the scenes. Isaac did the same but blocked some of it out because it depressed him. He could've had a good life if he had stuck it out. Even though Isaac didn't want to remember his childhood, he thought about his future. The notion of Moses' possible success would crush him. Bob bragged about his history, Shereza, being a child, consistently asked him questions. And like her mother, Shereza's eyes widened. She gasped at every detail of Bob's past life.

Shereza pinned pictures of houses on the wall, where she slept every night. Whenever Isaac went to the store, he would pick up a free copy of a cheap real estate magazine for Shereza. She loved the properties located in Manhattan, Queens, and Long Island. Shereza reminded Isaac of himself when he was a kid. He had fallen in love with the beauty of real estate. Isaac wondered if Bob fabricated this tale to feel better about himself because he lived in darkness. Isaac had gotten used to his new environment. *What else was out there in the world for him?* Nothing but dirty stares, strangers brushing past him, disrespect, and even getting beaten up. Getting attacked hadn't happened yet, thankfully. Isaac got off the streets before sundown and spent much time in the murky tunnels. They would spend so much time in their world of gloom that they didn't know what day it was, or even the month.

Moments later, Jessica kissed Shereza while she slept in her sleeping bag. Jessica wanted to keep her daughter in this world of darkness to protect her. She didn't want her to witness anything horrible, like her or her mother being harmed. Isaac and Jessica had to go into the world and find whatever they could to eat. Isaac stood to his feet and asked Jessica if she was ready to go on to the streets of New York to face the cruelty that awaited them. Shereza tossed and turned, sitting up and yawning. "Are you going out, Mom?"

"Yes, I can't let you starve honey," Jessica fixing her clothes.

"Why can't I go? I want to see the world," Shereza opened her arms waiting to receive a hug from her mother. And she got just that. Jessica kissed her daughter on the forehead, wrapping her arms around her. When she was younger, she begged her mother not to go. She'd cry and cry. Not only did Shereza want to be with her mother, but she wanted to see the outside world. Jessica kept her daughter in the absence of light, shielding Shereza from the ugliness that dwelled within it.

"I'll be right back, Sherry." Jessica insisted as she and Isaac were ready to go.

"Okay, Mom," Shereza shrugged her shoulders, frowning.

"Bring me back another real estate magazine, Isaac," Shereza said.

"Alrighty," Isaac nodded.

"Alright!" Isaac and Jessica smiled at Shereza. They bolted down the steps passing Bob as he lay on his back with his bubbling mucus in the chest.

Isaac couldn't wait to escape from this area and into some fresh air. He raced out of the condemned construction, removing the piece of concrete from the wall. He squeezed his body through the hole as Jessica followed him out. She placed the concrete chunk back in the space in the wall as if she had closed the door to her actual home.

In no time, Isaac and Jessica weaved in and out of the crowd of busy New Yorkers who were either going to work or sightseeing. Isaac needed to figure out what day it was. He wanted to ask someone, but that would be a task. Of course, Jessica hadn't any idea either. Isaac worried about getting food for Shereza, Jessica, Bob, and himself. Isaac glanced over his shoulder as he kept walking and saw that Jessica wasn't with him. Suddenly, he stopped. He noticed her on the corner holding a cup and begging for change.

"What the fuck!" Isaac charged toward Jessica and grabbed her by the wrist.

"Don't touch me like that!" Jessica cried as if Isaac was going to cause physical harm. He released his grip and stepped back. *"I guess that brought back memories of her husband putting his hands on her,"* Isaac thought.

"I'm sorry, Jessica," Isaac looked around because he didn't want to be hauled off to jail.

"I'm going to get us some food," Isaac stormed away. Jessica ignored him and kept asking strangers for a handout. Isaac's eyes watered as tears trickled down his face. He balled his hands into fists. A murky life underground felt as if he were in hell, but it was a haven. Isaac loved the sun, trees, and grass. He loved the birds singing and being out during the day. He rushed to a small park and sat on a bench. Pigeons flew all over his head, where a sixty-something woman fed them. She smiled at Isaac but then frowned.

"Hello, young man," the pigeon lady asked. At first, Isaac didn't respond and ignored this woman. Isaac didn't know her from Adam. She spoke about smiling every day and praying. *"Oh, not another Jesus freak. Is she planning on stealing from me?"* Isaac asked himself. He didn't glance at her. Instead, Isaac nodded and stared at a luxurious building right before him. He wondered about this building and what it had in it. Luxurious apartments were where some rich and famous spent their lives or fancy offices where the big shots conducted business. Isaac was dazed at this structure as the loquacious woman kept on. He couldn't understand the gibberish about Jesus Christ as if it were going out of style. "You're not the only one going through things, young man," the bird lady bellowed. Her statement caught Isaac's attention as he glared at what seemed to be a mentally disturbed female who sat three benches away. She cried for no reason.

"Ma'am, what's the problem?" Isaac asked with an attitude. The bird lady sobbed while tossing pieces of bread at the pigeons.

"How long have you been living out here? Isaac asked curiously.

"Over thirty years and still counting," she pouted.

"I've been in a similar situation for over a decade," Isaac told this woman as she cried.

"I understand your pain. You have no idea what I've been through. I can tell you don't have a scratch or a bruise. "Or even have your only friend set on fire right in front of your face," the pigeon lady expressed her horrifying experience on these cold-hearted streets. Isaac's eyes bulged out of his head in disbelief. Isaac looked at his hands and arms. She was right. He neither had a bruise nor a scratch. He realized how blessed he was even while living beneath the Earth. Isaac softened his tone of voice and asked her name. This lone woman, Margaret from Pleasantville, New York, lifted her sleeve and exposed the bruises she got from some crazed man who stole the little change she had in her pocket. Isaac couldn't bear to hear any of her sorrows, so he went and sat on the bench beside her. Margaret kept crying and crying. Isaac wished he had a tissue for her to dry her eyes. Instead, she wiped her tears with her hand. The senior citizen had a dingy face, and old, stained clothing, just like Isaac did. There were also balls of sweat surfacing on her forehead because of the sun's rays. Isaac asked her the date without meaning to get off the subject.

"It's June twenty-first," Margaret answered as she grinned.

"I'm sorry. You're right, Maggie. Is it all right if I call you that?" Isaac asked with caution.

"Yeah, that's what my friends in school called me for short," She giggled and looked at the pigeons that approached her. Maggie proceeded to throw the last slices of bread at the animals.

"I'm sorry about your friend. I know we just met. I'm staying underground with other people in a similar situation," Isaac said.

"What do you mean, underground?" Maggie cowered on the bench. Isaac described where he resided and how the conditions weren't excellent. Still, that would be the safest place for her to be.

"Isn't it dark down there?" Maggie frowned and imagined the unsanitary conditions.

"Yes, it is. But it sure does beat the weather whether it's cold, hot, sleet, rain, or snow," Isaac said grimly. Then Maggie shook her head. She was uncertain about leaving the park.

"What about my friends here? There will be no one to feed them," Maggie referred to pigeons. She cried at the thought of the birds starving to death. Isaac wanted to embrace this older woman who was on this park bench alone. *"Who was going to look after her? The birds can take care of themselves?"* Isaac thought. He wanted to avoid persuading her to go into unfamiliar grounds. Still, Isaac had concerns about her being on the streets by herself. He wished that Maggie would trust him and stay in a safer place. But still, the answer was *"No."* She was someone's grandmother or a mother who had no idea about her whereabouts. Maggie fixed her mind on these pigeons that would be here way after she even passed on. She cried and cried and wouldn't stop. Isaac had to figure out something to cheer up this bird lady.

"How about I try to get you an iced tea? How's that sound?" Isaac promised with a smile. He knew he had no money on him, but he knew what to do. Maggie wiped her tears and nodded her head. "I'm working on it right now," Isaac rummaged through the garbage bin for plastic bottles and aluminum cans. He held about four cans and searched for a plastic bag to store them.

"Do you have a bag, Maggie?" Isaac asked. She grabbed a wrinkled plastic bag from her cart and handed it to him. Isaac smiled and collected more recyclables for another person. A stranger he knew absolutely nothing about. People had to do everything they could to help one another, and Isaac did this without even thinking. He remembered giving his taco salad to the homeless man in the diner's parking lot when he was a kid. Today must be his blessed day. Isaac kept loading the plastic bag with bottles and cans. Then, he asked Maggie for another plastic bag to load more recyclables. Isaac swaggered over to another garbage bin on the other side of the park and searched through it.

"Maggie, I'm going to need another bag!" Isaac hollered across from this pudgy woman who hustled a couple of more plastic bags to him.

"Here you go, Isaac. Do you need some help?" Maggie asked.

"If you like," Isaac said. Surprisingly, this woman willingly stopped feeding her friends and chose to aid Isaac in going through public trash cans for bottles. She dashed back to her shopping cart and grabbed some plastic bags, filling them up. Isaac scoffed at Maggie shoving every plastic bottle and cans into the bags. She aggressively bolted from sanitation can to sanitation can, filling the bags around her arms.

"Whoa, she's really off her rocker," Isaac thought. He then overlooked this sixty-year-old's mental handicap and continued collecting the recyclables. *"Oh, shit! Jessica! I hope she's alright,"* the thought dawned on him.

"Maggie, I've got to go and get the cash for these bottles, okay? I'll be right back. I promise," Isaac's voice quivered. He rushed off to check on Jessica. Maggie sat back down slowly on the bench, pouting. Isaac hated leaving this poor woman vulnerable to this heartless world. He hustled with five bags of plastic to where he last saw Jessica.

On the street, Jessica still held out her cup, receiving a few dollars she earned. Isaac walked up behind her with caution.

"Jessica," Isaac called to her.

"Yes, Isaac. Why did you leave like that?" Jessica stomped her foot on the ground. She continued to rattle her cup full of coins with a few dollars in it.

"I've got some bottle receipts that I can cash in. Come on," Isaac said. Jessica then held her paper cup and followed Isaac to the upscale supermarket on the other side of town.

In the rear of the supermarket stood the bottle machine. Just like before, a few homeless people inserted their bottles and cans. An available machine stood waiting for some business. Isaac pushed his bottles and cans one by one into the machine. Jessica impatiently paced back and forth, frowning and glancing over her shoulders.

"Isaac, can you hurry it up, please," Jessica's eyes wandered.

"I'm going as fast as I can," Isaac wanted to tell Jessica to go back underground; he'd take care of the rest. Next time, he would do just that. Jessica's eyes kept shifting back and forth, and the pacing made him nervous. She felt her ex-husband's presence in the air and wanted to dash off. "Jessica, do you want to leave? I'll meet you back underground," Isaac said.

"No, No, I can't," Jessica's face trembled with shifty eyes.

"What's scaring you, Jess?" Isaac inserted the recyclables into the bottle machine as quickly as he could. She scanned the back alley as an African American male, dark-skinned with a bum-like appearance, seemed like a familiar face to her. A guy in his mid-thirties rode his bike into the alleyway toward the bottle machines. He observed this pretty Latina female, standing right before him flinching. She sprinted into the store, leaving Isaac behind.

"Jessica!" Isaac finished placing all the bottles inside the machine and grabbed his receipts. Isaac recognized the menacing black male, who freaked Jessica out.

Within minutes, Isaac paraded up and down the aisles of fancy foods, searching for his friend. He zigzagged between customers with their carts full of food in the frozen aisle. A well-to-do Asian female in her mid-twenties felt Isaac's presence approach she immediately became startled and sneered at him. He didn't pay any attention because he was used to it.

The less-crowded meat department was where the butchers packed the shelves with freshly cut steaks, chicken, pork, etc. Isaac glanced at that rib steak; he couldn't get it because he needed a stove. Right now, he had no time to look at food. Instead, Isaac had to locate Jessica. Having his bottle receipts in his hands, Isaac needed the money. Isaac almost exited the store, but then he made a bow face and stood in line for the receipts. Isaac looked at the cashier; she was pretty. She gave Isaac a friendly smile as he was fourth in line. The lines moved quickly, and he returned the smile. For over a decade, Isaac has cashed his recycling receipts with different clerks, or even stole. He and Bob brought every little thing they could for the past four years, and then Isaac did the so-called seeking food for the clan. Jessica started coming with Isaac within the previous year, but now she's freaking out. When it was his turn, Isaac gave the receipts to the cashier. He grimaced because he didn't want to intimidate the clerk. She rang up his receipts with a smile remaining on her face. It was as if this clerk was another mentally ill person as well. Her name tag read: Teresa. This Latina female wore a beautiful foundation on her face, mascara, and burgundy matte lipstick.

"Here you go, sir," Teresa placed the cash into his hand, six dollars and forty-five cents. She didn't cringe at the fact Isaac's hands being filthy, and she looked him in the face. Teresa proceeded to smile. She then realized he was pale-skinned and blond-haired with googly eyes.

"Thank you, sir. Have a nice day," Teresa continued with her politeness.

"Thank you," Isaac said in return. He exited the store, grabbing a local real estate magazine.

"How could she run out on me? Dammit," Isaac stomped down the street and began having vile thoughts. *"Man, I see why her husband beat the shit out of her. Jessica does stupid shit. She rushes off, makes you panic, and makes you forget things! Now, where do I look?"* Isaac murmured. Already Isaac was a bum on the streets of New York. Who cared if they noticed him talking to himself? That was nothing new for a homeless person or anyone who wasn't homeless. He proceeded to stomp his foot on the ground and curse. "Shit!"

Isaac promised Maggie an iced tea when he returned. He stopped at a bagel shop and purchased an ice-cold beverage for his new friend.

Within the hour, Isaac strutted across to the park, where Maggie remained on the bench feeding the pigeons. She seemed to be in good spirits.

"Maggie!" he cried out to this bird lady. She noticed her new friend with that iced tea she desired. He approached Maggie and placed the can in her hand.

"One iced tea for you," Isaac said. Her eyes widened as she gulped the iced tea down and belched.

"Excuse me. Thank you so much. I've been looking forward to this. It's like I've died and gone to heaven. You're such a good friend, Isaac. My good and new friend," Maggie chattered. Isaac tapped his foot on the ground, unaware of how to tell Maggie the news.

"Are you going to be here tomorrow, Maggie, "Isaac interrupted her enjoying her iced tea. Maggie took another sip and stared into Isaac's eyes. She didn't receive lousy news easily. Though, this wasn't exactly bad news. He was going to visit her the next day.

"Yes, I will be here. Where am I going? This park is my home, and the birds are my family," she whined. Tear after tear rolled down her dirty cheeks. Maggie wiped them away. Each one streamed down before she could finish drying the other away.

"I'll be back tomorrow. I swear," Isaac promised and did the sign of the cross.

"Pinky swears?" Maggie asked.

"Pinky swears," Isaac intertwined his pinky with hers.

"I can assure you of that," Maggie grabbed a stale loaf of bread to feed the birds.

Returning to his home beneath the earth, Isaac dashed down the staircase. Anyone could tell he wasn't pleased. Isaac then stopped where Bob laid their heads. Bob noticed Isaac wasn't in a good mood. Jessica saw Isaac not smiling. Jessica rocked Shereza in her arms. She kept apologizing to her baby girl for not getting her something to eat. Isaac scoffed as he carried a small paper bag and gave Bob a delicious golden apple. Then, he sat on the other side of Jessica. She felt the tension in the air. His eyes shifted back and forth between Jessica and Shereza. Jessica unwrapped her arms from around Shereza and rushed to Isaac. She clasped his hand. "Isaac, I'm sorry. I got freaked out," Jessica whined. The more and more she explained, the more Isaac seemed to become irate. Jessica clasped his hands even tighter and tighter. Isaac wanted to snatch his hand away, but he didn't.

"First, you stop on the corner and start panhandling, which is fine. You didn't even tell me what you were going to do. I turned around, and you disappeared, only to find you on the corner. I thought I lost you for a second. You screamed at me," Isaac argued.

"You have no idea how paranoid I would be if I came across my ex-husband," Jessica laid her head on Isaac's chest. He embraced this scorned woman who experienced every form of pain. In his head, Isaac was going to have to be the one to search for food for everyone. He didn't want any harm to come to Jessica or Shereza. He kissed Jessica on the forehead as a gesture of *"it's okay."* Shereza wondered why her mother was crying. This eleven-year-old didn't ask any questions, but she knew something was wrong. Isaac noticed this mini version of Jessica gawking at him and her mother. Then Isaac grabbed the brown paper bag and gave it to Shereza.

"Here you go, Shereza. There's an apple and your magazine in there," Isaac said.

"What do you say, Shereza?" her mother glared at her.

"Thank you, Isaac," the little girl took a bite out of the pink lady apple. She flipped through her magazine of apartments and homes throughout New York City.

Jessica looked into Isaac's googly eyes and shook her head, "Thank you." Isaac wanted to kiss her, but she immediately rushed out of his arms. That was a clear sign right there, a "No."

CHAPTER TWENTY-THREE

Double French doors opened to a sparkling cottage swimming pool in Northampton Beach, Long Island. The Atlantic Ocean's waves washed onshore back and forth, contacting the land and sea. Screeching seagulls soared in the blue sky on this privately owned beach. This summer day in July was eighty-eight degrees and counting as Moses dressed in business attire. He wore a white dress shirt, a navy-blue vest, matching trousers, and Armani shoes. He strolled onto the furnished patio with an outdoor kitchen and a large windmill with its vanes twirling in the light wind. NBC's *Open House* camera tracked Moses as he proceeded with his tour of this twenty-one-million-dollar residential property. In the background, Calvin watched the entire shoot as he wore a three-piece black business suit. He also joined the Remington team by taking the New York state six-week real estate exam. Within a few minutes, the NBC *Open House* camera focused on Calvin as the cameraman. They followed him through the living room, detailing the furniture, its walls, and ceilings. As Moses' stepfather finished up the mansion tour, Moses exited through the front of the mansion. He swaggered towards his business partner, Barbara, embracing her.

"I'm so proud of you. Now, I just got off the phone with the producers from NBC. This episode will broadcast within a week," Barbara enthused, clutching Moses's hands.

"His childhood dream is now a reality. Moses was in disbelief. He exhaled and snatched his cell. "Barbara, excuse me. I've got to make a call," he scrambled a few feet ahead of his business colleague. He spoke with caution as he moved as far away as possible.

He addressed the Valley Stream precinct operator about reopening his brother's case. The operator was rude about his brother being gone for so long and inquired why the family didn't report it sooner. Moses' face turned red having to deal with police again who didn't care. "What am I, a fortune teller? How was I supposed to know my brother was going to vanish!" Moses bickered with the operator. From the petty words exchanged, it then became intense.

Suddenly, Moses ended the call. He glared at the ground, breathing heavily as his eyes watered. Tears flowed down his cheeks. He choked back his tears; he didn't want his colleagues to know about the situation. Moses didn't tell his team that he had a brother missing. Nor did he mention that he was trying to find him. He recalled he had a birthday coming up and wanted to pursue it on that day, maybe. But why spoil a celebration? It wasn't only his birthday; it was Isaac's as well. Moses turned around, and to his surprise, no one interrupted his call for this critical mission. He guessed God ensured Moses made plans on his and Isaac's birthday. *"What if I find my brother on our day? Right now, I don't want to be around anyone,"* Moses said. His company would relocate to Mid-town Manhattan, around Grand Central Station or Park Avenue.

"Moses! The cameraman must get you and Calvin's shots together, introducing yourselves and the company," Barbara exclaimed as she reached out to Moses. She escorted him back towards the cottage. Barbara noticed his watery eyes but didn't ask any questions. They had a television shoot and didn't want to ruin it. All Barbara did was place her hand on his shoulder as a gesture of "It's going to be okay." He sensed the divine energy coming from her heavenly persona.

In no time, Moses and Calvin were side by side in the cottage's foyer, the NBC cameras rolling. Calvin spoke about the cottage's price and how to contact Remington Realty for a grand tour of the sumptuous residence. As Moses looked at him, he envisioned Isaac by his side. A heavenly light brightened the foyer as Moses glared at his sibling next to him. *"Was this real estate business going to take place in Heaven?" Due to this godly glow, would he and*

Isaac be God's real estate agents when a person made their way to heaven? It would be their reward for doing good, keeping His word, showing compassion for their fellow man, and accepting Jesus Christ as their savior. Then Moses returned to reality. Calvin finished his piece, and it was Moses' turn. Barbara, the cameraman, and his stepfather tried to get Moses' attention. He was still in a trance, but then he snapped out of it. He gave the final word for the presentation of the Northampton home. Moses did his part without messing up at all.

"And cut!" the *Open House* director shouted. Barbara scrambled to Moses and asked, "What was happening with you?" She could tell that Moses was in emotional distress. Moses sobbed and sobbed. Without any words or questions asked, Barbara consoled her colleague. She wrapped her arms around him as he released watery tears onto the sleeve of her light blue blouse. Calvin glared at his stepson. He didn't attempt to embrace Moses. He knew Moses had thought of his brother all these years, ever since he'd been missing in action. Calvin stood there, not reacting to his stepson's pain. He acted as if nothing was wrong. Moses had helped Calvin get his New York real estate license, and this was the thanks that he gave. Because of Moses' success and even Isaac's indirect success, the dreams of these two young men provided for their freeloading stepfather from the start. Now, Calvin had more money in his pockets while he and Irene dwelled in a lavish home in Manhasset – all due to Moses and even Isaac's success. If it weren't for their dream, Calvin would be eating out of garbage cans.

Two weeks later, a moving truck parked in front of the Forest Hills Remington Office while movers loaded up an eighteen-wheeler with desks, tables, chairs, computers, and other office equipment. The last man closed the double doors of the truck as the roaring engine revved. He hopped into the passenger's seat, and the vehicle pulled off. In a matter of time, these movers carried the furniture into a high-story building in Mid-town Manhattan. Moses had gotten a tour from another real estate investor/agent, billionaire Valentin De La Rue, a Frenchman from Cannes, the South of France. He had connections to contractors, interior decorators/designers, and architects who specialized exclusively in luxury real estate. Valentin showed an interest in Moses' company and its reputation, especially the episode of the company on Open House. Also, Valentin came from a long line of contractors. His great-grandfather was a contractor, while his grandfather and father had also invested in real estate. And now, Valentin inherited a world of homes and properties - whether they were built from the ground, flipped, or purchased. He gave Moses a grand tour of the new office. The office had three floors, spiral staircases, white blanketed walls, marble floors, beautiful light fixtures and built-in speakers in the ceiling.

Within a month, Remington Realty based in midtown was transformed into an alluring place of business. From top to bottom, pictures of homes, plants adorning the atmosphere, and a few pieces of leather furniture gave a fabulous touch. The Remington Realty group photo was nailed on the wall along with an individual photo of Moses, Shawnette, Barbara, and a couple of other high-ranking people with the company. The realtors got down to business, taking care of clients over the phone or in person. House music played from the speakers in the ceiling to put their clients at ease. Jocelyn swerved in her recliner, jotting down some notes. Then a Reality TV celebrity, April Berry, sporting a skimpy tight outfit, hair-styled nicely, waltzed through the double glass door, approaching the receptionist's desk.

"Hello. How are you?" Jocelyn greeted.

"I'm here to see Moses Remington," this somewhat celebrity answered.

Jocelyn noticed the uppity wannabe A-list actress, not making any eye contact with her.

"Moses, April Berry is here to see you," Jocelyn said over the phone.

"That's Miss Berry," April Berry gave Jocely a dirty look.

"I apologize, Miss Berry," Jocelyn smiled in return. She hung up the phone.

"You can have a seat, Miss Berry. Moses will be right with you. Would you like something to drink?" Jocelyn asked.

"No, thank you," Miss Berry shook her head, sashaying to the leather sofa. She sat next to a table with a stack of magazines on it. Miss Berry flipped through one of the real estate magazines. Then Calvin entered through the heavy glass door with his backpack on his shoulder. As soon as he saw Jocely working at her desk, Calvin smiled devilishly. He was about to address Jocelyn but then recognized April Berry residing on the sofa with her legs crossed. Her black catsuit hugged her body from head to toe. Calvin turned, approaching this woman cautiously.

"Miss Berry?" Calvin addressed this star.

"Yes," Miss Berry looked Calvin up and down.

"It's a pleasure to meet you," Calvin approached Miss Berry. Jocelyn looked up from her desk, witnessing Calvin flirting with the reality star. He stood over Miss Berry with his pelvis directly in her face. From Jocelyn's angel, it looked as if Miss Berry was doing something inappropriate. Moses rushed into the waiting room, noticing the scene. His eyes widened. "What the fuck is he doing?"

"How are you, Miss Berry?" Moses inserted his way between his stepfather and Miss Berry.

She placed down the magazine, extending her hand to shake this successful real estate genius' hand. She stood on her feet, sashaying out of Calvin's sight.

"Step right into my office," Moses escorts this celebrity out of the waiting room. He sneered at Calvin. "I hope that wasn't what I thought I saw. All I know is that it wasn't good. Especially, not for me," Moses' thought.

"Don't you have some Open house coming up?" Moses patted his stepfather on the back, hard.

"Yes, I do. I've got to make some calls to some very important clients," Calvin smiled, playing along.

"Yes, you do. Let me know how things go," Moses exited the waiting room.

'I sure will, "Calvin laughed it off. His smile dropped to a sneering expression. The hate Moses must have for him was very real. Calvin continued to play along. He noticed Jocelyn stroking the keys on the computer receptionist's desk. Again, a fiendish grin surfaced on Calvin's face, and he waltzed over to Jocelyn.

"You look mighty fine today," Moses complimented in a seductive tone.

"Thank you," Jocelyn smiled at him. She continued with her work.

Calvin stares at her breasts, licking his lips. He grabbed her hand tight, kissing it. Jocelyn pulls away.

"Stop, please," Jocelyn's hands began to quiver while she continued to work on the computer.

"I love the way that blouse fits you. All in the right places," Calvin laughed like the devil.

Jocelyn turned fiery red in the face because she knew what he was getting at.

"Please go away, Calvin! I am working!" Jocelyn clenched her teeth, keeping her voice low.

"I apologize. How about you and I go somewhere to get more acquainted?" Calvin continued to cackle.

Jocelyn wasn't laughing at Calvin's jokes. She stopped typing the keys of her computer, glaring at him. Jocelyn then grasped a sharpened pencil in her hand. Calvin put his hands in the air, taking a step back.

"Whoa! Have a nice day," Calvin walked away.

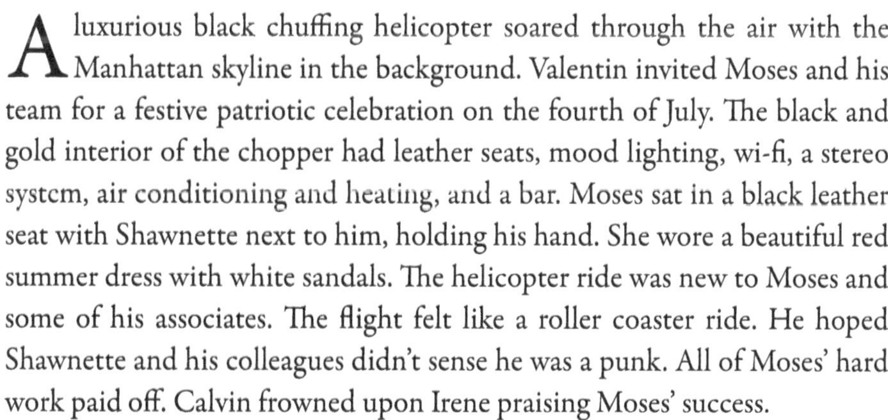

A luxurious black chuffing helicopter soared through the air with the Manhattan skyline in the background. Valentin invited Moses and his team for a festive patriotic celebration on the fourth of July. The black and gold interior of the chopper had leather seats, mood lighting, wi-fi, a stereo system, air conditioning and heating, and a bar. Moses sat in a black leather seat with Shawnette next to him, holding his hand. She wore a beautiful red summer dress with white sandals. The helicopter ride was new to Moses and some of his associates. The flight felt like a roller coaster ride. He hoped Shawnette and his colleagues didn't sense he was a punk. All of Moses' hard work paid off. Calvin frowned upon Irene praising Moses' success.

A black swan yacht with its helicopter launching pad on top docked in the East River. The ship looked like something out of a James Bond movie. Moses was flabbergasted at seeing a majestic vessel docked in New York's famous river. He drew Shawnette's attention to it, and she became excited. "Is this your yacht? How gorgeous!" Shawnette complimented.

In seconds, the helicopter landed on the yacht's top, and the rotors began to slow. A robust gentleman opened the chopper's door. Valentin stepped off with Moses, Shawnette, and the rest of Moses' business colleagues. The yacht's crew stood in line, ready to meet and greet Valentin and his guests, giving them the best comfort possible on their holiday boat ride. Moses, Valentin, and the guests were dressed in red, white, and blue outfits. All looked very patriotic for the occasion. Shawnette held Moses by the arm as they loaded into the elevator and went to the main floor. When the elevator doors widened, more stewardesses lined up to greet the guests. The yacht crew consisted of twenty-eight beautiful brunettes, both male and female, including the captain and crew. Then, there was the stewardess, her team, and her deckhand. Mr. De La Rue's group dressed accordingly. All were ready to accommodate the guests.

Meanwhile, a dis jockey blared house music from the massive speakers with virtual imagery of the Manhattan skyline. Moses and Shawnette grabbed each other and began laughing. They decided to stroll on the cruiser. There was a cushioned booth with a floral setting, nicely set plates, utensils, glasses, and menus. The couple dashed on deck, looking at the East River and the city.

"Wow, this is something," Shawnette said.

Moses was at a loss for words. He kept to himself a bit, but he knew that as the night approached, he would have to come out of his shell.

Valentin tapped Moses on the shoulder. "How do you like everything?" Valentin asked in his accent, a smile from ear to ear.

"Very good!" Moses exclaimed with a burst of laughter.

"Good. We should be setting sail within thirty minutes. The crew wants to ensure everyone is comfortable," Valentin shook his hand.

"Thanks, Valentin," Moses said graciously.

"You're very welcome, my friend. See you in a bit," Valentin strutted away. An attractive female stewardess approached them, handing them two glasses of Pina Coladas.

Thirty minutes later, the yacht's engine set sail along the East River with majestic skyscrapers in view. Moses and Shawnette clanked their drinks and sipped their beverages. They weren't verbose; they were overwhelmed by this uniquely crafted ship. As the yacht sailed, Moses peered his head over the side and eyed the boat's structure. The silent engine had a low moaning sound. Moses turned and caressed Shawnette's shoulder, moving down to her bare arms to her red dress. He wanted to tell her that red looked good on her. The color complimented Shawnette whether the outfits were for an occasion or a season. Even the different shades were becoming of her. When she and Moses met in college, she wore a pretty cherry-red shirt with some studs. The color certainly captured Moses' attention.

"You look good in that color. I never told you that red looks good on you," Moses cleared his throat. Shawnette smiled and kissed him on the cheek.

"You don't look too bad yourself, Moses," Shawnette complimented.

"This is just a plain old shirt I had from last year," Moses said, unostentatious about his attire.

"It doesn't look like some plain old shirt to me," Shawnette squinted at Moses' modest attitude. Then he got quiet again.

"Baby, what's wrong?" Shawnette asked.

"Nothing," Moses kept his eyes focused on the water.

"Moses, you roamed around the swimming pool at home like a zombie the other night. What's up, honey," Shawnette pleaded.

"I'm going to find my brother. I haven't told my mother yet," Moses said.

"You haven't talked much about him. What happened?" Shawnette raised an eyebrow.

"All I can say is that we were tight as kids. Gradually, our bond broke. Isaac should be here on this yacht with me. I don't know if he's dead or alive," he tried his best to fight his tears. This was no time to get choked up over family issues.

"Did you call the police?" Shawnette asked.

"They can't do anything about it. Isaac is an adult, and even when my family contacted the authorities, he was already eighteen. Who knew that he would vanish," Moses leaned his body against the balcony.

"Right now, you should be celebrating. You've got a new business partner who has all this and more. So, stay focused, Moses. Your brother will turn up," Shawnette grimaced.

"Hello, Mr. Remington. Do you need anything?" the stewardess asked humbly.

"Not really; I finished my drink," Moses handed the stewardess his glass, and so did Shawnette.

"Thank you," Moses said.

"Thank you, "Shawnette said. The stewardess strutted away.

Without any words, Moses wrapped his arms around Shawnette like an octopus. He embraced his girlfriend tighter than he did the other night. He then released the tightness of the hug and made it breathable. "Let's enjoy ourselves," Moses said.

As night approached, so did the Macy's Fourth of July Fireworks Show. Red, white, and blue lit up the sky. Moses, Shawnette, Valentin, and their business colleagues clanked their fancy bubbly champagne glasses. Moses kissed Shawnette passionately under booming, sparkly, loud fireworks, where a person couldn't even hear themselves talk. Calvin had his hand around Irene's waist as these two lovers kissed. He notices his stepson and girlfriend kissing. Calvin glared at Shawnette's buttocks and then eyed her down to her feet while moving up to her rear end once more. Moses opened his eyes, catching his stepfather red-handed. Calvin quickly turned away, laying a kiss on Irene's cheek. He hugged her like never before. Moses' face turned fiery red while still engaged in a lip lock with Shawnette. He had to control his fury. Moses then kissed his girlfriend on the forehead as they watched the patriotic celebration. But then, he peeked over at his stepfather, who turned away again. Again, Moses' heart raced in his chest. His grip tightened around the thin champagne glass. He had to control his temper to avoid breaking his business partner's property.

"A womanizer! There's a possibility he's cheated on my mother. Over the years, I've seen shit firsthand," Moses cursed in his head while the summery breeze tickled his nose with Shawnette's Chanel allure fragrance. Even though Calvin wasn't physically touching Shawnette, his glaring eyeballs were troubling enough.

⁂

At dinner, Moses and Shawnette gathered with everyone at a beautifully set booth. They ate steak, shrimp, lobster, veggies, ribs, and fancy summery dishes. The stewardesses served their guests wines and beer, both alcoholic and non-alcoholic. More house music continued to blare throughout the yacht. Isabella strutted over to Moses with more champagne. She filled up Calvin's wine glass, and he smiled while glaring in her face. Moses peered at his stepfather again, catching him in the act. He wondered how many times he'd cheated on his mother. *"He's been eyeing the stewardess since we stepped on this ship. Fuckin' asshole,"* Moses screamed in his head. He gave his attention to Valentin, who had discussed purchasing apartments and townhouses in Manhattan.

"We'll discuss more business later. Right, Moses?" Valentin guffawed. He and Moses high-fived one another. The stewardess again waltzed to the table and served slices of red velvet cakes with red, white, and blue sparklers.

"Oh, this is nice," Irene cried.

"Happy fourth, baby," Shawnette said. She pecked Moses on the cheek. While Isabella continued serving cake to the rest of the table, Calvin peered at her waistline and the rest of her frame. Moses kept his attention on his girlfriend and everyone else at the table, but from the corner of his eye, he saw Calvin. Moses shook his head in frustration as Shawnette took notice.

"What's wrong, Moses? Shawnette whispered.

"Nothing," Moses held his head down to avoid drawing attention to Calvin. He focused his eyes on Calvin. Again, that cardiac muscle raged in Moses' chest with closed fists. If he could get away with it, Moses would beat the shit out of his stepfather without any words exchanged, without the authorities involved. Like the asshole Calvin was, he peered over his shoulder without any discretion. He watched the stewardess make her way to the bar. Moses threw his napkin on the table and stormed away.

"Moses!" Shawnette cried.

"What's wrong?" Barbara asked.

"Something's irritating him," Shawnette said.

"Is he okay?" Valentin said as his face trembled.

"I'm pretty sure it's nothing. He's fine." Barbara advised.

Moments later, Moses paced the floor in the men's room, punching his fists in the air like a mentally ill person. Luckily, no one was in there to observe him throwing a fit alone. They would've put him in a straitjacket. Then Valentin stormed through the swinging.

"Are you okay, Moses?" Valentin asked.

"I'm all right. I've got a lot on my mind," Moses continued to pace.

"Did I say something wrong?"

"No, Valentin. You're fine. We're going to be fine, and I'm blessed to have you as my partner," Moses shook his hand.

"Okay,'" Valentin agreed. Both men exited the bathroom. They strolled along the deck, where the Manhattan skyline was before them. The yacht sailed under the Brooklyn Bridge along the East River. The world's most famous bridge was up close and personal as vehicles drove across it. The sightseeing made Moses forget about his flirtatious stepfather for the moment. He couldn't bring his issues to Valentin. That's bad for business. Since people weren't around, Valentin thought he'd talk a little one-on-one with Moses about their plans. Moses didn't mind since nobody was around. Valentin knew of an old, abandoned mansion in Cannes, France where the owner fell ill and wanted to sell. Valentin showed photos of the property on his cell phone and the land surrounding the estate. This mega-mansion is in foreclosure, and Moses wanted to fly to France first thing in the morning. Valentin planned their journey on his private jet the next day and left Moses's side. Moses gazed into the blackened waters of the river while the yacht's humming relaxed his body. He smiled to himself, having been successful so far. It was like a dream. Then Moses heard a masculine voice echoing from the lower deck. He followed the familiar tone. He crept down the steps to the lower deck and noticed Calvin seated on a stool at a small bar. The stewardess wiped the counter with a white cloth while Calvin tried to impress her with his Italian. He couldn't speak well. He grabbed her hand; she pulled away. Moses stormed to his stepfather's side.

"What's up, Calvin? Let's chat up on deck," Moses bellowed as he startled Calvin. He splashed some of his drink on the counter.

"I'm sorry, darling," Calvin apologized.

"I bet you are, Moses added. The two men trotted up the steps to the main deck. As the two men reached the main deck, shit hit the fan. "What are you doing? Don't jeopardize my business. I pulled your ass in here! You're flirting with my partner's stewardess and checking out Shawnette. And don't play it off. I saw you looking at her ass," Moses bitched.

"I don't know what you're talking about," Calvin snickered, not making eye contact with Moses.

"Don't disrespect my mother," Moses turned blood red.

"It won't happen again," Calvin pleaded. He reached out to shake Moses' hand. Moses didn't reciprocate the gesture. He gave his stepfather the cold shoulder and fixed his eyes on the East River.

The next morning, a matte black jet landed at Nimes International Airport as its screeching wheels touched the runway. Valentin sure did have a lot of toys for Moses to see, from a helicopter ride to a yacht. The plane taxied to the gate while Moses laid his head on the headrest of the silvery leather seat. The jet's interior had gray leather recliner seats, white walls, and ceilings, and added black décor to bring contrast to the setting. He was impressed by the decorator, who only used three colors to make this surrounding worthwhile. Moses glared out of the small window, hoping to see something different. But the airport was like every other airport worldwide; aircrafts landing and taking off. Moses prayed to see mountains and hills in the distance, but he had to wait until he hopped in a car. Only then did he see some sightseeing around Monaco.

In minutes, Moses and Valentin sped through the airport, steering his navy black Mercedes onto the road. Moses glanced over both shoulders, admiring the beautiful homes on the hillside. The colors were bright and gave a Hollywood vibe like Double O Seven. Very vibrant flowers aligned the streets, leaving a perfumery whiff in the air. Valentin drove the car where the steering wheel was on the right side. Moses' eyes almost jumped out of his head. This was something new to him.

"Doesn't it feel funny driving with the steering wheel on the right side?" Moses watched how his colleague handled the vehicle like a race car driver.

"It's the same thing. Just on the opposite side," Valentin said, shrugging his shoulders.

Seconds later, the black Mercedes pulled up to an enormous fence, and Valentin beeped the horn. The gate opened slowly, and Valentin drove the Mercedes Benz onto the curvy path to the foreclosed manor. The two-story maestoso estate was constructed of concrete and stone with a light yellow and beige finish. The vehicle's brakes squealed as it stopped short before the property. An eighteen-wheeler moving truck sat in front of the property. Moving men loaded elegant, plastic-wrapped furniture into the truck. Moses didn't allow the monster truck to spoil his view of this unique home. He remembered envisioning a mansion in the South of France when he was a kid. Moses pictured every house he saw in magazines, on YouTube, on mainstream television, and in the flesh back in the States. He got out of the car, still in a trance.

Valentin didn't engage in any verbal communication either. He was also in a trance-like state of this magnificent house. Moses stepped towards the structure as if approaching a giant looking down on him. This home overwhelmed him to the point where he got nauseated. He took sharp breaths and tried not to let his colleague see him in another one of his episodes. Moses hoped this property didn't have a supernatural presence. If so, then he wasn't interested. Valentin and Moses swaggered to the heavy wooden door. As it swung open, they were greeted by the former lady of the home – a woman of her mid-seventies, a beautiful Rachel Welch type, and a Bridgette Baptiste. She stood in the doorway of her Chanel taupe-colored jumper while a light wind blew her unique fragrance. It was created by her husband, Perfumer Pierre Baptiste. Moses had never smelt anything like it before; it was beautiful. He didn't know what the notes were but wanted to find out.

"Hello, Valentin," this Hollywood look-alike greeted her dear friend with a hug and kiss.

"Bridgette how are you?" he greeted her in return with a hug and kiss. Bridgette's husband had suffered several strokes during the past several years because he had been a heavy smoker. Then, Mr. Baptiste met his demise.

Valentin introduced Moses to this “Plein aux as” woman, who only turned up her nose when she or her husband met new people. Moses’ heart raced in his chest upon meeting Bridgette. Meeting an affluent person residing in Monaco made him almost have an accident in his pants. This meeting was far more paramount than any Hollywood personality. Mrs. Baptiste shook Moses’ hand. Moses didn’t get the sense she was astonished, nor did she realize he was a real estate investor. Instead, Bridgette handled it like a professional and acted like she was meeting another businessman.

Moses and Valentin followed Bridgette into the foyer, where a mover removed a large painting from the wall. More movers in the living room wrapped a sofa in plastic and carried it outside. Haulers proceeded with their task throughout the entire mansion. They removed lounge chairs, beds, desks, armoires, wall décor, vases, carpets, plants, etc. Mr. and Mrs. Baptiste had dwelled in this residence since the mid-sixties, having entertained their guests throughout the years. Pierre had grown his flowers, herbs, and plants on the estate grounds. All were used to create his unique scents. Moses saw the floral gardens on the property through the open double doors of the family room. He saw movers haul more chairs, bookshelves, and table decor. Surprisingly, Valentin and Bridgette didn’t engage in French; therefore, they wouldn’t be rude. She gave the gentlemen a tour of the mansion as Moses zigzagged out of a mover’s path, carrying a large painting.

On a second-level concrete balcony with panoramic views, Moses and Valentin used binoculars to spot every detail. Moses observed a yacht sailing along the Mediterranean Sea with a couple of model-type girls. Both were in their early twenties and were skinny dipping in the ocean.

“Check it out, Valentin!” Moses captured the view through binoculars with pleasure on his face. He gave the binoculars to Valentin. He observed the naked girls swimming in the ocean.

“Oh, that’s nothing. That happens every day,” Valentin gave the binoculars back to Moses. Moses looked through them again and saw a girl water skiing with the boat speeding along the sea.

“Water skiing, that’s cool,” Moses said, a smile on his face.

"Water skiing, polo, golfing, wineries - all that good stuff. Nice, but there's nothing like having real true people in your life. Monaco, Beverly Hills, Park Avenue, the Hamptons. There's nothing like having a true friend to share wealth. When I was eight, you know my family had generational wealth. We had an estate with many rooms, furniture, and gardens where vegetables and fruit trees grew along the property. Also, the estate had heating, air conditioning, and electricity. I had a friend named Hans, the opposite of me. His mother, Estelle, cleaned my mother's Chambre, her bedroom. Hans and Estelle lived on the other side of town, where life wasn't so great. A lot of drugs, prostitution, and violence. Ghettos. Ghettos are everywhere in the world, not just in the United States. They're also not only full of black and brown people. White people grow up in these environments as well. Whenever Hans and I played together, my parents disapproved, so they wanted me to act accordingly. But I kept my friendship with Hans over the years, even after his mother retired. We kept in touch until he and I went our separate ways in life. He didn't want to be around me anymore. Hans changed and got involved with some bad people. So, I had to cut off my friendship because I didn't want to jeopardize my life or my parents. From that experience, I don't judge a person on their economic background or race," Valentin lectured.

Moses squinted his eyes and tried to figure out where he was getting at. Valentin took notice of his colleague's expression.

"What I'm trying to say is, I don't have much time left. And I wanted you to have the best that life has to offer. As for my friend Hans, I wanted to give him a better life. From one human to the next," Valentin concluded.

"So, this billionaire tycoon comes out of nowhere and chooses me. Why?" Moses asked himself.

"Valentin, why me?" he asked the billionaire, who was confident in his decision. He paced a little and then stopped in his tracks.

"Because God told me to do so," Valentin responded positively.

A Remington Realty sign sat on the lawn of a Little Neck middle-class brick home on Long Island. The neighborhood was surrounded by trees, giving a fairytale ambiance. John Dalton, his wife, and two young sons waited for the realtor to give them a tour of their new home. Mrs. Dalton held her kids close to her. She glanced over both her shoulders, nervously. Her husband, Mr. Dalton glanced at his watch and shook his head.

"Dad, I'm tired," his youngest stomped his foot on the concrete. Mr. Dalton pressed the button on his keys to unlock the car door. The mother and kids rushed back to the vehicle.

"Find out where the realtor is, John!" his wife demanded.

"I am. I am," Mr. Dalton dialed the phone number for Remington firm on his cellphone. There was a connection.

"Hello. Remington Realty, this is Jocelyn speaking. How can I help you?" she greeted from the other end of the phone.

"Yes, hello. This is John Dalton and I'm waiting for the realtor Calvin Mitchell. It's been over two hours," Mr. Dalton paced the ground.

CHAPTER TWENTY-FOUR

Soon after Moses' business trip to Monaco, he and Valentin checked ads for potential sellers of upscale apartments and condos in Manhattan. Both businessmen checked out an apartment in Soho with its large rooms, long corridors, and detailed ceilings and walls. Moses caressed his hands along the walls and loved their smoothness. He took significant steps towards the living room window, where he enjoyed the city's panoramic view. Valentin checked out other parts of the residence.

"Moses!" Valentin cried.

"Where are you?" Moses cried in response.

"The kitchen," Valentin hollered as his voice echoed. Moses swaggered down the long, bright corridor. Then, he walked into the large gourmet kitchen with an island table. It had see-through cabinets, two stoves with fourteen burners, two ovens, and a microwave. Valentin ran his finger along the marble top of the island. Moses then opened the doors of the cabinets, ovens, and glass refrigerator with a virtual monitor. The bathroom had an old-fashioned tub, toilet, and sinks. An enormous master suite had a sunken sitting area and a concrete balcony with a slide-in door. Moses stepped onto it with patio furniture. He viewed the building before him without any disturbance from his colleagues. The urban view seemed like the scenery in Monaco a few weeks earlier. Then his cell phone vibrated on his hip. The caller ID read: Private. Moses took a deep breath and answered the call. On the other end of the phone was a heavy-spoken gentleman who seemed to be dying. Though, he was interested in talking to Moses about Isaac's case. Moses wanted to meet with the Valley Stream detective as soon as possible. Both men agreed on that.

The next day, elevator music played on the speakers in the ceiling of a diner in Valley Stream. The detective resided at the table for two with an unoccupied chair across from him. He scrolled through her email on her cellphone. Moses hurried into the empty chair before this pudgy gentleman and shook his hand. He introduced himself, fidgeting in his seat with a smile. The Valley Stream detective initiated the conversation. He placed his cell phone on the table and jotted notes about Isaac's case on his iPad.

"Where do we begin? I don't even know where to start your brother's search." The detective doubted.

"I don't have a clue either," Moses scratched his head. The search seemed hopeless, and the last person to see Isaac was his girlfriend, Clarissa. But what would she know? The only thing the detective could do was to talk to Clarissa, his mother, Irene, and his Uncle Tyler. In the short term, Moses didn't want to jeopardize the business he had worked so hard to get. He had to take business trips, hold conferences, and attend meetings with some extraordinary people. The detective suggested that Moses post Isaac's case on social media, but Moses didn't like that idea. Someone could fabricate information on Isaac's whereabouts to extort money out of him, especially by him being a real estate tycoon. That was a risk he didn't want to take. And if the detective interviewed his mother, it wouldn't help any. Irene wasn't the last to see him, but she was the one who slapped him across the face, which caused his disappearing act. Moses hadn't heard from Clarissa in years. "*She probably moved to another state and started a new life. When Isaac first went missing, she stuck around for a little while, but after that, we never heard from her again. I didn't think she loved my brother. I know I loved him. I know I slacked off during our high school years, but eventually, we were going to patch up our relationship,*" Moses thought to himself. He apologized for wasting the detective's time. Searching for Isaac wasn't going to work. He was now a grown man who had forgotten the whole thing. He pounded his fist on the table and stormed away.

At Remington Realty later that afternoon, Barbara helped Jocelyn with some duties in the office. The phone rang. Barbara picked up the receiver, "Hello. Remington Realty, this is Barbara Levi speaking. How can I help you? An older gentleman could be heard screaming on the other end of the phone. Barbara held the receiver away from her ear, so this upset client didn't deafen her. She tried to reason with this enraged woman who expected Calvin to give her a tour of a house in Bayside, Queens. "I sincerely apologize, Mrs. Kerron. I'm going to send an agent over there right away.

"But, you're all the way in the city!" Mrs. Kerron hollered.

"It doesn't matter. I'm sending an agent right now. It's going to take a while to get Bayside," Barbara beckoned Zahira to drive to Bayside for the Open house.

"What kind of real estate firm? I thought you guys had such a good reputation," Mrs. Kerron screamed even louder. Barbara placed her hand over the receiver while the client was still enraged.

"Zahira, I need you to speed to bayside and do the open house," Barbara insisted.

"Yes, ma'am," Zahira grabbed the folder about the property and rushed out of the office.

"My agent Zahira will be there, Mrs. Kerron. I sincerely apologize for the delay," Barbara sighed.

"Alright," Mrs. Kerron abruptly disconnected the call. Barbara complained about Calvin being irresponsible. She and Jocelyn chatted about the stress on the job. The realtors whispered around the water cooler about Calvin not showing up for open houses and Moses having issues with his stepfather's behavior. Also, the women discussed how he'd wink, grab them, and try to kiss them. Shawnette strutted in tiredly, wearing her red pumps, purse, and briefcase. She noticed how her colleagues gathered like a pack of hyenas feasting on food scraps. Shawnette sat down in the empty chair close to them. "Where's Moses?"

"I don't know. Calvin stood up another client at an open house," Barbara shrugged her shoulders, slamming a stack of folders on the desk. Then the boss stormed into the office, scowling and not making eye contact with anyone. His team scattered back to their desks. Everyone occupied themselves with their work. "Baby, what's going on?" Shawnette asked her lover as he ignored her concerns.

"Moses, I need to know what we'll do about Calvin. He stood up another at an open House in Bayside. I sent Zahira to fill in for him," Barbara gave chase. Moses stormed passed Kevin's desk as he took care of business on the phone with a client. He noticed his boss rush by his cubicle.

"Moses, I've got great news," Kevin shouted to Moses while he proceeded to his main office. He thrust the door open. Moses plopped his body in his lounge chair. He turned his back on his colleagues, facing the window. Barbara stood directly in front of Moses, face-to-face. "Calvin's, making you look bad here," Barbara advised. Moses swirled around in his recliner, facing Shawnette sitting on the edge of his desk. The search for Isaac was a done deal. What was Moses going to do now? He let it out, sobbing. Shawnette and Barbara automatically wrapped their arms around him, hoping to assist with whatever issues he had. Then Valentin swaggered, addressing Moses about some apartments that would interest the city. Shawnette and Barbara shushed them.

"I'll never find my brother. Ah, shit," Moses whimpered.

The boss's pain grabbed Valentin's attention. He squinted his eyes and cocked his head. "What's he talking about?" Valentin mouthed.

Shawnette motioned to him, placing her finger to her mouth.

"Moses, I took care of the open house in Jackson Heights, Queens," Kevin announced and dashed into Moses' office.

"Tell Moses later," Shawnette cut Kevin off.

"What's the matter," Kevin asked.

"Not right now, Kelvin," Valentin mispronounced his name.

"It's Kevin, not Kelvin," he corrected Valentin. Barbara escorted Kevin and Valentin as they bickered their way out of Moses' office. Barbara closed Moses' office door with ease. Shawnette consoled her fiancé in his time of need. Whatever it was, she'd be there for him. The exchange of words between Moses' colleagues didn't bother him. Moses wanted to be locked up in a dark room and die. He held Shawnette around the waist, smelling her alien perfume. He loved that fragrance on her, he didn't mind it going directly up his nostrils. Moses sunk into his world of darkness, where there was nothing. No hope, no love, no happiness, and no light. He had to open his eyes. Only then could they see the beautiful woman who gave him hope. And yes, he choked back his tears. Shawnette smiled at him, wiping his tears away. Moses' mind was blank. He held Shawnette around her waist and closed his eyes once more.

Then Calvin barged into Moses' office, acting like he was the big cheese in the firm. He smiled from ear to ear, announcing that he took care of the buyers at the Open houses. Calvin's annoying voice disturbed Moses' peace. Lie after lie after lie, Calvin talked about giving house tours to clients, which was false. His lies made Moses' blood boil. *"I could hop over the desk and beat the shit out of him! This is my fuckin' business. I'm not going to lose it,"* he said in his mind. Calvin was wrapped up in his own little world and didn't even see that his stepson was in emotional pain. Or he didn't care. Calvin was a liar. A romancer with fantasies in his head. His life is a lie. Calvin is the Isaac is out here in the world," Moses thought in his head. He released his hands from Shawnette's waist, glaring at his Calvin with tears in his eyes. Moses wiped his tears, quickly. He noticed Calvin kept talking and talking. Lie after lie after lie.

"You 're a fuckin' liar, Calvin. You stood up the clients at the Open houses!" Moses addressed him in a stern tone.

"What! Lying about what, Moses?" Calvin looked him dead in the eyes.

"You never showed up for the clients. I had Kevin, Zahira, and other realtors rush to the locations to take care of the situation! Plus, you've been making my lady colleagues and clients uncomfortable with your comments, glaring, and touching!" Moses pounded his fist on his desk. Shawnette took a couple of steps with a smirk on her face.

"Are you accusing me of sexual harassment? You've got to be shitting me," Calvin pushed his backside against the chair. He shook his head.

"You're terminated. Get out! Clean out your desk!" Moses pointed to the door.

Calvin pounded his fists on Moses' desk. "I'll sue you!"

"You don't have a fuckin' case! Go!" Moses marched to his office, gesturing him out. His stepfather took his time exiting the office. "This won't be the last you see of me."

Moses slammed his office door. "I hope this is the last I see of this fuck! I want to put this behind me and move forward with my business and life. And hope to find Isaac.

That night Moses lay in his California King bed with black satin sheets. He closed his eyes and didn't want to open them. Now, he was back in the real world. A place with real anguish that hadn't a brother and a family that was about to fall apart. God forbid that he has his business. "I don't have a clue how to find my brother. What could I do? I gave up on Isaac's case. And maybe that's why Isaac was gone. My family's fucked up!" Moses opened his eyes as the fancy ceiling fan blew fresh air over him. He is worried, as Moses smiled at Shawnette, snoozing peacefully. She slept in his fuchsia satin short gown, and jet-black hair with a cute bob cut. Moses leaned in close, getting a whiff of Shawnette's Alien fragrance. He recognized Shawnette's closed eyes. *"Shawnette's got to be dreaming. What is she dreaming of? "That's a stupid question, me, of course,"* Moses proudly smiled. That dream of Shawnette's must be good. Her eyeballs shifted left and then right slowly. It must be a wet dream or something relating to Moses. Whatever it was, he allowed her to sleep. He shut his eyes, trying to imagine something pleasant as an escape.

Darkness has a place in everyone's life - whether you're black, white, Latino, Asian, rich, or poor - this entity devours everyone. The seven train chugged along the tracks with screeching brakes, pulling into Grand Central Station. The subway car's double doors widened as the passengers got on and off the train. "Next stop, Fifth Avenue, and Forty-Second Street. Please watch the closed doors," the automated conductor announced as the bells chimed. Then the double doors shut. The train chugged through the tunnel without light, its horn totting. Eight staircases below, Isaac slept on a flattened cardboard box as he woke up to the train's horn from above. Hearing the horn of the subway was a first for him since he's been living in the shadows for almost a decade. As he squinted his eyes, Isaac recognized only candlelight, where Jessica and Shereza slept. He lifted his head from the landing on the bottom staircase, where he rested. Isaac had no idea what time it was; he figured it was either the middle of the night or the witching hour. Bobby snored as if he slept comfortably in his home without a care. A rat scurried into the corner close to where Isaac and Bob resided. Isaac raised his head from the cardboard, trying to chase the rodent away. He threw one of his shoes at the vermin. The pest scrambled up the staircase, squeaking. Bob sat up and looked around, smiling at his friend Isaac.

"What happened, my friend?" Bobby asked with his half-opened eyes.

"Nothing, Bob. Go back to sleep," Isaac suggested to his friend. Bob yawned and fell asleep. Surprisingly, that bump didn't wake Jessica and Shereza. Nothing seemed to startle this youngster. She probably never heard of monsters' tales. Everyone down here could be eaten alive. Isaac had a pounding headache due to the eighty-nine-degree temperature. He laid his head on the sleeping bag slowly and closed his eyes. Isaac wanted this headache to go away; maybe he needed some food. Rummaging through New York's trash cans sometimes couldn't make ends meet. People drank their beverage, saved the bottle, and got a five-cent refund. Other times, some other hobo would beat him to it. He'd have to steal. Right now, he needed to rest awhile. Later, he would see what happened.

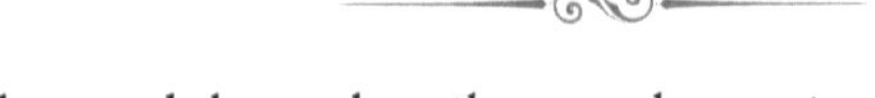

Sun rays beamed through a silver steel grate into the subway below Grand Central Station. A possum scurried in the garbage, searching for food, and large cockroaches crawled in and out of holes. Isaac was on a mission to find some food. He noticed the sunshine from a distance as he went to the eight staircases. He swaggered to grate and glared up at the outside world above him. Isaac wished he could be on the beach in the Caribbean or California, living it up. He'd rather be a homeless beach bum than a subway bum, but Isaac and his cronies needed to be safe. It was hot with no humidity, which wasn't so bad. Isaac made it his business to subside this headache of his, which still pounded in his temple.

Later that day, pigeons pecked at pieces of bread thrown at them. As always, Maggie sat on the park bench. She wore her old Beatles t-shirt with John Lennon's face, paired with old, faded jeans and old beat-up sneakers. This old bag woman glanced over her shoulder, hoping to see her friend Isaac. A kind stranger gave her a couple of dollars and brought her some food. Maggie generously saved one of the sandwiches for Isaac if he came to the park. Then she noticed her friend swaggering across the two-way street and towards the park. Isaac waved to Maggie. He placed his hand on his head due to the pounding headache that wouldn't stop.

"Hey, Isaac. I'm returning the favor. Here's a chicken sandwich for you," Maggie shoved the food in his face. Isaac had no problem taking the sandwich. He immediately unwrapped it and took a big bite.

"Thank you, Maggie," Isaac said with his mouth full. He swallowed his food and then took another bite.

"I haven't seen you in a couple of days," Maggie proceeded to feed the birds.

"I've been struggling with migraines," Isaac swallowed easily. He chewed his food slowly before it went down the wrong way.

"Migraines! Whoa, they're the worst!" Maggie said.

"Tell me about it, "Isaac continued eating his sandwich.

"What's on your agenda for today?" Maggie asked, smiling, exposing her blackened teeth. Isaac couldn't answer Maggie because he still crammed the sandwich in his mouth. He then gulped the Italian bread, chicken breast, cheese, red onions, lettuce, tomato, and black olive.

"I planned to collect some bottles and cans. I must get some food for them. Thanks for giving me this sandwich. My headache is going away. And I've got some energy right now," Isaac said.

"You're very welcome, my friend," Maggie smiled and nodded. Isaac shoved the last piece of sandwich into his mouth. Then, he looked around for a garbage can. He threw the sandwich wrapper in it. He almost forgot that he had to collect bottles and cans. Isaac rummaged through the trash can. "Maggie, do you have any plastic bags by any chance?" Isaac asked humbly.

She grabbed some plastic bags from her shopping cart and gave them to Isaac. Isaac grabbed two plastic bottles and then an aluminum can. He kept digging his hands further into the trash, but then Isaac gave up. He didn't want to search any further. He didn't want to come across anything gross. Isaac hustled to the trash can a few feet away while Maggie did what she loved most - feeding the birds. He cautiously ran his hands through the trash and found another soda can, along with another plastic bottle. That was it.

"What the fuck," Isaac sucked and exhaled, heading to a third trash can.

"Any luck, Isaac?" Maggie shouted from a distance.

"Not really," Isaac replied. He then went to a fourth, fifth, sixth, etc., seeking more bottles. There were no bottles to collect. "Where the fuck did they go?" Isaac said. The sanitation workers were out in full force, cleaning up the streets and parks and emptying the trash cans.

"That's where the money is," Isaac said to himself. A sanitation worker dumped garbage from a public can into the garbage truck. Isaac had to have some food for his friends by any means necessary.

That same morning in an office building a few blocks away, Moses and Shawnette were in his office alone. Instead of checking out the properties suggested by Valentin, the two love birds kissed. They caressed and undressed one another.

"Baby, we have to finish looking at these homes," Shawnette pushed Moses off her, trying to get him to look at the computer screen.

"We can look at them later. I want to see you. You're my property," Moses said in a low, sensual voice. He kept kissing her on the lips, face, neck, and then her hand.

"Moses! Moses! Come on!" Shawnette hollered. Then he focused his attention on his business. Moses scrolled through the homes in Beverly Hills, Bel Air, Palm Springs, London, Tokyo, Milan, and the remainder were in the south of France.

"Oh, look at this in San Francisco. This house is built on the side of a cliff! What if there's an earthquake or something? The house will crash into the water," Shawnette said, noticing the house had the Golden Gate Bridge in the background.

"That won't happen," Moses shook his head. Then his stomach rumbled and growled.

"Fuck! I need some food, Shawnie," Moses indicated.

"Alright, babe. Do you want to eat out?"

"No. Let's grab some takeout and bring it back. I've got a lot of work to do," Moses said.

Minutes later, Moses and Shawnette clutched hands as they strolled along the Manhattan sidewalk. They looked like the ideal couple with the perfect life. Shawnette wore her fuchsia jumpsuit, carrying her wristlet purse.

"Your birthday is coming," Shawnette reminded her lover as she kissed him.

Meanwhile, Isaac entered the supermarket and headed to the bottle machines. As he marched past the aisles, Isaac imagined he and his friends having something good to eat. Customers sneered at him and moved out of his path quickly. "I'm used to this treatment. Humans have always given me the cold shoulder, rolled their eyes, and whispered. When I was born, the nurses probably whispered about how awkward I looked. People would treat me better if I were an upscale businessman," Isaac thought. He approached the recyclable bottle machines, where one was available. Isaac inserted three of the plastics and got his tickets. Altogether they were worth fifteen cents. Then he pushed in two of the aluminum cans in the vendor machine. Isaac got two receipts for ten cents. "Only twenty-five cents. What am I going to do with a quarter?" Isaac murmured.

He opened his hand with a plastic bag balled up. Isaac's heart pounded heavily in his chest because he was risking his freedom. Isaac strolled around the produce, glancing over his shoulder. He shoved two apples into the plastic bag. He approached the deli department, where there were sandwiches, salads, and already prepared foods. Again, Isaac tried to make sure that no one was watching. He shoved a pack of buffalo wings, chicken salad, and a sandwich in his bag. Isaac's eyes shifted around as he stormed away.

The deli manager noticed Isaac stealing, and he phoned security. "There's a gentleman stealing from the deli department," the deli manager notified the general manager.

Moses and Shawnette strolled into the deli department and picked two chicken wraps.

"Do you want a Snapple?" Shawnette asked in her loving voice.

"Yeah, that's cool," Moses responded as he glared in the distance. On a long stretch of customers at the cash register, he saw a pale-skinned young man with blond dreadlocked-matted hair and shabby clothes. Moses gazed at the dreadful-looking human being waiting for his turn on the line. Also, Moses noticed the plastic bags of items this destitute person tried to conceal. Chances were that this young man, who looked down on his luck, had no money to pay for the food. Moses continued to stare at the line of people. Then Shawnette had a bunch of cumbersome items in her arms. "Moses, I need a basket," Shawnette alarmed her boyfriend. His girlfriend's scream snapped him out of his trance which could've wakened the dead.

In the line, Isaac waited for his turn when a fancy-dressed woman finished ahead of him with lots of food. The general manager stood before the cash register, eyeing Isaac while standing in line. The assistant manager guarded the entrance, and a security guard waited in front of the cashier. They had their eyes all on Isaac. He glanced over his shoulders, balls of sweat dripping on his face.

Moses and Shawnette took their place on the line while Moses kept his eyes fixed on this stranger that looked like his long-lost sibling. He then saw the plastic bag with the items in it. Isaac kept his eyes on the floor, but then it was his turn; he handed the cashier his bottle receipts. The clerk smiled and keyed in the amounts of the bottles on her register. Then the robust guard approached Isaac and snatched the plastic bag away.

"Do you think we're stupid? You don't think anyone is watching," the guard bellowed, which caught the customer's attention. And, of course, the guard's aggressive tone made Moses and Shawnette look.

"I'm starving, and I have to get some food for my friends and me," Isaac whimpered. By that recognizable tone, Moses' eyes widened. He suddenly intervened in the dispute. When he got closer to this depraved man, he said, "Isaac!" The general manager entered, dumping the food on the empty register next to another one.

"I'll pay for the items, sir," Moses grabbed his wallet.

"It's me, Moses. Isaac, we've been looking all over for you," Moses said. Isaac's heart pounded hard as he dashed through the entrance.

"Isaac!" Moses threw forty dollars at the cashier.

"Moses, where are you going?" Shawnette screamed. She dropped her food basket and gave chase.

Isaac sprinted through the streets of Manhattan traffic, glancing over his shoulder with his brother on his tail. Isaac heard his name being called repeatedly by the well-dressed gentleman claiming to be Moses. Isaac's name echoed through the streets for all of New York to hear. Isaac couldn't go home, face his mother, or deal with the bullshit from his fucked-up stepfather. "I'd rather live with the filth, rodents, and trash than live where it's clean. I can't endure abuse from a man who never claimed me as his own. Why doesn't he give up and leave me alone?" Isaac said to himself but kept his pace up.

The general and assistant managers chased Moses and Isaac through the packed streets; then, an NYPD van with eight officers took notice of the pursuit. "Police! He's a thief," the general manager of the supermarket shouted. All eight New York police officers joined in the chase. Isaac tried his best not to knock anyone down, but he had to get away from this man on his heels. As Isaac glanced over his shoulders, the NYPD officers also chased him. He started to weep and ran and ran as fast as he could. Not only was Moses after him, but so were the boys in blue. "God, please help to get me home. The home that I dwell in. Please make these people go away. Who are they?" Isaac wept aloud. The tears in his eyes caused his vision to become very blurry. He snatched his glasses off, throwing them to the ground. Isaac wiped his watery eyes to see better. His sight was more apparent as he ran down the steps of Grand Central Station. He scrambled down the long corridors of the station, hopped the turnstile, and weaved in and out between straphangers waiting for the number seven train. As Isaac got to the platform's edge, he turned and stopped. The people waiting looked at him in wonder. Then Moses did the same thing that his brother, who was dashing through a station corridor, had done. He jumped the turnstile and made his way to the platform. Moses looked over both shoulders and noticed Isaac.

"Isaac!" Moses shouted as he gave chase.

Isaac ran down those small flights of yellow steps in the middle of the tracks. Moses stopped and hesitated to enter the forbidden territory. The NYPD officers ran to the platform, looked, and saw Moses.

"Hey, you!" An officer shouted.

Moses stuck his chest out and went after his brother. He tried to catch up to Isaac as fast as possible, but Isaac was too swift. Moses then realized that he could lose his life. He glanced over his shoulder, and no subway approached. Moses heard the police officers' radios echoing and flashlights shining through the dark tunnel. Then he saw Isaac running to the side of the train tracks with a flashlight and to the condemned area with "DO NOT ENTER" tape. Isaac tore the strip of tape, removed the piece of concrete from the hole, and slid his body through it. But he didn't place the large chunk back. Moses ran to the area with the "DO NOT ENTER" tape.

"What the fuck is this?" Moses couldn't understand what was going on with Isaac. *"Is he living down here?"* he asked himself. Police radios echoed. They got louder and were getting closer and closer. "Holy shit!" Moses slid his body through the hole.

As Moses entered, there was some light. He cautiously crept to the staircase's landing and heard heavy footsteps descending.

"Isaac," Moses cried. He ran down the first flight and continued to chase his brother down eight flights of steps. On the way down, Moses smelt the stench of human waste, blood, and garbage. Rats and enormous cockroaches scurried in it. He grabbed his cell, realizing he had no signal. He couldn't use the flashlight on it. Moses leaned over the balancer and saw his brother's shadowy figure.

"Isaac! Isaac!" Moses cried to his brother again.

He proceeded down the staircase; it became darker. Moses watched where he stepped due to the pitch blackness. Heavy footsteps tramped down each flight of staircases. Then Moses halted in his tracks. He did not know if he was in the stairs' middle, top, or bottom of the stairs. His heart raced in his chest, and he breathed heavily. *"What the fuck is this? Does he live down here?"* Moses asked himself. He wanted to call his brother's name again but hesitated.

Moses carefully took his time going down the staircase, where he couldn't see a thing. There was a glow as he got down close to the last staircase. Moses stopped on the landing, where he noticed Bob snoozing on a piece of cardboard. More and more sewage surrounded the premises. He looked straight ahead of him, seeing Isaac standing his ground. Isaac guarded the condensed space that Jessica and Shereza occupied. Moses took caution, heading down the steps and holding the railing. The two brothers glared at each other. Moses had found his other half, with whom he shared birthdays, holidays, secrets, hopes, and dreams. *"How the fuck did this happen?"* Moses wondered. He inhaled and got teary-eyed.

"Isaac, I've looked all over for you. We've been looking for you. Mom's been worried sick for almost ten years. How did you wind up like this?" Moses whined.

"You should know the answer to that," Isaac replied with an unpleasant expression. Moses recalled his high school years that sabotaged their bond and, mainly, their stepfather.

"I got caught up in the girls and my popularity...I," Moses started, lost for words.

"It was all about you. And look at you now. GQ style. What's your line of work?" Isaac raised an eyebrow. Moses couldn't answer because it was apparent. The whiff of Moses' Spice bomb Cologne by Viktor and Rolf contacted Isaac's nose every few seconds. Bergamot, Grapefruit, Cinnamon Leaf, and Pink Pepper were some of the notes that made Isaac furious. "You and I had a dream. And we were supposed to do this together," Isaac whimpered.

Moses rushed over and embraced his brother simultaneously; Isaac didn't reciprocate the affection. The echoes of police radios got louder with tramping footsteps approaching. Moses knew he had to protect his brother. NYPD officers stopped at the bottom of the staircase, brandishing their firearms at Moses and Isaac.

"Mommy," a cry blurred out. Shereza woke up as she noticed bright flashlights and guns drawn. Jessica then coughed and awakened to the barrels of cops with flashing lights in their faces. Moses used his body as a shield to protect Isaac. Isaac did the same for Jessica and Shereza.

Moses held both hands in the air. He hoped these officers didn't pump any bullets into him, Isaac and whoever was down there.

"Don't shoot!" Moses reached for the sky even higher. Isaac didn't put his hands in the air. Instead, he glared at the boys in blue from over his brother's shoulder.

"What's going on?" the officer asked. Then, he realized the homeless people lived in the sub-level of darkness. The officers' sergeant radioed in.

"McGreevey! What's going on down there?" NYPD sergeant asked in a loud, demanding tone. Officer McGreevey didn't know how to respond, so he answered as best he could.

"We...got...a...colony down here," Officer McGreevey stuttered.

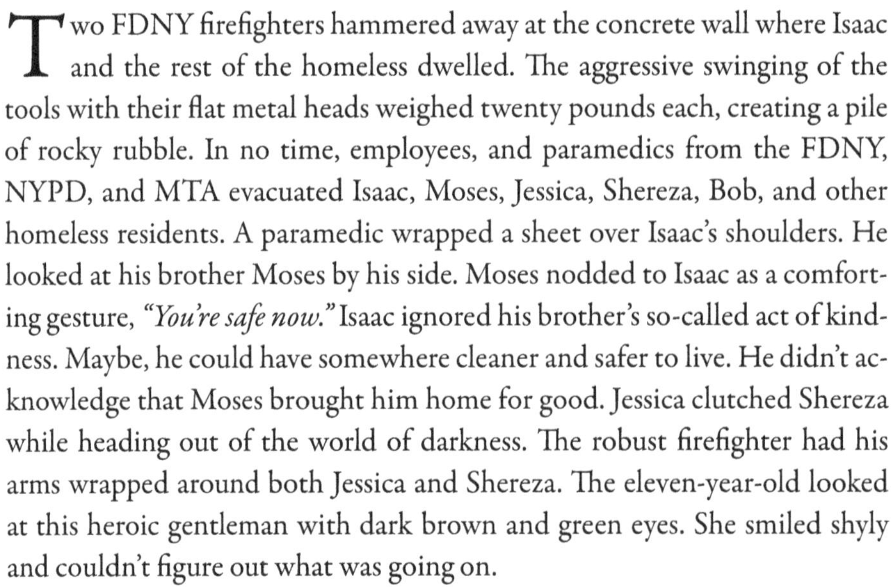

Two FDNY firefighters hammered away at the concrete wall where Isaac and the rest of the homeless dwelled. The aggressive swinging of the tools with their flat metal heads weighed twenty pounds each, creating a pile of rocky rubble. In no time, employees, and paramedics from the FDNY, NYPD, and MTA evacuated Isaac, Moses, Jessica, Shereza, Bob, and other homeless residents. A paramedic wrapped a sheet over Isaac's shoulders. He looked at his brother Moses by his side. Moses nodded to Isaac as a comforting gesture, *"You're safe now."* Isaac ignored his brother's so-called act of kindness. Maybe, he could have somewhere cleaner and safer to live. He didn't acknowledge that Moses brought him home for good. Jessica clutched Shereza while heading out of the world of darkness. The robust firefighter had his arms wrapped around both Jessica and Shereza. The eleven-year-old looked at this heroic gentleman with dark brown and green eyes. She smiled shyly and couldn't figure out what was going on.

"Mommy, what's happening?" Shereza gripped her mother's hand tight.

"We're going somewhere safe," Jessica assured her baby girl.

The sun beamed down on a crowd of spectators capturing the scene on their cell phone's video cameras and the live coverage from the local media and CNN. Isaac and Moses ascended the subway cemented stairs as a gurney awaited them. Two paramedics assisted Isaac as he lay on the stretcher and was wheeled into the ambulance. Moses was right by his brother every step as they entered the back of the ambulance. Then, it sped away. Isaac didn't have the chance to say goodbye to his friends with whom he had shared the same murky environment. He could only see the slightest bit of light from a candle, their struggles, fears, hopes, and dreams. Isaac placed his arm over his eyes and sobbed. Moses patted his brother on the shoulder.

"You're going to be fine, Isaac. When you leave the hospital, you're coming home with me. We're twins. "We're family," Moses whimpered. His cell phone vibrated. The caller ID read: Shawnette. "Shawnette," Moses answered his cell as the noise of the ambulance drowned out his call. So, he had to shout.

"Where are you, Moses?" Shawnette asked with a nervous quiver in her voice.

"I'm going to the hospital."

"What hospital!" Shawnette screamed over the cell.

"What hospital are you taking my brother to?" Moses asked the paramedic.

"New York-Presbyterian," the paramedic answered.

"New York-Presbyterian!" Moses shouted on his cell phone.

"Go get my mother and meet me at the hospital!" Moses demanded.

"For what!" Shawnette asked, not knowing what was going on.

"Listen to me, Shawnette. Do as I say!" Moses ended his call.

In the intensive care unit, doctors and nurses tried to subdue Isaac. He fought them off while they were trying to insert the IV into his hand. Moses had to help restrain his brother. Isaac then spat at one of the nurses. "What the hell! You bastard!" The nurse stuck the IV needle in his hand. Moses' face turned fiery after hearing the nurse insult his brother. Isaac regressed to a kid and cried like a baby. "I want to go home," Isaac whined.

"After you get better, you're coming with me like I told you," Moses promised. Moses saw the bitchy nurse storm away from Isaac's bedside. Moses gave chase. He pulled the curtain, concealing his brother. "Excuse me, what the fuck was that!" Moses hollered. The nurses and doctors took notice of the verbal exchange between Moses and the nasty nurse.

"How would you like it if someone spat on you," the nurse said, brushing him off.

"Where the fuck are your superiors!" Moses bellowed. The doctor approached Moses, apologizing for the nurse's rudeness. The male physician hounded him with questions about his brother's condition. Moses told her how his brother had lived sub-level within the subway system. Isaac needed a thorough check-up to make sure he was alright. Then Shawnette and Irene arrived. Moses embraced them.

"Your son's alive," Moses pointed to Isaac's bed area. Irene pulled the curtain open, seeing her baby boy in such a horrific condition.

"Isaac," Irene called to her son.

"Mom," Isaac responded. Irene embraced her son and kissed him regardless of his situation. She apologized for her ways and blamed herself for it all. As mother and son rekindled their relationship, Moses and Shawnette embraced each other. She figured out the same long hug they had at the house was like this one. And Shawnette knew the reason why.

CHAPTER TWENTY-FIVE

After a day and a half in the intensive care unit at the hospital, a medical staff member wheeled Isaac's bed into his eleventh-floor room. Isaac tore the IV from his hand. He leaped out of bed, stripped off his hospital gown, and sprinted nude into the bathroom. Isaac left a trail of blood on the floor, so the nurses hurried to clean it up. Isaac left the bathroom door cracked open. He stood under the showerhead and turned on the hot water. He grabbed the soap and cleansed himself. The nurse snatched the hospital gown from the floor as she and Moses waltzed to the bathroom doorway.

"Are you alright, Isaac," Moses stood against the wall adjacent to the bathroom. Isaac lathered the soap on his dirty body. He rid himself of the sewage, rotting garbage, waste, and rodents where he had laid. The black water swirled down the drain as Isaac scrubbed himself even harder with the soap. Moses noticed a steamy mist flow from the door opening and knocked on the door. "Isaac, isn't that too hot for a shower!"

"Let me shower in peace," Isaac hollered to Moses. Moses didn't say a word. Instead, he closed the door tight and left Isaac alone.

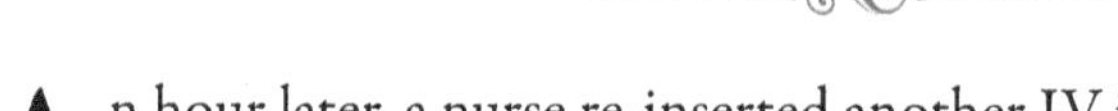

An hour later, a nurse re-inserted another IV into Isaac's hand. He didn't put up a fight this time. Isaac stretched in a hospital bed, wearing the patient gown. The nurse attached wires to Isaac's back and chest area, connecting to a heart rate monitor. He then rested his head on his pillow and noticed Moses watching him from a couple of feet away. Moses swaggered to his brother's bed with a smile. "How are you feeling?"

"Better," Isaac looked towards the window, not having much else to say. Moses noticed the frown upon Isaac's face; something vexed him. Moses dragged a chair to Isaac's bed and wanted to get into his brother's head.

"Whatever you have to say, Isaac, you can get it off your chest," Moses said in a sympathetic tone. Isaac ignored his brother. He kept his eyes on the outside world beyond the glass window.

"I know you're pissed at Mom and me for turning our back on you when you needed us the most," Moses continued while Isaac focused his eyes on the world beyond his reach.

"Should I tell Moses what's on my mind or let bygones be bygones? He's my other half, and I've got to move forward," Isaac said in his mind, peering at his brother from the corner of his eye. Moses repeatedly took deep breaths to get Isaac to acknowledge his presence.

"Isaac, I'm sitting right before you. I'm not outside!" Moses stormed out of his chair and paced the floor. Then Isaac looked at his brother as if Moses wanted to leave.

"Are you going to leave me again," Isaac asked, still gazing out the window.

"You left us, Isaac! I was going semi-crazy trying to figure out where the fuck you were!" Moses blared out without thinking before he spoke. Isaac focused on Moses standing close to the door.

"You were the only one who was there for me when everyone else gave me the cold shoulder, including Mom," Isaac expressed.

"Why didn't you stay with Uncle Tyler and Aunt Melissa? Sub-level of Grand Central?" Moses sighed.

"I had to do what I had to do," Isaac inhaled.

"Doctors must run all kinds of tests on you to ensure you're disease-free! You think this is a fuckin' joke," Moses paced the floor and eyeballed Isaac.

"I was a joke when you and Ryan were buddy, buddy. You were the popular one with all the pussy thrown in your face! Mom and Calvin played favorites with you. And I'll never forget that slap I received across the face. That fuckin did it!"

"So, what do you want me to do, Isaac? If I could change the past I would. And Ryan and I aren't buddy, buddy anymore," Moses hollered.

"But you can change the future. I know you went into real estate. Did you?" Isaac asked. Moses paced the floor and turned his back.

"I know you did. I could tell by the way you dress and your confidence. You've always had that. When you were selling your properties. Did you think of me?" Isaac whined.

"Yes, I did, Isaac," Moses turned abruptly to his brother with watery eyes. Tears cascaded down his cheeks as Moses wiped them away.

"Can you find a real estate course for when I get out of here, brother?"

Moses slowly made a three-sixty-degree axis and smiled at Isaac. Isaac's question heartened the brother moving forward. Irene, Shawnette, and Barbara waltzed into Isaac's room with balloons, cards, and food. Shawnette and Barbara didn't know Isaac, but they did it from the bottom of their hearts. When the three women surrounded the bed, Isaac recognized his mother. He didn't know Shawnette and Barbara. Moses introduced Shawnette, whom he had romanced. He introduced Barbara, an investor in his company. Isaac had to get to know Barbara since she was the foundation of Remington Realty.

Barbara shook Isaac's hand, placing his balloons in the corner of the room. Irene placed a Tupperware bowl on the bed table and moved it towards Isaac. She lifted the top as hot roasted chicken, rice and beans, and broccoli steamed in the air. He grabbed the plastic fork, scooping the rice and beans into the bowl. Then, he shoved the food in his mouth. Isaac chowed down on his mother's cooking. The nurse carried hospital food on a tray. She didn't know where to place the meal, so Moses took the tray and handled it. He sat at the hospital on the windowsill. While Isaac stuffed his face, Irene wanted to get a few things off her chest. Shawnette and Barbara strutted out of the room, but Moses remained for their family moment. He dragged the heavy chair with its metal legs screeching along the floor for his mother. Irene sat in the hard chair. She smiled from ear to ear while Isaac kept eating. Moses dragged another chair close to his brother's bed. "I missed you very much, son," Irene patted Isaac's dreaded matted hair. Isaac pulled his head away from his mother's hand. He proceeded to gobble the chicken and broccoli.

"Calvin's not in our lives anymore. Moses got rid of him," Irene, teary-eyed, touched her child's face. Isaac pulled away again and glared at his mother. She knew what it meant and respected her son's wishes. Moses witnessed the unwanted affection coming from Isaac. He glared at Moses with a slight smile after hearing Moses had banished Calvin from the home. Now, Moses had the opportunity to give details to Isaac about his business and plans. The brothers planned on going into business as kids, and right now, Moses had no partner. He wanted his brother Isaac.

"How many people go homeless, go home, and start a bright new life — not many. I'm fortunate," Isaac put his arm behind his head and rested on the pillow. Moses rambled on and on about things he had planned for his brother. Isaac wasn't bothered, as his brother – older by five minutes – took charge. He never felt threatened by Moses' leadership as a kid. He sat erect in his bed and gaped at Moses and his mother. "My friends!" Isaac pressed the nurse button.

On the eighth floor, Moses and a nurse escorted Isaac out of the elevator. He wheeled his heart rate machine alongside him. Screams echoed through the hallway, and Isaac's eyes bulged out of their sockets. He knew Jessica's cries and noticed two police officers guarding a hospital room. Isaac wheeled closer and closer. Jessica was handcuffed to her bed, tears cascading down her face. She was screaming her head off. An exchange of words was occurring between Jessica and a woman in her mid-fifties, business suit-clad. She jotted notes on her iPad that reverberated through the entire floor. Isaac stopped before Jessica's room, witnessing the social worker condemning her for harboring Shereza in deplorable conditions. The workers of the Department of Children's Services wanted to know the father's whereabouts, but Jessica told them stories about her abusive and irresponsible husband. Jessica pleaded for her family to take Shereza with God's blessings. And they agreed. Authorities arrested and charged Jessica with child endangerment. She would have to serve jail time and fight her case in court. Isaac stared into the doorway of Jessica's room, hesitating to enter because of the police presence.

"Jessica! It's going to be alright!" Isaac clutched his heart rate machine for dear life. Isaac cringed like an older adult, seeing his friend in emotional anguish.

"Isaac, they're going to lock me up!" Jessica tossed and turned in bed, trying to wiggle her wrists from the handcuffs, but no luck. She laid back, sobbing. That's all she could do. The hefty social worker woman, having an expression that could kill a thousand men, sashayed to Isaac. Isaac reciprocated the unpleasant feeling. She hounded Isaac with hostile questions about himself. Moses wanted to curse this miserable female with a chip on her shoulder. Isaac explained the situation, where he, Bob, Jessica, and Shereza dwelled in the sub-level of Grand Central Station. He didn't want Isaac to give too much information that may jeopardize Jessica's case. Isaac could only testify on Jessica's behalf in court. For now, Jessica and Isaac waved to each other and kept in contact.

Bob's adult son and daughter surrounded his bed on the ninth floor. Other family members also came to visit. Isaac wheeled his heart rate machine into Bob's room with Moses and the nurse behind him. "Isaac! How are you, my friend!" Bob stretched his arms to embrace his dear friend. Isaac clutched Bob as they shed tears.

"We're safe. We're home, my friend," Bob patted Isaac on the back. Isaac placed his rear end on the edge of Bob's bed.

Isaac cracked a smile and believed in a home for good. Moses had gotten rid of the drama in their lives, and Irene had more confidence now. Isaac introduced his brother to Bob and told him what he did for a living. Bob's eyeballs bulged from their sockets upon hearing of the exciting occupation that some well-to-do people have. Moses shared a little information about himself, while on the contrary, he did big things. Isaac had no idea how great Moses had made it in real estate. Bob also introduced his family to Isaac. He spoke about their lives being the mole people. Moses' cell phone vibrated on his hip. He checked the caller ID, which read: unknown. Moses swaggered out of Bob's room and down the hallway.

"Hello," Moses paced back and forth.

"I hope you can get used to public transportation, mother fucker!" The unknown caller disconnected the call.

"Who the fuck," Moses mumbled. He marched back to Bob's room; his cell vibrated again. He checked the caller ID: unknown.

"Hello!" Moses stopped abruptly in his tracks.

"You've got one fine ass lady. You better keep her close," The unknown caller used a muffled voice.

"Who the fuck is this?" Moses stomped his foot on the floor. The unknown caller disconnected. Moses stood there. He couldn't identify the caller. Moses summed it up as a crazy person making crank calls. Again, Moses' cell phone vibrated. He checked out the caller ID as it read unknown. He had no other choice than to ignore unknown or private calls. Moses marched back into Bob's room. He slowed his pace while his brother and Bob spoke of how people gave them dirty looks, sneered, cursed, and ignored their existence. "I've been treated that way since the day I was born. I counted on my brother to have my back. Right, Moses," Isaac's eyes wander around the room. Moses embraced his brother. "That's exactly right."

The orange evening sky released a summer glow throughout the atmosphere without any relief from the heat. Moses, Shawnette, Irene, and Barbara exited the hospital together and moseyed to the parking lot. Moses clutched Shawnette's hand. He didn't want to upset her with the anonymous calls he received. "You know I love you. Right, Shawnette?" Moses kissed her a zillion times. Irene smiled at Moses and Shawnette's love.

"Of course, I know you love me. You're the best thing that ever happened to me," Shawnette kissed Moses on the cheek a zillion times over chuckling. Shawnette's eyes widened.

"Holy shit, Moses!" Shawnette and Moses noticed his BMW with four slashed tires.

"What the fuck!" Moses released Shawnette from his arms and threw his keys to the ground. Irene's eyes watered as a tear streamed down her face.

"How the hell did that happen!" Barbara clunked in her heels over the parking lot attendant booth. Shawnette picked up Moses' keys from the ground and strutted to his side. Moses' face turned hell red as he embraced his girlfriend.

Minutes later, an auto mechanic loaded the damaged BMW onto the lever of a tow truck. Parking lot security and NYPD searched the area for clues. They asked Moses questions or if he had a dispute with anyone. Calvin popped into Moses' head but claimed he had no idea. The cop checked Moses' New York state driver's license and found information on him. "You're in real estate?" The officer squinted his eyes with a dubious expression.

"Yes, I am," Moses embraced Shawnette. Then officers glared at Shawnette and Barbara, questioning them the same way.

"I'm Barbara Sterling. I'm a real estate investor with Remington Realty, Mr. Remington's firm," Barbara handed the officer her driver's license. Shawnette knew to do the same, and she did. "I'm Shawnette, an agent at Remington Realty."

"And your relationship with him?" The officer held Shawnette's driver's ID along with Barbara's.

"I'm his girlfriend," Shawnette clutched Moses' hand tighter. The officer shook his head, and nothing out of the ordinary. He gave the women back the licenses.

"Mr. Remington, no one saw anything. I'm sorry," the officer handed Moses his driver's license.

"Alright. Thanks," Moses took his ID from the officer's hand.

"I'll drive you guys home," Barbara led the way to her car as they followed.

The next morning at the office, the agents sat at their desks. Everyone showed clients properties. But then, the receptionist answered the buzzing phone. "Remington realty, this Jocelyn speaking. How may I help you?"

"You can show more cleavage — bosses love that," the unknown caller said. Jocelyn slammed the phone on the hook. Her eyes shifted from left to right, hoping her colleagues wouldn't notice her nervousness. The phone buzzed again. Jocelyn's heart raced in her chest. She answered the call.

"Good morning, Remington Realty. This is Jocelyn speaking. How may I help you?"

"Good morning, Jocelyn. Valentin speaking, can you give Moses a message? Tell him I'll be a little late due to a doctor's appointment," Valentin explained over the phone.

"I will, Valentin. Feel better," Jocelyn jotted down Valentin's message and hung up.

Moses stormed through the heavy glass door of his place of business. He neither greeted his employees nor colleagues but instead frowned at the floor. He avoided eye contact. Jocelyn swirled in her chair and handed her boss the note. He halted, taking a few steps back. Then, he snatched the sticky note from Jocelyn's hand.

"Thanks," Moses said, proceeding to his office.

Shawnette lagged, carrying her briefcase, and pushing the heavy glass door open.

"Moses!" Shawnette stomped behind her lover.

Moses thrust open his office door and threw his body in his recliner. He rocked and turned his back on Shawnette as he faced the window. At least he had the Manhattan skyline to see. His girlfriend leaned against the window seal, facing him.

"Baby, you're going to have to let the company know about your brother," Shawnette folded her arms. Moses continued rocking in his recliner. He shook his head in disagreement.

"It's not the right time."

"Do you want me to get you some coffee or something," Shawnette caressed the back of her hand across his cheek.

"Go," Moses stopped rocking in his recliner.

"Take it easy, Mister," Shawnette grabbed her wristlet and marched out of Moses' office.

On the congested Manhattan sidewalk, Shawnette weaved between people keeping her eyes fixed on her destination. She collided with a good-looking gentleman in his mid-thirties, husky but menacing. He grabbed her around the waist to prevent her from falling. But Shawnette pushed his hands off her. "I'm sorry. How are you doing, Shawnette?" The stranger placed his hands on her hips again.

"How did you know my name?" Shawnette pushed his hands away again.

"Moses is your man. Right? It's nice to see a young African American couple in real estate instead of sports or entertainment," the stranger winked.

"Have a nice day," She stomped in heels, avoiding this unknown man. The menacing stranger blocked her path. She pulled away from this stranger, who had a tight grip on her wrist. "Let go of me! Please, let go!" Shawnette continued to wiggle her wrists out of the hoodlum's hold.

"I love the way you beg," the stranger snickered.

Shawnette slapped the menacing stranger in the face. She darted down the street, getting away from him as fast as she could. A sadistic smile surfaced on this stranger's face swaggering away.

Back at Remington firm, Moses rocked in his recliner. He gazed at the city's buildings. His cell phone vibrated on his desk behind him. He swerved around in his chair with ease. Moses saw the caller ID: unknown. He inhaled, ready to curse out whoever dared to threaten his livelihood. "Remington realty. Moses speaking," he said, handling his situation professionally. "Your girlfriend looks good in that pink dress. I would keep a close eye on her if I were you," The anonymous caller disconnected the call. Moses raised an eyebrow and leapt from his recliner, sprinting out of his office. He stormed through his office like a superhero on a mission. His colleagues took notice and wondered what happened. Moses thrust open the heavy glass door. He raced down the stairwell.

Shawnette raced towards the office where she worked. Luckily, she and Moses bumped into each other's arms.

Minutes later, police questioned Shawnette about the gentleman who accosted her. She told the authorities that this stranger knew her and Moses, what they did for a living, their place of business, and God only knows what else. A light bulb went off in Moses' head. The only person who knew all of them would be his stepfather. Moses told the cops about his stepfather and why he terminated him. The authorities got information on Calvin, and they began investigating the case. Moses wasn't going to let Shawnette out of his sight. His mother came to mind. Moses called his mother on his cell phone. "Come on, Mom. Pick up," Moses paced the floor.

"Hello," she answered.

"Mom, if Calvin comes to the house, don't open the door! And lock up!" Moses panicked.

"I will," Irene stirred iced tea in a glass pitcher with lemon slices floating on top. She hung up the phone and continued stirring the iced tea. Moses didn't allow his mother's abrupt disconnection to bother him. He focused on Shawnette, clutching her hand. Everyone in the company gathered around as Moses advised them that, should a stranger approach them in the street and claim to know them, to take caution. They should be aware of their surroundings and go together in a group.

A few days later, doctors released Isaac from the hospital. Moses, Irene, and Shawnette strolled down the hallway with Isaac. Yet, he seemed puzzled. Moses frowned. He could tell his brother, a brand-new man, had something on his mind. "I have to go to the eighth floor," Isaac stopped in his tracks. Seconds later, the elevator door on the eighth floor widened as Isaac swaggered out. He glanced over both shoulders on a mission to find Jessica. Isaac stopped right before Jessica's room, where a new patient occupied it. A nurse rushed past Isaac.

"Where's Jessica Teel," Isaac asked.

"The big house," the nurse mouthed, continuing her duties. Moses swaggered behind his brother. He could tell Isaac's friend had gone downhill. Isaac felt Moses' presence over his shoulder and shook his head.

"What could I do to help Jessica?" Isaac stood there, and it seemed he was asking that question to himself out loud.

"There's nothing you can do," Moses remained behind his brother.

"Yes, there is. There's no such thing as can't! Am I right?"

On the ninth floor, the elevator doors opened with ease. Isaac did the same as he did on the lower level. He prayed Bob remained in his room, or there would be good news that he was home. He halted in front of Bob's room, where inside, a nurse tidied the bed where he lay. Isaac took baby steps inside. His eyes shifted from left to right; Isaac at least hoped to see Bob sitting in a chair or hoped he'd be in the bathroom. "Hello. Where's Bob?" Isaac's heart picked up speed.

"I'm sorry. Mr. Clancy passed away," The nurse continued cleaning the room. Moses crept behind Isaac again, not to scare him but to give him some space. Teardrops cascaded down his face, and he sobbed. "Bob's dead."

Moses placed his hand on his brother's shoulder. "I'm sorry about Bob, Isaac."

Isaac closed his eyes, fighting back tears, and envisioned his friend's whereabouts. "Bob's in heaven serving the angels delicious meals that he served. And probably now lives in a mansion that God offered him. He probably has a spacious living room, a gourmet kitchen, a family room, and seven bedrooms for him and his loved ones." Isaac opened his eyes, and tears streamed down his face.

"Are you alright, Isaac? Let's get you a haircut," Moses patted him on the shoulder.

CHAPTER TWENTY-SIX

Pop music bellowed from the speakers of an upscale barbershop on Long Island, where prestigious white gentlemen, young and old, sat in the barber chair, getting cuts. There was just a sprinkle of men of color in this establishment. One or two, African-American gentlemen, one Latin, and an Arabian businessman. When Moses and Isaac swaggered in, the electronic bells chimed. The brothers were dressed in t-shirts, jeans, and sneakers. Isaac wore a baseball cap over his head, concealing his hair. He held his head down because he was back in the real world of judgments and stares.

The receptionist greeted Moses with a handshake. Isaac didn't make eye contact with anyone. He sensed that eyes were on him. He kept his eyes fixed on the floor. *"The respect Moses received from the receptionist was the red carpet treatment. I doubt if I will get that. Shit! My hair is matted. Who the hell is going to cut my hair?"* Isaac thought. He noticed how the other clients in the shop waved to Moses, rushing to shake his hand, and striking up conversations about business. Not just anybody, but mostly white men with power and privilege. Moses was well-known among the elite and had lots of connections.

"Here, we go again. Everyone loves Moses. I will have to get used to the fact that Moses has more pull than me. He pulled me out of the gutter! How fucked up is that!" Isaac's eyes shifted left to right, and he felt strange eyeballs still fixed on him. Luckily, a biracial gentleman, who was the product of a black mother and white father, agreed to serve Isaac. He and Moses chatted as if they were old friends. Isaac believed he would probably be another Ryan. He was the best one for the job. He extended his hand to Isaac, introducing himself. His name was Theo, and he had the same hair texture hair as Isaac. So, he understood. Theo chatted with Isaac and Moses as if he already knew

them. Theo knew Isaac needed a haircut badly just by him wearing that baseball cap. Isaac sat in the barber chair. Then, Moses snatched the hat off Isaac's head. Everyone's eyes jolted upon noticing Isaac's matted, dreaded hair. Some of them guffawed at Isaac's unpleasant-looking head. Isaac sneered as if he wanted to kill someone. Moses reciprocated the sneers and glared at everyone in the shop. "Please! My brother's been through a lot! Anyone here could wind up homeless! You never know in life," Moses' eyes watered. Theo took a deep breath and worked on Isaac's head. "Do your thing, sir," Moses slipped Theo a one-hundred-dollar bill.

Thirty minutes later, Theo trimmed Isaac's edges of his newly cut hair. Isaac looked like a GQ model ready to walk the fashion runway. He felt like a baby with the apron over him, but that's how barbers operate. Theo shaped the sides of Isaac's hairline after cutting off the dreadlocks. Of course, he got a shampoo, conditioning, and then cut and style. "You look good, bro," Moses glaring at his twin's reflection in the large mirror before them. Theo placed the handheld mirror in Isaac's face.

Isaac had the guts to admire himself for the first time in almost a decade. He loved it. Moses' image is reflected in the handheld mirror.

From there, Moses drove Isaac in his latest silver Audi and sped along Sunrise Highway. Traffic flowed fast without any vehicle slowing down. Isaac loved how smooth the car felt. He couldn't believe how comfy the seats and interior were. "This car is beautiful," Isaac turned on the radio as house music blared from the speakers with surround sound. "I've got a closet full of clothes for you that I haven't worn," Moses shouted over the music. He wanted to turn the volume down but didn't want to disrespect Isaac. Instead, Isaac lowered the music. "What happened, Moses?"

"I've got clothes for you that I haven't worn," Moses changed lanes on the highway.

"Where do you live?" Isaac asked.

"Brookville," Moses switched lanes again.

"Do you live around a lot of wealthy people?" Isaac asked as if you regressed back to a kid again.

"Yes," Moses' Audi halted at a red light.

"How's your vision, Isaac?" Moses spotted a Lens Crafters store.

"It's okay. I guess. I can probably get around," Isaac scoffed.

"Get around? The way you sprinted through down Times Square!" Moses pulled into the parking lot and found a space for his vehicle.

An hour later, an optometrist checked Isaac's eyes through the phoropter in his office. Moses stood in the background and recalled this same experience as kids. At eight years old, Isaac got his stylish glasses at Pearle Vision in the mall. "How history repeats itself when you lose touch with loved ones. Now we can watch television and movies, celebrate Christmas, Halloween, or our birthdays. And it's right around the corner. I want to do something special for Isaac and me. I'll figure something out," Moses watched the optometrist place a stylish pair of black glasses on him. "How do they feel, Isaac?" Moses took small steps closer to his twin.

"Good. They feel good. I feel good," Isaac admired himself in a mirror again.

The Audi parked in front of Moses' lavish manor, with a slated rooftop. It reflected on the passenger's side window. Isaac gasped as he opened the passenger side door of the vehicle. He felt like he had died and gone to heaven, where God granted him a mansion. Most people here are Earth pray they enter the Kingdom of Heaven. Therefore, they can dwell in a four-bedroom palace. The apples and pears whiffed from the trees as they continued to grow. Moses rushed to Isaac's side. He saw amazement in his face.

"So, what do you think?" Moses waltzed to the front door with his rattling keys in his hands.

"It's like heaven," Isaac headed towards the front door and stumbled upon the small brick steps before him.

"Watch your step, Isaac," Moses held the front door open. Isaac dashed in. Large chandeliers hung from the ceiling. Fresh-cut flowers were in a vase on a marble table. Rosa, Moses' housekeeper, catered to him. "Mr. Remington, how are you today?"

"Isaac, this is Rosa. Rosa, this is Isaac, my brother," Moses patted Isaac on the shoulder. Isaac couldn't figure out whether his brother patting him on the shoulder felt sincere.

"I heard so much about you. Would you like something to drink, Isaac?" Rosa asked.

"I would like a soda," Isaac then patted his brother on the shoulder. Rosa sashayed away, continuing with her duties. Isaac waltzed further inside, peering at whatever he could. "Give yourself a tour. This house is your home," Moses trailed Isaac into the living room. The beautiful sofa, cushioned chairs, a coffee table, and a fireplace weren't ready for use. Isaac noticed the large marble table with framed photos featuring him and Moses when they were kids. He picked up the black-framed photo of him and Moses at their fifth birthday celebration. Isaac had nothing to say to Moses. He only browsed at the pictures of him and Moses.

"You know we've got a birthday coming up," Moses lingered around the sofa before plopping into the chair. Isaac didn't say a word. He continued looking at more family pictures on another table. An eight-by-ten frame featured a photo of their mother, Isaac, and Moses many moons ago. Another eight-by-ten was a framed picture of Shawnette.

Additionally, there were individual pictures of her and Moses. "You sure do love Shawnette, don't you?" Isaac held the five-by-seven framed photo of Moses and Shawnette.

"That's my baby," Moses rose from the cushioned chair, swaggering to his brother's side.

"Are you going to get married?" Isaac carefully placed the framed photo down.

"I've got a surprise for her," Moses added. Isaac continued the tour of the home. A tomato sauce aroma emerged from the kitchen. Isaac's nose led him into the Old-World marble kitchen, where Rosa approached him with his soda in a fancy glass. "Here you go, Mr. Remington. I'm sorry I got distracted. Dinner will be ready shortly," Rosa bowed, continuing with cooking.

"Thank you, Rosa," Isaac gulped the soda down.

"Follow me. We must get you into some new gear," Moses dashed up the spiral staircase. Isaac gave the soda can to Rosa as he followed his brother to the second level.

In no time, Isaac stood in front of a full-length mirror sporting gray slacks, a royal blue dress shirt, a matching vest, and a black tie from Moses' enormous walk-in closet. He felt as if he had won the lottery. "We're twins. Identical that is," Isaac straightened his tie. Moses maneuvered to Isaac's side. "Fuck that! We already are twins." The brothers admired themselves in the full-length mirror and each other. Moses expressed how everyone bowed down to him as if he were Moses. From pre-school to higher education and then a skyrocketing in real estate, especially for someone in such a short period of time.

"You're probably still holding that cloud of guilt over my head," Moses pounds his fists on the dressing table in the middle of his walk-in closet. Isaac didn't flinch because of his brother's outbursts. He stormed out of the closet, leaving Moses.

"I'm gone!" Isaac raced down the winding staircase.

"Where the fuck are you going! Get over here!" Moses chased his brother down the beautiful staircase. "Get the fuck over it!" Moses raced to the front door, blocking it with his body. Isaac stood right before him, seeing his twin act like such an ass.

"Why didn't you just leave me be? That's why when I recognized you in the store I ran. Because all you're going to do is throw me to the wolves again! I was better off in the subway tunnels under Times Square," Isaac didn't move a muscle. Instead, he gazed at Moses with tears in his eyes.

"I'm sorry. My fault! I felt guilty over these years for not being there for you," Moses embraced Isaac, sobbing. "And you better not think about leaving either!" The brothers crying on each other's shoulders.

"Mr. Remington dinner is ready," Rosa wipes her hands in a dish towel.

"Thank you, Rosa," Moses choked back tears.

"Is everything ok, Mr. Remington?" Rosa raised an eyebrow.

"Everything's cool. We're starving, right bro?" Moses patted Isaac on the shoulders.

"Yeah, starved," Isaac wiped his eyes, quickly. Then the brothers headed into the kitchen.

It was yet another busy morning at Remington Realty as pop music played from the speaker ceiling. Agents showed clients properties, other realtors filed paperwork, typed the keys on the computers, or chatted at the water cooler. Meanwhile, the phone buzzed, and Jocelyn twirled in her chair. She reached her hand to answer the call but halted her hand in mid-air over the phone. Jocelyn inhaled, closed her eyes, and hoped it wasn't another crank call.

"Good morning, Remington Realty. Jocelyn speaking; how may I help you?"

"Jocelyn, it's me, Barbara. Tell Moses I'll be late getting into the office," Barbara's voice was muffled over the phone. Then Moses and Isaac swaggered into the office. Both were dressed the same. Black dress pants, royal blue shirts, matching vest, and black ties. Jocelyn's eyes usually widened whenever Moses swaggered in, but there was another peculiar gentleman. He seemed off due to his appearance. *Barbara and the agents in the office couldn't figure out this stranger. Was he a new investor? Or simply a kid enthused to join the team? Either way, this young man dressed identically to Moses.*

Moses swaggered into the office, Isaac behind him. "This is my office from where I have done all of my dealings," Moses pointed to his surname on the wall. Isaac didn't utter a word but caressed his hand along the receptionist's marble desk. He noticed the eight-by-ten photo of Moses on the wall. Along with Barabara and other top realtors in his company. Then a picture of Moses's entire realty team. The team of realtors was curious about Isaac and shyly smiled at him. Isaac gave a quick smile and turned away. He kept his eyes on himself. He hoped this didn't turn into another competition.

Minutes later, Isaac browsed Moses' private office, noticing more photos of him and Moses around Christmas time. Four beautifully framed pictures of Shawnette adorned the office. She resembled Clarissa.

"Hey, Moses!" Marques stormed in, greeting Moses with a handshake. Isaac held his head down, his eyes fixed on the floor. "Who's this? Your brother?"

Moses put his arm around Isaac, "This is my brother, Isaac," Marques extended his hand without any awkward feelings. Isaac reciprocated the greeting, feeling his brother's colleague was genuine. "I'm Marques."

"How are you doing?" Isaac pulled his hand away. Marques realized Isaac's quick snatch of the hand but ignored it.

"So, what's up for today?" Marques grabbed a sourball from the candy dish.

Moses' team of agents flocked around him with Isaac by his side. Isaac shifted his eyes from left to right, which he googled. He noticed the pretty women at his brother's place of business. Isaac would love to get next to one of these fine ladies. Still, he kept his cool. Isaac focused his eyes on the speaker in the ceiling, paying close attention to the instrumental music. He tuned Moses out, imagining himself somewhere in the Caribbean with a gorgeous female. Moses patted him on the shoulder before Isaac could get further into his fantasy.

"Everyone, this is my fraternal twin brother Isaac. We may have separate DNA, but he's my better half. And, he'll be joining our team," The twins embraced as the office of his colleagues applauded. Throughout the day, Moses and Barbara showed Isaac the ins and outs of running an office. As time went on, Isaac made new friends at the office. They were diligent, ambitious people. All strived to be the best at their job.

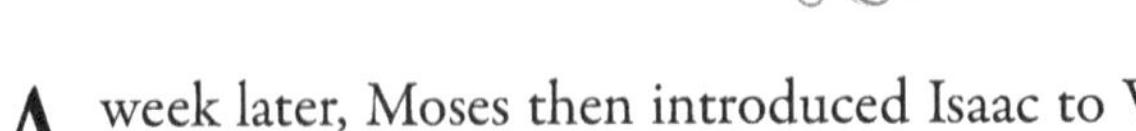

A week later, Moses then introduced Isaac to Valentin. All three gentlemen sought out luxury apartments in the city and townhouses. A nineteen-million-dollar mansion, with seven bathrooms and seven-and-a-half bathrooms, had an enormous kitchen. Its spacious living room stunned Isaac. More notable were its high ceilings and indoor swimming pool in almost every room. Isaac cautiously toured the apartment while Moses and Valentin stayed at a table, making plans. Moses could see Isaac from the corner of his eye, smirking. Isaac strolled into the pool house with its old Roman cathedral ceilings. The sparkling blue water of the sixteen-by-thirty-six-sized rectangular pool reflected in Isaac's face. He glared into the beaming, turquoise water, where Isaac stood on the swallow end and closed his eyes. Moses crept up behind his brother.

"Beautiful, right?" Isaac's eyes widened.

"It sure is," Moses sat in a patio chair.

"I'm proud of you, Moses. I really am," Isaac turned with his eyes fixed on his brother.

"I'm proud of you as well," Moses smiled, fidgeting in the uncomfortable chair.

"I'm nothing compared to you. Why would you be proud of me?" Isaac sneered.

"You're my brother, that's why," Moses stood from the chair and embraced Isaac. The brothers' shadowy figures reflected themselves in the blue water as they exited the pool house.

Rosa wheeled a three-layered red velvet cake with thirty glistening candles on this sultry evening of August 17th. Moses and Isaac stood beside each other as their family and friends sang: "Happy birthday to you. Happy birthday to you. Happy birthday, Moses, and Isaac; Happy birthday to you!!!" Their party guests applauded. Moses and Isaac's celebration took place on Moses' gorgeous patio with their outdoor kitchen. Black, royal blue, silvered pearl textured latex, and foil balloons adorned the patio, and some floated in the swimming pool. House music played from Moses' stereo system while guests ate cake and drank champagne. Valentin brought an expensive bottle of his own to share with his business partner, Moses, and a new friend, Isaac. The brothers devoured their big slices of cake as adults, reminiscing about their childhood. Moses felt nine years old again. He had no idea what Isaac thought at that moment. He saw that Isaac had transformed from a bitter young man, being down on his luck, and then was brought back to life from hell.

"Happy birthday, Isaac," a familiar feminine voice from Isaac's past presented a black box with a blue ribbon right before his eyes.

"Clarissa," Isaac dropped his fork and looked up. Clarissa stood right before him. Isaac laid a passionate kiss on her. Everyone noticed the moment and applauded as if Isaac had kissed his bride at the altar. "How did you know where to find me?" Isaac held Clarissa tight and placed the gift on the table. He had gotten his present; his first love, Clarissa. "HAPPY BIRTHDAY, BRUH!!!" Moses patted him on the shoulder. Isaac embraced Moses, knowing he brought his girlfriend back into his life.

Valentin gently tapped a fork against the wine glass to get the guest's attention. Everyone held their wine glasses in the air with the bubbly French champagne. "I would like to propose a toast to the most ambitious, fruitful young man I have ever met – and to his brother, to whom I believe is as determined and prolific as Moses. Happy Birthday, gentlemen, and all the best." Valentin, Moses, Isaac, and the party guests clanked their glasses. Everyone sipped the champagne and applauded. Moses sipped his fruity champagne and noticed a shadowy figure reflecting. "What kind of wine is this, Valentin?" Moses sipped again with his arms wrapped around Shawnette's waist.

"It's grapey," Shawnette sipped the expensive beverage again. Moses drank more champagne from his glass. He noticed a shadowy figure that emerged through his sparkling drink as three more silhouettes materialized.

"Happy birthday, Moses and Isaac," The four masculine voices greeted. Then four menacing figures became clear to Moses' eyes. Isaac turned and recognized the voice. The party guests wondered about these menacing gentlemen dressed in black, brandishing arms. Valentin's eyes shifted left to right as his hands quivered. Moses stomped towards Calvin, his brother Troy, an older man, and his two sons, Winston and Ronnell, thugs who amounted to nothing. Winston stuck the nine-millimeter firearm under Moses' chin. "Remember when we fucked up your occasion? Funny how history repeats itself." Winston noticed Shawnette as she pleaded with him to withdraw the gun from her boyfriend's chin.

"How are you doing, sweetheart? Remember, we met last time," Joe grabbed Shawnette by the waist.

"Please, don't shoot him," Shawnette whined.

"Don't move, Isaac," Ronnell pointed the nine-millimeter in his back. Isaac felt as if he experienced being robbed in Central Park again. Ronnell had a husky, menacing build with a face that could be used for Halloween. Isaac trembled. His heart pounded, and he hoped this hoodlum didn't squeeze the trigger. Isaac wasn't ready to die. He had already been through enough. He reached his hands to the high heavens and cooperated with this roughneck. "You and Moses are rich now?" Ronnell pointed the gun harder into Isaac's back.

"I don't have anything," Isaac tried making eye contact with his so-called cousin.

"Don't try it. I know your brother must have a safe in this house, somewhere," Ronnell waved the gun in the air. Then, he pointed it to Isaac's head.

Meanwhile, Troy and Calvin brandished their guns at Moses' family, friends, and colleagues. All huddled in the corner of the patio. Jocelyn eyed Calvin as he made visual contact and devilishly smiled. He scanned Jocelyn from head to toe. "How are you doing, Jocelyn? I see that you love wearing shirts that reveal cleavage. Jocelyn's eyes widened. She knew Calvin had made those perverted calls to the office. His brother, Troy, asked Valentin about his business, lifestyle, and how he had made his billions. Valentin refused to answer his audacious questions. Instead, he gave Troy a nasty attitude. Calvin noticed this Frenchman's snobbish ways and encouraged his brother to do whatever he could. So, Troy hit Valentin in the face with the butt of the gun. Valentin fell flat on the cement patio. Barbara, Jocelyn, and the others rushed to comfort him.

"What the hell are you doing, Calvin?" At only five feet tall, Barbara stood on her feet.

"Barbara, sit down before I blow your little head off!" Calvin pointed the rifle to her forehead. Barbara teared up, backed down, and rushed to Valentin's side.

"Why are you doing this, Calvin?" Irene stood to her feet and approached him. Calvin pointed right at everyone gathered on the patio.

"I'm doing this for us. Just you and me," Calvin wrapped his arms around Irene and kissed her on the head.

"This isn't about us. It's about your family. I didn't want to believe it initially, but you didn't love me. You sure didn't love my sons, especially Isaac," Irene pushed him away.

"Get your ass back there with the rest of them. Otherwise, I will blow you to kingdom come," Calvin cocked the rifle. Irene cringed, along with the rest of Moses' colleagues.

"Do you have money and jewelry? I want it all," Winston pointed the gun to Moses' head. Winston forced Moses into the house while Joe grabbed Shawnette. Winston hauled Moses through the kitchen like a large mannequin. "Where do you keep your valuables?" Winston shoved Moses onto the family room couch. He took sharp breaths and had to open the vault behind the Caribou painting above the fireplace. Moses had spent a lot of money on Shawnette's engagement ring and planned to propose to her. "I've got some things in the safe behind the painting," Moses pointed at the piece of art.

"Get it!" Winston cocked the gun, aiming it at his forehead.

"Sit your ass down, sweet thing!" Joe pushed Shawnette into the lounge chair. Shawnette's eyes watered. "Why are you doing this?"

"Shut the fuck up before I beat the shit out of you right here. I'll beat you in front of your man and he can't do a fuckin' thing about it!" Joe brandished the gun to her head. Shawnette closed her eyes and wept. Moses felt utterly helpless, seeing some thug pointing a gun at his girlfriend. He didn't want to lose his life. At the same time, he wanted Shawnette to see him as a heroic figure, even though it wasn't real. Moses had to face reality. He had to open the vault and give these assholes what they wanted. Then they would be on their merry way. Seconds later, Moses punched the numbers for the safe's combination lock. Shawnette watched in fear, hoping a bullet wouldn't go off. Moses fooled around with the combination. He didn't punch in the numbers but played around with them.

"What the fuck is taking you so long?" Winston cocked the gun as he raised an eyebrow.

Moses proceeded to punch in the keys of the vault. "I forgot."

"Bullshit! How did you forget!" Joe took a few steps towards Moses but kept the gun pointed at Shawnette.

Moses proceeded to punch the numbers. Then ... *BOOM!*

Isaac and his party guests/colleagues heard the gunshot, as they were being held at gunpoint on the patio. "Moses!" Irene attempted to see what happened. Calvin blocked her path. Then, he slapped her across the cheek. "Take a seat, Irene!"

"That's my brother in there! Isaac attempted to get into the house, but Calvin blocked Isaac's path. He pointed the gun in his stepson's face. Out of nowhere, Isaac attempted to wrestle the rifle out of his stepfather's hands. Isaac shot Calvin in the chest as he collapsed to the ground. Calvin held his hand over his bleeding chest, taking sharp breaths. Then Isaac shot two bullets into Troy's abdominal area. His body plummeted to the concrete ground, lifeless. Isaac dashed through the patio glass door.

Moses lay in a pool of his blood on the wooden floor, and unconscious.

"Moses!" Shawnette rushed to her lover's side as he lay in a pool of blood. Joe grabbed Shawnette by the collar, forcing her back into the chair as she cried.

"Shut the fuck up before I bust a bullet in you like your man!" Joe pointed the gun at her again. Shawnette took a deep breath, fighting back the tears. She eyed Moses stretched out on the floor. Shawnette clasped her hands, praying.

Isaac hurried to the family room, where he saw Moses on the floor. Isaac pumped Winston's body with bullets. Winston plummeted to the floor injured, hanging on for dear life. Shawnette ducked for cover, holding her ears. Joe aimed the gun at her. Isaac and Ronnell then participated in gunfire in the family room. Then several bullets were pumped into Ronnell's body. Blood was everywhere.

"I've always envied you and Moses. Both of you are so smart, but I'm a fuck-up," Ronnell's body dropped to the floor. Joe's eyes widened. He couldn't believe the bullet had missed Isaac. Out of the blue, Shawnette knocked Joe in the head with a vase from behind. He collapsed to the floor, blood dripping from his head.

Outside, Irene, Barbara and their colleagues heard the gunfire. Then dead silence. "Let me go in there! My sons!" Irene rushed into the house. Barbara gave chase. Jocelyn grabbed a bat and hit Calvin in the legs. "You nasty, dirty dog!"

Silence overwhelmed the luxurious home inside and out. Barbara embraced Irene and Shawnette wept over Moses's body.

Silence overwhelmed this luxurious home, inside and out. Isaac noticed his family and friends were still breathing. "Oh, no! God, please let my brother live! Please!" Isaac begged God. Tears streamed down his cheeks. Clarissa embraced Isaac, sobbing.

An hour later, red and blue police and paramedic lights flashed through the night. Officers asked Isaac questions about the incident. Two paramedics hauled Calvin out in a stretcher while handcuffed. He couldn't walk after being shot in the chest and hit with a bat in his legs. Then two more paramedics wheeled Moses to the ambulance with Shawnette and Irene by his side. They loaded him inside, shutting the double doors. Officers had asked Isaac to come down to the precinct for questioning. While in the interrogation room, Isaac told the officers everything about his relationship with his stepfather Calvin. He elaborated on the bad experiences he and Moses encountered as kids years ago.

This top cop believed Isaac's words were credible. Troy, Winston, and Ronnell had been involved in several burglaries and attempted murder. And now deceased. Before that, the father and his sons served time for drug possession and selling to an undercover cop. Joe had evaded the law for years. He already had back child support for about fifteen years, so he'll serve a long time behind bars. Calvin has no priors. Still, he was going to go down for attempted robbery, assault, and additional crimes. Isaac hoped his mother would finally get rid of this worthless man. Calvin had done nothing but cause a divide between him and Moses, not to mention abusing his mother mentally and physically.

Moreover, Calvin was why Isaac and Irene's relationship wasn't as tight as before Calvin entered their lives. Isaac wanted to leave that police station and go to the hospital. He had to call the shots now.

CHAPTER TWENTY-SEVEN

"D*amn, how the tables reverse! Moses is now stretched in his hospital bed. Meanwhile, I'm dressed in gray trousers, a black dress shirt, a gray vest, and black shoes, and ready to conquer the world,"* Isaac shook his head with his neatly trimmed facial hair on his head. He dragged a chair with its metal legs, screeching along the floor to his brother's bedside.

Irene, Shawnette, and the twins' Uncle Tyler gathered around Moses' bedside. Melissa, Barbara, Valentin, Marques, and Moses' colleagues joined them. "Get well" balloons sat in the corner of the room. Shawnette held Moses' hand, hoping for a fast recovery. Irene prepared some home-cooked food, which Moses ate from a Tupperware container.

"I'll start that real estate course next week. Luckily, I paid for the class on time," Isaac said, scratching his head and eyeing Moses. That was good news coming from his brother. Knowing that Isaac was taking New York's state real estate exam made Moses smile, despite his pain. Doctors had to remove the two bullets from his abdominal area; one of his lungs almost collapsed. Thank Heaven Moses pulled through. Otherwise, this unhappy birthday could've not been a happy occasion. Speaking of good news, Irene filed for divorce. She had spent years and years with Calvin. Despite this, she hardly knew it made their lives hell. Irene never told anyone about the hell she went through with Calvin. In hindsight, Irene didn't want her sons to risk their freedom. She would have never forgiven herself if Moses had died. Irene can't forgive herself for Isaac being homeless for over a decade. She prayed to God that her family crisis would go away. Irene had taken responsibility for bringing these hardships to her sons.

"The office feels weak without you there, Moses," Shawnette opened a small container of ice cream and fed it to him.

"You can run it," Moses glared at his brother.

"I've got to study for my exam. That's too much to handle," Isaac held his hands up in the air, surrendering.

"Stop being a fuckin' wimp, Isaac," Moses insulted him with mouthful of ice cream.

"Watch your mouth, Moses!" Shawnette slapped Moses' hand and fed him more ice cream. Isaac snickered at his brother being corrected for cursing. Shawnette nagged about Moses' bad habits like an old married couple. Hopefully, his girlfriend's engagement ring remained in the safe. Moses wished he had a moment to slip it on Shawnette's finger. She already acted like a wife. Shawnette would be a good mother as well. Moses thought highly of his girlfriend. Moreover, he didn't allow his mother's bad decisions to affect his relationship.

Isaac, Shawnette, his mother, and his investors - Valentin, Marques, and Barbara - could've lost their lives. Yet, they were all alive and well. Moses proceeded to apologize to his colleagues for putting them through this ordeal. Marques had primarily understood since he had grown up in a rough area. He told Moses stories of how he would sit on the building's rooftop and stare at the Manhattan skyline. He dreamt of doing something prolific when other young people his age were screwing their lives up. Marques had taken the real estate course in the late spring, finishing it up in midsummer. He'd go on the roof and study for hours; others would go to the roof to smoke weed or have sex. And now, Marques had achieved his goals. He hoped to help Moses and Isaac build an enterprise. These brothers had to stay focused. Neither brother could allow anything to divert them. As visiting hours ended, Moses' team showered him with kisses, and hugs and promised more visits. As the group sashayed out of the hospital room. Isaac, the last to leave, stood over Moses' bed. "Let your investors handle your affairs, Moses. I know nothing about this, so don't call me a fuckin' wimp."

"Why are you so insecure, Isaac? You're the strong one now. Handle it," Moses attempted to sit up in his bed but got a pain in his chest. Quickly he laid down with ease.

"Take it easy, man," Isaac fluffed Moses' pillow and pulled the sheets over him.

Moses fixed his eyes towards the window and didn't utter anything. Isaac knew this scenario. His brother would ignore everything he asked of him. Isaac would talk and talk to his sibling until he turned blue in the face. He swaggered away, hoping to hear his brother spew some words. Isaac slowed his pace down, waiting for Moses to say something. He didn't care if he cursed him out. Isaac stopped in his tracks and abruptly made a 360-degree turn. "Aren't you going to say fuckin' something!" Moses kept his eyes fixed on the window without moving a muscle. Isaac scoffed and stomped towards the doorway.

"You're such a fuckin' wimp!" Moses insulted Isaac. Isaac heard his brother's words, which weren't endearing. He stopped again.

"You're such a fuckin' wimp, a baby. You can't do anything on your own. I always had to bail your ass out," Moses continued.

"I told you not to call me a fuckin' wimp. You're the one laid up!" Isaac raised his voice to the heavens.

Moses slowly turned to Isaac and smirked, "Exactly! Now go and get your license." Isaac had a glum expression on his face by his brother lighting a fire under his feet, encouraging him. His brother insulted and encouraged him. Isaac had to take charge and run the business they dreamt of as kids. "I'll call you later man," Isaac inhaled, smiling at Moses before exiting the room.

That night, Isaac hit the books hard. He read chapter after chapter about flipping homes, low-income to higher-income rentals, and wholesale and luxury properties in bed. He checked the time on his cell phone: 2:13 a.m. His eyelids had become heavy; he had to get some rest. So, he closed his real estate textbook, turned off his light, and lay down.

A few hours later, Isaac woke up and checked the time on his watch. "Holy shit! I'm late!" Isaac sprung from his slumber, dashing into the shower. Ten minutes later, Isaac didn't have anything to wear since he had stayed at his mother's house. The clothes Moses gave to him were back at his home in Brookville. Isaac smelled the whiff of coffee in the air. He heard his mother stirring in the kitchen. "Mom!" Light footsteps ascended the staircase. Irene opened the door with ease. She noticed her son standing in the full-length mirror in his boxers.

"Sorry! I didn't know you were getting dressed," Irene shied away.

"I have nothing to wear," Isaac glared at his pale-skinned corpse. Irene thought about Calvin's clothes but then changed her mind. She wanted to trash his things; he wasn't coming back. Then Irene had second thoughts. "Calvin-"

"Fuck, no!" Isaac punched his fist into the palm of his hand, turning blazing red in the face. "Why would you ask me that! Throw his shit out!" Isaac demanded. Instead, Irene found some old clothes belonging to Moses. A pair of black pants, a white shirt with a black tie, and old dress shoes that didn't fit. An hour later, Isaac strutted into the Remington Realty office pigeon-toed. He wanted to take the shoes off so bad. Jocelyn greeted him with a wave as the team smiled. All nodded and gave him high-fives. Isaac wondered why he got such a warm welcome. He guessed it was because he was now in charge. *"They all know Moses is coming back soon. I'm temporary,"* Isaac swaggering to Moses' office. He opened the door.

Meanwhile, Barbara worked on his brother's computer. She kept track of the business's financial records. "Good morning, Isaac."

"How are you, Barbara?" Isaac rushed into a chair and snatched the shoes off his feet. The shoes forcefully hitting the floor startled Barbara. "What was that?"

"I'm sorry. These shoes are killing me," Isaac rubbed his feet. He marched along the carpeted floor to his brother's desk, where Barbara stroked the computer keys. She lectured Isaac about the company's finances. Then, she worked on filing and taking calls from interested buyers. She further set up meetings with the buyers and business investors. Isaac felt like a receptionist, but he shared space in Moses' office instead. He sat at a smaller desk. It had a phone, an old computer, and other office supplies. Bookkeeping wasn't exactly Isaac's cup of tea, but he had to start from the bottom like everyone else. Isaac enjoyed seeing the real estate team every day. He got to work alongside Valentin, Marques, and Barbara. All sought-out luxury apartments and homes within the Tri-State area. Without Moses present, Valentin and Isaac got to know each other one-on-one. Both men loved the city's panoramic views, whether it was a building or a home. Valentin and Isaac's eyes shifted left and right. The Manhattan skyline was displayed right before their eyes on the balcony of another luxurious apartment in mid-town Manhattan. "I can't get over this view," Valentin strolled the stucco patio with Isaac alongside him. Isaac kept his trap shut, taking in all the info this tycoon knew. "The south of France has a gorgeous view with the whiff of floral and citrus in the air; the weather is beautiful year-round. So, tell me, how's that course of yours going, Isaac?" Valentin stopped and turned to Isaac with a delightful smile. "It's going great. I'm learning the different levels of the business and enjoying the class," Isaac made visual contact with Valentin, his eyes crossed. Isaac hoped his handicap didn't cause this affluent realtor to underestimate him. "Since Moses and I were kids, we always wanted luxury real estate because of the beautiful homes here in New York and abroad. You heard of Unique Homes magazine, right?" Of course, every realtor knows that periodical. I know the editor," Valentin and Isaac continued their stroll. "How long have you been a real estate investor, Mr. De La Rue?' Isaac scratched what little hair he had on his head, looking down.

"It's okay to be blunt with me, Isaac." The gentlemen proceeded to walk on the patio. "I come from generational real estate. During my life, I realized how blessed I was to have a loving family from money passed down from my great-grandfather to my father and then to me. I had a childhood friend, Hans, who came from a disadvantaged background. His mother worked for my family. Every holiday, I wanted to share my generosity with Hans. As I grew older, I followed in my father's footsteps. I wanted to show the ropes of real estate, but Hans got involved with some terrible people. And so, I had to cut off our friendship. I always looked forward to giving a person a chance in life instead of not only giving charity. Someone like you and Moses are the best men who could carry the entire planet into wealth," The gentlemen halted at the corner of the patio. Isaac loved the idea of the thought, sharing wealth and helping those in need. Isaac knew plenty of needy people personally.

"I love the idea. It's not hard to make it work," Isaac wondered about Valentin's story.

"And I don't have very much time," Valentin took a few steps away from Isaac. Isaac raised an eyebrow. It seemed as if he implied his demise. After saying it, Valentin wouldn't look Isaac in the face and then stepped away from him.

Two weeks later, Moses stayed at his mother's house. He lay in bed, glaring at the ceiling. A half-eaten bowl of chicken soup sat on the nightstand. Isaac poked him in the doorway with his real estate textbook in his hand. Of course, Isaac invited himself in and sat by Moses' bedside. "What chapter are you studying?" Moses tossed in bed. He tried to get comfortable.

"Chapter nineteen," Isaac rocked back and forth in his chair.

"And what's the chapter about?" Moses glared up at the ceiling and looked at his brother.

"Wholesale properties," Isaac scoffed.

"Do you understand what you're studying?" Isaac proceeded to glare at Isaac.

"Yeah, I'll be finished in another month. I wanted to ask you something about Valentin. Did he tell you the story of his friend, Hans, who he was supposed to help back in France?" Isaac focused his eyes on Moses while walleyed.

"Bullshit! I'm not going to try to figure out what Valentin is getting at," Moses coughed, grabbing a napkin. He spat up some blood.

"Shit!" Isaac rushed from his chair.

"It's normal, Isaac. Stopping being a-"

"Don't say it!" Isaac pointed at Moses.

"Look, I'm not going to figure out what Valentin is saying. He's on some bullshit," Moses proceeded to cough.

"Anyway, I wanted to go back to the house and get some of your clothes from your house. Although I couldn't face seeing your blood on the family room floor," Isaac comfortably sat back in the chair.

"Why didn't you?" Moses snapped at Isaac.

"I told you. Shawnette and I can't face your house again," Isaac's voice lowered and quieted.

"I'm going to get my belongings," Moses sat up in bed.

"I know you're not going to stay in that house! Right?" Isaac gave Moses a dead-hard stare.

"I'll sell it to another company," Moses fidgeted in his slumber.

Moses, Isaac, and Shawnette pulled up in her Saturn to Moses' Brookville home. Three police cars surrounded the property as if they were investigating a murder. Moses stepped out of the passenger's seat, alive and well. He was ready to relive this experience, which could have been fatal. An officer stepped out of the driver's seat, approaching Moses. "Mr. Remington?"

"Yes, that's me," Moses kept walking towards the front door with rattling keys.

He inserted the key in the keyhole and turned the knob. Moses inched his way through the foyer with Isaac right behind. His blood dried on the floor, a broken vase not too far away. Moses noticed his safe was untouched. The caribou painting artwork had swung open like a door. Moses exhaled and cracked a smile.

"This would've been the worst birthday if you had died, Moses," Isaac eased into the foyer to the living room. He saw the safe in the wall untouched.

Moses turned to his brother, "I'm alive, Isaac. Happy birthday to us."

In the background, a few cops entered through the front door with static radios. Officer McConnell, a top cop, approached Isaac and nodded to him. He stood in between Isaac and Moses. "How are you feeling, Mr. Remington?" Officer McConnell had a pad and pen handy.

"I'm alive," Moses said with a smile.

"I came by the hospital, but you were out cold. Besides, I was busy with your stepfather and his kin's case," This top cop had the point of the pen close to the notepad. He eyed the living room despite the crime that had occurred. He took notice of the opulent home.

"What do you do for a living?" Officer McConnell asked.

"I'm a real estate investor," Moses set the record straight. The top cop raised an eyebrow. "What's the name of your firm?"

"Remington Realty," Moses answered gladly.

"Where are you located?" Officer McConnell dubiously raised an eyebrow.

"Fifty-Third Street, between fifth and sixth avenues. Around Rockefeller Center," Moses smiled from ear to ear, along with Isaac. Officer McConnell looked at Isaac with his smile. "And you do the same thing, yeah. I'm getting my license," Isaac dropped his smile to a straight face. Another Officer keyed in the information about Moses on his iPad. The officer waited for the information, and then Moses' handsome picture appeared on his website for his firm. Officer McConnell looked over the shoulder of his fellow officer at the Remington Realty website. He read Moses' story, how he started in the field and clicked to see his properties. The twenty-three-million-dollar mansion in the Hamptons popped on the screen and another home in Westhampton for eight million dollars. Then, the video of Moses and his stepfather on *Open House* appeared.

"I saw you and your stepfather were on *Open House*. What happened between you two?" Officer McConnell waited to jot down whatever Moses told him.

"He neglected his responsibilities to the job and family issues. And he abused my mother. She doesn't want to speak on it," Moses glared the top cop right in the eye.

"So, she never reported the abuse?" Officer McConnell continued.

"No. Are we finished here?" Moses scratched his head.

"Alright, that's it," Officer McConnell and his comrades waltzed towards the front door. They hopped in their patrol cars and sped away. Moses closed the front door. He looked at the caribou painting, swinging back the picture with the safe on the wall. Moses punched the combination for the safe. It clicked, and he pulled the small, hefty door open. There was necessary documentation like a birth certificate, an old driver's license, and some credit cards with his name. Then, there was a ring box. Moses opened the red velvet ring box. The fourteen-karat rose gold ring sparkled before his eyes.

In no time, two enormous moving trucks parked in front of Moses' new home for him and Shawnette so they could raise a family. Robust movers carried a sofa wrapped in plastic, loading it into the truck. Also, movers packed boxes of clothes, pots, pans, utensils, and additional items into eighteen-wheelers. "Please be careful with those paintings and vases!" Moses watched the movers like a hawk. Shawnette and Isaac stood in the background, watching Moses take charge like always. Then Rosa eased her way into the house towards her employer.

"Mr. Remington?" Rosa asked, teary-eyed.

"Rosa," Moses embraced her.

"Thank God, you're okay. I couldn't come back to this scene," Rosa sobbed.

Moses put his arms around. "It's alright."

Moses didn't want to pressure Rosa to work for him again. He gave Rosa the pay that was due to her. They would take it from there.

A week later, Moses drove his BMW. It was equipped with brand-new tires. Moses parked in front of a middle-class home in Smithtown, Long Island. Two young men, ages twelve and thirteen, tossed a baseball back and forth to one another. They noticed Moses and Isaac stepping out of the car slowly. "Dad, grandpa's friend is here," The thirteen-year-old tossed the baseball into the air and caught it in the baseball mitt. Stuart Clancy, a slender gentleman in his early forties, had brownish-auburn hair and green eyes. He exited the front door and recognized Isaac from the hospital. "How are you, Isaac?" Stuart shook Moses' hand. "How are you doing, Moses? Do come inside," Stuart showed them the way into his home.

"I do apologize for not attending your father's funeral," Isaac handed the fruit basket to Stuart. "Thanks. That's alright. I'm sure my father would've understood," Stuart set the fruit basket on the coffee table while they sat in the living room. "Twenty-six years ago, I lost my mother to breast cancer, which hurt my father. In my junior year of high school, my father sent my sister and me to stay with our grandparents for a while. Because he couldn't take care of us, days and days passed. Then, weeks and weeks passed from there. I knew something didn't sit well with my grandparents or me. So, we went to our home, and he wasn't there. My sister and I stayed in the house, and again, days and days passed. Weeks and weeks passed, and then my grandfather called the police. The authorities posted my father's pictures everywhere, but nothing," Stuart glared ahead without making eye contact with Isaac. Stuart's father's disappearance was like Isaac's. Bob's son discovered his father couldn't handle his mother's death. Instead, he wanted to crawl under a rock and die. Instead, Bob crawled under the New York subway system, got sick due to the sewage, and transitioned from the Earth to the heavens. Isaac and Moses could do nothing but listen and hopefully reach out to them in the future if they needed anything.

On a bright sunny spring morning, Isaac stood in the office of Remington Realty, holding his New York state real estate license. Moses and his team applauded Isaac's success. "I knew you could do it, bro," Moses' embraced his brother. Later that morning, Isaac gave a tour of the eight hundred-fifty-thousand-dollar home in Garden City to an African-American married couple, Mr. and Mrs. Douglas Respass. They and their three kids were from Georgia. Isaac and the couple strolled into the kitchen with its black wood cabinets, and a marble island table with a second sink. "Please, boys calm down," Mr. Respass approaches his sons, gazing out the large window into the backyard. Isaac proceeded with the house tour as Moses stood outside, allowing his brother to handle his business. Moses accompanied Isaac due to his not being able to drive. Therefore, he would have to arrange for someone from the company to take Isaac to the open houses. He leaned against his BMW and heard screaming from the house. The Respass boys dashed along the spacious green grass to a large oak tree. Moses witnessed these wild young men; he thought of his and Shawnette's future. They'd live in a beautiful home with some savage ass kids terrorizing them daily. Their kids begged for all the candy and toys in the world. His phone vibrated as Moses sat in the driver's seat of his BMW. The caller ID read: Valentin. "What's up, Valentin?" Moses leaned back in his leather seat.

"I'm on my way to France. My doctor must run some tests," Valentin was escorted by baggage handlers to his private jet.

"What kind of tests?" Moses sat erect in the chair. His heart pounded in his chest.

"It's nothing serious, Moses. I'll be back in New York in no time," Valentin boarded his jet plane with its loud rumbling engines.

"Call me while you're there, Valentin," Moses said.

"I will. Talk to you later," Valentin turned off his cell abruptly, boarding his jet.

Moses glared at his cell phone in his hand due to Valentin hanging up so suddenly. He leaned back in his driver's seat again. Moses recalled the indirect stories Valentin had told him. Moses wanted to block that out of his mind. He already had enough problems. Moses was trying to get rid of his stepfather, to help him and Isaac on the right track. Moses couldn't handle any more shit. "I did it! Sold!" Isaac opened the passenger's side door, hopping into the car.

"Yes," Moses embraced Isaac and high-fived him. From Isaac's first sale, he continued to give more and more open houses to potential buyers. Isaac gave a tour of an apartment in Forest Hills, Queens, to a twenty-something-year-old woman. She was a New York Times bestselling author who needed a place to get inspiration. On Seventh Street in the heart of Greenwich Village, Isaac showed a home to a middle-aged same-sex couple. Both were art dealers. They loved the roomy home and made their decision fast. Isaac laughed all the way to the bank, making deposits after deposits of his commission. As Isaac proceeded with his open houses, he and the newlywed couple toured a two million-five hundred-thousand-dollar home in Brooklyn. They sashayed into the family room, admiring the detailing of the ceilings and walls. Isaac's cell phone vibrated on his hip. He ignored it for a second to point out the cozy fireplace. But then, his cell kept vibrating.

"Excuse me, I have to take this call," Isaac stormed through the family room to the living room and the foyer. His caller ID read: Private. "Who the hell is calling me private," Isaac mumbled.

"Hello,"

"Isaac Remington?"

"Yes, this is he."

"My name is Faith Kaplan. I'm a lawyer representing Jessica Teel. You are a friend of hers?" The attorney's voice muffled over the cell.

"Yes, I am," Isaac paced the floor.

"When can you come into court to testify on Jessica's behalf?" Mrs. Kaplan paced the carpeted floor of her firm.

"Whenever you need me," Isaac said.

"Okay, good. I'll be in touch," Mrs. Kaplan hung up. Isaac knew Jessica's case would soon arise.

In a halfway-crowded courtroom, Jessica sat in a wooden chair. Alongside her sat Mrs. Kaplan. Isaac swaggered in on a mission to help his friend out. He slid his rear end across the empty bench right behind Jessica. Moses followed his brother, losing him amongst the packed courthouse guests. Then, he spotted his brother and hurried to Isaac's empty seat. "I'm here, Jessica," Isaac whispered to Jessica as she faced forward. Isaac leaned back on the bench with sure confidence.

She turned slowly and teary-eyed. Jessica tried to restrain teardrops from streaming down her face. "You're here," Jessica grasped Isaac's hand.

"All rise!"

Jessica, her lawyer, Faith Kaplan, and a small group of spectators stood to their feet.

"The honorable Tara Bowman is presiding," the bailiff, a husky and good-looking Caucasian male in his mid-forties, introduced. Gerard Teel, Jessica's estranged husband, was a dark-complexioned African-American male in his early thirties. He sat alongside his lawyer. Isaac eyed this woman beater, noticing him giving Jessica dirty looks. Jessica held her head down, avoiding eye contact. Isaac saw goosebumps surfacing on the back of her neck as she trembled.

"Jessica, calm down. It's going to be alright," Isaac whispered. He hoped she heard his words. Then, she'd take his advice and could get through this trial. Isaac wanted to beat the living daylights out of Gerard, putting the mother of his child through such pain. She had to live underneath the subway for her safety and her child. "This bum sits beside his lawyer, his eyes fixed on Jessica. Stop looking at her and face forward," Isaac balled his hand in his fist. Gerard had no idea the two men in Jessica's corner wanted to pound him with their fists. Moses felt the tension this heartless fuck caused Jessica. Still, she proceeded to keep her eyes clear of seeing him. But then, she sensed his presence like a demonic entity ready to dominate her existence. The brothers saw Jessica tremble more and pounded her fists in her lap. She rose to her feet. "Stop staring at me! Take your eyes off me!"

Judge Bowman banged her gavel twice. "Mrs. Kaplan, please restrain your client!"

Mrs. Kaplan wrapped her arms around Jessica as she sat Jessica back in her chair. The bailiff handed Jessica bottled water to drink. Then Judge Bowman fixed her eyes on Gerard, at which point she saw the devilish expression on his face. Isaac and Moses observed Jessica's estranged husband's vile persona. Anyone would think he'd play it off in front of the courtroom, but he didn't care. "Mr. Teel, I saw you mad dogging your estranged wife," the judge stared at Gerard with her glasses halfway off her eyes. Gerard's pompous attitude made the judge, and the little spectators that were in the court cringed. "Someone needs to fuck him up," Moses leaned to Isaac. Isaac nodded and wanted to hurt Gerard, just like he wanted to do to his stepfather. Though, that was another issue. Isaac realized he'd gone through trial and tribulations with his friends Jessica and Bob. Now, Bob was in a better place. "Mrs. Teel, why on God's green Earth did you have your child living underneath the New York subway? That's where all kinds of diseases and rodents dwell. Can you explain that to me?"

Gerard abruptly stood from his chair.

"You're not the only one, Your Honor. She needs to do a lot of explaining to me. She took my baby girl away from me for over a decade. You must be out of your mind!"

Judge Bowman banged her gavel. "Counsel, your client's out of order!"

"I have no idea what my baby girl even looks like now. I knew this bitch was crazy from the day we stood at the altar," Gerard continued his rant. The court officer approached, trying to calm him down. But then, Jessica's out-of-control husband proceeded and punched the bailiff. This husky man hurled punches at one another, causing the courtroom to erupt into mayhem. Gerard had the best of the fight with the court officer. Then, six more bailiffs sprang into action. Isaac wanted to intervene in the brawl since he and his brother had a mother who had dealt with an abusive man.

Within a matter of minutes, the court officers took control of the situation. They cuffed Gerard with his bloodied face. He looked like something out of a horror movie, with blood streaming down his face. Gerard had the most diabolical face ever. Jessica, of course, saw this crazed man's face which caused terror in her heart. Tears cascaded down her face as she quivered. Isaac placed his hands on her shoulders. "Don't look at him, Jessica!"

Jessica held her head down, sobbing. As the officers led him out of the side entrance of the courtroom, this beast from the underworld still ranted. "I'm coming for you, Jessica! You're mine. You will always be mine! I'm in your mind, your nightmares! You're mine!"

Isaac rose to his feet. He was ready to go toe to toe with this fool while his heart pounded. "Don't make threats! You fuck!"

Judge Bowman noticed Isaac continuing to exchange words with Gerard. Once again, she banged her gavel. Sir! Sir, who are you?"

"I'm a friend of Jessica Teel's, your honor," Isaac remained on his feet. His eyes were fixed on the judge as best he could while cock-eyed.

"And how are you acquainted?"

"Jessica and I, along with her daughter, Shereza, and others, lived underneath Times Square Station," Isaac explained. Judge Bowman suggested Isaac take his seat. She'd get back to him later. Then, this dark robe goddess gave Jessica a tongue-lashing. Jessica and her lawyer, Mrs. Kaplan, stood to their feet. "Mrs. Teel, I've got your child's medical records. Shereza's healthy by the grace of God. Raccoons, possums, giant cockroaches, maggots, worms, human waste, and toxic waste are underneath the sidewalks on this planet. How old is the child?"

"Shereza's eleven years old, your honor," Jessica sniffled.

Judge Bowman shuffled through files of Jessica's medical records and her child's. A photo of Shereza had been taken for the first time in her life. The judge shook her head and held up the picture of the eleven-year-old, "Do you see this photo, Mrs. Teel?"

"That's my daughter, Shereza?" Jessica murmured.

"I can't hear you, Mrs. Teel. Speak up!" the judge's face turned red with fury. Isaac didn't like the judge being so hard on Jessica, but he and Moses kept their mouths shut.

"That's my daughter, Shereza!" Jessica choked back her tears. She wiped her eyes with a Kleenex.

"Shereza's first picture. Your daughter has no baby pictures because you took the cowardly way out of a situation. Why didn't you go and stay with your family? "Why, Mrs. Teel?" the judge rocked in her recliner.

"I loved him. I guess," Jessica shrugged her shoulders, crying.

"Why didn't you call the domestic abuse hotline?"

"I wasn't thinking. And I thought my father had the wrong idea of Gerard. When the abuse started, I didn't want to feel stupid. So, I stayed away from my family," Jessica held her head in shame.

"Mrs. Teel, I'm up here," The judge pounded her fist on the bench instead of the gavel.

Jessica shifted her attention to Judge Bowman.

"Do you mind repeating yourself!"

"My family was right about Gerard because he wasn't good. I would have felt stupid if I had told them they were right," Jessica spoke louder.

Judge Bowman shuffled through Jessica and her daughter's files once more. "Your father was right. Mr. Teel isn't an upstanding man by his behavior in this courtroom. I know this child needs you. Do you have anywhere to go?" The judge glared at Jessica. Jessica couldn't answer, so Isaac cleared his throat and stood up.

"Alright, sir. What is your name?"

"Isaac Remington. I'm accompanied by my brother Moses."

"Moses Remington? Moses Remington, the real estate investor?" The judge glared hard through her spectacles. "I noticed you looked familiar. I have seen you on television."

"Good morning, Your Honor," Moses stood up and nodded.

"Proceed, Mr. Isaac Remington."

My brother and I had our story, but that's not the case now. It's about Jessica and her child getting into a safe place where they can grow. Moses and I can place them in a comfortable environment free of charge," Isaac nodded to Moses. He gestured to Isaac in agreement. Again, the judge quieted and fidgeted in her chair. She shuffled through Jessica and Shereza's paperwork. "Mrs. Teel, many women in your situation aren't as fortunate. While you and Isaac lived within the filth of the Earth, he overcame his condition. You're blessed to have him as a friend who will give you a chance at life. I'm granting Shereza to you, Mrs. Teel. And I'm posting a restraining order against your estranged husband. Will you be filing for divorce, Mrs. Teel?" The judge rolled her eyes.

"I'm filing right now," Jessica spoke clearly.

"This case is closed. Good luck to you, Mrs. Teel," Judge Bowman banged her gavel, leaving the bench. Jessica embraced her lawyer. Then, she rushed into Isaac's arms. "Thank you, Isaac. Moses, thank you so much." He wrapped his arms around Jessica.

"We've got you and Shereza covered," Isaac and Jessica hugged again.

Red, yellow, and brown leaves fell from the trees in this well-kept community of American reality. Moses parked his BMW in front of a magnificent upper-class home fit for someone making a yearly income of over a hundred thousand dollars. Shereza's eyes widened as she stepped out of the vehicle's rear seat and stood before the property. She noticed the white framed window, the red front door, and the natural surroundings of her new house.

"This house is like in the magazine, Mom!" Melodies of songbirds echoed throughout the atmosphere. Full green trees could be seen with each step, and trimmed grass was under her sneakers. Jessica stepped towards the home. Moses and Isaac exited the car, closing the doors. Jessica squinted her eyes, sneering at Isaac. He dangled a set of keys in Jessica's face. "You've got to be kidding, Isaac!" Isaac laid a kiss on her lips. From that kiss, she knew this home belonged to her for good.

"Welcome home," Isaac placed the keys in the palm of Jessica's hand. Jessica and Shereza dashed through the cherry red door while inserting the key into the lock. She heard the click and pushed the heavy front door open. The mother and child stepped into the foyer. Fresh-cut roses were in a fancy vase. Raymour and Flanigan had furnished the living room with a sofa, a loveseat, two recliners, and a fireplace. A large, framed picture of Shereza and a flat-panel screen television was on the wall. "Look at that picture of you, baby," Jessica ran her fingers through her daughter's hair and hugged Shereza. "Is this the living room?" Shereza stepped to the center of the floor.

"Yes, baby," Jessica answered.

Moses and Isaac allowed their friends to familiarize themselves with their new surroundings. Jessica closed her eyes and shook her head in disbelief. She continued to grasp the set of keys in the palm of her hand. "Someone pinch me so I can wake up from this dream."

Isaac pinched Jessica's arm very hard while standing behind her. "Ouch!" Jessica's voice echoed through her new home. Her screams got Shereza's attention. "What's wrong, Mom?"

Jessica shook her head as Isaac appeared from behind. "It's real, Jessica."

"Are you serious, Isaac? Moses?" Jessica looked at the brothers.

"It's a gift," Moses sat on the loveseat.

"A gift? For what? I can't afford this, Isaac, and Moses. You guys know that." Jessica placed the keys in Isaac's hand.

"Jessica, it's fine. You don't have to do anything for this," Moses added.

"Why me?"

"With the blessings Isaac and I have, we're giving to you."

Jessica, dumbfounded, couldn't utter a word. Who would deny a gorgeous home fully paid for and furnished? The new environment provided everything humans needed - heat, air conditioning, food, and a place to lay their heads at night.

"Mom, it's my favorite apple. Pink Lady," Shereza munched on the rosy-colored fruit. She dashed back into the kitchen. Jessica gave chase as she stopped in the middle of a gourmet kitchen with glass cabinets. Cabinets filled from top to bottom with cookies, cakes, canned goods, sugar, flour, salt and pepper, and other spices. Jessica noticed Chips Ahoy cookies appearing through the window like an invitation. She thrust open the cabinet, grabbed some cookies, and bit into it. Isaac and Moses strolled in, seeing the mother and child check out the kitchen. "Do you want one, Moses?" Jessica took another bite of the cookie.

"No, I'm on a diet," Moses said.

Isaac frowned at his brother's bullshit story. He grabbed a cookie from the pack.

On the second floor, Shereza entered the white bathroom with squinting eyes. She had no idea about this space. The sink, clawfoot bathtub, toilet bowl, and separate shower drew her to test these things out. She turned the hot knob for the sink as the burning hot water contacted her hand. "Ouch!" She immediately turned off the water. Jessica, Isaac, and Moses strolled into the bathroom.

"You like it, Shereza?" Moses laughed.

"What is this space?" Shereza's eyes wondered at everything in the bathroom.

"It's the bathroom. You can take a bath and shower to get clean, brush your teeth, and make pee-pee and do-do, "Jessica points her finger to different restroom areas. Moses and Isaac eyed each other. Both snickered at Jessica, speaking old-fashioned to her daughter.

"Go check out your bedroom, Shereza," Isaac pointed down the hallway. She frowned, not understanding all these brand-new things. The child opened the door to a red and pink colored girly room. There was a full-sized Tiffany bed with a red-ruffled bedspread, pink blanketed walls, and a white ceiling fan. The mirrored dresser reflected her image. She cringed for a moment, scaring herself. Then, she crept towards her vision in the glass before her eyes. Jessica appeared in the background of the mirror and took baby steps. "Look at how beautiful you are, Shereza." Jessica got closer and closer to the vanity mirror, noticing her mother's image.

"Look at how beautiful you are, Mom," she ran her fingers through her mother's hair. Jessica looked and the brothers as they led the way to the rest of the home.

Jessica swung open the double doors of her master bedroom. A king-sized firm mattress adorned with a gold and white bedspread, and many plush pillows. Her eyes widened, caressing her hand along the silky comforter and the velvet headboard. Shereza watched her mother's every move. She then stroked her hand along the bedspread and the headboard. Jessica opened the double glass doors, which led out to a balcony. She took baby steps to see the large backyard with surrounding trees and manicured grass. The birds proceeded to sing. The fresh air gave her tranquility. She and Shereza should've had this suburban home from the beginning. Jessica's eyes bulged as she grabbed her daughter's hand. "Come on, Shereza!" Moses and Isaac stood back and watched these two get a kick out of their new home. A majestic oak tree sat on the grass with a swing tied on its robust branch. Jessica regressed to her childhood as she dashed towards the swing. She hopped on it and pushed herself back on it, swaying back and forth through the air. Moses and Isaac headed out on the grass, watching Jessica and Shereza. "It's what I always wanted, a swing," Jessica swung as high as she could. "It's all yours, Jessica!" Isaac waved.

"Moses, we did a good thing here. With our blessings, we can give that to others, especially the less fortunate," Isaac patted Moses on the shoulder.

Moses smiled and knew who had coached Isaac on this lesson of giving back. "Valentin told you his life story. Right?"

"Who else?" Isaac shrugged his shoulders. "Have you heard from Valentin?"

"I called and left some messages, but he hasn't returned any of my calls. I hope he's alright," Moses scratched his head. The frats focused their attention back on the mother and daughter. Jessica pushed her little girl on the swing. "This is fun, Mom! Look at me, Isaac, and Moses. The brother swaggered on the lawn and watched the family enjoy their new home.

CHAPTER TWENTY-EIGHT

Down a long gloomy corridor of a jailhouse, inmates' verbal noises echoed throughout the entire floor. A correction officer roamed down the dark hall without noticing a giant cockroach crawling up the wall. Following the insect, an oversized rat scurried alongside the wall, squeezing its body into a hole next to a cell. Calvin lay in his cot with his eyes half-opened. He thought about the pain he had caused Irene, Moses, and Isaac. He had no television for entertainment, no comfortable plush bed to sleep on, and no good food to devour. So, he reminisced about the money he made from his stepsons' firm. Calvin smiled to himself, pleased that he had done a job well. Calvin gave tours to clients when they thought about purchasing with Remington Realty. In hindsight, he had made a wrong decision. How could he convince a jury he had meant no harm to his stepsons' special day? He heard the squealing of a rodent. His heart raced in his chest, and he sat up in bed, clutching his pillow. The fatty rodent sprung upon his chest, glaring at him. Balls of sweat emerged on Calvin's forehead and streamed down his face as if he struggled through the hot sands of the Sahara Desert. This creature knew about his hard life and sins from the time he came into the world. The rat knew Calvin had beaten, and verbally abused, Irene and her sons. Though, he did not realize it until now. The hellish red tint of the pest's eyes glistened as Calvin whimpered. He hit the pest with the pillow, jumped out of bed, and crawled on his knees into a corner beside the sink. Calvin placed his trembling hands over his eyes, hoping this fiend would vanish. Calvin opened one eye slowly and peered through two of his fingers. He released a scream for help that only echoed through the facility. No one heard Calvin's agony. Besides this beast, that is. It crept closer and closer to him, still glaring into his eyes. "What do you want? I didn't mean to break those little boys' bond. And I loved Irene so much; you know that. Please don't take me to hell," Calvin whined. He made visual contact with this demonic entity that came to put fear in his heart. He had to figure out a way to get this monstrosity out of sight. Calvin grabbed the bed sheets from his cot. He twisted and knotted them and wrapped them around his neck. He tied the extra sheets around the pipes of the sink and radiator, continuing to cover the bedding around his neck. Calvin gasped as much air as he could while attempting to free his spirit. The rat proceeded to wait for him to take his last breath. Calvin finished balling the sheets around and had a short piece of fabric in his hand. He held the sheet tightly, pulling, pulling, and pulling. Calvin heard the rat squeaking loudly in his head. Calvin yanked the cloth, snapping his neck. His head tilted, blood streaming from his mouth, and his eyes opened. The rat scurried away through the hole of the cell.

Meanwhile, Irene threw Calvin's dress shirts, trousers, ties, sweaters, and other garments in a trash bag after removing them from the master bedroom. She felt the world being lifted off her back. Irene shoved this past of pain into the hefty bag. Isaac descended from the third floor of his mother's home. He crept towards his mother's bedroom, noticing her removing Calvin's things.

"Isaac!" Irene was startled, holding her hand on her chest.

"Sorry, Mom," he leaned in the doorway with his arms folded.

"You scared the daylights out of me," Irene kept packing the GQ apparel. Isaac didn't bother to respond to his mother's fears. He had lived with her after Calvin and his kin interrupted their birthday celebration. Isaac watched his mother like a hawk. He was willing to do anything it took to keep her safe. Another pair of feet made their way down the hallway. Moses made his presence known.

"Good morning, Mom."

"Good morning, baby," She paused the packing momentarily and embraced her twins. Moses also moved into the house with his mother to keep an extra set of eyes on her for her protection. He sold his home to a separate company and thought about selling the home his mother and Calvin occupied. They wanted no recollection of bad memories of the abuse, turning them against one another or cheating. But none of Calvin's immoral ways affected Moses' enterprise.

"Thank God." If it did, Moses' firm would've been a done deal. Moses dreaded another court case. He and Isaac had to run back and forth to court over some bullshit his stepfather did. If it came down to that, he and his brother would have to be there for their mother. Spring La Primavera played on Irene's cell phone. She sprinted across the bedroom, answering the call.

"Hello," Irene paced the carpeted floor.

"Is she going to throw all his shit out!" Moses rummaged through the trash bags.

"I told her to," Isaac peered into the plastic bag.

"What the fuck do you mean you told her! These are good clothes, expensive," Moses held the trousers in his hand.

"So, you're going to wear them?" Isaac smiled.

"Hell fuckin' no!" Moses shoved the garments into the plastic bag.

"How did he die?" Irene questioned the person on the other end of the cell phone. The question got her sons' attention. The brothers eyed each other without saying anything. Neither brother could figure it out. For a second, Moses hoped it wasn't his Uncle Tyler because he had done everything for him and Isaac.

"I don't want to see him. Tell his family; it's out of my hands," Irene subsided her call. She smiled at her sons and inhaled. "Calvin's dead."

Her sons looked at each other for a second. Then, they looked to their mother for an answer. The twins could see her face lighting up. Death wasn't something someone should rejoice in, but when a person went through hell with that person, they were no longer in their lives. Death had separated them, and the weight had been lifted off them.

"How?" Moses asked.

"Suicide," Irene looked away.

"Good! Throw his shit the fuck out!" Isaac pounded his fist against the wall.

That night, Moses and Shawnette sat at a candlelit booth next to the window at Central Park's Tavern on Green restaurant. The loving couple grasped hands with glasses of wine beside them. Lite jazz played in the background. Guests chattered in the ambiance of the fancy hot spot. Shawnette and Moses made eyes at each other, but for some reason, Moses couldn't keep his focus off her. She did the same. In fact, Shawnette could sense that her boyfriend had something in mind. She snickered.

"What, Shawnette?" Moses caressed her hand. He figured she knew something special might advent itself, not like the last time when he gave her a finger orgasm. Shawnette took a deep breath and sighed. "What, Moses?"

"Why are you so shy all of a sudden?" Moses chuckled.

"You're up to something." Shawnette laughed.

"What? I have no idea what talking about," Moses continued to caress. "Do you want me to go under the table," Moses rubbed his middle finger in the palm of Shawnette's hand. She snatched her hand away, guffawing. Shawnette held her head down, keeping her composure. She hoped not to attract any attention.

"Are you out of your mind, Moses?" Shawnette noticed the red velvet ring box on the table. "What's this?"

"Open it," Moses said.

His girlfriend lifted the lid as the fourteen-karat rose gold engagement ring sparkled. Moses slipped it on her finger. He bowed on one knee. "Marry me, Shawnette," Moses held her hand. He knew the guests in this upscale place noticed this man bowed down. He didn't care. Tears cascaded down her cheeks. She and Moses engaged in a kiss. The restaurant erupted in applause.

Three weeks later, a clean-cut, medium-height gentleman dressed in a three-piece designer suit, holding a briefcase strutted through the Glassdoor of Remington realty. The unfamiliar man approached the receptionist's desk, where Jocelyn stroked the keys on the computer. She swerved in her chair. "Good morning, sir?"

"Hello, I'm Alexandre Lacome, Mr. Da La Rue's avocat. His lawyer," the French lawyer explained.

"Okay," Jocelyn gave her undivided attention to this man.

"May I see Moses and Isaac Remington?" he asked in a submission tone.

"Yes, sir. Have a seat," Jocelyn immediately got on the phone to inform her bosses about the visitor.

Within minutes, Moses resided at his large wooden desk as his mentor/investor's attorney seated before him. Isaac pulled up a chair to the side of his brother's desk. The brothers glared at the lawyer in the face. He waited to hear what this heavy-accented gentleman had to utter. His heart raced in his chest. Moses felt uneasy about the situation. The French attorney grimaced, shifting his focus between the brothers. Then, he took a deep breath.

"I'm here to inform you that Mr. De La Rue has sadly passed away."

Isaac's heart pounded rapidly, glaring at the lawyer through his glasses. He rose from his chair, pacing the floor. Moses pounded his fist on the desk, dropping his head in the palm of his hands. He sobbed.

"Fuck!" Isaac bellowed.

The next morning, a small aircraft took off on the runway. It soared through the air to Cannes, France. While the brothers sat in seats on the plane, they exchanged no words for the entire flight. Moses stared out the window, imagining the shapes of the clouds in the sky. One cloud shaped like a castle. Everything was made of clouds. He got childish thoughts in his head. *"What am I doing right now? I'm acting like a kid. My mentor is gone. Cancer! That's one sickness that can be cured. Or it will get you. Cancer got Valentin. Why didn't he try to save himself? He felt as if he had already gotten his blessing. Therefore, he left it for Isaac and me,"* Moses closed his eyes. Isaac's eyelids remained closed despite the soothing sounds of the private jet. He opened his eyes but had blurry vision. Isaac rubbed his eyes with his hands, blinking. He tried to make out a silhouette image seated beside him. The darkly outlined image became visible as a European masculine voice greeted him. "Isaac, how are you?"

Isaac couldn't believe a dead person like Valentin was sitting right beside him. Though he was looking at him in the face. Isaac looked around. He noticed a small group of passengers minding their own business. He didn't even think about Moses or his whereabouts.

"Isaac, you and Moses will be so blessed with what I've left for you. Go and enjoy life. Get married, have a family, and eat all the fat from the land," Valentin laughed with a heavenly smile. Isaac continued not to say anything. He wanted to but was frightened. Instead, he gave his dear friend the honors. "You and Moses, the fraternal twins, are something special. Both of you are destined for tremendous success. I know it. God made it possible. And you gentlemen give the blessing back to others less fortunate," Valentin's voice resounded, fading away. Isaac lifted his eyelids and wiped them. He saw Moses stretched out in the plane seat. His brother was asleep with the pillow over his face. Isaac snatched it from Moses' face. Moses woke up in wonder. "What are you doing?"

"Why are you sleeping with a pillow over your face? That's so fuckin' stupid," Isaac threw the pillow back at him.

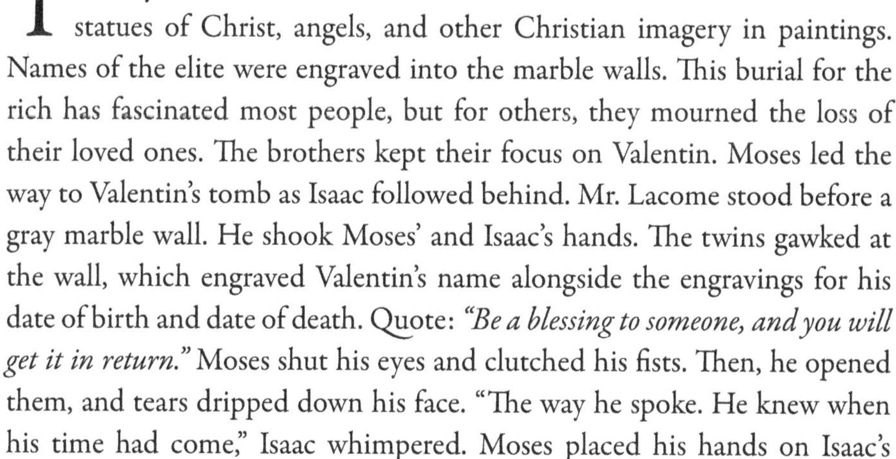

Two days later, Moses and Isaac waltzed into a French mausoleum with statues of Christ, angels, and other Christian imagery in paintings. Names of the elite were engraved into the marble walls. This burial for the rich has fascinated most people, but for others, they mourned the loss of their loved ones. The brothers kept their focus on Valentin. Moses led the way to Valentin's tomb as Isaac followed behind. Mr. Lacome stood before a gray marble wall. He shook Moses' and Isaac's hands. The twins gawked at the wall, which engraved Valentin's name alongside the engravings for his date of birth and date of death. Quote: *"Be a blessing to someone, and you will get it in return."* Moses shut his eyes and clutched his fists. Then, he opened them, and tears dripped down his face. "The way he spoke. He knew when his time had come," Isaac whimpered. Moses placed his hands on Isaac's shoulders for comfort. "Be a blessing to someone, and you will get it in return," Isaac read aloud. He envisioned when he gave the homeless man his food from the diner as a child. When he became homeless, an upscale gentleman gave him a twenty-dollar bill.

Moreover, he and Bob had met under harsh, cold, ruthless circumstances. Isaac further remembered living under the rumbling trains of Grand Central Station with Jessica and Shereza. Then, Isaac recalled searching for food for them, him and Bob. He will remember Maggie over in the small park near Times Square. Isaac prayed that she still was in good health and that no harm would come her way.

Valentin's black jet sat alone in an aircraft hangar, orphaned from its rightful owner, who had passed on. Moses, Isaac, and Mr. Lacome strolled alongside the giant bird that soared in the heavens. "Why are we looking at this plane? What's this about?" Isaac caressed his hand along the bird. The entrance with airstairs awaited the three gentlemen as a stewardess greeted them.

Moses marched up the flight of stairs, bumping into a stewardess.

"How are you, Mr. Remington?" the stewardess greeted, but his smile dropped after hearing the bad news.

"Hello, Mr. Remington," the stewardess then greeted Isaac. He smiled and saw the sadness in her face. Isaac saw the aircraft's interior, waltzed in, and looked around like a child in the toy aisle.

About an hour later, Isabella served poured coffee into cups. The men discussed some documentation before them. Moses poured a creamer into his coffee and read the page in his hand. "Is this for real?"

"What's for real?" Isaac shoves a cookie in his mouth. "Holy shit!" Cookie crumbs flew from Isaac's mouth. Moses and Mr. Lacome moved from the table because of Isaac's bad manners. Luckily, no cookie bits got on Valentin's will. Moses sat down in his chair. "Finish eating, please, Isaac. Damn!"

Isaac swallowed the pastry and cleared his throat. "So, Valentin left his estate to us?"

"Yes, Mr. Da La Rue left his real estate properties in Monaco, Beverly Hills, The Hamptons, Long Island, the Virgin Islands, the Fuji Islands, and so forth. He further left his stocks and bonds, bank accounts, cars, plane, and yacht," Mr. LaCome went through the documents word by word.

"His yacht?" Moses leaned back in his chair, dubious.

"What, yacht?" Isaac's eyes widened.

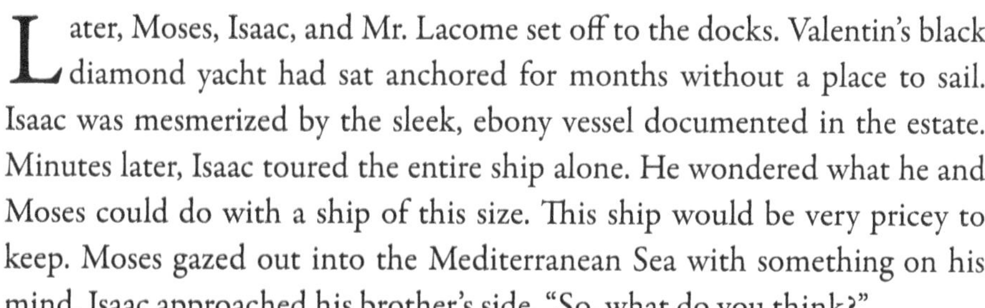

Later, Moses, Isaac, and Mr. Lacome set off to the docks. Valentin's black diamond yacht had sat anchored for months without a place to sail. Isaac was mesmerized by the sleek, ebony vessel documented in the estate. Minutes later, Isaac toured the entire ship alone. He wondered what he and Moses could do with a ship of this size. This ship would be very pricey to keep. Moses gazed out into the Mediterranean Sea with something on his mind. Isaac approached his brother's side. "So, what do you think?"

"This is beautiful. I'm speechless right now," Isaac turned away from the sea on the ship.

"Do you want to keep all this, Moses? These toys are too overwhelming," Isaac shook his head.

"We'll keep the jet and sell the yacht. We'll donate seventy-five percent of the proceeds and build homes for needy people," Moses focused on the sea.

"Bet," Isaac embraced Moses.

Months later, dozens and dozens of homes had been flipped by Remington Realty. They placed homeless families and individuals in the homes for free. Permanent homes were renovated across Queens, Manhattan, The Bronx, Brooklyn, Long Island, and New Jersey. Isaac visited his friend, Maggie, who remained on the park bench. She still fed the birds. The black BMW parked on the sidewalk as Isaac hopped out of the passenger's seat. He spotted her right away. Maggie still smiled and talked to these flying creatures like they would talk back. Isaac dressed dapper, approached Maggie with caution. "Maggie, how are you?"

"Isaac! Look at you! You're so handsome," Maggie stopped tossing bread to the pigeons.

"How are you?" Isaac sat on the bench's edge.

"I'm fine. Where are you going so dressed up?" Maggie placed her hands on her hips.

"I'm working," Isaac said.

"Good for you. Where?"

"I'm a real estate agent," Isaac nodded.

"You're so smart. You made your way off these cruel streets," Maggie said, teary-eyed.

"Maggie, I know you don't trust anyone or even me. But I've got a beautiful place for you to stay," Isaac said.

"No, I can't. I'm so afraid," Maggie sobbed. Isaac stopped, respecting her wishes. He grabbed a one-hundred-dollar bill from his wallet.

"Take this, Maggie," Isaac placed the money in her hand and his business card. She wiped her eyes, taking the cash and business card. He had no other choice but to walk away.

"Take care of yourself, Maggie."

Maggie checked out the business card, where she saw Isaac's photo. Moses' photo was on the other side. Then her eyes bulged; her cardiac muscle raced in her chest. Maggie noticed Isaac swaggering towards the BMW.

"Hey, wait Isaac!" Maggie wobbled as fast as she could. Isaac turned, hearing his friend's cries. He stopped in his tracks as Maggie approached him. She looked at the black car and fixed her eyes on Isaac.

"You better not be shittin' me. Is this a trick?"

"No, it's for real," Isaac glared at her in her eyes.

That day, Maggie entered a nicely furnished apartment in Greenpoint, Brooklyn. Volunteers had fixed up the place and bought clothes in Maggie's size. They had installed cabinets and a refrigerator filled with food while sporting "MANY MANSIONS" homeless foundation t-shirts. Neighbors had also come to introduce themselves. Everyone helped her get acquainted with her new home. Maggie cried, turning to Isaac, and hugging him. She then noticed Moses in the background. "This is your brother. Oh, he's beautiful, just like you, Isaac."

Maggie sobbed. "I can't believe it; my apartment. Rent?"

"Free of charge," Moses smiled.

"Thank you both. I had a feeling about Isaac," Maggie sobbed.

Los Angeles' skid row became nonexistent due to volunteers placing homeless residents into permanent housing, including in San Francisco and Oakland. There, a homeless shelter filled to the roof was now a run-down block. It had been flipped into a line of homes for low-income families nationwide. Birds sang the same old song; children played the same games. Adults gossiped about nonsense and current events. They mowed lawns, trimmed the hedges, and had cookouts. This was a blessing to humankind made possible by the "MANY MANSIONS" a foundation founded by Moses and Isaac Remington.

Months later, NBC cameras for the television lifestyle series *"Open House"* were on location at a villa in the heart of Cannes, France. Moses and Isaac were giving a grand tour of the luxurious property. Make-up artists and wardrobes prepped the brothers like big Hollywood stars. Both were ready for the scene. The twins wore gray trousers, matching vests, white dress shirts; paired with black shoes. They wore their signature style. The director clapped his hands. He was ready for the siblings to give a tour of this fifty-five-million-dollar estate overlooking the Mediterranean Sea. The brothers raced from the chairs. They dashed towards the double doors of the dining room.

"Remember when we were kids, we said we were going to be on this show," Moses said.

"You made it happen," Isaac smiled.

"We made it happen," Moses gave a high-five to his brother. Then the double doors swung open to the pool area. Moses and Isaac swaggered out onto it.

"I'm Moses Remington," he started.

And I'm Isaac Remington. My brother and I'll give you a grand tour of this fabulous villa on eighty acres of land. "Come on and look," Isaac spoke to the television audience. As the cameraman tracked the twins of this French mansion.

THE END

About the Author

Alexis Soleil has been writing for over three decades and has written two books "FROM THE OTHER SIDE OF THE TRACKS" and "IRATE". She loves to write stories that move people and make them dive into a whole new world. Alexis hopes to continue to write tales about love, family, and wherever her heart takes her.

www.ingramcontent.com/pod-product-compliance
Lightning Source LLC
Chambersburg PA
CBHW020500310726
48979CB00016B/2730/J

* 9 7 9 8 2 1 8 2 9 0 8 5 6 *